Critics and Readers Praise

PARADOX

"Pulse-pounding . . . Coulter fans will have a tough time putting this one down."

—*Publishers Weekly*

"Action is nonstop . . . Perfect reading for the beach and beyond."

—*Booklist*

"Catherine Coulter remains one of the very best at what she does, and *Paradox* is some of her very finest work yet . . . Eerie, unsettling, and breathlessly terrifying."

—*The Real Book Spy*

"Each and every Coulter book is out-of-this-world good, but *Paradox* is the very best book, to my way of thinking, that ever came out of her brain. This book simply blows your mind away. It's a captivating, intriguing, hold-on-to-your-britches book. Simply put, this is the best book of the year."

—P. L. Berry

"I just finished *Paradox* and loved it. I've read all your books and I hope you never stop writing!"

—C. McClure

"I finished *Paradox* and loved every minute of it. It was very hard to put down—stealing fifteen minutes to read it in the parking lot before going into the grocery store is now my new norm. Great twists and turns."

—J. Davis

"*Paradox* is another winner! Your skill at creating two independent stories and weaving them together into a single novel is amazing, and your strong characters keep the book flowing."

—S. Smith

"I just finished *Paradox* and as usual it was excellent. I was sucked in right from the beginning straight through to the end. The characters, the pace, the plot—I enjoyed every page of it!"

—M. Wascom

ENIGMA

"Bestseller Coulter is at the top of her game in her twenty-first FBI thriller . . . Twists and turns galore in both investigations ensure there's never a dull moment."

—*Publishers Weekly,* starred review

"A master of smooth, eminently readable narratives."

—*Booklist*

"*Enigma* is a new seductive and menacing thriller that sets new standards . . . This must be next on your reading list if you love to read thrillers."

—*The Washington Book Review*

"I give *Enigma* five stars. I couldn't put it down. Another page-turning thriller."

—A. Konieczka

"I just finished *Enigma*. You've done it again! A fabulous read with enough twists and turns to keep the adrenaline meter on HIGH! Congratulations on another success. I really enjoyed this book and can't wait for the next."

—N. LeComte

"*Enigma* was wonderful! Your descriptions and how the scenes play out are fantastic. Thank you again for writing a wonderful story, bringing everything together and making me lose sleep because I couldn't put the book down."

—C. Storzum

INSIDIOUS

"Coulter keeps the two plotlines equally engaging—and the reader guessing—all the way to the satisfying resolution of each."

—*Publishers Weekly*

"Two very intriguing mysteries . . . You can't go wrong with a Coulter book, as she has proven time after time."

—*RT Book Reviews*

"Catherine Coulter knows how to weave and web incredibly heinous crimes that make you think and shudder."

—*Mrs. Leif's Two Fangs About It*

"You outdid yourself on this one. The best one yet. I had a very hard time putting it down. I had to take my wife to the doctor today and while I was waiting, I was getting almost to the end of the book. I was so engrossed in the story that I did not realize my wife was leaving."

—T. Muller

"Wow! I finished *Insidious* last night. I didn't see that [ending] coming. Great job of keeping me and all the other readers in the dark. Keep up the great novels. I can't wait for the next one."

—D. Riker

"I could not put [*Insidious*] down. Both of your story lines were well thought-out and the characterizations were so thorough I could picture each person and their attitude in my mind. You gave us enough to try and figure out the villain but twist it just enough that we might be close but not close enough. You write such compelling stories."

—S. Lavalais

THE FBI THRILLERS

Enigma (2017)

Insidious (2016)

Nemesis (2015)

Power Play (2014)

Bombshell (2013)

Backfire (2012)

Split Second (2011)

Twice Dead (2011): *Riptide* and *Hemlock Bay*

Whiplash (2010)

KnockOut (2009)

TailSpin (2008)

Double Jeopardy (2008): *The Target* and *The Edge*

Double Take (2007)

The Beginning (2005): *The Cove* and *The Maze*

Point Blank (2005)

Blowout (2004)

Blindside (2003)

Eleventh Hour (2002)

Hemlock Bay (2001)

Riptide (2000)

The Edge (1999)

The Target (1998)

The Maze (1997)

The Cove (1996)

A BRIT IN THE FBI THRILLERS (WITH J.T. ELLISON)

The Sixth Day (2018)
The Devil's Triangle (2017)
The End Game (2015)
The Lost Key (2014)
The Final Cut (2013)

CATHERINE
COULTER

PARADOX

G

GALLERY BOOKS
New York London Toronto Sydney New Delhi

Gallery Books
An Imprint of Simon & Schuster, Inc.
1230 Avenue of the Americas
New York, NY 10020

This book is a work of fiction. Any references to historical events, real people, or real places are used fictitiously. Other names, characters, places, and events are products of the author's imagination, and any resemblance to actual events or places or persons, living or dead, is entirely coincidental.

Copyright © 2018 by Catherine Coulter

All rights reserved, including the right to reproduce this book or portions thereof in any form whatsoever. For information, address Gallery Books Subsidiary Rights Department, 1230 Avenue of the Americas, New York, NY 10020.

First Gallery Books trade paperback edition February 2019

GALLERY BOOKS and colophon are registered trademarks of Simon & Schuster, Inc.

For information about special discounts for bulk purchases, please contact Simon & Schuster Special Sales at 1-866-506-1949 or business@simonandschuster.com.

The Simon & Schuster Speakers Bureau can bring authors to your live event. For more information or to book an event, contact the Simon & Schuster Speakers Bureau at 1-866-248-3049 or visit our website at www.simonspeakers.com.

Manufactured in the United States of America

10 9 8 7 6 5 4 3 2 1

The Library of Congress has cataloged the hardcover edition as follows:

Names: Coulter, Catherine, author.
Title: Paradox / Catherine Coulter.
Description: First Gallery Books hardcover edition. | New York : Gallery Books, 2018. | Series: An FBI thriller ; 22
Identifiers: LCCN 2018007876 (print) | LCCN 2018009811 (ebook) | ISBN 9781501138126 (hardback) | ISBN 9781501138133 (trade paperback) | ISBN 9781501196409 (mass market) | ISBN 9781501138140 (ebook)
Subjects: LCSH: United States. Federal Bureau of Investigation—Fiction. | Sherlock, Lacey (Fictitious character)—Fiction. | Savich, Dillon (Fictitious character)—Fiction. | BISAC: FICTION / Suspense. | FICTION / Espionage. | GSAFD: Suspense fiction.
Classification: LCC PS3553.O843 (ebook) | LCC PS3553.O843 P37 2018 (print) | DDC 813/.54—dc23
LC record available at https://lccn.loc.gov/2018007876

ISBN 978-1-5011-3812-6
ISBN 978-1-5011-3813-3 (pbk)
ISBN 978-1-5011-3814-0 (ebook)

To Dr. Anton Pogany, a man for all seasons.

—Catherine

ACKNOWLEDGMENTS

To my goddess at the FBI, Angela Bell, for her continued support and invaluable help in hunting down the right resource and hooking me up.

To Dr. Richard Thomas, FBI forensic anthropologist, who told me what he would do if a pile of disarticulated skeletons were brought to him for analysis.

To Dr. Angie Christenson, FBI forensic anthropologist, who gave me a quick course on what happens to bodies thrown into a lake.

To Karen Evans, my woman for all seasons. Thank you.

If I made any mistakes, I cannot, in good faith, blame either Dr. Thomas or Dr. Christenson.

PROLOGUE

SAVICH HOUSE
GEORGETOWN
WASHINGTON, D.C.
WEDNESDAY NIGHT

Wake up, wake up. Something's not right. Sherlock's eyes snapped open, adrenaline surging. But why? She didn't move, listened. There—three beeps coming from the security monitor beside the bed. She'd never heard them before, but she knew what it meant: the security system was off. The beeps would get louder and louder. Possibilities scurried through her brain, none of them good. Dillon was on his back beside her, stirring now from the noise. She leaned down, whispered, "Dillon, the alarm's off."

He was instantly awake. He heard the beeps and turned off

the alarm. "You check on Sean. I'll see what's going on." They'd had this protocol in place since Sean had been born, but this was the first time they'd had to use it.

Savich unlocked the closet safe, handed Sherlock her small ankle Glock and a suppressor. The last thing either of them wanted was for Sean to wake up to a gunshot, terrified. He fitted a suppressor on his own Glock and racked the slide. He prayed for a simple malfunction as he pulled his pants on, but he knew it was unlikely. "Be careful," he whispered against her cheek. He ran down the stairs, and Sherlock, her bare feet whisper-light on the hall carpet, headed to Sean's room. His door was partially open, as it always was at night. She stopped, leaned in to listen, heard him make a little snort in his sleep. He was all right, no need to alarm him.

She heard a soft footfall and her heart seized. Someone had disabled the system and that someone was now in Sean's room. Sherlock slowly pushed the door inward, her heart pounding, her adrenaline spiking even higher. Moonlight poured through the window, silhouetting the man bent over Sean. His head looked distorted—no, he'd pulled a stocking over his face. She ignored the toxic punch of fear, raised her small Glock, and said very quietly, "Get away from him, or I'll blow your head off."

She saw the gun clutched in his gloved hand, a Ka-Bar knife in the other. He jerked up but didn't turn. "I'll shoot him before you can kill me." A young voice, low and hard. And something else. It was fear she heard, she knew it.

"Move away from him, and I won't shoot you. Drop the gun and the Ka-Bar and back away."

He slowly turned, but the gun still pointed at Sean. "How did you know I was here?"

"I've got bat ears. Who are you? What do you want?"

He looked undecided, then said, "You try to shoot me and he's dead, you got that?"

She wanted to vomit, she was so scared. *Hold it together, hold it together.* Again, she saw indecision. "You fire and you'll see, I'll still shoot him!" But he didn't. He ran six feet to the open window and jumped through a gash in the screen and onto the roof.

Sean jerked up, rubbed his eyes. "Mama? Mama? What's wrong?"

She had to move, had to go after him, but she had to soothe Sean. "Everything's all right, sweetie. Don't move." She ran to the window and jumped onto a thick oak branch that nearly touched the house. She saw him below, nearly to the ground now. She didn't have a good shot through the thick leaves and he was juking and jiving from branch to branch, but she fired anyway, missed, the bullet gouging tree bark a foot from his head. He didn't fire back.

He swung from the lowest tree branch six feet to the ground, landed on his side, rolled, and ran, not all-out because he was limping. She fired until her magazine was empty, but he was zigging and zagging, the limp even more pronounced now.

He disappeared around the corner of Mr. McPherson's house. She heard McPherson's puppy, Gladys, barking her head off.

Dillon's quiet voice came from behind her. "Sherlock, stay with Sean. I'm going after him."

They heard a car engine fire up. Sherlock grabbed his arm. "We can't get him now."

He helped her back through the slit in the screen. He studied her face, ran his hands over her arms. "I called 911. The police will be here soon."

Sherlock cupped his face between her hands. "Dillon, I'm not hurt, I'm fine." But of course she wasn't. Her heart was pounding, fear for Sean pouring off her.

"Mama! Papa!"

Savich quickly slid his Glock into his waistband and grabbed up Sean into his arms, hugged him tight against him. He whispered against his small ear, "Everything's all right, Sean. Don't worry, okay?" He closed his eyes as he rocked his small son.

Sean reared back in his arms and looked over at his mother. Sherlock pressed her own Glock against her leg so he wouldn't see it. "I heard you yell, Mama. Did you have a nightmare? What were those loud popping sounds?"

Her heart still pounded, her adrenaline still pumped wildly, but she could deal with that. She could deal with anything because Sean was all right, the danger was past. She looked at his small beloved face and said a thank-you prayer. She smiled, lightly patted his face. "Like your papa said, sweetie, everything's all right. The popping sounds, it was probably somebody's car backfiring. Some messed-up car, right? Too loud for our neighborhood. That's what woke up your papa and me." Did her smart son buy that whopper? Or would he realize the popping hadn't happened until after she was in his room? Well, she'd lied as clean as she could. Savich brought Sean close again, rocking him, breathing in his sweet child smell until Sean pulled back. He put his hand on his father's cheek, cocked his head.

"There's something wrong, isn't there, Papa? I dreamed I heard a man talking. And Mama, you said something, too, and you sounded angry. And then someone was running to the window. His head was all weird-looking, like a spaceman, and you were running after him, Mama. I saw you going out the window. It wasn't a dream, was it?"

Savich knew he had no choice. "There was someone here, Sean, but your mama took care of him. He won't be back. Now, it's time for you to go to sleep." While Dillon was speaking to Sean, Sherlock scooped the Ka-Bar off the Winnie the Pooh rug by Sean's bed. She hadn't even seen the man drop it.

"But—" Sean gave a jaw-cracking yawn.

Savich kissed him and tucked him under a single light sheet. He saw Sherlock quietly closing the window over the slit screen. He hoped Sean wouldn't notice it in the morning, but chances were good he would. Savich would have to figure out what to tell him without scaring him. He waited quietly until he heard his son's breathing even into sleep.

He went to Sherlock, saw her give a little shudder of reaction. The words burst out, low and controlled, but Savich heard the thick fear coating every word. "He was standing over Sean, Dillon, a gun in one hand, a Ka-Bar in the other." She swallowed. "He wouldn't tell me who he was. I couldn't shoot him—he said he would kill Sean. Then he ran to the window. Was he a pedophile who wanted to steal him? Or someone who wanted to kidnap him for ransom? Or some random crazed lowlife?"

His brain immediately latched onto *pedophile*, a word that scared every parent to his toes. He didn't want to say it aloud, or it would bow him to his knees. He felt violence stir in his gut, rancid and black. He pulled her close, whispered against her curly hair. "No," he said, more to himself than to her, "whoever he is, he had to believe we're rich because of my grandmother's paintings."

"Well, your Sarah Elliott paintings do make you rich, and a lot of people know it. They also know you'd sell one or all of them in a flash to save Sean."

"No matter who or what he is, we'll get him, I promise you. You saved our boy. Sean's safe. You're my hero."

That brought a hiccupping laugh. "I tried to shoot him, but he got down that tree in a flash." Her breathing hitched. "I wondered why he had both a gun and a Ka-Bar, but he needed the knife to slit the screen. Was he going to kill Sean?"

They held each other, saying nothing now, their eyes on their sleeping son, but only for a moment. The Metro cops would be here very soon.

While they stood in the open front door, waiting, Savich said, "I asked the dispatcher—it was Jordan Kates—to send them in silent." He kissed her forehead. "They'll be here any minute now. Did anything about him seem familiar to you or strike you as different?"

"It happened so fast—I don't think so. Wait, his voice was young, Dillon, and he moved young, too. Something else—when he told me he could kill Sean even if I shot him, I think I heard fear in his voice. But then again, he hadn't expected any trouble."

"Maybe he'd talked himself into coming after Sean, but he didn't have another plan if he was challenged."

She nodded. "Well, at least we have the knife, for all the good it will do us. He was wearing gloves. Dillon, I went after him, emptied my magazine, but I missed him. I actually missed him—me!—can you believe that?"

He loved hearing the outrage in her voice. It meant she was getting back on an even keel. "Even *you* have to miss sometimes. You were terrified for Sean, pumping out adrenaline, and so hyped you could have rocketed yourself to the moon. I hear a car coming. You can fill in the blanks when we tell the police what happened."

"Okay, I've got it together—well, I'm close. Thank heavens we had a plan in place if those three beeps ever sounded, otherwise—" She paused, then, her voice shaking. "Without the suppressor, I think Sean would have freaked. Even so, it was loud. So fast, Dillon, it all happened so fast. I wonder why he never fired back at me."

"He knew if he hesitated, turned back to you, you'd nail him."

A Metro squad car pulled into their driveway, cut its lights, and two officers climbed out. "Agent Savich?"

After introductions, Sherlock gave them a quick rundown, then Officers Pattee and Paulette headed out to search the neighborhood. They were back ten minutes later. No sign of their intruder, not that Savich or Sherlock expected them to spot him.

Paulette said, "No lights on in any houses, so the sound of the car engine didn't wake anybody up."

"And no neighbors standing on their porches to tell us anything," said Pattee.

Savich was studying his security system beside the front door. He called, "Come look at this." Both Paulette and Pattee looked over his shoulder to where he pointed.

"That's more wires than the back of my TV," Paulette said.

"Looks untouched to me," Pattee said, leaning in. "But how can that be possible? The guy got into your son's window. It's alarmed, right?"

"Oh yes," Sherlock said.

Dillon said, "I'm thinking we've got a guy with major computer skills."

"You think he disabled the alarm system remotely, using his computer?"

Savich nodded. "To do it, he'd have to be very good, because I upgraded the system myself. But he succeeded, and now I'll have to figure out how he did that and fix it."

The three men studied the complex mess of wires for another couple of seconds, then Paulette turned to Sherlock. "Could we go inside? You can tell us exactly what happened."

They went into the living room and Officer Paulette switched on a recorder. Sherlock went through it all again, answered their questions, and finished with "I can't tell you what he looked like. He wore a stocking mask, but I do believe he was young, twenty-five at most. When he ran across the yard, I saw he was limping a bit. From the jump? Maybe. I didn't notice a limp when he was in Sean's bedroom." She closed her eyes, pictured him. "It was his left leg."

They asked questions, Sherlock gave more details, and finally

Officer Paulette switched off his phone recorder and smiled at her. "You really told him you'd shoot his head off?"

Paulette, no more than twenty-five himself, had a great smile, and Sherlock found herself smiling back as she nodded. "That's what came out of my mouth, yes. Come on, guys, if someone was leaning over your sleeping child with a gun and knife, what would you say?"

"I don't know if I'd say anything," Pattee said. "I'd probably just shoot him."

"Yeah, sure, Joel," Paulette said, and smacked him on the arm. "That's what you'd want three-year-old Janet to wake up and see—blood and gore all over her bed."

Pattee pointed. "Yeah, okay, you have a point. I see a dog toy over there. But no wild barking?"

Savich said, "Astro would have brought the house down if he'd been here. But he's in love with a neighbor's new puppy, so our son let him do a sleepover."

Paulette said, "From now on out, I'll bet it'll be the new puppy sleeping over here."

"You're right about that," Sherlock said, "and yes, we're going to cut those branches off first thing tomorrow."

Officer Pattee said, "You guys had this plan in place in case something like this happened?"

"Yes," Sherlock said. "It sure paid off tonight."

"Now that's something I'm going to talk about with my wife," Pattee said. "You know, it would have been easier and cheaper for him to snatch your son off the sidewalk or out of a neighbor's yard or from the playground at school."

Sherlock said, "Yes, it would. I hadn't thought of that."

Pattee said, "You said, Agent Sherlock, you heard fear in his voice?"

She nodded.

Paulette said, "Well, he wasn't expecting her to walk in on him with a gun."

Pattee said, "That isn't the point. This doesn't sound like a pro someone hired to kidnap your son for ransom. Those guys have metronomes for hearts, nothing shakes them." No one had to say it, but everybody was thinking it—maybe the guy was a pedophile.

Savich said, "Officers, we'd like to speak to Detective Ben Raven in the morning. Will that be a problem?"

It wasn't a problem. Savich wanted Raven to check for any recent break-ins remotely like this one.

Pattee paused at the front door. "I've got to say something you already know. The guy who tried to take your son? I'll wager he'll keep trying. All his preparations show a big commitment. I'd say he's in for the long haul."

Both Savich and Sherlock hated it but knew he was right. Sherlock said, "At least we have the Ka-Bar. I'll get it to our FBI lab people in the morning."

Paulette said, "You'll let us know when you catch the guy?"

What faith. Sherlock smiled. "Yes, of course we will."

1

WILLICOTT, MARYLAND
FRIDAY MORNING
LATE JULY

Four years in Vice at the Seattle PD and Police Chief Ty Christie had never seen a murder, until this moment right after dawn on what promised to be a hot, sunny Friday. She was standing on her weathered back deck, sipping her daily dose of sin—thick-as-sludge Turkish coffee—and looking out at the patchy curtains of fog hanging over Lake Massey, man-made, like every other lake in Maryland, 1,800 acres. Lake Massey wasn't the largest of Maryland's lakes, or the deepest, only fifty-six feet, but it was still a popular vacation destination with thirty-three miles of shoreline and water warm enough to swim in during the summer. Fishermen loved Lake Massey with its walleye and large- and smallmouth bass eager to leap on their lines. As for Ty, she loved the impossibly thick maple and oak trees, a solid blanket of green covering the hills on the east side of the lake.

The only sign of life was a small rowboat floating in and out of the gray fog near a hundred yards away. She could barely make out two figures, seated facing each other, both wearing jackets and one a ball cap. She was too far away to tell if they were male or female, talking or not talking, or how old they were. Could they be out fishing for largemouth bass this early in the morning? She was starting to turn away when one of the figures abruptly stood, waved a fist in the other's face, and brought an oar down hard on his head.

She froze, simply couldn't believe what she'd seen. She watched the man slump forward as the fist-shaker leaned over him, jerked him up, and shoved him out of the boat. She yelled, but the killer never looked toward her. Rather, he looked down into the water, then at his oar. Checking for blood? He straightened, threw his head back, and pumped his fist.

Pumped his fist? He was happy he'd killed someone? That made it unlikely to be in the heat of the moment. So she'd seen a cold-blooded murder? Had the fist-shaker brought the other man out in the lake with the intent to kill him? The shock had Ty's heart kettledrumming in her chest. She watched the killer row smooth and steady back toward shore, quickly disappearing behind a curtain of fog. She hated that her hand was shaking when she pulled her cell out of her shirt pocket and dialed 911. Operator Marla Able always picked up on the first ring. Ty took a deep breath, cleared her throat. "Marla, it's Ty. I saw what I think was a premeditated murder on a rowboat in the lake a minute ago. One man struck another with an oar and threw him overboard. You heard me right. I think it was a man, but I can't be sure. Listen now, we've got to move fast. Call Ted Mizera, have him order out the Lake Rescue Team. Tell him the boat was about one hundred yards out into the other side of the lake directly across from my house. Tell him to hurry, Marla. I'm going out in my boat now."

She grabbed a flashlight, a jacket, and binoculars, pulled on gloves as she ran down her twenty wooden stairs, out onto her long, narrow dock, unlooped her mooring lines, and jumped on board her fifteen-foot runabout. She fired up the outboard engine, carefully steered away from the dock, aimed the boat at the spot where the killer had thrown the other person overboard, and floored it. Within four minutes she was at the edge of a sheet of fog, watching three mallards swim toward her, followed by four more, flapping their wings over the still water, then settling in with their brethren.

She slowly motored in, idled the boat, and searched the area with her binoculars, chanting, "Clear off, clear off." Miraculously, within minutes, only wisps of fog dotted the water around her. As for the fist-shaker in the rowboat, he was long gone, the offshore fog blanketing his escape.

She began searching for the body, praying the person was only dazed and still alive. The water was smooth, the surface unruffled except for the kick-up waves made by her runabout. She cut the engine, pulled out her cell again, and took pictures, but she knew there wasn't anything to see. She lined up one shot with the ancient oak tree standing sentinel in front of the abandoned Gatewood mansion on Point Gulliver to document her own location. Only its top branches were visible through the fog. She listened carefully but heard only mallards squawking and the soft lapping of the water against the sides of her boat. She scanned the eastern shore with her binoculars, but the fog was too thick offshore to make out any sign of the rowboat. Through a small pocket, she now saw Point Gulliver clearly, the pebbled beach, and Gatewood, three stories of stark gray stone, forbidding in the early morning light, its wooden dock stretching out into the lake. She saw nothing and no one. She knew the fist-shaker could dock the rowboat at any of the dozens of cottages lining the beach, tie up, and run, or pull the rowboat up onto the sand, hide it in bushes, and then disappear. He couldn't know she'd seen him. Had both people in the boat been staying in one of the rental cottages?

She called her chief deputy, Charlie Corsica, jerked him out of a deep sleep, and told him what had happened. He and the other four deputies would head to the eastern shore, scour the area for the rowboat, and interview all the cottage tenants. Most cottages along the eastern shore were rentals. Some of the vacationers had to be up, someone had to have seen something, even though it was barely 6 a.m. Maybe when her deputies went door to door, they'd find him. Had anything ever been that easy when she'd been in Vice in Seattle? Not that she could remember.

Even though she knew it was hopeless, Ty turned on the engine and began a slow grid search. She saw nothing until minutes later, when the three boats of the Lake Rescue Team circled her and cut their engines. All four members of the team were lifelong residents of Willicott. Ted Mizera, a local contractor, was big, beefy, and strong as a horse, rumored not to spare the rod on his kids. He'd formed the rescue team long before Ty had accepted the city council's offer to become the first woman police chief in the town's long, fairly peaceful history.

Mizera shouted, "Chief, Marla said you saw someone get whacked with an oar from your house? You see anything, like a body, since you got out here?"

"If my visual memory serves, I'm near the spot," she called back, "but so far no sign of a body. After the killer hit the victim on the head with an oar, he dumped the body overboard and rowed back to the eastern shore, toward Point Gulliver. I couldn't see anything because of all of the fog. I haven't seen any sign of a body. Did the killer have a brick tied around his victim's waist? I don't know, I was too far away."

Harlette Hensen, a retired nurse, grandmother to six hell-raisers, and owner of Slumber House B&B, shook her bobbed gray head. "You think the killer changed his mind, pulled the man out of the water?"

That was Harlette, always the optimist, wanting to think the best of her fellow man. Ty said, "Sorry, Harlette, I'd have seen it if that had happened. I saw him fist-pump after the victim went overboard, which says to me he rowed his victim out onto the lake to murder him and dump his body. It was premeditated." She shook her head. "That fist pump. I couldn't believe it."

Ted snorted. "Harlette, you wouldn't recognize the devil even if he perched on your rocker. Ty, I think you're right. The victim's probably weighted down. Or maybe held by the water reeds."

"The reeds aren't that thick this far out, Ted, too deep," Congo Bliss said. "I'm betting on a brick tied around the victim's waist to keep him under." Congo was the owner of Bliss's Diner, going on twenty-five years now, known far and wide for his meatloaf and garlic mashed potatoes. He was tall, fit, good-looking, going on fifty, and as proud of his physique as his meatloaf. Congo was on his fourth wife and his fourth rat terrier, all former terriers choosing to depart with the wives. More important, he was the group's designated diver, and he was already dressed in a partial wetsuit. He spat over the side. "Water's about twenty-five feet deep here. I'll do some free dives, see if I can find him before you call Hanger to drag the lake."

Congo pulled on his mask and fins and made four dives. No sign of the murdered man, but he brought up a present for Harlette and tossed it to her. Harlette caught it, let out a yell, then cursed. "Not funny, Congo." She held up the skull he'd thrown to her. "This sure isn't your guy, Chief. I wonder how old this skull is. Could be fifty years, who knows? I haven't heard of any local disappearing, ever. Some long-ago tourist, you think?"

Ty pulled her boat closer and took the skull from Harlette, turned it over in her hands. "No bullet hole, no crushed bones, and three teeth left. I'll take the skull to Dr. Staunton later. Right now we need to find the man I saw murdered an hour ago."

She handed the skull to Albert Sharp, owner of Sharp's Sporting Goods, with Harlette in her boat. He was the designated provider of any necessary water equipment and once a champion swimmer. Albert looked like he wanted to hurl, but he knew he couldn't because he'd never live it down. He swallowed half a dozen times. Nobody said anything. He carefully wrapped the skull in his daughter's blue polka-dot beach towel and laid it on the seat, wiped his hands on his pants, and attempted a manly smile.

"You said it was a rowboat," Harlette said, shading her hand over her eyes as she searched the water. "Did you recognize it, Chief? Was it one of Bick's rentals?"

"I was a good ways away, but it could have been. Yes, of course it was—it was painted an odd green, sort of an acid green."

Congo nodded. "That's it. I remember Bick got that green paint on sale a decade ago, long before your time, Chief. Everyone in town had a good laugh." He looked down at his watch. "Sorry, Chief, I can't do any more dives. I gotta get back to the diner. Willie's the only cook there. He can't fry an egg worth spit and he's always burning the toast."

Ty thanked them all, sent them home, and set everything in motion. She called Hanger Lewis over in Haggersville, set him up to drag this part of the lake in his ancient pontoon boat with its big dragging net. She called Charlie to check in. Nothing yet, no one had seen anything, no sign of one of Bick's acid-green rowboats and no sign of anyone who didn't belong there. She said, "No surprise, though I really did hope someone might have seen something. Okay, Charlie, keep the others scouting the east shore. Hanger will be here in about an hour. You go out with Harlette and Hanger, she'll show you guys the exact spot. And Charlie, be on the lookout for loose bones. Congo found a skull when he dived to look for the man I saw shoved overboard."

2

Ty got back to her cottage ten minutes later, grabbed a slice of toast, smeared on some strawberry jam, and ate it while she drove to downtown Willicott. She played over and over what she'd seen. What burned her was that she'd been nothing but a bystander, unable to do anything, only watch the murder unfold like a movie on the screen. Ty wondered what the odds were of a chief of police actually witnessing a murder. She prayed Charlie and Hanger would find the body when they dragged the lake.

As if a missing body and a skull weren't enough to keep her running, tomorrow was the first day of the yearly Willicott Book Festival. Despite everything, she had to make sure it went off without incident. She admired the banners already flying over High Ginger Street, snapping in the morning breeze, announcing the festival on Saturday and Sunday. Signs were everywhere hyping books, authors, attractions, signing venues, workshops, and panels. A gigantic banner in the middle of it all advertised Osborn's BBQ, the best barbecue in the area, honey from Osborn's own bees jazzing up the sauce.

The stores lining High Ginger Street were buffed and shined, showcasing their best goods behind sparkling glass windows. Kismet's Lingerie had enjoyed its yearly paint job, white with killer red trim to match a daring red satin teddy on display surrounded by six artfully arranged colorful thongs.

Most of the publishers, agents, and the sixty or so visiting authors had already arrived with mountains of luggage, their entourages, and signing pens. Marv Spaleny, president of the Willicott Festival Committee—the WFC—and owner of Spaleny's Best Books, had informed the city council and the *Willicott Weekly Informer* they were projecting at least seven thousand visitors this year, coming from as far away as Seattle. Visitors to the festival had begun arriving in Willicott earlier in the week in a nice steady flow, with few complaints and no gridlock, all smooth sailing so far. Since this area was a tourist destination, there was sufficient housing for the visitors—motels, B&Bs, three high-end resorts—many booked months in advance. In addition, some of the area locals rented out rooms, which meant the surrounding towns would enjoy the annual economic windfall along with Willicott. The festival committee even hired on more water taxis to ferry visitors staying on the east side of the lake.

Ty had brought on twelve volunteer deputies to smooth any troubled waters and to help the other volunteers answer visitor questions. She'd had only six extra deputies on hand last year, and that hadn't worked out—too many unexpected kerfuffles. She still shuddered at the mayhem that had erupted when Ponsy Glade, owner of Glade's Gas, had gotten into it with a reader who'd cut in a long book-signing line. Ponsy actually belted him in the chops, the line of readers cheering him on.

Everything was set, all the schedules were nailed down, everyone knew where he was to be when, and if a visitor had a question, there were dozens of volunteers to help. She decided she and Willicott were ready. She could focus on finding the body in the lake.

Ty stopped at Dr. Staunton's office, carrying the skull still wrapped in the polka-dot beach towel under her arm. Dr. Morgan Staunton was a transplant from New York City, the borough of Manhattan, she'd announced upon arrival. She'd been a general practitioner here in Willicott for ten years now, had learned to water-ski and fish, and served as the local volunteer medical examiner, a service she didn't provide often. Everyone called her Dr. Scooter, after her Vespa, a common sight in Willicott.

Dr. Staunton wasn't in her office yet, so Ty left the skull with her nurse, Pammie Clappe, eighty years old and still going strong. Pammie opened the towel, looked down at the skull with complete indifference, wrapped it up again, tagged it, and set it in the inbox tray. She said in her scratchy smoker's voice, "Kismet would sure like that skull to be her mother-in-law. Have you seen those thong things she displayed in her window? I'm thinking I might get the purple one. You all ready for the festival, Ty?"

"All's good. I saw Kismet's mother-in-law yesterday," Ty said, "tossing a Frisbee, so Kismet is out of luck."

"A pity. I don't much like her, either. This is exciting, Ty, one of my favorite horror authors is coming."

Ty said over her shoulder as she left, "Purple'd be a cool color on you, Pammie, go for it." She headed to Bick's Bait and Rental on South Pier, wondering if Pammie read horror novels in bed at night. Talk about gruesome nightmares.

It was eight thirty in the morning, the sun was bright, and the temperature would hit the high eighties today. Lots of business for Bick and his rental rowboats, but not for a couple of hours, until he opened at nine thirty. His store always smelled like Lysol, to kill the fishy odors, Harlette had told her, but fish and Lysol weren't a happy combination, not that Bick seemed to care. He bought the Lysol wholesale by the case. Bick was an energetic seventy-five, with tufts of white hair sticking out of his ears, nose, and eyebrows and a love of Jim Beam. He was standing behind his counter, eating a corn dog loaded with mustard and coated with sweet relish, a Diet Coke at his elbow, his daily breakfast, since his seriously vegan wife didn't work in the shop in the mornings and so wasn't around to throw the hot dog to the walleye in the lake. "Hey, Chief, what's up?"

Ty told him what had happened, described the rowboat she'd seen.

"*What?* You actually think it was one of my boats?" He sounded outraged, like she'd accused one of his children of dealing meth to the local teenagers.

"Can't be one hundred percent sure, Bick, since the fog was

so thick, but I think the rowboat was acid green like the paint you use. Did anyone turn in a boat in the past couple of hours?"

"Don't know, but I tell everyone where the boats go and they can bring 'em back at three a.m. for all I care."

"Let's check names against boats," Ty said.

It didn't take long. Rental boat number six, the *Green Gaiter*, scheduled to be returned at 6 a.m. this morning, wasn't parked in its slot beside rowboat number five, the *Green Lantern*.

The name of the renter of the *Green Gaiter* was Sala Porto of Washington, D.C.

"Yeah, I remember him," Bick said. He ate the last bite of his corn dog after dipping it into the small bowl of mustard Ty knew he would wash and put away before Mrs. Looney came in. "He rented the *Gaiter* for a week, fishing, lolling around with his girlfriend, drinking beer and swimming, that sort of thing, not here for the book festival. He said he had to be back in Washington today, so he'd return the *Green Gaiter* no later than six o'clock this morning.

"I told him his name was real interesting, I mean, how often do you hear the name Sala Porto? He smiled, said he heard that a lot, but he wasn't a *gangsta,* didn't hail from Sicily. He was an FBI agent, and the name was good because the bad guys thought he might be Mafia and that scared them lots more than a federal cop with a vanilla name and all those rules and regulations to worry about. You think he might be the guy you saw get hit over the head and thrown into the lake?"

"I don't know, Bick. He actually told you he was an FBI agent?"

"Yep, he showed me his ID. 'Creds,' he called it."

"Was anyone with him? This girlfriend?"

"I never saw the girlfriend, only this FBI agent, Sala Porto." Bick showed her his signature.

"Credit card?"

"Yep, let me find it for you." Bick scrounged in a small steel box, flipped through piles off credit card receipts, and pulled one up, waved it at her.

Ty studied the receipt. American Express for $240. His signature was bold—that was the first word that popped into her mind. More than bold, dominant.

"He used his own pen," Bick said.

Black ink, of course, to go with that strong signature. Ty left Bick cleaning up a spill of mustard and walked to her white Silverado in the pier parking lot, shining bright under the morning sun. She leaned against her truck door, pulled her hat down to cut the glare, and pulled out her cell. She didn't have any contacts at the Hoover Building, so she called the main number and asked for Special Agent Sala Porto. After being passed around for ten minutes, Ty ended up with a summer intern named Mindy who said she'd heard Agent Porto was with his girlfriend, Octavia—didn't know her last name—on vacation, and who wanted to know? Ty put on her best cop voice, low and hard, and finally ended up transferred to the Criminal Division, where Agent Porto was assigned, according to Mindy. Agent Sala Porto's unit chief was on vacation, and no one else wanted to talk to her. She was eventually passed to Executive Assistant Director James Maitland's office. She grinned into the phone at that coup. She'd managed to get to a top dog. Ty used her most intimidating voice when she identified herself and asked to speak to Executive Assistant Director Maitland, stating it was a matter of great urgency. The woman said without pause, "All I've got to say, Chief Christie, is that this had better be good or I might be visiting you in your own jail cell."

A man's deep, impatient voice came on the line. "Maitland here. Goldy said this was urgent. Who are you, and what do you want?"

Maitland sounded like her kind of cop: no nonsense, straightforward, hard as nails. Ty identified herself as the police chief of Willicott, Maryland, then described what she'd seen three hours before and what she was doing about it. "The murdered man could be an FBI agent, Sala Porto. Or Porto could be the murderer. Or neither. I need your help."

Maitland snapped out questions until she was wrung dry. She wouldn't have been surprised if he'd wanted to know about her birthmark (a lovely strawberry on her left hip), her marital status (still thankfully single after two broken engagements), and if he did ask her age, she'd have no problem telling this man she was turning twenty-nine on the fourth of November.

Jimmy Maitland was silent a moment. "All right, Chief Christie, here's what we're going to do."

3

WILLICOTT BOOK FESTIVAL
WILLICOTT, MARYLAND
SATURDAY, LATE MORNING

It was warm and sunny, an altogether perfect day for a book festival. Savich gave the smiling, fresh-faced parking attendant Jimbo a ten-dollar bill and parked Sherlock's Volvo in Lot B beside an SUV filled with a half dozen enthusiastic young women, all talking, laughing, and gathering book bags, purses, water bottles.

Nearly-five-year-old Sean and his longtime girlfriend, Marty Perry, who was still on schedule to be one of his future wives, were so wired they bulleted out of the car, their goal to hunt down their favorite author, Remus McGurk, the creator of Captain Carr Corbin, intergalactic space marauder, and his sidekick, Orkett, a terrier with sharp teeth who filched chocolate bars.

Sherlock met Dillon's eyes over the roof of the car. She knew he was as worried as she was. It had been only three days since the man had broken into their house and threatened Sean. The FBI lab hadn't found fingerprints on the Ka-Bar, not that they expected to, and had determined the knife could have been purchased from dozens of stores in the D.C. area. Every agent in the CAU was working in his spare time on trying to identify the intruder. Most of Dillon's agents believed it was either a pedophile who'd seen Sean, or a kidnapping for ransom, knowing Savich could sell one of his grandmother's paintings. Or, he thought now, an old enemy here for payback. Oddly, that felt like it could be right. Detective Ben Raven of Metro was working different sources, and as of today, still nothing had popped. Even though Savich had moved the security system box to behind one of his grandmother's paintings in the dining room and put a dead bolt on the front door, it didn't alleviate the nerve-racking low-level fear. Savich had hoped the kidnapper or pedophile, or whatever he was, might be moved to make contact, but as of this morning, there'd been no communication of any kind and no further attempts on Sean.

Sherlock hadn't wanted to take Sean to a public place where thousands of people would be milling about, but he'd been so excited about today, a promised treat for more than a month now, she and Dillon couldn't say no. What was worse, Dillon wouldn't be with her for extra eyes and protection. He had a job to do here in Willicott with a Chief Ty Christie, assigned yesterday by his boss, Jimmy Maitland.

Sherlock said, "I figure three hours should do it. Then we'll head to Osborn's BBQ, to be followed by the Dali Lama ice cream shop, then, if you're done here, we'll take Sean to his grandmother's for the rest of the weekend."

Savich nodded, knowing he'd spend more hours tonight hunkered over MAX searching for the intruder. He looked toward the rocket-fueled kids. "Sean, Marty! Hold up. Do. Not. Move."

Sean knew the serious voice, grabbed Marty's hand to hold her in place, and began confiding to one of the six young women from the SUV he was going to take a zillion photos with his iPad of Remus McGurk. Didn't they admire Orkett, Captain Carr's terrier sidekick? Had they read his latest adventure on the planet Mumbo? Were they going to see him? Get his autograph? The women were charming and happy to pose when Sean told them he would like to practice taking their pictures before he shot his masterpiece of Mr. McGurk.

Marty was jealous and poked Sean in the side. One perceptive young woman invited Marty to stand in front of them, made her one of their group. Sherlock saw Sean send admiring looks to the young woman and she'd bet most of his photos would be centered on her.

After oohs and aahs over Sean's photos, Sherlock took each child's hand while Savich locked the Volvo and wished the girls a fun day.

Savich told Sherlock, "If you see anything that alarms you, anyone suspicious, call me immediately." He kissed her. "I owe you big-time." He peeled off to meet up with Flynn Royal in front of the police chief's office on High Ginger Street. Flynn was a sharp agent Maitland trusted and Sherlock's major competition at the shooting range. Mr. Maitland had sent Flynn to Willicott right after the call from Chief Christie the previous day to assess the situation, gather facts, and make himself generally useful, trying not to step on the chief's toes. In short, Flynn was here to be Maitland's eyes and ears. As for Savich, he was here to consult, if needed, and if they found the body in the lake, to identify Sala Porto, an agent he knew personally, if he'd been the murder victim. Maitland was concerned. No one had been able to locate Sala. A photo likeness wasn't good enough for Maitland.

Savich wove through the crowds and finally spotted Flynn. He was called the intellectual pirate because of his black-rimmed glasses set over smart, dark eyes and his too-long black hair and lithe build. Savich could easily see him on the deck of a ship wielding a sword and laughing maniacally. Flynn was speaking with a tall, fit woman holding a Mariners baseball cap in her hands. She wasn't wearing a uniform but black pants, low-heeled black boots, and a white shirt, her badge over her left breast pocket. He recognized Chief Christie from the candid photo Detective Harry Anson of the Seattle PD had emailed him yesterday afternoon. He'd texted Savich: *Christie's smart, a dirty fighter with serious skills, hated being a big-city cop. No gray areas for her, always either black or white, but admittedly, in Vice, there are few gray areas. She knows only one direction—forward. Her daddy's a captain in the Washington State Patrol, so nope, the acorn didn't fall far from the tree. Oh yeah, she's popular and a looker. Good luck, Ty's also a frigging bulldog.*

Savich heard Christie say to Flynn as she slipped her cell back into her pocket, "That was Charlie Corsica, my chief deputy.

They found the body, not where I thought it would be, but there was a lot of wind chop yesterday afternoon, stirred up the water. He's taking the body to Dr. Staunton, our local medical examiner. Charlie said no ID, but I was in for a big surprise. He wouldn't tell me, for which I am going to bust his chops."

Flynn said in his honey-soft Alabama drawl, "I don't know Porto, but Agent Savich does. As soon as he gets here, we can go to Dr. Staunton's office." He paused a moment, added, "If the body is Porto's, we'll have him taken to Quantico for autopsy. Of course, then it'll be a federal case." He turned, saw Savich, and grinned. "Good to see you. Let me introduce Chief Ty Christie."

Savich and Ty shook hands and took each other's measure. Ty saw a big, tough, good-looking man, maybe five years her senior, with intelligent eyes she imagined saw most everything, eyes so dark as to be nearly black. He had thick black hair, a bit on the long side. She'd bet her new LED TV he took no crap and would joyfully dive into a fight.

Savich looked at a woman far more vibrant than the photo Harry Anson had emailed him. Tall, sharp green eyes, dark brown hair nearly to her shoulders, pulled back from her face with two clips. He really liked the stubborn chin, and a line of freckles across her nose. Harry hadn't mentioned the freckles or how she radiated energy and focus. He was right that she was a looker. She was a frigging bulldog? Savich found himself smiling at her—impossible not to—and stuck out his hand. "Call me Dillon."

"I'm Ty, and no, I won't tell you what Ty is short for. It's too embarrassing. A pleasure, Agent Savich—Dillon."

She had a lovely smile that made an immediate connection to the person she was talking to. Ty said, "Glad you're here. I understand you know Agent Sala Porto?"

Savich nodded. "Yes, four, five years now. We're the same age. He was on the Washington SWAT team, then transferred to the Criminal Division at the Hoover." He drew a deep breath. "I'm hoping it isn't Sala. He's tough, an excellent agent, a good man."

"If it isn't Sala Porto," Ty said matter-of-factly, "then it's no longer federal." She eyed them both. "And you two can go about your business and enjoy the book festival."

4

Flynn said, "Certainly, Chief, although Mr. Maitland told me to offer my assistance if you asked for it. Excuse me. Hey, Sherlock, hold up!"

"You can shake my wife's hand," Savich called after him, "and that's it, Flynn."

"Yeah, yeah," Flynn said over his shoulder, not looking back, his eyes on Sherlock standing next to a book stall, holding both children's hands, no mean feat since each kid wanted to go in a different direction.

Ty was staring at Sherlock, her curly red hair a beacon. "Sherlock? Oh my, I recognize her now, she's the agent who brought down the terrorist at JFK, then shot that Brit terrorist at the Lincoln Monument. She's your wife?"

Savich felt the familiar burst of pride, then impatience because he wanted to get to the medical examiner's office, wanted to be able to say the murdered man wasn't Sala. He nodded. "And the little boy is our son, Sean. The little girl is one of Sean's future wives. No, don't ask, like your name, it's complicated." Savich called out, "Come on, Flynn, get away from my wife, and let's get moving."

But Ty was already striding after Flynn. When Savich reached the group, he heard Flynn say, "So Savich assigned you the kids while he's off playing with me and the chief?"

She grinned up at him. "Bless his heart, Dillon's going to miss all the fun." She turned to Ty with interest, and Flynn introduced them. The kids got in on the act, and it was a good two minutes before Marty saw a photo of a favorite children's book author and tugged on Sherlock's hand.

Savich said quietly to Sherlock, "They dragged the lake, found the body. We're off to see if it's Sala."

She laid her hand on his arm. "If it is, I'm sorry, Dillon."

The crowd noise didn't matter, Sean had Vulcan ears. "What body? Who's Sala? What happened, Papa?"

"Somebody's dead? Drowned?" Marty closed in, her eyes steady on Savich's face.

Savich came down on his haunches, took the kids' hands. "Agent Flynn and I need to make sure someone who died isn't an FBI agent. You guys go have fun. I'll catch up with you later."

Sean said, "I'm going to ask Mr. McGurk if he wants to eat lunch with us. I want him to tell us about Orkett's next adventure. Don't worry, Papa, tacos and chips don't cost very much. Marty and I will pay for his lunch. We've got sixteen dollars."

Sherlock said, "I thought we were going to Osborn's BBQ, Sean."

Marty said, "I wanted to try sus-shi, but my mama said it cost a lot and the raw fish could make you die."

Sean's opinion of raw fish was clear on his face. "No raw fish, Marty. All right, Mama, maybe we can afford to buy Mr. McGurk a small basket of barbecue ribs."

As for Sherlock, she couldn't wait to see how McGurk handled the kids' invite to lunch. She'd bet he had learned long ago how to let a kid down easy. She said low to Dillon, "Everything's okay, haven't seen anyone remotely interested in Sean. Or in me, for that matter. Well, except for Flynn," and she gave him a fat smile.

"He's a horndog, keep your distance, Sherlock." Still, Savich worried. He watched her lead both kids away and thought again about payback, that the man who'd broken in on Wednesday could be someone he'd sent to prison who was now out.

Savich, Chief Christie, and Agent Flynn Royal headed to Dr. Staunton's office on Wintergreen Avenue, Ty telling them that so far it appeared no one in the rental beach cottages had seen any stranger or any rowboat, either too early in the morning or too much fog to see anything.

Ty said, "Charlie Corsica said he's got a big surprise for me. Like I said, if I don't like it, I'm going to belt him."

Ten minutes later, Savich stared down at the draped body lying on top of an examination table. Dr. Staunton pulled back the sheet. Crushed skull, facial features obliterated. There was no blood, it had all been washed away. Dark hair was flat around the ruined skull, but there was something off—the face was narrow, fine-boned, and despite the destroyed features . . . Savich said, "This isn't Sala Porto. In fact—"

Dr. Staunton said, "That's right, not only isn't this Agent Sala Porto, it isn't a man." She pulled back the sheet, and they looked at a woman's body.

So this was Charlie's big surprise. Ty glanced back at him, standing by the exam door, looking like he'd aced the hand and won the pot. Well, he was only twenty-five. His hair was so blond it was nearly white in the sun, and his light blue eyes made him look like an angel, which he wasn't. "Your big surprise?"

He started to grin, but at Ty's expression, he dropped his eyes, studied his boots. "Yeah, one of them."

Dr. Staunton said, "There was ID in an inner pouch on the inside of her jeans' waistband." She handed Ty the driver's license. "She had two bricks tied around her waist to keep her down."

Ty read aloud, "Octavia Millsom Ryan. Age thirty-six, address in Washington, D.C." She looked at the photo. "Her face, it's hard to tell. When I called the Hoover Building, a summer intern told me Sala Porto was with his girlfriend, Octavia—no last name—and they were on vacation. You don't forget a name that unusual." She passed the driver's license to Flynn.

Flynn said, his voice emotionless, "Yes, it's Octavia. I was a witness in one of her cases, maybe three years ago. Did you know her, Savich?"

Savich shook his head, pulled up her info on his cell. "Octavia Ryan is a criminal defense lawyer in Washington, known as the Patroness of Lost Causes, according to this article in the *Post*."

"Looks like it's my case after all," Ty said. "Now I've got to find Special Agent Sala Porto. He's my prime suspect."

Savich read further, raised his head again. "Sorry, Chief, Octavia Ryan left her private practice last year. You didn't know, Flynn? She became a federal prosecutor six months ago."

5

Dr. Staunton said, "Ty, maybe you not running this case is for the best, given what I've got to show you now. Everyone, come with me to see Charlie's second surprise for you."

They followed Dr. Staunton to another room, watched her unfold a tarp on an exam table. They stared down at dozens of human bones jumbled together.

Dr. Staunton said, "Charlie and Hanger found these bones when they dragged the lake. You can see there are at least enough bones to form close to a dozen people, maybe even more. The FBI forensic anthropologists should be able to make a count."

Ty felt like she'd been slammed in the face. It was incredible, unbelievable. All these bones at the bottom of Lake Massey? She said blankly, "There's a shoe and a foot inside it."

Dr. Staunton nodded. "Unfortunately there's no soft tissue left. The shoe's still got some shape, so I'd say it hasn't been in the lake longer than, say, ten years. As for the rest of the bones, I have no idea how long they've been in Lake Massey, maybe fifty years. Fish clean the bones quickly, particularly largemouth bass and walleye. They're both efficient scavengers. As you can see, there aren't enough skulls for this number of bones. So there are more down there."

Ty couldn't look away. The most heartbreaking to her were the three skeletal hands, fingers outstretched, the bones white as snow. "All these bones—they belonged to living, breathing people—" She swallowed. "Hanger needs to do a wider drag of the lake."

Savich said, "Chief, shall I see what the FBI can do, or can you handle another lake drag locally?"

She only shook her head and turned to Charlie, standing by the exam room door. "Charlie, get ahold of Hanger, go out with him on another drag. This time do a wider grid. Be very thorough."

Charlie had his cell phone out before she'd finished talking, then he was gone.

Flynn said, "Dr. Staunton, I know you've only begun, but have you noticed any obvious possible causes of death?"

"I did examine the one skull Ty brought me. No injuries I could see. As for the rest, I haven't had time to examine them. And besides, you know I'm no forensic anthropologist—I could easily miss something important. As I said, the FBI forensic anthropologists are the ones to examine these bones."

Savich looked at Ty. "Chief?"

"Yes, Dr. Staunton's right. Thank you."

Flynn nodded. "I'll arrange to have the bones picked up to take to Dr. Richard Thomas at Quantico. He's one of the top forensic anthropologists in the country."

Ty waved her hand toward the pile of bones. "It doesn't make sense. I haven't gotten any reports of missing persons in the three years I've been here. Well, there was one, a teenager, but we found him." She picked up a skeletal arm. "Who are you? Who are they? Why are they on the bottom of Lake Massey?"

Savich lightly laid his hand on her arm. "They'll do DNA tests. It will take time, but we will find out who these people were and give closure to their families."

Ty swallowed. "The man I saw murder Octavia Ryan, maybe he's a serial killer, maybe she was his latest victim."

Flynn said, "It's possible. If we are talking a Serial, Chief, he's killed a lot of people over what could turn out to be a long period of time. If no one's gone missing locally in your tenure as police chief, then he could be drawing on towns all around Willicott and simply using Lake Massey as his dump site."

Dump site. It sounded obscene. Ty said, "It means going back over missing persons files plus contacting all law enforcement in, what, a fifty-mile radius of Willicott, telling them the situation, asking them to go through their missing persons files as well."

Savich said, "What makes things hard is if we're talking about a Serial, he could be from Pittsburgh or Boston, for all we know, but it's a good start."

Ty said, "True, but I have to treat this like it's local or semilocal until we know if these people were murdered and who exactly they were." She drew a deep breath. "You think the forensic anthropologist will find perimortem trauma, don't you?"

Savich hated to say it, but had no choice. "Yes."

Ty agreed. A serial killer, or a Serial, as the agents referred to the kind of monster who'd murdered people and thrown their bodies into Lake Massey, dusted off his hands and walked away smiling.

She looked again at the bones. "I wonder how many people he dumped in the lake we'll never find? They're simply gone, forever." She looked at Agents Savich and Royal. "I've read there are hundreds of serial killers running loose around the United States, killing and getting away with it, sliding seamlessly back into their everyday lives, and no one ever seeing what they really are. Cops in Seattle, where I'm from, still talk about Gary Ridgway, the Green River Killer."

They stepped out of Dr. Staunton's office and nearly ran into a panting Charlie. "Chief! Congo called me. They found Bick's missing rowboat, the *Green Gaiter*!"

Ty said, "Where?"

"Sunk right off the Gatewood dock. Actually, it was Buzzard." He added to Savich and Flynn, "Buzzard is Davie Coursey's nickname. He's a snot-nosed little teenager, always causing trouble. He was busting around with a couple of friends up at Gatewood, probably daring each other to go inside and settle in and talk to the ghosts. Buzzard said he saw something in the water, and sure enough, it was the *Green Gaiter,* sunk in sixteen feet right off the dock."

"Good," Ty said. "We'll go winch it out of the water. Charlie, did you tell Hanger I'd authorize the additional hours and his costs for another lake drag?"

Charlie said, "Yeah, and he said if he's to do a bigger search, he'll need his sons, and they'll want time and a half."

Ty thought of her straining budget. The city council was covering all the expenses for the additional deputies for the book festival, but only an idiot would think that as important as finding the bones of murdered people in Lake Massey. "We'll have to do it, Charlie. If he's got his sons, he won't need you. You can stay with me."

Flynn pulled out his cell, turned away. A couple of minutes later, he turned back and said, "I've called it in. An FBI forensic team will be here in a couple of hours. They don't want anything touched, including the boat. They want to be the ones to bring it up."

Ty said, "Not a problem. Octavia Ryan's killer must have known only kids go near Gatewood, to scare themselves silly, so he wouldn't expect anyone to find the rowboat, at least for a while."

Savich said, "What do you mean the boys would dare each other to go inside the house and talk with ghosts?"

Ty rolled her eyes. "Gatewood is supposedly haunted, and of course a big-time draw for both kids and teenagers. They prowl around the house and yes, make their dares—spending the night inside. From what I hear, none of them have."

Savich remembered clear as day that long-ago winter night in the Poconos when he'd searched the Bannister house, empty for nearly thirty years—only it hadn't been. "Why is it haunted? What happened there?"

Ty nodded. "It's quite a story. Since we've got lots of time until the forensics team gets to Gatewood, everyone, come to the station with me. Charlie can tell you what happened at Gatewood, then we can go out there and look around. You were a kid when it happened, right?"

Charlie gave a little shudder. "I'll never forget."

6

The station house door opened into a long, narrow room, a high desk sitting squarely in the middle, benches lined up against the wall. Behind the desk sat a large gray-haired woman wearing a bright red flowered muumuu, rhinestone glasses sitting on her nose. She was well north of sixty, and she had a great smile. Ty said, “Agent Royal, Agent Savich, this is Marla Able, my dispatcher, my 911 operator, and my enforcer. Any citizen of this fine town runs afoul of the law, they have to deal with her first. Marla, our murdered man wasn’t a man. He was a woman, and her name was Octavia Ryan, a federal prosecutor. It’s no longer our case, but we’ll be assisting the FBI.” She shot Savich a look that told him she wasn’t backing away from this. He understood: a murder in her town, a murder she’d witnessed. It had to burn her to her toes not to lead the investigation.

Marla shoved up her glasses and gave Savich and Flynn a thorough study. "I hate to hear it was a woman, Chief. But these two sure look tough enough to lasso the bad guys."

"Thank you," Flynn said and cracked his knuckles.

"And you," she said, looking at Savich. She cocked her head at him. "You've got something else going on, too, don't you? Pretty smart, aren't you?"

Something else going on? He wasn't about to ask. Savich said only, "Some would agree, some wouldn't."

She laughed, a hacking smoker's laugh. "Ty, now I've got to state the obvious. Both of these boys are young and good-looking, and that could be a problem if the Cougar Club gets a whiff of them."

Flynn stared down at this amazing woman, her plump hands loaded down with rings his mom would really like. "Cougar Club, ma'am?"

"Our town's finest," Marla said. "I'm a longtime member myself. Ty here is what we call a cub cougar, far too young to break loose and run wild with us, but she'll be a fine addition someday. Our motto is 'Cougars Forever.' "

Ty said, "I heard the motto is 'Feed the Cougars.' "

"That's the naughty submotto," Marla said. "Now, what about all the bones Charlie found? Some yahoo using our lake as a dumping ground?"

Ty said, "I'll fill you in soon, Marla. We'll be working with Agent Royal on that situation. We're all heading out to Gatewood in a few minutes." She herded them into her office, paused a moment. "Marla, is everything going all right at the book festival?"

"A couple of loud arguments with a political author in Tent C, but Willie shut it down fast, said he'd put them all in jail unless they piped down. They did."

"That's good," Ty said. "We've only got two cells. That's the only problem reported? All the deputies are doing what you tell them to?"

"They'd better," Marla said. She cracked her own knuckles, watching the diamonds in three of the rings glitter and sparkle. "Don't you worry, Chief, I've got it covered. I'll get you special agents some coffee, all right? Tea for you, Chief?"

"Yes, thank you, Marla."

"And for me, too, please," Savich said.

"A tough guy who drinks tea, now isn't that a kick? You can get yourself a Diet Coke, Charlie." Marla waved the hand sporting those three big diamond rings toward Savich and Flynn. "You take care of those boys, Chief."

Ty closed the door of her good-size office, rectangular with two small windows that gave onto the civic parking lot in the back. A battle-scarred wooden desk of ancient lineage stood in the middle, three institutional wooden chairs with cushions in front of it. The cushions looked new. On the desktop sat a telephone, a printer, and a computer about five years old, which made it ancient. Behind the desk was an IKEA credenza with a coffeepot on top and a framed photo showing a younger Ty, her arms around a teenage boy, a man, and a woman—presumably her parents and her brother. An iPad with a banged-up red cover and a new MacBook Air lay beside it, looking like a sleek greyhound next to a grandfatherly bulldog. A beautiful Christmas cactus sat on the windowsill, blooming wildly in July.

When everyone was seated, Ty said, "Okay, Charlie, while we're waiting for the tea and coffee, tell Agents Savich and Royal about Gatewood."

Charlie sat forward and clasped his hands between his knees, readying himself to tell a story he'd told many times. "My mom told me all about it. Since she's the smartest person I know, I believe her. She told me it all started way back in 1965 when an oil tycoon, a Major Samson Gatewood, built this huge house and named it after himself. Word was he wanted it to look like the nineteenth-century houses in Newport built by those New York magnates.

"Gatewood died suddenly in the late eighties, and local folk suspected the wife killed him. But it didn't go anywhere. The wife lived alone at Gatewood until she died in the early part of this century. Their only son didn't want the place and sold it to a Methodist minister from Boston, Reverend McCluen, and his wife and three kids. My mom said Reverend McCluen told everybody the General Conference—that's the governing body of the Methodist Church—was paying to fix up the house, but she didn't believe him because the contractor let slip over beers at the Timberline Bar that the price to restore the place was several hundred thousand dollars, and what church had that kind of money to give to a single minister to fix up his house? So there was lots of gossip about where the money came from, rumors he had to be stealing from the church, or even the collection plates.

"Anyway, Deacon Pitter went over there one day, found the entryway of the house splattered with blood, and called Chief Dickerson. They found the whole family murdered, dumped in Lake Massey, right off the end of the Gatewood dock, all of them stabbed to death. Come to find out there were two violent escaped prisoners from Springville in the area at the time—that's an institution for the criminally insane, about fifty miles from here—and everyone believed they'd killed the McCluens. They found the escaped prisoners and locked them back up. Mom didn't know if the prisoners really did kill the McCluen family, but maybe they were too crazy to even remember if they'd done it."

Charlie paused for effect, and Savich nudged him along. "What happened at Gatewood after the McCluens were killed?"

7

Before Charlie could continue, Marla knocked and came into Ty's office, carrying a tray with tea and coffee and exactly four lovely big chocolate chip cookies.

Once everyone had their drink and their single cookie, Charlie said, "Well, now, Reverend McCluen's younger brother inherited Gatewood and sold it the next year despite the scary stories about McCluen family ghosts. This was the Pierson family, and they were rich. Mr. Pierson was some sort of venture capitalist, my mom said. They had two kids, teenagers, the older one a boy, a popular jock, good student, and a younger girl, also very smart, pretty, good grades, every bit as popular as her brother. Mrs. Pierson was active in local politics for the short period of time they lived here—before they were killed, too."

"The Piersons were killed at Gatewood?" Savich asked.

"Yes, maybe six months after they moved in. Mom said the Piersons thought the whole ghost and haunting thing was funny, though. The son, his name was Robert, he liked to tease people about hearing screams when he was alone in the house. But that was it. Everything seemed fine, the family fit into life here in Willicott. Everything was normal.

"Then a UPS man delivered a package and found the front door open. There was blood in the entry hall and in the living room.

"Chief Dickerson found their bodies thrown off the end of the dock like the McCluens, and stabbed like the McCluens, all except for the daughter, Albie Pierson. They couldn't find her body. They dragged the lake, but there was no sign of her. Then the rumors started, like gossip does, that the father and brother were sexually abusing her and the mom only wrung her hands and did nothing. The idea was that Albie must have snapped and killed them, dragged their bodies to the dock and kicked them into the lake, and ran.

"No one wanted to believe that, I mean, everyone liked the Piersons, thought they were nice. But there weren't any other leads and no word about Albie Pierson, so Chief Dickerson put out a BOLO on her, sent her photo out everywhere, asking for information about her as a person of interest in the Pierson murder case. But no one ever saw her again. She was only fifteen years old when all this happened. The case is still open."

Ty said, "Charlie, is this what your mom believes?"

"My mom said she didn't believe there was any sexual abuse

going on. She said the family were nice people, Mr. Pierson sort of standoffish, but he was smart, worked mainly from home. She told me Albie wouldn't hurt a fly. It was obvious to her Albie was terrified the killer would come back for her, so she took the money out of her dad's safe and ran. There was some talk that the killer took her—who knows?"

Charlie shook his head. "Imagine, everyone was looking for her, and she was only fifteen years old." There was admiration in his voice. "She sure had to be smart, like her dad, to stay out of sight like that."

Ty said, "Gatewood has been empty since the Piersons' murder, fifteen years ago."

Charlie swallowed, showing a prominent Adam's apple. "That's right. Mr. Pierson had a sister. She and her husband tried to unload Gatewood, but couldn't. Its reputation had spread far and wide. They even tried to donate it to Willicott, but the city council turned them down. There've been some ghost hunters from out of town here over the years, and they reported out what you'd expect—cold spots and odd noises, doors opening and closing on their own, stuff like that. So it's stayed empty for fifteen years."

Savich rose. "So now we know what's out there. Are we ready to take a look at the boat and the house?"

They all piled into Ty's official police car, a five-year-old mud-brown Crown Vic. Savich called Sherlock, told her where he was headed. "I'm hoping we'll find something to lead us to Sala. Take care of yourself and the kids." He paused, then, a smile in his voice, added, "I'll give you whatever your heart desires tonight."

Flynn heard Sherlock's laughter. He said, "Yeah, I used to make promises like that to Beth."

Ty looked at him in the rearview. "Your wife?"

"Yes," Flynn said, "back when." He said nothing more.

Everyone had baggage, Ty knew, herself included. She let it drop.

Gatewood stood on Point Gulliver, a low promontory that stuck out into Lake Massey like a fat thumb. It was the perfect movie poster for the classic haunted house, made of unrelieved pale gray stone quarried from Scarletville, sixty miles east. There was a wide porte cochère along the side, a detached garage beside it. The driveway wound through the trees to a narrow two-lane road. There was a long, skinny beach of pebbled coarse brown sand dotted with tumbled piles of driftwood and rocks strewn about. A long dock looking ready to collapse stretched fifteen feet over the water.

A half dozen oak trees faced the lake, stalwart sentinels, misshapen and bowed from years of winter storms. A wide gray stone path led from the dock to six deeply indented stone front steps. The porch was narrow, and Savich could see from twenty feet away that vandals had ripped up many of its dark wooden planks.

Savich paused, stepped back, studied the house, and opened his mind. He felt nothing but the sun's warmth on his face and a cool breeze off the lake. He'd bet the gray stone hadn't looked this grim when people still lived here. He could picture colorful flowers in the beds and boxes hanging from the ceiling of the porch, a rich green lawn, a good-size boat tied up at the dock. He turned slowly and looked back over the lake. He pictured the murderer wearing a ball cap and dark jacket, rowing the *Green Gaiter* through the early morning fog away from the dock. Had he forced Ryan to hold still while he tied weights around her body to keep her under once he'd killed her? Why hadn't she fought him? Had he parked a car in the porte cochère? Or hidden it in the garage? What did he do with the oar he'd struck her with? There had to be blood on his jacket. What did he do with it?

Ty pointed. "That's my house, directly across. See the dash of bright red? That's rhododendron in one of my flower boxes."

Savich stowed the questions for the moment. "You've got quite a location."

"I was lucky. The lady who lived at Bluebell Cottage—no, there aren't any bluebells around here—decided to move to Florida. She gave me a great deal. Let's have a look at the *Green Gaiter*."

They walked the stone path down a slight incline covered with tall blue lobelias, pale purplish-pink Joe-Pye weed, swatches of black-eyed Susans, and other plants Ty couldn't identify. Charlie walked to the end of the dock and pointed down. They saw the hazy outline of the *Green Gaiter*, sitting upright on the rocky bottom some fifteen feet down. A simple rowboat, its only distinctive feature the acid-green paint job. Charlie said, "I don't see any oars. I guess they floated away."

Ty said, "Even if we did recover the oar he used to kill her, it wouldn't help, the lake water would have washed it clean."

Savich said, "I gather you haven't been inside the house?"

Charlie shook his head. "No reason to since the teenagers found the rowboat in the water."

Savich could tell from Charlie's face he wasn't eager to go inside the house. The chief said in a cool voice, "Okay, sure, let's take a look. I've only been downstairs. You'll see it's been trashed."

She paused on the first step and turned toward Charlie. "Charlie, would you stay here, keep a lookout for the FBI forensic team?" Since he'd been raised on the stories of Gatewood's bloody history, she imagined the last thing Charlie wanted to do was go into Gatewood. Charlie looked relieved, but he tried to be cool about it. "Sure, not a problem, Chief, I'll keep an eye on the *Green Gaiter*."

Savich followed the chief and Flynn up the steps onto the wide-oak planked porch and into the house through the double front door, once beautifully carved and now so battered it looked ready to fall off its hinges. It creaked when Flynn pushed it open.

8

Ty laughed, hating that her voice sounded high and jumpy. She said, "I hope the script doesn't have us going down the basement stairs."

Flynn said, "Hey, there are three of us, and we're armed. No self-respecting ghost would want to take us on."

Savich stopped dead in his tracks when he stepped into the entrance hall. He felt a bone-numbing cold.

Ty cocked her head at him. "Is something wrong?"

He realized no one else felt it. Only him.

She asked again, "Dillon, are you all right?"

He drew a deep breath. "Yes, of course, Ty. You were right about the desecration."

She nodded. "Some morons even smashed the beautiful

etched front windows, at least I think they were once etched. I've always wondered why people, kids especially, get off on destroying things." She pointed to the floor. "Look at those Italian tiles. You know they were beautiful once, but now they're filthy, gouged, and chipped. And the white walls, covered with graffiti that probably goes back years. See, here's one dated 2003 and signed, *Motown*. Go figure."

Flynn said, "Kids are all hormones and bravado, and the house can't fight back." He grinned, waggled his eyebrows. "Or maybe it can." He checked his iWatch. "Forensics might already be in Willicott to take the bones and Octavia Ryan's body to Quantico. They should be out here soon. When will this Hanger start dragging the lake again?"

Ty said, "Not much longer, I don't think. He's good, don't worry. Any more bones, he'll find them." She swallowed, cleared her throat. "I've been told bones take a very long time to disintegrate. I can't help but think about all those people who were thrown in out there." She shook herself. "Okay, through there is the living room—big, beautiful once, you can see traces—the high ceilings and the elaborate moldings. You'll see some lowlifes ripped out the appliances in the kitchen, tore off the doors to the cabinets. It's really sad. So I guess we'll split up. Look for any signs that someone's been here lately."

"Yes, that's fine. I'll check upstairs." Savich headed for the wide, once-ornate staircase.

"Don't let a ghost grab you by the throat," Flynn called after him.

Savich waved his hand and walked slowly up the stairs, careful where he stepped because the oak boards were scuffed and scarred, some scored with knives, some ripped up entirely. Many of the banister posts were broken, tossed onto the floor below. The wall beside him was covered with a science fiction landscape, all done by one hand. The aliens were very inventive, their tentacles heaving and intertwining in what looked like violent copulation.

At the top of the stairs, Savich found himself on a wide landing. To his right stretched a long, narrow hallway, the light dim because all the doors were closed. To his left was a shorter hallway, shadowed as well. He turned right and walked to the door at the very end of the hall. It was the master bedroom. He stepped into a large, perfectly square room, empty of furnishings. He stood in the doorway, disbelieving. There was no graffiti on the walls. They were painted a soft cream color that had held up well, looked almost freshly painted. He walked to the center of the room and stood quietly, looking around, not understanding. There were no broken windows, no gouges in the oak-planked floor, no dust he could see anywhere. The room looked frozen in time, as if waiting for its occupant to walk in. He looked into an enormous adjoining bathroom. The sink, toilet, shower, tub, and counter were dated, but stark white and clean, again, without a hint of dust. Like in the bedroom, nothing looked touched, again, as if waiting for someone to come in and brush his teeth. He stepped back into the bedroom, trying to make sense of it. Why wasn't this room trashed? Because someone had to have been there recently. He walked to French doors that gave onto a deep covered deck looking out at the lake, glistening beneath the noonday sun, his hand outstretched to turn the shining gold handle.

Suddenly, as if someone on the remote had changed the channel, the scene in front of him morphed into something else entirely. He saw a fog bank, gray and thick, rolled nearly to the shore, and a figure in an acid-green boat rowed toward him out of the fog, dipping the oars rhythmically. He couldn't tell if it was a man or a woman. The person was wearing a ball cap pulled low, a dark jacket, and jeans.

The rowboat touched the end of the dock, and a man—Savich was certain now it was a man—stepped onto the dock and laid the oars down beside him. Savich couldn't make out his features, he was wearing dark sunglasses, and now his ball cap was pulled even lower. He watched the man step off the dock and onto the beach. Savich watched him pick up a large rock, carry it back, and place it in the rowboat. He worked quickly, made three more trips. Satisfied, he tipped the side of the boat until water started to pour in. He watched the *Green Gaiter* slowly sink. He picked up the oars and hurled them out into the lake. He turned back, stopped, and looked up, directly at Savich. He yelled something Savich couldn't hear, grinned wide, pumped his fist in the air, and walked back toward the house. Savich would swear he heard whistling.

He heard the front door open and close.

His heart skipped a beat. Savich didn't want to believe what he'd seen, but there was no choice. He knew to his bones he'd witnessed the killer coming back after murdering Octavia. He stood motionless, drew a deep breath, let it all sink in. This sort of phantom re-creation of a violent deed had happened to him before, but this time he hadn't seen the actual violent deed, only the aftermath. Had he imagined hearing the door, too, or had he heard the murderer come into the house? No, it had to have been the police chief or Flynn. He turned to look out again at the lake. He saw Charlie standing at the end of the dock, looking down at the sunken rowboat, the chief and Flynn standing beside him. Neither of them had closed the front door. Who had?

9

WILLICOTT BOOK FESTIVAL

Remus McGurk called the nearly eighty children to sit cross-legged in a semicircle on the floor in front of him. The tent was large enough to accommodate all of them and their parents. McGurk settled himself in a big armchair. Sherlock soon realized he was a master showman, mesmerizing the children with a brand-new Captain Carr Corbin and Orkett adventure in a deep, booming voice. Every young eye was fastened on him, enthralled. Remus McGurk was at least twenty years older than his author's photo on his book jackets and looked, in fact, a great deal like Santa, with his head of thick white hair and comfortable paunch. Unlike Santa, he was wearing a yellow nineteenth-century lawman duster over jeans, a *Star Trek* command red shirt that stretched over his belly, and shiny black boots. Like Sherlock, parents, both standing and seated on the grass, seemed to be enjoying the show.

Sherlock didn't speak to any of the other parents, she was too much on alert watching over Marty and Sean. She spotted a young man with dark hair and a long face, wearing chinos and an untucked plaid shirt, who didn't look like a parent. She looked for any sign of a gun under his shirt, looked to see if he was showing any interest in Sean or simply watching the spellbound children, listening to their gasps and laughter, amused at their absolute focus on McGurk. Was she being paranoid? Maybe, but all she had to do was think about the man standing over Sean with a gun and a knife, and she didn't care. The young man pulled something out of his shirt pocket. She was ready to take him down—no, it was a small notebook. She watched him write as he looked and listened. A reporter? She drew a deep breath, heard Sean's laughter when McGurk read how Captain Corbin threw a bar of chocolate in the air and Orkett caught it in his mouth and made great chewing noises. She found herself wondering if Remus McGurk was a pseudonym, decided it had to be. She listened with half an ear to the scary situation Captain Corbin was in. Not to worry, Orkett came to the rescue. He gnawed through his ropes, freeing Captain Corbin to drive off the bad alien who was trying to steal all the water on the planet Ark. McGurk bowed, and the children went wild, clapping and cheering.

She heard a dad whisper to his neighbor, "Guess what the kids are going to demand for lunch?" They laughed. "Yeah, I'll have to keep my boy from feeding chocolate to the dog."

Sherlock wanted to tell him to make a big point of the chocolate, when she saw a man step into Tent A and stand quietly, looking at the mob of children. He was wearing dark sunglasses and a ball cap, but Sherlock saw he was searching through the excited children talking and shoving as they formed a long line with their parents for McGurk to sign their books. Was he looking for his own child? He didn't look like a parent. Sherlock kept a hand on each child's shoulder as the line moved slowly forward until they had nearly reached McGurk. She looked again at the man in the sunglasses and cap, and knew to her gut he was staring at Sean. She turned to the woman behind her, large, fit, with no-nonsense mother's eyes, herding three young children. Sherlock jerked her creds out of her pocket and lowered her voice. "I'm FBI. Please keep an eye on this little boy and girl. You can all speak to Mr. McGurk together." She lowered her voice. "I have to go check on someone."

The woman looked squarely at Sherlock. "Go. I've got them."

Sherlock worked her way through the crowd, circling around behind the man. He was walking slowly toward the children, toward Sean. It was still crowded, kids with signed books pressed to their chests milling around, not wanting to leave. Sherlock's heart pounded despite her brain telling her he certainly couldn't hope to take Sean here, in this tent, surrounded by other children and dozens of parents. It would be madness.

She managed to get behind him, no more than three people between them. She couldn't make out his features with the sunglasses and the ball cap, but he moved young, like the man who'd stood over Sean. He was also slight—like the man who'd stood over Sean. Wait, hadn't he been taller? She couldn't be sure. He stopped, pulled something out of his jacket, and Sherlock went for her Glock. He held up a large solid bar of chocolate, waved it around, shouted, "All of you know Orkett loves chocolate. Whoever can tell me how old Orkett is wins this incredible nut-filled five-pound chocolate bar!"

The children moved like a tsunami toward him, yelling out numbers. A little boy screamed, "Twenty-one! He grew up!"

A little girl, not to be outdone, shouted, "No, Orkett's only a puppy! He wets the floor!"

Parents trailed indulgently after their kids as they shouted out numbers, obviously thinking this was part of the McGurk show. And was it? Sherlock saw the woman she'd asked to watch Sean and Marty, keeping a tight rein on them as well as her own three. She wasn't laughing with the other parents, she was watchful.

Suddenly the man turned, saw Sherlock was close, and without hesitation, he threw the candy bar to her. She automatically caught it. He yelled, "She's got Orkett's chocolate! She'll pick the winner!" Dozens of excited, yelling children, their parents behind them, changed direction on a dime and swarmed toward her. Sherlock quickly lost sight of him. She threw the chocolate bar as far as she could toward Mr. McGurk, who was staring at the spectacle, looking bewildered and a bit pissed at losing his worshipful audience. Sherlock slipped past the throng of people and made her way out of the tent. She heard a little girl yell, "I've got it! Orkett's chocolate bar!"

Outside the tent, she stopped, panting, looked around, but she didn't see him. There were too many people blocking her view. She wondered if she caught a glimpse of him ducking behind a lemonade and cookie kiosk. She heard Sean shouting behind her, "Mama! This lady won't let us go! Help!"

Sherlock slowly turned back. She doubted she'd have caught him, not in this mad jumble of people. Ditch the ball cap and the sunglasses, and she wouldn't know him from Orkett. She calmed as she turned back to see the woman holding Sean's arm in one hand and Marty's in the other, her own three kids staring at her, their eyes big. Sherlock trotted up to them. "I'm here, Sean. She was keeping an eye on you two for me. Please thank her, kids."

Sean and Marty gave Sherlock a confused look, but they thanked her. The woman said low, "Did you think that man with the candy bar was up to something? Maybe a pedophile?"

Sherlock swallowed. "I don't know, it's possible. Thank you very much. I'm Agent Sherlock." She stuck out her hand.

"I'm Maureen Jernigan."

Sherlock shook her strong, capable hand and gave her a card. "Mrs. Jernigan, if there is ever anything you need, call me."

Maureen studied the card, but only for a moment because her little girl was pulling on her leg, demanding a chocolate bar with nuts, like that man was waving around. Maureen was soon trotting away with her children. She turned her head, gave Sherlock a smile, and disappeared into a crowd.

Sherlock took Sean's and Marty's hands. "Time for lunch. Is Mr. McGurk going to join us for barbecue?"

Marty shook her head. "I asked him when he signed my book. He said he was meeting Captain Corbin for lunch and couldn't let him down. I told him Captain Corbin wasn't real, Mr. McGurk had made him up, and he gave me that look, like Grandpa does. But then he smiled and patted my head and called me precocious. What does that mean?"

"It means you're too smart to be almost five years old," Sherlock said. "Okay, kids, we're on our own. What would you like for lunch? Barbecue or tacos?"

Say tacos, please say tacos.

"Is Papa coming with us?"

"I don't think so, Sean. He's still meeting with his friends."

Sean looked up at her with big, dark eyes, his father's eyes. "Mama, who was that man with the big candy bar? I saw you go after him."

Her eagle-eyed son. Sherlock looked him straight on and lied clean. "Turns out he was part of the show, not a problem. Come on, guys, let's eat. I'm starving. What's it going to be?"

"Barbecue!" they shouted together.

Oh well. Barbecue was fine, but truth was, she'd never met a taco she didn't like. Sherlock wanted to call Dillon, tell him what happened, but how could she with Marty and Sean next to her elbow, all ears? She couldn't be sure it was the man who'd broken into their house three nights ago. She wasn't even sure he'd meant any harm. She tried to picture the man bending over Sean's bed. She hemmed and hawed, going back and forth, until she wanted to kick herself. Of course it had to be the same man. Finally accepting it settled her. She couldn't be sure, but she didn't think she'd seen him limp. *No, don't second-guess*—it only meant his ankle may have healed in three days.

Sean and Marty were flying high as kites on a windy day, each stuffing down pork ribs, barbecue sauce smeared all over their faces and T-shirts, comparing their books but not touching them, on Sherlock's order, while she studied every single man she saw come toward the stand. When would Dillon get back?

10

GATEWOOD MANSION

Savich paused on the second-floor landing, listened. He looked down into the large entry hall. He was alone. The house was silent.

He knew why the killer had looked directly at him and pumped his fist. *Because someone else was standing at that window, waiting for him to return. He'd looked up, pumped his fist to show that person his pleasure, to signal his success.*

Had he avenged someone Octavia Ryan had prosecuted during her tenure as a federal prosecutor? Or had he killed her in revenge for failing to get an acquittal when she'd been a defense attorney? Savich remembered the man whistling, happy as a clam, as he'd hurled the oars out into the lake, one of them the murder weapon, with no remorse, no regret, pleased with what he'd done.

Savich already knew one thing for sure. The killer hadn't been Sala, no way. And Sala was a big man, strong, tough, and taller than Savich. This man was slight, no more than five foot eight. So where was Sala? Savich didn't want to consider it, but he had to. Chances were good Sala was already dead. But that fist pump had been for killing Octavia Ryan, not Sala. Had he come back to kill Sala? Had he believed it necessary to kill him? Or was he collateral damage? Was his body in the water off the Gatewood dock, like the Piersons' had been fifteen years before?

Savich walked up a narrow set of stairs to the third floor. It was colder up there, a natural cold, the air still and silent, the light dim. It smelled old, musty, uncared for. It was a good place to hide. He shook his head at himself. Both the McCluens and the Piersons had been killed inside the front door, the reason, he thought, for the cold spot. Had the Piersons' killer or killers known there was another Pierson child and searched for her up here? Was Albie Pierson still alive? Or had she died on the streets of some city?

He methodically opened each door along the narrow corridor—three small bedrooms, for maids, he supposed, and two old-fashioned bathrooms, all the rooms empty. Like in the second-floor rooms, there was no graffiti, only faded cream-colored walls and a thin coat of dust. The last door on his right, facing the lake, was locked. Interesting. Why lock this particular room? He shoved, but the door held. He knocked, felt foolish even as he called out, "Anyone in there?" He knocked again, louder, shook the doorknob.

He heard something, a muffled sound, garbled, and a series

of thumps, like shoes banging against wood. He knocked again, called out louder, "Is there anyone in there?"

The muffled sounds were louder this time. More wild thumps and garbled noises. He stepped back and kicked right below the doorknob. The door shuddered but held. He kicked again harder, and the door flew inward, slammed against the wall.

He stepped into the small room, momentarily blinded by the brilliant sunlight pouring in through the large front window. Like the other rooms, this one was also empty. He heard more violent kicking against wood. Savich saw the closet door shudder. He twisted the knob, but the door was locked. "Get back, I'm going to kick the door in."

The closet door gave way on the first kick but didn't slam all the way inward. Someone was in the way. He got the door open enough to see inside the closet.

Savich met Sala Porto's eyes.

11

Agent Sala Porto drank the entire soda Charlie handed him and ate a half dozen Oreo cookies Ty kept stashed in her truck. Finally, he wiped his hand across his mouth and chased it all down with a bottle of spring water. Blood matted his hair over his left temple, and his face was bruised. But Savich hadn't found anything broken. He was sitting on the edge of the front steps of the house, the four of them gathered around him. No one had suggested they stay inside the house.

Ty said, "Drink another," handing him a full bottle. "You're still dehydrated. Don't drink too much, just a bit more. Yes, that's good. Now let me see how bad it is." Ty came down on her knees beside him, examined his head wound. "Bleeding's stopped, but you'll need some stitches. In the meantime, let me clean it out and put a couple of butterfly bandages over it to keep the wound together. Your wrists are raw. I've got some antibiotic cream and some gauze. Then we'll get you to Dr. Staunton. She'll take care of you. Are you ready to tell us what happened?"

Sala Porto held up his hand, and looked over at Savich, who'd carried him firefighter style over his shoulder down the two flights of stairs, since Sala's legs were numb. Sala rubbed his legs, feeling the pins and needles and the cramps. He said simply, "I owe you my life. Thanks for searching me out. How did you know I was up there? Did you see me in one of your visions?"

Charlie came to attention. "Visions? What do you mean, Agent Porto?"

Savich said easily, "Agent Porto is joking. I was checking the upstairs, went to the third floor, and found a locked door. I heard something, broke in, and found Agent Porto tied up and stuffed in a closet." He thought about the series of unlikely events that had led him to Sala. It had been too close. He said a silent prayer of gratitude and squeezed Sala's shoulder. "You hung in there, that's what was important."

Sala was so grateful to be alive, so relieved Savich had found him, that for a moment, he couldn't find any words. Then he said, his voice thick, "The truth is I didn't think I was going to make it. When I woke up in the closet and got my brain working again, I thought he'd come back and kill me after he murdered Octavia, but he didn't. I don't know why." Sala didn't tell them how close he'd been to giving up, accepting he'd die of thirst in that closet. He'd tried to make peace with himself, prayed his parents and his brothers and sisters would be all right without him. He didn't tell them he'd have rather had a bullet in his mouth, over and done with instantly, than have to face his own death like that, knowing it would take days upon days of knowing, of waiting, of trying to come to terms with it. He said, "Chief, he hated Octavia. He killed her, didn't he? How?"

12

It was difficult, but Ty kept her voice matter-of-fact. "He took her out in a rowboat, struck her head with an oar, and threw her body in the lake. We found her this morning, identified her."

Sala looked down at his wrists, raw and bleeding because he'd tried hour after hour to loosen the ropes. But there'd been no give at all. At least he now had feeling back in his feet and legs. He realized it felt odd to be alive and know he'd be all right. But Octavia wouldn't be all right, the bastard had killed her. He swallowed. "He was after Octavia. I was only an extra on the set. He told me I was in the wrong place, wrong time, and he laughed and said 'Sorry, Agent, but *c'est la vie*.'" He looked at Ty. "How do you know exactly what he did to Octavia? It was so early, barely dawn when he took her."

Ty said, "Against all odds, I was the one who saw him kill her. I live directly across the lake and I was standing at the railing of my back deck, admiring the beautiful dawn over the lake, like I do nearly every morning, and I saw him strike her with an oar. If I hadn't happened to be on my deck at that particular moment, neither of you would have been found for a long time. Agent Porto, if you feel up to it, tell us what happened. Can you identify this man, at least give us a good description of him?"

"I never saw his face. I'd know his voice anywhere, though, some Southern in it. He screamed at Octavia that she'd told lies about him, that it was time for her to pay. He screamed it over and over, cursing her." Sala felt pain spike through his head, thought he probably had a concussion and closed his eyes a moment. No one said a word. When he opened his eyes, he managed a crooked smile. "Some FBI agent I am. Let me try to be coherent and tell you what happened from the beginning." He knew it would be easier said than done. He let his rage come to his rescue, let it focus him on the here and now. The pain, the guilt, the grief over Octavia could come later. "I've got to speak to Octavia's parents."

Flynn said, "I'll handle that. What's important now is getting a handle on this man who killed her. Start at the beginning."

Sala nodded, took a sip out of the bottle of water Ty handed him. "Yes, all right. Octavia made all the arrangements for our week's stay here at her aunt's cabin near Lake Massey. She asked me to join her and both of us could de-stress, she said. I'd just finished up a difficult case, and she was deeply involved in a federal money-laundering case coming up. She wanted us to be alone, even cook our own meals, swim in the lake, lie around, and drink margaritas. And that's what we did, except the rowboat, I guess. I rented it from a guy named Bick, told him I'd return his boat early yesterday morning, no later than six a.m. Octavia had to get back to Washington for a deposition. When I was in the closet, I was hoping Bick would come looking for it, realize something was wrong, but that didn't happen.

"The killer got into the cabin when it was still dark, maybe half an hour before dawn. I jerked awake at the sound of a board creaking, and my hand went automatically to my Glock on the bedside table.

"A man's low voice said, 'Don't, Agent Porto. Touch that gun and you're going to die sooner than you have to,' and he laughed.

"I still made a grab for my Glock. He screamed at me, 'Put that gun down or the bitch is dead,' and I saw he had the tip of a knife not an inch above Octavia's neck. It was barely light enough in the cabin for me to see he was wearing a stocking mask over his face. Octavia moaned and woke up, tried to jerk away. He grabbed her, and I jumped out of bed, my Glock in my hand, when he yelled again, 'Didn't you hear me, moron? Drop the Glock, Mr. Agent, or the bitch dies.'

"He pressed the knife into her neck, pinning her to the bed. I could see blood running down her neck. I dropped my Glock.

" 'Get back in bed. That's good. Don't move.'

"Octavia made a slight mewling noise, and he looked down at her. 'You're finally awake, are you? Time to party, you lying bitch. Put your hands on top of the covers, Agent, or I'll do her right here and now!'

"I put my hands on the outside of the covers, waited, assessed. Octavia asked him what he thought she'd done to him. She pleaded with him to tell her who he was, but again, he only laughed. She kept trying to talk to him, telling him she could make things right.

"All he ever said was 'No, bitch. I'll tell you everything, but not yet.'

"He laughed again and pushed the knife in deeper, told her to shut up until Octavia stopped making a sound. He grabbed my Glock and told us to put our clothes on.

"I knew it was crunch time. I leaped at him, but I wasn't fast enough. He hit me on the head with the butt of my own gun, and I was gone.

"When I woke up, I was alone, my arms tied tight behind my back with rope, my ankles duct-taped together, a gag in my mouth. I realized I was in a small closet and I couldn't move." His voice hitched, then smoothed. "I'd about given up when I heard your voice, Savich.

"I've played it over and over in my mind." He looked at each of them. "I want to break him apart. I want to kill this guy."

Ty opened her mouth to spout some line about the courts seeing to justice but realized it would only sound hollow, even ridiculous. In his shoes, she'd want to kill the man, too.

Sala said, "As I told you, I finally decided he was going to leave me there to rot in that closet." He took another sip of water. "I have no idea why he didn't kill me at the cabin. Maybe he was coming back to haul me out to the rowboat, like he did Octavia."

Savich said, "He sank the rowboat after he came back from

murdering Octavia, so it's obvious he wasn't planning on taking you out in it."

"How do you know that?" Flynn asked him.

Because I saw him do it. "It makes sense, don't you think?"

Sala said, "Sitting there in the dark, trussed up like Houdini, I had a lot of time to think. A lot of time to listen. I swear to you I heard laughter, not anywhere close to me, but it was clear and distinct. And I know I heard voices. One of them was the guy who killed Octavia."

"And the other voice? Did you recognize it?"

Sala shook his head. "No. But I do know one thing for certain. I did hear a girl laughing. Not a woman, a girl, crazy laughing, and it went on forever."

13

Ty rose when the FBI forensic crime team pulled up in a large white van. She said, "Flynn, if you'd introduce me, we can get them started. Dillon, I'm sure you have a lot to talk about with Agent Porto."

Savich and Sala watched her stride toward the van with Flynn. Savich knew he would keep close tabs on the operation without putting the chief's nose out of joint. He was good working with locals and keeping the peace, which, Savich supposed, was why Maitland had sent him. Savich laid his hand on Sala's arm. "I'm very glad you're alive, Sala. Trust me on this, we'll find him."

Sala was rubbing his hands together, the pins-and-needles feeling nearly gone. "It was close, Savich, closer than I've ever been to getting my plug pulled. But Octavia, I couldn't protect her. I know he told her who he was before he killed her, probably jerked off that stocking mask and laughed at her. I forgot to ask the chief if she saw him pull it off on the lake."

Savich could tell him the man hadn't been wearing a mask when he'd rowed back to the dock, but he didn't. He looked to the group who now stood on the dock, gazing down into the lake. He could hear the chief's voice explaining what they would need. Sala looked out over Lake Massey and said in a low voice, "Octavia and I drank too much wine Thursday night, her favorite, Leaping Frog chardonnay." He stopped, shook his head. "I remember her laughing her head off at something a kid said at the gas station outside Willicott Thursday afternoon. It was her last day.

"Sure, she asked me here so we could both relax and forget about work, but she had another reason, too. Her ex-husband, Bill Culver, was putting on a full-court press for her to come back to him. We talked about the situation between them, but she hadn't made up her mind what she was going to do. She was still wavering. She said she hadn't believed people ever changed, but now it looked like he had, or at least he was trying. He'd told her he loved her, but she wasn't sure if she still loved him." Sala swallowed, turned to Savich, tears pooling in his eyes. "And now she's gone." He snapped his fingers. "Just—gone."

Sala looked down at the bandages from Ty's first-aid kit wrapped around his raw wrists. "If it hadn't been for you and the chief, we both would have simply disappeared. No one would ever know what happened to us. Sure, the FBI would have tracked us here, found the cabin, but after that, no one would have known where to look.

"I wonder why he ever bothered with the stocking mask if he was going to kill both of us."

"No matter his bravado, coming alone, he couldn't be sure how it would go with you there, Sala, an FBI agent. He used the mask in case he had to run."

Sala stared at Savich, and then he grinned. "That's excellent B.S. Maybe it's even true. Sorry, Savich, I'm not very proud of what I am or what I did, right now."

"Then help us find him. We can start with the criminals Octavia was assigned to prosecute and the criminals she defended before that. It had to be one of them. This was payback."

"Most of the scumbags she defended ought to be offering to buy her Christmas presents for the rest of her life, not trying to kill her."

Savich nodded. He thought about the girl Sala had heard laughing. "He was with someone, Sala, the girl you heard laughing. Maybe she helped him get you over here, get you up the stairs. You don't remember anything until you woke up in the closet?"

"No. I suppose I could have been going in and out for a while, but I don't remember."

"You need to tell us where you and Octavia stayed. We'll get the forensic team over there next."

"It's a small clapboard cabin Octavia's aunt owns out past the rental cottages, right on Shoreline Way. Number 357, I think."

"What car did you use?"

"We came up together in Octavia's Volvo. It was parked at the cabin last time I saw it."

He and Sala were silent a moment, looking out over the placid lake, a warm summer breeze against their faces. Savich saw Hanger's pontoon boat out in the water, its big nets dragging for more bones.

Sala looked back at Savich, his eyes bleak and filled with pain. "You remember my wife, Joy? She died so needlessly, too, in that helicopter accident."

"Yes, I remember," Savich said.

"And now Octavia's dead. I couldn't save either of them." Sala gave an ugly laugh. "I guess I don't rank very high on the good prospect list. A woman would have to be seriously desperate to hook up with me."

Savich wanted to tell him what he'd said was ridiculous, but there was never much sense in raw emotion, it spewed out without reason or logic. Sala hadn't been able to save either his wife or Octavia, and he blamed himself. Savich said, "That kind of thinking is a waste of time, Sala. Time for you to focus, to put the blame where it belongs, and use that fine brain of yours to help me find her killer."

They sat in silence, side by side on the top step, watching chief forensic tech Tommy Raider—tall, skinny as a parking meter, a cloud of black curls on his head—direct his team winching the *Green Gaiter* out of the water and settling it onto the wooden dock. They took their time going over the boat. At last the group walked back to Savich and Sala.

"Nothing to help us," Tommy said, waving back at the *Green Gaiter,* now lying on its side on the dock. "Not that we expected to find anything, what with the boat being in the water so long.

What is with that green color?" He called to his team. "Pete, Rand, Gwen—we're going to head upstairs to that bedroom where Savich found you, Sala, see what we can find. After we're done processing this humongous place, Savich, you can take us to the cabin were Sala was staying." Tommy gave Savich and Sala a salute, said, "Upstairs to the third floor first, bambinos, bambina!"

Tommy leaned close to Sala as he passed him, lightly touched his hand to his shoulder. "If there's anything useful in there, we'll find it." He studied Sala's still face, gave his shoulder a squeeze, then turned. "Savich, you wanna show us which bedroom closet?"

Savich started to rise, but Sala grabbed his arm.

"No, I'm okay. Let me show him. I heard you speaking to Sherlock on your cell. It sounds like you need to get back to her. Oh, and Savich, whoever this guy is, you know he's got to be bat-crap crazy." Sala rose slowly, testing out his feet and legs. No more pins and needles, no more cramping. He frowned a moment. "I know I'll never forget that girl's laughter. I bet she's as crazy as he is."

Savich remembered the man he'd seen waving to where he stood in the upstairs window. Had that girl been standing at that window?

Tommy said over his shoulder, "Don't worry about Sala. Gwen has some medic training. She'll keep an eye on him. Sala, when we're done here, the chief's deputy, Charlie, said he'll take you to the local doc and get you checked out, get your scalp stitched up."

Ty walked away to answer her cell. She turned back after she'd punched off. "That was Hanger, calling from the lake. He and his sons have already found more bones from at least six people, he estimates. He's going to take all the bones to Dr. Staunton to give to the FBI." She paused, drew a deep breath, looked from Flynn to Savich. "I don't see any other explanation. It has to be a serial killer using Lake Massey to disappear his victims."

Savich saw panic in her eyes before she quashed it. He said easily, "It seems the likeliest scenario, but, Chief, one step at a time."

Ty looked back out over the lake. "A serial killer. It's tough to think there might be one of those monsters anywhere near this beautiful lake."

Flynn said, "Savich, I know you and Sherlock are up to your earlobes in alligators, so we'll drop you off."

Ty came to attention. "What alligators?"

Savich said, "We had a home invasion three nights ago, and we still haven't caught the guy." Because Sherlock hadn't been sure of it, he didn't tell them the man might be in Willicott.

14

TY'S COTTAGE
WILLICOTT, MARYLAND
SATURDAY NIGHT

Ty clicked her beer against Sala's. "Here's to a fricking toilet paper rod."

"May Charmin rule the world," Sala said, and they drank. "You know what's amazing?"

"As a matter of fact, I think I do. Everything was spotless, but he missed a fricking empty roll of toilet paper that probably has his fingerprints on the roller bar, and like that"—Ty snapped her fingers—"he's busted."

"You nailed that one."

"A huge hunk of luck for the good guys." She toasted him again, and they drank.

Sala said, "If the killer was one of Octavia's clients, he'll be in CODIS. He'd have been arrested, fingerprinted, probably gotten jail time."

They were sitting together on Ty's back deck facing Lake Massey, each holding a Coors, looking at the lake glistening beneath a half moon and a dazzling display of stars casting diamonds on the still, dark water. House lights across the lake began to wink out as tourists and book festival fans hung it up for the night. Every time a light went out, the starlight display over the lake became more brilliant.

Sala looked over at the chief. "Imagine you're camping out in an abandoned house. It's time to hit the road, so you're careful cleaning up after yourself. You don't want to leave anything for anyone to find, even though you doubt anyone will come looking through the house for years. You and your girlfriend—yes, I think that mad laugh had to be the killer's girlfriend—both of you pick up every single hair, wipe down every surface, scrub the bathroom. You're thorough. When you drive away, you're pleased with yourselves for a job well done, your plan perfectly executed. No one will ever find Octavia Ryan. Her body will be eaten by the fish, and her bones will lie on the bottom of the lake forever. As for Porto—" He swallowed, couldn't help it. "He'll die of thirst, tied up in a closet." He felt her hand lightly touch his arm, for comfort, for reassurance that he was alive and here with her, that it was over. He drew a deep breath and leaned back in the wooden deck chair, closed his eyes. He'd survived because of Savich.

They fell into a comfortable silence. Ty heard night sounds she was used to—crickets chirping, the movement of small animals in the undergrowth, the gentle lapping of the water against her dock, the rustling of tree leaves in the night breeze, sounds that soothed and comforted.

Sala took another drink of his beer. His throat still felt razor dry. *No, don't think about those hours in the closet. Put it behind you. Focus, like Savich said. The headache is fine. It means you're alive.*

Ty said, "I like the bandage over your forehead. Looks rakish, like a badass pirate."

He lightly touched a fingertip to the large adhesive bandage. "Dr. Staunton is good. I didn't feel a thing when she stitched me up." He paused, then said, "I can't stop thinking about this. Why didn't Octavia recognize his voice?"

"You weren't conscious for very long. What, a minute or two? She probably did recognize him, once they were on the lake." Ty sipped her beer. "I wonder if his girlfriend was with him when he came to your cabin."

"I don't know. I never saw her, and forensics couldn't help us. They only found the window he broke in through, some of my blood on the floor, and our smashed cell phones."

Ty said, "They must have used the Volvo to get you to Gatewood and then dumped it somewhere in the woods. We were lucky to find you after only a day."

She smacked her head. "What a dummy. That toilet paper rod means the Gatewood plumbing still worked. And to use the toilet means they had to have the water turned on, right?"

"Maybe, or they could have simply brought in buckets of lake water to flush the toilet." He watched her pull her cell out of her breast pocket, then sigh and put it back.

"I forgot. It's Saturday night. At best I'd get a maintenance worker. On Monday, we'll find out. Fake name, but it'll be something."

Sala said, "Maybe they turned the water on themselves, and we'll find prints on the main water valve."

"Good thought."

He grinned at her. He felt good, but only for an instant, then a slap of guilt swamped him and he fell silent, rolling the beer between his palms. "Thanks for letting me stay here with you, Chief. I appreciate it."

"You know Dr. Staunton said you've had a concussion, and she ordered you to rest. I couldn't have you driving back and forth on the highway, and I doubt there are any vacancies in town at all. Besides, I can keep an eye on you this way, make sure you're all right. So don't worry about it. It's not a problem." Didn't he realize that available rooms or no, she'd have insisted he stay with her? No way would she let him be alone after what he'd been through. "Since you're staying in my guest room and I put clean sheets on your bed, even plumped up your pillow, you should call me Ty."

He nodded. "And since I'm sleeping on those clean sheets, call me Sala."

She smiled, nodded.

"What does Ty stand for?"

"Don't go there, too scary. Now, your name, it's very unusual."

"My dad's responsible, at least that's what my mom always swore when I'd come home from school with bloody knuckles and a black eye." He paused, smiled again. "Never really bothered me, though. I really liked to mix it up when I was a kid. Never lost a fight after the age of five, when I learned not to mess with a third-grader. My dad was a marine, a real scrapper back in the day, so he taught me, my mama rolling her eyes in the background." He paused. "My mom gave me lessons, too, she was a pretty dirty fighter herself. She grew up on Chicago's South Side with three brothers."

Ty sighed. "My mother went hysterical when I told her I was going to be a cop. She gave it her best shot to talk me out of it, but it was no use. Needless to say, my dad was all for it. He's a captain in the Washington State Patrol. So why didn't your parents change your name? Save the spillage of blood on all sides."

He laughed. "Dad and Mom said I should be proud of my name, so I learned to fight."

She gave him a huge grin, cracked her knuckles. "One of these days, we can see at the gym which of us is the dirtiest fighter, Mr. FBI."

"Yeah, yeah, blah, blah."

They fell silent, both looking out over the lake. Sala said after a while, "He has my Glock. It's like missing a limb."

That was a tough one because it was never supposed to happen. She said with no hesitation, "You'll get it back."

"You're that certain we'll get him?"

"He has no idea how close we are, no idea we probably have his fingerprints, and pretty soon we're going to know his name. A couple more days and we'll have both him and his girlfriend."

Sala tapped his head, then thumped his fist to his chest. "I know that in my head, but not here, not in my heart, not yet."

15

Ty couldn't imagine what it would be like to be tied up and helpless in a closet no one would ever open, struggling to finally accept that you were going to die, all the while grieving for a woman you were close to and believed had been murdered. She reached over and touched his arm again, kept her voice calm. "I'm very sorry for what happened to Octavia and to you, Sala. It was a horrible thing to go through. I saw him murder Octavia on the lake, and that was bad enough. But the bottom line is we'll catch him and find his girlfriend with him. There will be justice."

Sala was tempted to dismiss what she'd said because he didn't care about justice right then. What he really wanted to do was squeeze his hands around the killer's neck and choke the life out of him. For Octavia and for himself. He said, "I wondered about his girlfriend when I was in the closet. That mad laugh—I wanted to see her face." If he was honest with himself, Sala wanted to kill her, too.

"Try to let it go, Sala, at least for tonight." She wondered where the two of them were that night. A hundred miles away? Believing they'd pulled everything off perfectly?

She pulled out a grin, gave a dramatic sigh. "That was a sigh of relief since nothing dramatic happened at the book festival today—well, other than the deal with Sherlock in the children's tent. Whatever that was, thankfully none of the parents or kids seemed to realize anything had really happened."

She looked at the few remaining lights across Lake Massey. "Some seven-plus thousand visitors to the festival are tucked in their beds now, maybe reading books they bought, talking about the authors they met. What happened to Octavia won't be in the local paper until tomorrow. Like you, they can be happy they have clean sheets."

Sala tried to smile, but couldn't manage it. "We turned off our phones when we arrived, told our families not to bother to call or check in. I'm not ready to talk with her parents yet about what happened. Bless Mr. Maitland for dealing with her family and her boss." He fell silent again, staring at nothing really, remembering, seeing stark images in his mind of Octavia's face, the fear in her eyes that she might die. "I know you're right—he took off the mask before he killed her, in case she hadn't recognized him."

"I imagine he did, otherwise he wouldn't get his full quota of revenge. Octavia had to know who he was so she could fully appreciate how clever he is. I couldn't tell if he was still wearing a stocking over his face on the lake. He was too far away."

Sala looked at his bandaged wrists, scarcely felt the welts and bruises with the cream Dr. Staunton had smeared on. "No matter the time lag, months or years, it still surprises me Octavia didn't recognize his voice right away. Octavia remembered how her termite exterminator talked, so why not him? Like I said, he had a Southern accent." He swallowed. "But she was very frightened."

"And fear can freeze you up. Maybe he disguised his voice, I don't know."

"I really like—liked—Octavia. She had guts, she was bright, and she really cared about helping people who couldn't help themselves."

"Which law firm was she with?"

"Jacobson, Wile, and Corman, in D.C. They'll be served with a warrant for their records of all the cases she was involved in. You know the lawyers are going to shout client confidentiality, no matter that one of their own was murdered. We're talking court orders, delays—I mean, that's what they all do, stall as long as they can to show their clients they tried. The bastards."

"No disagreement from me." She lightly patted his leg. "No more cramps?"

"No, I'm fine, good to go." He looked back at the lake again, sitting perfectly still, and she knew what had happened to him, to them, was running on an endless loop. How long would it take for the experience to fade? A long time, Ty imagined. He'd known Octavia, slept with her, laughed with her. Ty couldn't imagine what he was feeling. What Ty herself felt was wrung out and sad. She got to her feet. “It’s late. You ready to sleep?”

Sala rose to stand beside her, looking down at his bandaged wrists, not at her. “I guess I’m a coward, me the tough FBI agent, but I don’t want to close my eyes. I’ll see Octavia’s face. I’ll see that closet.”

She said matter-of-factly, “Tell you what, let’s haul a mattress and a couple of blankets and pillows out here. I’ve done it myself, and it’s a great way to get to sleep. You can look up at the stars, listen to the crickets, maybe drink another beer. I’ll drink another one with you.”

He really looked at her then, realized she was tall, at least five ten, nearly to his nose. The moonlight cast shadows on her face, but her eyes were clear and bright and compassionate. “Thank you,” he said. “That’s a great idea.” He paused. “Too bad I don’t have Lucky with me.”

“Lucky?”

“My cat. She’s a sweetheart. She’s pure black with big green eyes and she sleeps on my chest at night, purrs so loud the rhythm puts me right out. I had to leave her with my sister. My sister adores Lucky, so I’m wondering if she’ll want to come back home. It’s been a long time.”

“Lucky will race you back to your house, you’ll see. Where’d you get her?”

“I rescued her as a kitten, not even three pounds, found in an alley in Georgetown. Her first night, she tucked herself in around my neck, happy as a clam. And she’s been around my neck ever since.”

"I'd like to meet her."

"Then I'll make sure you do."

Before Sala fell asleep thirty minutes later, he wasn't thinking about his cat. He was thinking about that single forgotten toilet paper roll and praying the fingerprints on the rod weren't from some local teenager who'd broken into the house and left it there.

16

SAVICH HOUSE
GEORGETOWN
SATURDAY NIGHT

Savich was sitting up in bed, pillows behind him, working on MAX. He looked up and forgot what he was doing. He didn't think he'd ever get used to seeing Sherlock in those tiger-striped sleep boxers and flowy top, silhouetted by the bathroom light, her hair pulled up on top of her head in a riot of curls, her face scrubbed clean, looking about sixteen.

Sherlock paused a moment, cocked her head to one side, listening. "I can't get used to the quiet. Not a single sleeping-kid snort, no little feet padding down the hall to say good night to us or crawl in between us after a nightmare." She stopped cold and swallowed hard. "I thought I'd come to grips with what happened today at the book festival, that man trying to take Sean again." She shook her head. "It scared me to death, Dillon. And I didn't catch him. Again."

He patted the bed beside him. "Come here." He gathered her close, kissed the top of her head. "I should have been with you, shouldn't have gone off with the chief of police."

It snapped her back. "Then you wouldn't have found Sala, so all in all, I'd say we were all lucky. You know it was the same man, Dillon. How did he know we'd be at the book festival?"

"Best guess, he followed us, or maybe hacked the car's GPS or tracked our cell phones. Then he waited for his chance, waited until you were with Sean and Marty by yourself. But a chocolate bar? Seems like he didn't think it through very well. He had to know you'd be watching for him, and you were."

"Dillon, if he followed us there, then he could have followed us to your mom's house."

"Don't worry. Senator Monroe is sleeping at Mom's house for the duration, and so is one of his aides. Sean will never be alone."

He closed down MAX and laid him on the bedside table, plugged into the charger next to their cell phones. "You know what I'm missing right now? Singing him his nightly country western song. He always wants another verse and he can't ever stay awake for the last verse, even with his current favorite, 'Elvis in the Chariot.' " He kissed her forehead, her nose, her ear. "Well, at least my mom's a happy camper. Do you think she's singing to him now about Elvis waving for the chariot to swoop down and fetch him up?"

"She doesn't have to go that far, she's the goddess of freshly baked chocolate chip cookies." She saw his smile, and for a moment, she felt one on her mouth as well, but soon it fell off. She felt her fear return, familiar to her now, always with her. Would he try again? When? Tonight Sean was safe, but what about tomorrow? Would he try to kidnap Sean from his day camp? Hard to imagine, everyone was alerted now.

They were both quiet a moment, then she whispered. "Octavia Ryan's dead, and Sala's got to be a mess. At least he's staying with the chief. She'll make sure he's all right."

Savich kept his voice calm, although he felt like hitting something. "I spoke briefly to Ty—Chief Christie. Concussion or not, I don't think she'd have let Sala come back to Washington by himself. She's a good woman, levelheaded, smart." He remembered Detective Harry Anson in Seattle saying Ty was a bulldog. He knew to his gut now Anson was right. "Let it go for a little while, sweetheart. We should both try to let it go."

But she was caught up in it. "Dillon, I still can't get over that vision you had—the murderer coming back to the dock. And Sala hearing a girl's mad laughter? Who was that? Maybe it'll be her prints they found on that toilet paper rod."

Savich wanted to distract her, distract himself. "All I can think about right now is getting you out of your tiger stripes."

She tried to laugh and hiccupped.

"That's a start." He breathed in her light rose scent, saw a red curl work its way out of the high ponytail to curve around her face. His heart kicked up. She pulled the rubber band out of her hair and shook her head, ending up with a wild nimbus to halo her head. He couldn't wait to run his fingers through the curls, feel them tickle his nose. She pushed him down on his back, leaned down to bite his neck, and kissed his chin. His mouth got the full treatment. He eased his hands beneath that tiger-striped top, loving the feel of her, but then his brain skipped again to the man who'd been in McGurk's tent waving a chocolate bar at the children, the same man he knew had been in Sean's bedroom Wednesday night. *Turn it off, turn it off.*

He felt her hair cascade over his face, her warm breath against his cheek. "You're letting me down here, Dillon. I'm doing my part, giving you my all, but I can see your brain going a zillion miles an hour." She tapped her fingers to his cheek. "Pay attention." Her fingers glided over his belly, taking all the blood from his brain.

When his breathing finally calmed, Savich leaned up on his elbow, bent down, and kissed her mouth. He saw she was nearly out, and so he tucked her in close beside him, whispered against her cheek, "I wouldn't be surprised if my mom tried to seduce Sean to the dark side. You know, promise to teach him how to drive, pay all his speeding tickets, to keep him with her."

Sherlock mumbled something. He kissed her again and eased down beside her, her head on his shoulder. He heard her breathing even into sleep. He closed his eyes and quickly fell asleep himself.

He was walking into the master bedroom at Gatewood, only now it was a long, skinny room. He saw science fiction graffiti on the white walls, not people, but video game monsters. They writhed, their tentacles reached out to him, trying to escape the wall to get to him, but he paid no attention, all his focus on the front window.

He looked out at an early morning patchwork fog over Lake Massey, though it didn't really look like the lake. There were waves that pulsed and seemed to twist in on themselves, and he knew something scary was beneath the surface, something deadly, that gave no quarter. He saw a narrow raft glide out of the fog, a man standing on it, staring down at the pulsing waves, and he was smiling. He didn't have an oar. The raft seemed to be moving on its own. It pulled in at a dock with parking slots all around it, and the man jumped out. He straightened, turned slowly, and looked up at Savich. He gave a rictus of a grin, pumped his fist, and yelled something, but Savich couldn't make out the words. The man kept staring at him, that mad grin still on his face, and gave Savich a deep bow. Savich felt a sudden, bitter cold. Black shadows roiled out of the cold, coming closer and closer. He wanted to run, but he couldn't move. Bony fingers slithered out of those shadows and stretched toward him, bone-white fingers that had come from the bottom of the lake. He heard an excited laugh—a girl's laugh—high and vicious and manic, and the skeletal fingers reached for his throat, closed around his neck. He couldn't move, couldn't fight. In the distance he heard a girl shout, "Kill him! Kill him!"

A sharp slap on his face, and another. His fingers grabbed Sherlock's wrist. She shouted in his face, "Wake up, Dillon! Come on, that's it. Everything's okay. You were having a nightmare. That's right, come back to me." He let her wrist go, sucked in a breath, and the black shadows faded away. Though he couldn't see Sherlock's face in the dark, he knew she was close, knew she was real. He calmed himself, breathed in the soft, quiet air of their bedroom, and felt his heart begin to slow its mad gallop, felt himself settle. She was kissing his face, holding him close, and whispered against his cheek, "What happened? What did you dream?"

Savich turned his face into her palm, kissed her smooth skin. It was dark, deep in the night, so he told her all of it, his voice scratchy, as if he hadn't spoken in a long time.

Telling her about it calmed him down. "Do you know, I heard the girl's laugh. It sounded familiar, but I can't remember."

She kissed him again, stroked her hand over his face. "A dream like that—I'd scream the roof down. But Dillon, given what happened today, it makes sense you'd have a doozy of a nightmare, don't you think?" She paused, cupped his face in her palm, studied him. "I think your mind is trying to fit the pieces together."

Such faith she had in him. How could he fit any pieces together when he could barely breathe? He still felt the lingering fear, the sense of helplessness. He concentrated on her hands stroking him instead.

Sherlock wondered how the girl's laugh in his nightmare could sound familiar to him. He'd figure it out, he usually did. She said, "Remember Tommy Raider's face when he FaceTimed us earlier, waving that toilet paper rod? 'We'll know tomorrow if this goombah's prints are in CODIS!' Utter disbelief and joy at finding that gift from heaven. He laughed like a hyena. Can you imagine all that work, and you miss the TP? Talk about irony."

Finally, Savich's heart was steady again. He said against her temple, "He did sound like a hyena, didn't he?"

She snuggled against him. "Sorry I had to slap you so hard." Her words were mumbled, she was nearly back to sleep. Savich waited another couple of minutes, then eased away carefully so not to awaken her and took MAX to his study. He'd been checking Octavia's cases in the public record before Sherlock had come out of the bathroom, a long and tedious job. Now he decided he didn't want to wait for fingerprints, didn't want to wait for the warrant for all of Octavia Ryan's client files, even those that hadn't made it to trial yet. Not when he knew Octavia Ryan's former law firm would fight the warrant tooth and nail to keep her files private.

It was time to move justice along.

17

Savich made himself some tea and got to work. It took him less than a half hour to break through the firewall at Jacobson, Wile, & Corman in D.C. and access Octavia's client files. He wondered if he should let them know how crappy their security was as he sipped his tea.

He methodically pulled up her former client files, concentrating on criminal cases. Fifteen minutes later, he stared at the familiar face of a young man Octavia Ryan had taken on as a pro bono case, Victor Nesser. She'd convinced a judge he wasn't competent to stand trial, so he'd been sent to the Wharton Facility for treatment a year and a half before. Victor Nesser was an only child, American mother, Jordanian father, gifted computer hacker, still only twenty-three years old. Savich remembered that

Victor was a mess at that time, uncommunicative, disinterested in everyone and everything around him. Had he even realized Octavia Ryan had convinced the judge the state couldn't legally prosecute him until he was able to more fully grasp the charges? He'd loved a thirteen-year-old girl, Lissy Smiley, and Savich knew she'd seduced him, an eighteen-year-old boy, and bound him to her. He'd then been brought in by Lissy's mother to drive the getaway car for the Gang of Four, as they were called. There was no doubt, though, that when Savich had been forced to kill Lissy, Victor had been a lost soul.

Victor Nesser fit the profile, but he should still be incarcerated. Savich brought up the patient database of the Central State Hospital, where he'd been transferred. Victor had escaped six weeks before. Law enforcement had been notified, notices had been sent out, but Savich hadn't seen them nor had there been any mention of his escape in Octavia's client files to indicate her former law firm had ever been notified. Victor had managed to disappear. Savich had no doubt Victor's fingerprints would be on that toilet paper rod.

But who was the girl Sala had heard laughing? The teenager who was Victor's soul mate, Lissy Smiley, was dead—Savich had shot her himself. Victor could have found another girlfriend since his escape, but Savich wouldn't, couldn't, believe it. He'd never forget Victor's howl of agony when Savich had told him Lissy was dead.

He looked down at his Mickey Mouse watch. Not yet midnight.

He went to their bedroom, turned the bedside lamp on low, leaned down, and kissed Sherlock awake. When she smiled up at him and touched her palm to his face, he kissed her hand, slipped in beside her. He said quietly, "Octavia Ryan's murderer is Victor Nesser. And it's Victor who's been stalking Sean."

She was instantly awake, blinked up at him. "Victor Nesser? You're sure?"

"As sure as I can be without the call verifying his fingerprints are on that toilet paper rod. I sent MAX into Octavia's files at her former law firm. She took over his case from the lawyer in L.A. She must have been happy she'd gotten him committed, saw it as a great victory, despite the fact he'd been the driver for the bank robberies and was as guilty of murder and robbery as any of them."

She stared up at him. "The Gang of Four, of course I remember. Jennifer Smiley and her sixteen-year-old daughter, Lissy, her nephew Victor the driver, and two guys from out west. And you brought their bank-robbing rampage to a close at our Georgetown bank. All of them now dead except Victor. The man who tried to take Sean Wednesday night—he limped. I shot Victor in the ankle two years ago.

"Dillon, that means Victor has a hit list, everyone who helped take down the gang, everyone who helped lock him up. He tried to take Sean first, but when that failed, he went after someone else on his list, Octavia Ryan."

"And after he killed Octavia, he must have driven back to Washington and followed us back again to Willicott. Victor must have thought our returning to the same town where he'd murdered Octavia a piece of irony. Maybe he saw it as karma." He frowned. "But why was Octavia on his hit list? He must be as crazy as they say to want to kill her. She did a brilliant job, getting him into treatment in a medical facility rather than life in prison. I remember he was a mental and emotional wreck after we brought him in. I suppose Victor couldn't have liked how she did it, pointing out he was mentally unstable to begin with and that was why he'd been easily manipulated. She made Lissy out to be a teenage Lolita. I suppose he couldn't bear to hear the truth, and so by killing Octavia, he gained—what?"

"I guess he had only one plan going for him, Dillon, and for whatever reason, he wanted her dead. If he wasn't crazy before, he is now. I saw him in McGurk's tent, a man wearing sunglasses and a ball cap, and I should have recognized him, maybe even his voice. But I didn't, Dillon. What he did wasn't very smart, but unexpected enough he got away with it."

Savich rubbed his hands up and down Sherlock's tiger stripes. "So who else could be on Victor's radar? Probably Buzz Riley, remember, he was the one who shot Lissy's mother in the bank robbery."

Savich would remember that day at his Georgetown bank for as long as he lived, lying on his stomach, face to the floor with everyone else in the bank when Lissy Smiley recognized him. He could still hear her high, excited voice, crowing how she was going to kill her an FBI agent. Then very suddenly, crunch time, and he and the security guard, Buzz Riley, had managed to survive. He said now, "It was Buzz who killed Jennifer Smiley. If Victor wants to go after anyone else, it'll be Buzz."

Savich grabbed his cell off its charger and scrolled through the numbers until he found Buzz. "Buzz? It's Agent Dillon Savich.

I'm sorry to wake you. But Victor Nesser has escaped from the psychiatric facility where he was being kept, and we believe he murdered his lawyer, Octavia Ryan, Friday morning. You saw this on the news, right?"

Savich listened, nodded, and explained exactly what was happening. Then he said, "What do you say to another vacation in the Caribbean? Can you get on a plane tomorrow? Good, I'll clear it with Mr. Maitland." When he hung up, he was breathing more easily. "Buzz said he'd sleep with his Beretta on his pillow. He said he really liked the sound of Saint Thomas, heard they were coming back from the hurricane damage."

It was only a little past midnight when they settled down to sleep. It was very quiet without Sean. He hated to say it, but he was used to telling her everything. "That girl's laugh, Sherlock, in my nightmare. She sounded like Lissy."

She wanted to tell him it was impossible, Lissy was long dead, but instead, she leaned up, kissed him, and said only, "You're not going to puzzle everything out tonight, Dillon. Try to get some sleep."

Both of them hoped there would be no more nightmares.

18

CAMPGROUND NEAR GREENBRIER LAKE
GREENBRIER STATE PARK, MARYLAND
SATURDAY NIGHT

Victor sang "We Are the Champions," nearly screaming the words as he thumped his fist on the steering wheel in rhythm. That's what he was, a winner, a champion of the world. He pulled his Kia smoothly to a stop at the Greenbrier State Park entry kiosk and was told by the snotty girl park ranger the campground was full, and why didn't he go to the Lorelei Motel back up the road, not more than ten minutes away? He felt a leap of rage, thought about sticking her with his new Ka-Bar knife right between her ribs, but he managed to quash it, even managed to smile and thank her nicely. She was nothing, a pebble in his path.

How dare the cow turn us away? Go back, Victor, shoot her in her stupid face with that agent's Glock.

Victor shook his head at her. Lissy would shoot everyone in the world if he let her.

He drove back to the exit and parked out of sight around a corner. He slipped through the trees until he could see the ranger in the entry kiosk. He waited nearly thirty minutes until she left for a break. Fast as a lick of spit, as Lissy always liked to say, Victor drove past the empty kiosk to the very end of the visitor parking lot and parked the Kia next to a big SUV.

I didn't think the bitch would ever leave. That was well done, Victor.

"Yeah, that's always been your problem, you have no patience."

Victor unloaded the camping equipment he'd bought, locked the car, and trudged well beyond the designated campsites. As he walked, Victor smelled hamburgers and barbecue being cooked over fire pits, heard children laughing, whining, several parents' exhausted voices scolding, two guys yelling at each other about the Yankees. He walked until all the people and their noise were far behind, deeper into the thick maple and oak forest until the trees were so close together their branches and leaves formed a canopy over his head. His arms were tired, but it didn't matter, he knew he had to walk until no one could hear him. Finally, it was silent, no one close. He found a small opening in the trees, set up his tent, dug a small fire pit, and sprinkled in dried leaves, a couple pages of wadded-up newspaper, and some small twigs. He laid a match to the pile, watched a small flame leap up. He said,

"You rest, Lissy. I know that was a long walk for you. I'm sorry I don't have any more pain pills. I'll make some nice strong tea for you, warm you up."

She was silent. It didn't take him long to get a fire going strong, the twigs snapping and popping. It wasn't quite dark yet and still warm, but the fire felt good. He felt the soft air against his face, and he breathed in deeply, stared up at the darkening sky. Soon there would be a white half-moon and brilliant stars shining down on him. He smiled. Everything was perfect.

It's beautiful here, Victor, nice and warm. And the best thing is none of those brain-dead yahoo cops have a clue who we are, not a single fricking clue.

"That's because we were thorough, Lissy. We cleaned up after ourselves, wiped everything down." He paused. "Not that anyone is likely to go up those stairs at Gatewood for the next fifty years. I mean, why would they? If by some crazy chance they do, they won't find a thing. Well, maybe that FBI agent's body, eventually. Then they'll know what we did, how we fooled them, but they still won't know who we are."

Victor raised his fist to the heavens and sang out, "I am the champion! I am the champion! Of the world!"

You mean we, *don't you?*

"No, I'm the one who did the heavy lifting in Willicott. Give your mouth a rest, Lissy, I'm tired."

You're not the only one who's tired. Drive, drive, drive. I was bored, and you know my belly hurts. The staples dig in and pinch.

"I know. I'm sorry." He could practically see Lissy getting ready to blast him even more and said quickly, "Okay, both of us are champions." He sat cross-legged on a blanket and watched the fire bloom, tried to distract Lissy by whistling Sonny and Cher's "I Got You Babe," an ancient song from the hippie era Lissy's mom was always humming, until she got shot through the neck. He hadn't minded that at all, the crazy witch. But he'd never say it to Lissy.

He'd picked a good spot, quiet and peaceful. They could even see a slice of Greenbrier Lake through the trees, its flat dark water smooth as glass. His only worry, a small one really, was that the girl park ranger would come sniffing around, threaten to fine him or toss him in jail. Victor cracked his knuckles. Let her come, maybe he'd strangle her with her ridiculous long hippie braid. He knew he could do it, no doubt in his mind, not since he'd whacked Octavia Ryan on the head and shoved her overboard into Lake Massey, two heavy bricks tied by a rope around her waist so she wouldn't float to the surface. That was what you had to do to keep a body under the water. He pictured himself standing in the rowboat, looking down at the flat surface of Lake Massey for any sign of her, and he'd felt better in that moment than he had in a long time. He was a winner. He sent his fist again to the sky. Yes, he'd thought of everything.

He looked through his small, cold bag and frowned. He didn't want to eat the last two hot dogs for dinner. No, it was time to celebrate. That meant dessert. He hummed as he made himself a s'more and set it on the small grate he'd carefully placed over his fire pit. The graham crackers were on the stale side, but the marshmallows and the Hershey's chocolate bar were prime. Lissy loved s'mores, a treat her mama had always made her when she was thirteen, licking her lips, to tease him, he knew.

He chewed slowly, swallowed, wiped his mouth. It was a wonderful reward for a guy who'd gotten the job done, accomplished what he'd set out to do. And better yet, he had the money to prove it. He looked into the small fire and said softly, "Don't worry, Lissy, I'm making you a s'more, too. Mine are better than your mama's."

About time, Victor. You *ate the first one, didn't even think to offer it to me. I don't know, Mama's were pretty good.*

"Sorry, Lissy, but I wanted to celebrate my success. And it was mine, not ours—you saw what I did." He preened. "I killed that bitch lawyer like I promised. And don't feel bad about that FBI agent who was screwing her, either—the guy tried, I'll give him that, came close but he failed. After that, I kind of liked stuffing him in that closet. I decided he deserved to die long and slow. I mean, he had the rotten taste to hook up with that lying witch, didn't he? I even have the agent's gun. Not that he'll ever need it again."

To his surprise, rather than criticizing him like she always did, she said, *I like what you did to the FBI agent. You made the punishment fit the crime. You know what else I like? I like how you waited for that girl park ranger to take a break. That was smart. You fooled her good.*

Victor felt a burst of warmth inside. He'd pleased her. She'd actually praised him, without reservation, without criticism. It had to be a first. He smiled into the glowing embers. Victor realized he'd been smiling a lot today. He could get used to it. "I wonder what the FBI agent is thinking about now, all cozy in his closet? About his mama? About Octavia, wondering what I did to her? Hey, I wonder if fish eat lawyers?" He laughed and began constructing another s'more for Lissy.

Nah, Porto's thinking about himself, no one else, not even that frigging lawyer he was screwing. He finally understands there's nothing he can do. He's helpless. It's all over. He's toast. I bet he's wondering how long it will take him to die.

"A good long time," Victor said, "at least three days."

She fell silent, but it wasn't a comfortable silence. Victor knew she was examining every action he'd taken to find fault, as she usually did when something was his idea, not hers. First praise, then the spurs. Sure enough, she pulled close and said, her voice sharp and critical, *Lookie here, Victor, what you did may have felt good, but I'm thinking you should have put his lights out with a nice clean bullet, instead of trying to prove you can think on your own. You know how hard it was for you to haul him up those stairs and leave him in that stupid closet. He weighs lots more than you do. He could have got his brains back together at any time and taken you down. Did you even think about anyone coming to Gatewood, maybe finding him before he's croaked? I mean, you did sink the rowboat right there off the Gatewood dock. What if someone saw you or finds that sunken rowboat? They'd investigate, wouldn't they? They'd look around and they'd find the agent, and maybe he wouldn't be dead yet. You tried to be cute. You should have shot him with his own gun, wham, right between the eyes, and that FBI bastard would be gone forever, no chance for him to rat you out. It was stupid, Victor.*

"Shut up! Stop your criticizing, Lissy. You know I hate it. It was my idea, my plan, and it was perfect. Keep your trap shut. You remember how sometimes I had to punish you for not respecting me?"

19

She didn't say anything. Maybe that would shut her up for a while. Maybe it meant she was ready to see him now as he was, as he saw himself. Victor smoothed out his fists, flattened his palms on his legs.

Suddenly, she laughed, right in his face, a match to the flames. *Yeah, that's you, Victor—the big man. You think you're so cool. Without me you're a putz, and don't forget it.*

He nearly burst with rage. He began hitting his fists against his legs, once, then again and again. "Don't rag on me, Lissy! It was a good plan. Just because it was my plan and not yours, you have to criticize me, make me feel bad. No matter what you think, I got it done, didn't I? You know as well as I do nobody's going to find the lawyer's body, nobody's going to see the stupid rowboat, and nobody's going to go to the third floor of Gatewood. Everyone's scared of that big old house. Porto will rot in that closet, long and slow. I did that without you, without your crazy mama. One dead and gone, one left to rot. What more could you want?"

My mama wasn't crazy! She was smart—

"Your mama got her head nearly shot off! You told me how her neck exploded and blood spurted out everywhere." He heard low shattered sobs. He whispered, "I'm sorry, Lissy, I know you loved your mama. I'm sorry. She wasn't crazy, exactly. She was different, that's all."

The sobs stopped. Silence, then, *Well, dead is dead, after all. Mama went out in a blaze of glory. I heard that once in a movie*—a blaze of glory. *She would have liked that, maybe.*

Victor, you know what I want. I didn't care about that lawyer, Ryan. She was your demon, not mine. I never could figure out why it was so important for you to kill her. So why did you?

"Be quiet, Lissy. You don't know anything."

She laughed, high, vicious, and too loud, right in his ear. Then her voice became a sneer, and he could feel her hot breath against his cheek. *All that poor cow Ryan ever did was tell the truth, Victor. You couldn't stand to hear the truth, could you? It made you feel small, like a worm. But Ryan didn't hurt you, not like Savich hurt me. He didn't only hurt me, he killed me.*

Ryan saved your butt, made the judge cry for poor little Victor Nesser, bossed around by his sixteen-year-old girlfriend, mashed down under her dainty thumb. Ryan played the judge perfectly, got you declared incompetent to stand trial. I would have sent her a bottle of champagne. Face it, Victor, you killed her because she told the truth and you couldn't stand it.

I didn't think that loony bin was so bad. Plus it gave us time to plan our revenge. And you fooled all those stupid shrinks, made them feel sorry for you, made them feel you were recovering. You were smart, Victor. You hid those pills under your tongue and slipped right out of that place in a nurse's uniform, the guards nodding good night to you on your way out. I was proud of you.

He smiled into the dying embers. "No, the place wasn't bad." He paused, then, "Like I said, Lissy, you don't know everything. In this, you don't know anything. Shut up now and go to sleep."

I don't want to go to sleep! I want my belly to stop hurting. I don't want all those fricking staples digging into me. I hate it! And here you are, acting all righteous for killing that bitch for some stupid reason you won't tell me.

I want Savich and Sherlock. They're the ones who ruined everything. He's the one who kicked me in my belly, he's the one who shot me in the chest. You could have gone right after him, but you went after his kid first. And look how that turned out.

She made him so mad he stuttered. "Th-that was all b-bad luck. You know that, Lissy. It wasn't on me."

Bad luck or not, trying to take the Savich kid out of his own house was a stretch. Like I told you, you should have gone after Savich or Sherlock.

He rubbed his ankle, remembering how he'd had to shinny down that oak tree outside the kid's bedroom and jump, hurting the same ankle Sherlock had shot. "That wasn't my fault! They shouldn't have heard me, shouldn't have known until the next morning when the kid was gone. I didn't make a sound, so how did they know?" He realized he'd nearly screamed the words and went silent, sat very still, listening. Nothing, no one had heard him. And he wondered again how they'd known he was there. It still baffled him.

Don't give yourself a stroke, Victor. Yeah, okay, maybe it was a good plan, maybe it was bad luck. I know why you went after the kid first. I mean, Savich shot me. And you love me more than anybody in the whole wide world, so you wanted to take away his little boy. It was a good idea. It would have made him real scared, that's for sure.

She was being nice now, but Victor was still shaking. He took slow, deep breaths. It had been a long day, and his ankle hurt—it always hurt, only much more today.

Your ankle hurts, always makes you grunt and groan and feel sorry for yourself. So why don't you put the blame where it belongs? That redheaded agent Sherlock was the one who shot you in the ankle to bring you down, not that poor old cow Ryan. Sherlock—what a stupid name that is, but I really liked her hair. I think she lied to me, that red color wasn't natural, she dyed it red and curled it. I could have done that.

Victor knew Lissy was preening, fluffing her hair. He shook his head. The past and the present, always bumping against each other, mixing things up. He couldn't let himself forget which was which. Now was now. He had to stay focused. There was so much more to do.

Victor heard something, maybe sneakers walking quiet as a ghost through the leaves. The girl park ranger? Was she tracking him? Had she seen him drive in, followed him? Did she have a gun? He got on his feet, the agent's Glock in his hand. He racked the slide, and it made him feel less afraid, ready for a fight.

A small burning branch exploded in the fire pit, made him jump. He nearly pulled the trigger, maybe shot himself in the foot. He cursed but didn't move, stood still as a beam of light and listened.

There, movement, off to his left, a rustling sound. He brought up the Glock and whirled around. He very nearly fired again when he saw the flash of an animal as it ran all-out away from him through the trees. Maybe a fox. He slowly slid the Glock into his waistband and sat back down by his fire pit, forced himself to calm again.

I knew no one was there, Victor. All you had to do was ask me. You got all scared, nearly peed yourself over a little animal. It was afraid of you, but you got all wigged out. For what? Nothing. And the stunt you pulled at the book festival, buying a fricking chocolate bar to help you grab up the Savich kid? How lame was that? If it wasn't for that kid stampede, you would have been caught.

Victor wanted to slap her, that'd get her attention. He fought for control. She was right, really, a lot of things had gone sideways. And today at the book festival, if only he'd had time to think it through, he could have ironed out the possible wrinkles. He would have realized the bitch agent would be on her guard, ready for him. But he'd had to move fast, too fast. No, it was nothing. Less than nothing. Today was an A+ for him. "Give your mouth a rest, Lissy. We've got a big day tomorrow."

Victor? I lied. I really didn't like that crazy ward they put us in. I don't want to go back. I like being free. Smell the fire, Victor. Feel the warm air on your face. Yes, this is much better. Can you hear the crickets? Noisy little buggers. And there's an owl hooting. It's so lovely here and so quiet, no screaming kiddies or arguing parents like at the campground sites. I'm tired, Victor, and my stomach still hurts. I wish I could get the staples out, always itching and tugging, and I can feel my skin pulling. Savich's fault, all his fault. And Sherlock's the one who shot your ankle, made you a cripple. Where are your priorities? Sometimes I don't know what to do with you.

"I'm not a cripple."

Face it, Victor, you need me. I always know what to do.

He hit his leg with his fist, once, twice, three times. "Look, I got us here to a nice isolated campsite, carried in all the crap we need, and you didn't hear any whining from me about my ankle."

Yeah, okay, you're a real macho.

"And you're a real pain, Lissy." Victor watched the small fire slowly die, and brooded. He'd get it all done.

She whispered, *I liked our time at Gatewood, Victor. Ghosts live there, you know. I could feel them roaming around, going from room to room. That's why I wanted to make our room shine and sparkle, let them know we were there and to stay out. I kinda felt sorry for them, but I guess they didn't have anywhere else to go, nobody to care they're holed up in that creepy old house. They're not free like you and me. I'll be with you forever.*

"Yes, you will, and I'm glad, Lissy."

You know I always wanted to go to Montana. I figure we can leave soon now, as soon as you take care of business. I wish you'd tell me why you bothered to kill that lawyer.

He only shook his head. Victor picked up a s'more from the

grate. Perfect. The marshmallows and chocolate were melted, but not too hot, and they stuck to his teeth. He licked and licked, closed his eyes with pleasure. Before he let sleep drag him under, he whispered, "I love you, Lissy. I'm sorry about the staples in your belly."

It's okay, Victor. I'll live.

20

NORM'S FISH & BAIT
BOWMAN, MARYLAND
SUNDAY MORNING

"Hi, young fella. I'm Norm. This all ya need?"

Victor nodded. He stood at the banged-up wooden counter in Norm's Fish & Bait in Bowman, a small town not five miles from Greenbrier State Park, and lined up his purchases. Norm, a grizzled old dude with an unlit cigar hanging out of his mouth, studied each item and its price, then punched them with arthritic fingers into an old-fashioned cash register. Fritos, bean dip, carrots, crunchy peanut butter, and white bread. Victor saw a stack of Milk Duds and felt his mouth water. Did Lissy like Milk Duds?

He jumped when she whispered against his ear, *Of course I like Milk Duds. That's a stupid question. I like anything chocolate. I wish you'd gotten me one of those big chocolate bars you threw to all those little kiddies, what a waste.*

She wouldn't ever let up, he knew it. He wanted to tell her buying the huge chocolate bar from the kiosk opposite the big tent had been creative, it was genius. He'd pictured it in his mind—using it to create chaos. But the redheaded bitch had been hovering over the kid, on red alert.

Victor laid two Milk Duds on the counter, one for him, one for Lissy. He watched Norm slowly press the ancient keys to ring up each little box on that ridiculous cash register from two centuries ago. He felt Lissy close, knew she was waiting to remind him she'd known Sherlock would be on the lookout for him at the book festival, watchful and ready if he tried something. *Would you look at that old varmint, chewing on that nasty cigar, his breath toxic and his teeth yellow. I want to get out of here, Victor. He's giving me the creeps.*

Victor heard his name and froze.

He looked up at a grainy old TV set on a shelf behind Norm, surrounded by boxes of cigarettes. Victor's brain went blank, his breath hitched in his throat. How was this possible? He stared at his booking photo from two and a half years ago, heard the newswoman saying: "Victor Nesser, aged twenty-three, is wanted for questioning in the murder of federal prosecutor Octavia Ryan in Willicott, Maryland, on Friday." She said he'd escaped six weeks ago from the Central State Hospital and was being sought by police.

Victor couldn't breathe. He felt poleaxed. They'd found Ryan's body? Already? But how? He'd seen no one on that freaking lake when he'd rowed her out. Not a soul, and the fog, it was thick, like veils lifting up and down. It was barely daylight. And they knew his name? It was impossible. He'd done everything right. He was shaking, his breath coming fast and hard.

Norm said, "That'll be fifteen dollars and thirteen cents." He looked up at Victor as he loaded up a bag. "Hey, what's wrong, kid, you sick or something? You're white as my Maude's bridal sheets." He laughed. "I guess by now they'd be as yellow as her teeth, they're so old. What's wrong?"

How? He'd been so careful. He'd wiped everything down, left nothing that could be connected to him. What? The old coot wanted money. Victor's hands shook as he pulled his wallet out of his back pocket and peeled off a twenty-dollar bill.

"You got thirteen cents? Make it easier, you know?"

"No." Victor couldn't look away from his face on the TV. How could they possibly know?

"You watching the news about that escaped murderer? He's a kid, like you, imagine that, and the little psycho's already been in a mental hospital. Who raises a boy to rob banks? And now he's killed his own lawyer. His parents should be in the cell next to him." He waved his hand back at the TV. "They've played it three or four times already. As if a murderer would stop in here to buy some junk food for a campout. That's what you're doing, right? Camping out? You're too young to have kids yet." The cigar moved and shifted, and a moist piece of tobacco fell onto his chin. Victor couldn't stop staring at it.

The newswoman's voice droned on in the background.

"Hey, you look familiar. Have I seen you before?"

Kill him, kill him! Shoot him between the eyes, Victor. You can't let the stupid old geezer live. Do it now!

But Victor grabbed his bag and bolted out of the store.

"Buddy, you forgot your change!"

Maude stuck her head through the curtain dividing the store from the small office. They watched the dirty Kia peel out of the parking lot in front of the store. "Hey, Norm, what's with that skinny young kid?"

Norm carefully took the cigar out of his mouth, picked the fleck of tobacco off his chin, shrugged. "It was weird. The kid turned white and ran out of here, forgot his change." Norm saw a box of Milk Duds had fallen on the floor. He picked it up, placed the box carefully in a straight line with the others. He stuck his cigar back between his lips as he turned to look at the TV again.

"Holy crap," he said. His cigar dropped to the counter and rolled against a bag of Fritos.

21

LAKE MASSEY
WILLICOTT, MARYLAND
SUNDAY MORNING

Sala and Ty followed well behind Hanger Lewis's pontoon boat as its net slowly dragged the next narrow slice of the lake.

Ty didn't need to be here in her runabout. It was wasted time, really, with the book festival still going on, but she knew Sala needed distraction. And this was as good a way as any. "Here, you steer," she said to him, "I'll get us some water."

Sala changed places with her, took the rudder. "They haven't found many more bones in the last half hour, so that's good, I guess."

Was it? How few was good? How many bones was too many? Ty remembered the Green River Killer in Washington, how the detectives still argued over the details of the case. So many women murdered, so many never found. She remembered her father telling her mother to never be out alone. Ty drew in a deep breath. Had she come across her own Green River Killer here at Lake Massey? She was terrified she wouldn't catch him, because more people might be murdered, and it would be on her head now. She was in charge, and she would have to bury her doubts, her private fears so deep, she herself couldn't find them. Like her dad always said, one step at a time. It was time for her to take that first step. Ty handed Sala a bottle of cold water from the ice chest. They both drank. It was going to be a scorcher today, no fog left to cool things down, only brilliant sun overhead. She'd given him a hat. They wore sunglasses and had so much sunscreen slathered on their faces, their noses were white.

Sala looked tired. Ty didn't know when he'd finally fallen asleep the previous night, but she'd been aware on some level that he'd tossed and turned, undoubtedly reliving what had happened, churning with guilt even though none of it had been his fault. But otherwise, he was holding up. The fresh air was good for him, not to mention the two cups of her Turkish espresso she'd given him. It was almost as thick as sludge and would jump-start anything with a pulse.

Ty looked out toward the pontoon some twenty yards ahead of them. They had to stop every few minutes and pull in the big net, clean it out. How many morons had thrown their beer bottles into the lake? She said, "So far this morning they've found the bones of maybe ten more people. Ten people, Sala, human beings, murdered and tossed into the lake like they were refuse.

And we never would have found them if I hadn't seen Octavia killed."

At the sound of Octavia's name, Sala felt his throat close up. He swallowed, made himself focus on Charlie and Hanger sorting through garbage in the net. There were only the two of them today. Charlie raised a femur, showed it to Ty. Sala said, "If I know Dr. Thomas, he's at Quantico right now—Sunday—examining the bones they took to him yesterday."

Another few minutes passed. Hanger had pulled the pontoon closer to shore, nearer the Gatewood dock, and hovered a moment there. They watched Charlie lean over the side of the pontoon, straighten, and shout, "Chief, I see more bones."

Ty kicked up the motor and eased her runabout alongside the pontoon. Hanger had pulled up the net. "Look, it's another man's loafer, nothing inside. The loafer's nearly disintegrated. And look at this. A belt buckle." Hanger cleaned it off with a towel and held it up. "It looks like it's real gold. It's a Star of David belt buckle. Never seen anything like that before. No belt, guess it rotted away a long time ago."

Ty felt a rush of hope. They hadn't found any ID's, the killer must have taken them. What had survived—some belts, shoes, bits of fabric—could have been purchased anywhere. But this belt buckle was unique. Hanger handed it to her, and she polished it even more before she studied it. "It's very distinctive. You're right, Hanger. I'll bet there aren't many of these around."

Sala said, "It looks handmade. This could be very big, Ty."

One step at a time. "We can start by announcing this belt

buckle to the media. Maybe someone will recognize it, and we'll have ID. It's a huge start."

Sala fished out his cell to call Savich. One ring, two, then—"Hang on, Sala. I've got to shoot my free throw in the brand-new net I put up a few minutes ago against my mother's garage." A moment later, "Nailed it." Sala heard Sean hooting in the background. "Okay, it's Sean's turn. Talk to me."

Sala told him about the gold Star of David belt buckle and their plan to publicize it. "We all agree, it's got to be one of a kind."

Savich heard excitement, not guilt or pain, in Sala's voice. "Yes, I agree," Savich said.

"Ty and I have been out on the lake all morning, so no TV. Did you get Victor Nesser's photo out?"

"Yes. His photo and bio are being plastered all over the networks in the tri-states."

"Do I want to know how you found him so quickly? Even before the prints were identified this morning?"

Savich said smoothly, "A hunch and I acted on it, got lucky."

Sala said, his voice just as smooth, "Thank MAX for me. You think it was Nesser who saw Sherlock with Sean at the book festival Saturday, took his chance? And missed?"

"Yes, thankfully, just as he missed taking Sean Wednesday night. We can't be sure, but it seems likely Victor followed us from Washington to Willicott."

Words clogged in Sala's throat, then, "Yeah," he said, and swallowed. "Searching the lake for bones with Ty. She won't let me alone."

"Sala, call Mr. Maitland and tell him what's going on. Tell

him about the gold Star of David belt buckle. He won't mind it's Sunday."

"Yes, all right."

"Wish me luck with my basketball game. My kid's got some moves, dribbling with both hands, trying to copy Steph Curry."

Sala punched off and called Mr. Maitland's cell. He answered on the first ring. "Yeah? This better be good. My wife handed me a dish of her potato salad. It's got kosher dills and olives. And I saw a cherry pie cooling in the kitchen."

Sala identified himself and said, "I really like cherry pie."

"So does the rest of the known world. Glad you called, Sala. Tell me what's going on there with the bone hunt in Lake Massey."

After Sala told him about the Star of David belt buckle, Maitland whistled. "A stroke of luck. Makes sense it belonged to one of the victims. We should get this out to the media. You got anything else to tell me?"

"I understand why I can't be out in the field looking for Victor Nesser, but I'd like to stay in Willicott, sir, maybe work with Flynn and the chief of police, try to find whoever murdered all these people and threw them in Lake Massey."

Maitland was silent. Sala wondered if he'd taken a bite of that potato salad with the kosher dills and olives. Or the cherry pie?

It came unbidden out of Sala's mouth. "Sir, I don't want to take time off or go see my family. Look, I failed both Octavia and the bureau. I've got to do something, focus on something other than what happened to her."

22

Maitland said, sarcasm thick in his voice, "Sure you failed—tell you what, wake me up out of a dead sleep and stick a knife in my wife's throat and see what I manage to do. Nesser had this planned out. Stop drowning yourself in buckets of guilt, it won't help us or anyone else. All right, Sala, stay and help the chief. Get the bones you found today to Quantico."

"All right. Sir, one of the chief's deputies will take the bones to Dr. Thomas. You know Dr. Thomas will be there. I've explained to Ty he won't be able to articulate all of the skeletons, but he will get a count on the number of bodies we find in the lake. Also, there might be DNA left in the bone marrow, and they can do facial approximations on the skulls we've found. That will take longer."

Maitland said, "I'll hurry the process along as much as I can. Knowing Dr. Thomas, security at Quantico will have to kick him out at night to make him go home until he's finished identifying those bones.

"Using a lake as a dump site is nothing new, but it's always very disturbing. Any evidence the Serial's a local?"

Sala said, "Makes sense, since the lake was convenient for him. Chief Christie told me there haven't been any missing persons in Willicott itself. She's reaching out to law enforcement all around here to begin with, see what that gets us."

"He could have trolled far and wide for victims. You know Chief Christie called the Hoover Building herself Friday morning and managed to work her way up to me? Goldy wants to meet her, thinks the chief's got guts. I hope she's got brains to go with the guts. Savich seems to think she does."

"I'd agree, but her biggest strength is her kindness." He swallowed, and said simply, "Ty is very kind."

Maitland heard the pain in his agent's voice. The chief was evidently dealing well with it. He made a decision. "Sala, I don't think we need both you and Flynn in Willicott. I'm going to pull Flynn back. We got handed multiple stabbing murders in Birmingham, Alabama, Flynn's hometown. He can assist the local field office."

Sala would miss Flynn, he never missed a detail, but Sala would take up the slack. "Yes, sir, thank you. I'll stay on, then."

"Where are you staying? Savich said the book festival had filled up every available room."

"I was with Chief Christie last night. I hope she lets me

continue on until I have to come back on Tuesday—for Octavia's funeral."

Maitland said, "Yes, of course. I'll be there myself. There will be a lot of people there. Octavia was well liked. Bring Chief Christie with you. I want to meet her. I want to meet the actual human being who got past Goldy."

"I'll ask her to come along."

"Good. Sala, keep your eyes open. When Nesser finds out you survived, he might come back."

"I will. Sir, I read up on him. I've dealt with him face-to-face, and I'll be ready. But I doubt I'm on his radar. It was Savich who killed Lissy Smiley, and Sherlock shot him in the foot. I only happened to be with Octavia."

"After he failed to take Sean Savich, I guess he decided to go on to Octavia, although, to be objective here, it still surprises me. No matter what she said that offended his manhood, she kept him from a life sentence.

"Don't worry, Sala, I've got protection on Savich and Sherlock." He heard what sounded like a forkful of potato salad going into Maitland's mouth, then Sala hung up, and turned to see Ty with her head cocked to one side. She'd been listening. She said, "Octavia Ryan kept Nesser from going to trial, got the judge to rule he was incompetent, so he was sent to Central State Hospital in Virginia. He was so young, only early twenties when he was sent to Central, and now he's only twenty-three. From what I've read, he was so infatuated with Lissy Smiley he'd do anything for her. And both Lissy and her mother were crazy as loons. It explains why he went crazy himself when Lissy died, why he's out to avenge her now. Do you know more about Victor or Lissy's family?"

Sala slipped his cell back into his pocket. "I remember Victor moved in with his aunt, his mother's sister, Jennifer Smiley, when he was sixteen. When Lissy turned thirteen, she seduced him. From all accounts she was the love of Victor's life. Savich believes she felt the same way. Only, well, she was crazy, so who knows? I guess you know, too, Victor was the driver for the Gang of Four, as they called themselves. Mother, daughter Lissy, and two other guys whose names I don't remember. When they hit a bank in Georgetown, Savich happened to be there. Lissy recognized him from a news show. She was ready to kill him, but he kicked her so hard in her belly that she had to have surgery on her duodenum. Victor managed to sneak her out of the hospital, and they ran, all the way back to where Victor had an apartment in Winnett, North Carolina. He tried to blow them up, took another agent captive. It was pretty hairy, lives on the line, as you can imagine, and in the end, Savich was forced to kill her. I heard he had help from a little girl, but when anyone asked him what little girl, he only shook his head. There was lots more, but those are the salients. Have I repeated everything you already knew?"

Ty laughed. "Only a little."

"And he tried for Sean again yesterday at the book festival. Go figure that. We've got to find him fast before he tries for someone else."

"What he did was pretty lamebrain, wasn't it, with Sherlock there ready for him?" Ty took another sip of her water. "I can't imagine the stress, your kid in danger right along with you and your husband. I wonder where Victor Nesser is hiding. I also wonder, if Lissy was indeed the love of his life, why he now has a new girlfriend."

"And I'm wondering if he knows he's been identified yet. You know it'll come as a real shock when he finds out. I only hope it doesn't send him on a rampage. Yeah, a new girlfriend. It doesn't make much sense to me. Doesn't to Savich, either."

23

EAST CAPITOL STREET NE
WASHINGTON, D.C.
SUNDAY MORNING

"Papa, Marty wants to know why I'm staying with Gran."

Sean and Savich were sitting in his mother's light, airy kitchen, Savich eating a late breakfast of spinach crepes, one of his mom's specialties, and a side of scrambled eggs. Sean was chowing down on Cheerios with his requisite sliced banana on top. Sherlock had said she wasn't hungry and excused herself to spend time with his mother in the living room, giving her an update on what had happened yesterday, well out of Sean's hearing.

Savich swallowed a bite of eggs, laid his hand over his son's small one. "It's almost your grandmother's birthday, Sean, and that's what she wanted for her present—you." Thankfully,

Sean knew very well his grandmother's birthday was next week.

Sean preened. "I'm a birthday present? That's awesome." Then he looked worried. "Don't we have to give her something else, Papa? I spent all my money yesterday at the book festival."

"Your present to her doesn't involve buying her anything. All you have to do is keep your room straight, enjoy yourself, and not be a pain in the butt. Senator Monroe is taking you to your day camp again tomorrow, then Gabriella will pick you up and bring you back here. Your grandmother said if it was okay with Marty's parents, she could come back here with you tomorrow after camp and have dinner. Senator Monroe will be here to take her home. What do you think?"

"Since I'm a present, do I have to wash the dishes?"

"It's nearly her birthday, Sean, so it'd be nice for you and Marty to help. Clear the table, like you do at home."

Sean said thoughtfully, "I'll tell Marty it's her job to clear the table." He gave his father a beatific smile. "I'll be the boss."

It was close, but Savich didn't roll his eyes. Sean telling Marty what to do? He'd like to see that. He said, "That's something you can work out with Marty. Now, after breakfast, you and Gran and Senator Monroe are going to Christ Church."

"I like going there. It's old, Papa. Gran told me it was old even when she was young. She says we can snuggle in with all those people who sat where we're sitting. She says lots of them were politicians, but what can you do?"

Savich laughed.

"Will you and Mama come with us?"

"Not this time. Your mother and I have some important work to attend to."

Sean forgot about Christ Church. He gave his father a long, serious look. "Are you going to catch that man with the big chocolate bar in Mr. McGurk's tent yesterday? Mama told a lady to grab me and Marty, and she ran after him."

No hope for it. "That's right. He wasn't a nice man, Sean, and we need to find him."

"And then I'll get to come home?"

When had Sean gotten so grown-up? "Yes, then you'll come home. So enjoy your stay here in Gran Disneyland. It won't last much longer."

It was quiet in the Hoover Building at noon on Sunday, the immense hallways echoing Sherlock's and Savich's footsteps. They walked into the CAU and saw Agent Lucy McKnight and two agents on loan from the Criminal Division, Dirk Platt and Jerry Barnes, manning the Victor Nesser hotline phones. The agents looked up when Savich said, "Thanks, guys, for coming in to handle the hotline."

They answered with some good-natured bitching, but only because neither agent had gotten any worthwhile calls that merited follow-up, one a Nesser sighting in Anchorage, one from San Diego. Dirk said, "Amazing how fast this guy can move. One woman claimed she saw Victor driving over the Mexican border. When I told her it couldn't be possible, she asked if I was single."

"I'm the one with the luck," Agent Lucy McKnight called out. "Wait'll you hear what I've got."

Dirk's phone rang. "Lots of folks out and about on a Sunday," he said, and picked it up. "Hotline, Agent Comptom. What do you have for me?"

When Lucy hung up from another call, she said, "Do you know my no-good husband is off fishing with his father and brothers at Cape Hatteras, like they do every single year? Okay, okay, so listen to this call I just got: a park ranger, Gina Clemmens, at Greenbrier State Park in Maryland is pretty certain Victor Nesser tried to get into the park late yesterday. Greenbrier is about sixty miles east of Willicott. She had to turn him away because there were no campsites left. I asked her if she was in the kiosk until she closed down the gate, and she said yes, of course. Then she backed up, said she did take a bathroom break, but it wasn't more than ten minutes. When she came back, she was on the gate for another half hour, then closed it down."

Savich said, "Still, Victor could have driven in while she was on break and parked out of sight, maybe away from the parking lot, taken his camping equipment into the woods for the night, and left this morning."

"Exactly. Ranger Clemmens said she saw some camping equipment in the backseat of the car. A Kia, she said, dark green, with a Virginia license plate she didn't write down, since she'd turned him away."

Sherlock said, "Did the ranger see a woman in the car?"

"I asked her, but she said she didn't notice anyone else. But she guesses there could have been someone hunched down in the backseat with all the camping gear."

Lucy gave them a fat smile. "But I haven't finished. Two minutes before you guys walked in, I got a call from a Mr. Norm Chitter, of Norm's Fish and Bait in Bowman, Maryland, right outside Greenbrier State Park. Victor was in his store to buy some junk food, saw himself on the TV, 'turned paler than a week-old trout'—his words—and ran. Dropped a box of Milk Duds on his mad dash out of the store."

Sherlock heaved a sigh of relief. "Thank goodness he didn't shoot Mr. Chitter."

"—or his wife, who saw him, too, came into the store from the back room as Victor was running out the front door."

"Did either of them see him drive away?"

"No. Mr. Chitter said it took him a minute to understand why Victor ran out of his store like 'a pair of hedge shears were after his tail feathers'—again I'm quoting. Then he looked at the TV and saw Victor's photo and that he was wanted for questioning in a local murder. By the time he got his courage up and went outside, Victor was gone. Do you think Victor went back to the park after Norm recognized him?"

"If he did, he didn't stay long," Sherlock said. She looked thoughtful. "If I were Victor, I'd dump the green Kia, since I'd have to assume I'd been seen in it, and find myself another car. He's got to be scared now, probably can't understand how we already know who he is."

Lucy said, "Maybe Victor hightailed it to another state park?"

Savich smiled at Lucy. "That's a good guess. If I were in his shoes, I'd get out of Maryland fast. Maybe Pennsylvania or Virginia."

"Or he could drive back to Winnett, North Carolina," Lucy said, "where he lived before you and Sherlock finally brought him and Lissy down."

Savich said, "Let's get an APB out on the green Kia in Maryland, Virginia, and Pennsylvania. The Kia's probably stolen, too."

Sherlock said thoughtfully, "I'm hoping Victor will be too frantic to get out of the area to bother dumping the Kia now. Maybe Virginia or Pennsylvania, if he makes it that far."

Lucy said, "You think there's a girl with him?"

Savich said, his voice expressionless, "I wish I knew." He looked down at his watch. "I've got a call to make." And he walked into his office.

Sherlock said to Lucy, "We're going to go out to Quantico soon, see Dr. Thomas. Maybe he's got something definitive to tell us about the bones they found in Lake Massey." She drew in a deep breath. "And we need to speak to Dr. Haymes. He called. He's finished Octavia Ryan's autopsy."

Lucy said, "Two months ago I worked with Octavia on the Wiliker case, you remember, the two-man team who killed those young women?"

"Yes, I remember the case, but I never met Octavia. Her funeral is on Tuesday, in Falls Church. Did you know she was seeing Agent Sala Porto?"

"Sure, she told me last week in the women's room she and Sala were going someplace to de-stress. Then she told me she was thinking about going back with her ex-husband, said he finally might be getting his head on straight. Her ex was really putting the moves on her. I think she was going back."

"But what about Sala?"

"She said she and Sala were good friends, with benefits, they understood each other, enjoyed each other." Lucy shook her head, swiped the tears away. "Now she's dead and she'll never have a chance to decide what to do—about anything. And what Victor Nesser had planned for Sala? Leave him to die in that closet? Where is Sala?"

"He stayed in Willicott to work with the local police chief. Everyone's thinking a Serial's been active in that area for a long time now, using Lake Massey as a body dump. We have no reason to think those bodies are connected with Octavia, but we don't know for sure."

Lucy laced her fingers over her stomach. "Why are some people evil?"

No answer to that question. Sherlock looked down at Lucy's fingers on her belly. "Lucy, you look different. You're all glowy. Oh my, you're pregnant, aren't you?"

Lucy gave her a crazed smile. "Yes, nearly three months. I was thinking about unfastening my jeans button. I was going to announce it next week, but now you know."

Sherlock gave her a big hug. "This is wonderful. What does your good-for-nothing off-fishing husband have to say?"

"Coop's strutting around the house, a huge grin on his face, talking about teaching his kid to fly-fish and skateboard. I gotta say, though, he does hold my hair out of my face when I'm puking in the toilet, so that's gotta prove I married a stand-up guy." Lucy tapped her pen on her desktop. "I hate this, Sherlock. Not only you and Dillon in danger from this Nesser, but Sean, too."

What could she say? Sherlock only nodded, patted Lucy's shoulder, and joined Dillon at the door of the CAU to walk down the empty hallway to the elevators.

"Lucy's pregnant. Coop holds her head when she hurls, so all is good in Cooperland. Beginnings and endings, life goes on. It's really quite wonderful." She stopped and looked up at him. "Don't you think?"

Savich cocked his head at her, gave her a quick kiss, and punched the elevator button. "I'm happy for them. I still can't get over Victor and that candy bar in McGurk's tent. I meant to tell you, Sean knew the man with the candy bar was bad. The kid doesn't miss much."

"No." She grabbed him when the elevator doors closed and held on tight. "We have to keep him safe, Dillon."

He kissed her hair and held her until the doors opened onto the lobby.

24

JEFFERSON DORMITORY
FORENSIC ANTHROPOLOGY LAB
QUANTICO, VIRGINIA
SUNDAY

Dr. Thomas stood beside a long stainless steel table covered with rows of matching bones neatly lined up. The next table held smaller bones, all of them still in a jumble. They reminded Savich of the wall of bones in the catacombs beneath St. Stephen's Cathedral in Vienna. Dr. Thomas waved Savich and Sherlock over, pointed down at the line of bones. "I've found sixteen right tibias so far, one obviously from a young adult, not yet fully grown, and one very long tibia, so a very tall man, about six foot six, I'd say. There are both men and women in this group of sixteen. There aren't enough skulls to attach to all these bones, so obviously there must be more at the bottom of the lake. Or in another lake," he added. "You never know what will and what won't show up. Over on that tarp are the bones they found this morning in Lake Massey. I'll get to them when I can, maybe tomorrow. My wife threatened this morning at breakfast to break my favorite antique turntable if I don't get home by three o'clock today."

They looked up when Sala Porto and Chief Ty Christie knocked on the open door. Dr. Thomas called out, "Come in, come in, we're just getting started." After introducing Ty to Dr. Thomas, Sala said, "Sorry we're late, ran into Beltway traffic. On a Sunday, go figure."

"Not a problem," Dr. Thomas said. "I was telling Savich and Sherlock the early count is sixteen so far, not including the bones you brought up this morning. None of the skeletal remains are nearly complete, of course, and there aren't enough skulls. All I can say with certainty thus far is that the bones I have here, as I said, are from a minimum of sixteen people, all but one of them adults. I haven't found any perimortem insults, but several orthopedic screws, two hips, two knees, which, unfortunately won't help me identify them. The half a dozen skulls have very few teeth, not enough to match with dental records.

"I've put aside the manufactured items—the few shoes, belts, remnants of clothing. We can probably identify some of the manufacturers, the range of dates those items were sold, but there's nothing unusual there. No jewelry or identification of any kind. Truth is, I have very little for you so far. Some of these bones could have been in the lake for as little as five years, some for decades."

They stood over the table looking down at the line of stark-white right tibias. Sherlock picked up the only smaller one. "He murdered a child, didn't he?"

Dr. Thomas said, "A teenage girl, actually. I've only begun to examine the bones closely for trauma, anything to indicate cause of death. One of the skulls appears fractured, but that's hard to say without closer examination." Dr. Thomas paused, ran his hands through his hair, thick brown with gray strands on the sides that made him look professorial. Rich was lean, a runner, Sherlock knew, with two kids and a wife with a local cooking show on TV. They were lucky to have him. He lived and breathed his work. And worshiped his wife's lasagna. He took off his glasses, cleaned them on his shirt. "I'll have done an examination in the next couple of days, then hopefully I'll be able to tell you what killed some of these folks." Dr. Thomas looked over at Sala. "You called me about some big break. What is it?"

Sala pulled the gold Star of David belt buckle out of a bag and handed it to Dr. Thomas. "I'm thinking it's fourteen-karat gold," Sala said, "which means lots of moolah was spent on that adornment. It might get us identification if the man was a local. I was wondering why the Serial didn't take it. I mean, he could have fenced it for at least a couple thousand."

Dr. Thomas fingered the belt buckle. "It's very beautiful and yes, unique." He said to Ty, "I know you want answers, Chief. Tomorrow, our people will start examining the bone marrow for traces of DNA. But you know, it will take time."

He handed the belt buckle back to Sala and looked over at the skulls. "Our artist Jayne will start the facial approximations tomorrow." He gave them a lopsided grin. "Although truthfully, they're not very useful yet. But hey, maybe in a couple of years, who knows? You could set MAX on it, Savich."

Ty picked up the Star of David belt buckle, studied it again. "When can we show this on local TV, Dillon?"

"Tomorrow," Savich said.

Ty said slowly, "Rather than some local police chief going on TV, namely me, I think the FBI would get more attention. Dillon, you should do it."

Sala added, "She's right, Savich. You and Mr. Maitland could appear together. It would give the announcement more gravitas, maybe more of the stations would run it, especially if you do it in Willicott. The belt buckle of a murdered man who lived in the area."

"I'll call Mr. Maitland, see if that's how he wants to run it." He looked over at the bones, at people whose lives had been ended so cruelly by an individual with no conscience, felt no remorse, who had probably felt nothing at all, except pleasure.

25

MARAUDER STATE PARK
NEAR PLUNKETT, MARYLAND
SUNDAY EVENING

I'm tired, Victor, and my stitches hurt. This place is pretty, I'll give you that, but why'd you want to come to another park in the same state?

"Lissy, think a minute. Nobody pays you any mind once you're cleared into a park. You walk past all the campers and the people with their tents and their kids and their barbecues, and it's nice and quiet. No one watching TV, not like that old buzzard at the bait store."

I can hear it in your voice, Victor. You're still peeing your pants, aren't you? That's because you didn't put out that old coot's lights like you should have. Stupid, Victor, and now you know he's already told the cops where we are. And he saw the car, and they'll track us. You know the dude couldn't wait to call them. That was a bad mistake,

Victor, really bad. I've told you, I don't want to go back to that brain-dead psych ward. And you dropped my box of Milk Duds, you were so scared. My mama never ran from anything.

"Shut up about your stupid mama! I don't want to hear about her anymore. Look, it took me by surprise, that's all. I mean, seeing myself on TV—I couldn't believe it. How'd they find out about me? How? And so fast? I was careful, scrubbed everything. You know that. You were watching and telling me how to do it. I wish we could get those staples out of your belly. They're ugly, and I don't like to see them, especially when you're scratching at them."

You *think they're ugly? Poor you. It's always you, isn't it, Victor? But what about me? They're clamping my guts in. I hate them. They pull and stretch and ache all the time.*

"It's because that bastard Savich kicked you so hard they had to cut you open and make repairs. Why'd you want to kill Savich so bad that first time when you saw him in the bank? I mean, he was lying there on the floor like the rest of the customers, right? He couldn't hurt you."

Lissy pulled out a slice of white bread and opened the jar of crunchy peanut butter. *I'd seen him on TV, realized he was that big important FBI agent, and I had this great chance to kill him.*

When I was with it enough to watch TV after the surgery, the news programs were still going on about how Savich had been some sort of hero, saved some worthless sods' lives. I hate him. I want you to kill him, Victor. Hey, there's sugar in this peanut butter. Why didn't you get natural? You know that's the only kind Mama ever bought.

"Peanut butter tastes better with sugar. Give me a slice, too, Lissy. And I want some of those Fritos and some bean dip."

The only fresh thing you bought are those limp carrots, probably older than that old coot, Norm. You should have looked closer before you bought them, Victor. They look like they'll taste nasty. And I don't have a peeler. Hand me that water so I can at least give them a wash. Then give me your new Ka-Bar. I'll scrape them down.

"Yeah, here's the knife. Look, even if I'd shot that old guy at the grocery, his wife was there, too, and she saw me. People could have come in, could have seen me. I had to run. You would have, too."

Me, run? You know better than that, Victor. Mama didn't raise no lame-butt coward. Pop! Pop! And the problem's solved. And you get the money in the cash register, and you wouldn't have to drive all day long, so scared you were sweating bullets. Look at you, happy now you're eating your peanut butter, with all that sugar on that poopy white bread.

Now they know who we are. You gotta be smart, no more making up things as you go along, like that stupid chocolate bar at the book festival, no more going cowboy. You could have got yourself caught, Victor. That agent, Sherlock, she got too close.

"How many times do I have to tell you? I followed them from Washington. They never saw me. I got this idea, thought I could get the kid. Why not? I would have gotten him if things had been different. How long are you going to rag on me about that, Lissy?"

All right, so you tried. Now we've got things to do, places to go. I'm thinking it's time to get Buzz Riley, that security guard who killed my mama. I'll never forget his name as long as I live. I want to shoot a bullet right up his nose, Victor. Okay?

"I'll think about it, Lissy. I'll buy you some natural peanut butter tomorrow."

26

WILLICOTT, MARYLAND
SUNDAY EVENING

Savich and Sherlock sat across from Ty and Sala in a booth, three of them eating Congo's famous meatloaf, Savich a corn-on-the-cob and three-bean salad, prepared for him by Congo himself. It was his granny's recipe from before the big war in Europe, he'd said. Ty had wondered if Congo was a nickname or if his parents had given in to whimsy or visited Africa at the time of his conception. Since Sean was at his grandmother's, Savich and Sherlock had wanted to come back to Willicott to touch base with Sala and Ty. And where they were touching base was at Bliss's Diner, a local landmark, Ty had assured them.

Congo sauntered to their table again and beamed a hundred-watt smile. "Well, now, what do you think of my special salad for you, Agent Savich? The beans are fresh, right out of my own garden."

Savich liked the good-looking older man with a crooked incisor and charming smile. "Nearly as good as my mom's."

"What can I say to that? A mom's a mom." As he poured iced tea into their glasses, Congo continued, "Did the chief tell you I was the one who found the first skull when I dived looking for poor Ms. Ryan? That was a shocker, I'll tell you, a skull on the bottom of Lake Massey. I thought poor Albert would mess his pants when the chief here handed it to him. Any sugar or lemon for anybody? No? Imagine, some crazy serial killer living in or near Willicott, Maryland. I mean, everyone knows they exist, but you don't expect it could be one of your neighbors down the street, right?"

Sherlock asked, "Is that what you think, Mr. Bliss? The serial killer lives in Willicott?"

"I was told that's what Charlie thinks, and Charlie's your right hand, Ty." Congo shook his head. "Hard to swallow he's risen so high in such a short time. I knew Charlie when he was a snot-nosed little dip, always blowing bubble gum, making a mess on his face. His mama—Lynn Corsica—was always peeling the stuff off, smacking his butt while she did. Smart lady, that Lynn, sees everything, knows everything, to be expected, I guess, being she runs the library.

"Anyway, I heard Charlie and Hanger Lewis and his boys hauled up a lot more bones in that creaky old pontoon boat of his. And more this morning when Charlie and Hanger went out again. I wonder why they haven't found more skulls.

The walleyes haul them away?" He shook his head. "Imagine finding that poor federal prosecutor down there with all those bones."

The perils of a small town. Everyone knew everything about Octavia's body being in the lake, right down to the number of bones they'd hauled up. At least she could hope anyone who'd heard or seen anything would come to her door. Would anyone come up and say something to Sala?

Congo gave them a salute and wandered to another table with his tea pitcher. Not three minutes later, he was back. "I heard the fancy folk at Quantico are looking at the bones. Chief, you gonna have Hanger take another run?"

She said, "Mayor Bobby and the council want to wait and see what the FBI is planning before they authorize more money for dragging the lake." Actually, Mayor Bobby had said, "What do we need more bones for, Ty? It's not like they can identify anybody from a skull like they do on the TV shows." He'd given her his patented winsome smile that had charmed her when he'd interviewed her and gotten him elected four times. He'd leaned close, patted her shoulder. "I know you want to do your job, Chief, and track down this maniac. The council and I, we've got your back." And what did that mean?

She smiled up at Congo. "Delicious meatloaf as usual, Congo. Look, Agent Sherlock and Agent Porto have nearly cleaned their plates, and hardly a bean left on Agent Savich's plate. Now it's on to your peach pie."

When he returned with an entire pie to cut at the table, Ty said before he could start up again, "Congo, do you know of anyone who's gone missing for, say, the last twenty years, and was never found or heard from again?"

Congo frowned as he meticulously cut the warm pie and served up the slices. Finally, he said, "Same question I've been hearing all day. There was Mr. Grover—went missing back in ninety-four, never heard from again. But he was old and had Alzheimer's, so he probably wandered off, maybe fell into Lake Massey and drowned. Can't think of anyone else myself. I'll ask around."

"Thank you. Guys, Congo's known not only for his meatloaf but his peach pie. Dig in."

Congo lightly laid his hand on Sala's shoulder. "Everyone's sorry about what happened to Ms. Ryan, and to you, Agent Porto. It was a horrible thing."

Marv Spaleny, the book festival committee president and owner of Spaleny's Best Books, walked over and introduced himself. He was always at Bliss's Diner on Sunday nights without his wife, although no one knew why. He was a tall man, thin as a nail, always full of bonhomie that kept customers coming in to buy his undiscounted books.

Marv looked down at the peach pie without a lick of interest and said in his deep, mellow voice that made him a favorite reader at the library, "The book festival was a big hit this year, despite all the trouble on the lake, Ty, biggest year yet. Your deputies did great. I saw the last of our authors off a bit ago. We'll find out how well all our shop owners did at the weekly council meeting. I know I sold more books than I'd expected. Hope you can make it."

Congo patted his shoulder. "Come on, Marv, I've got your tortilla soup all ready. Don't want it to go cold."

Marv gave them a small bow and left them, following Congo, though Marv stopped at every table to preen about the festival success.

The four of them adjourned to Ty's back deck. Ty served her Turkish espresso and Earl Grey tea for Dillon, talking him into a dash of cinnamon, which, to his surprise, he liked.

The sun was setting, the air warm and soft against their faces. The crickets had begun their nightly symphony when they settled on the deck and grew quiet to take in the evening.

"The water looks like glass," Sherlock said and sighed. "This is a beautiful spot, Ty. Do you ever miss Seattle?"

Ty was looking across the lake at Point Gulliver and Gatewood, remembering the murder, seeing it all again. She shook herself. "It's strange, but I sort of miss the incessant drizzle—liquid sunshine, Seattle natives call it. But Seattle itself? With all the Starbucks, all the crazy traffic, people going every which way, the drugs and the gangs I dealt with in Vice—no, I don't miss that. Willicott is exactly my speed." She saluted Sherlock with her coffee cup. "Except for everyone knowing what you eat for breakfast, it's perfect.

"Dillon, thank you and Mr. Maitland. I know it's my jurisdiction, but I don't have enough resources. Your bringing the FBI on board on TV tomorrow will be a big help."

Savich took his final drink of tea, with cinnamon. Who knew?

"I'll call you in the morning after I've got everything lined up, give you an exact time. Sala, I want you there, all right? I think it's time to set rumors straight about the Serial and about what happened to you and Octavia. I'm hoping the broadcast will go regional. I don't want either the Serial or Victor to be able to find a hole to hide in."

Sherlock said, "Something's been bothering me. Since Victor escaped from Central State Hospital, he couldn't have had much money. But look what he's done. Moving around in Washington, buying camping gear, weapons, coming up here. So he's either been robbing stores or—"

Savich finished it. "Or—he went back and picked up the stolen bank money Jennifer Smiley hid somewhere. Money we never found on her property, even after the FBI went over the place thoroughly, house and grounds."

Ty asked. "How much money?"

"Over a half a million dollars," Savich said. "You can bet the citizens of Fort Pessel dug up the property. So far we haven't heard about anyone finding a big load of cash, and we would have."

"Why is it important to you to know that, Dillon?" Ty asked him.

He said slowly, "Unless we know for sure whether Victor has that bank money, it leaves us with a mystery."

"As in where then did he get money after his escape from the psychiatric ward?"

"Exactly." Savich shook his head. "We'll figure it out, sooner or later."

Sala said, "Guys, here's what I can't get past. We know Victor's girlfriend, Lissy, is dead. You've said she was the love of Victor's life, so then who was that girl I heard laughing? Has he hooked up with some runaway teenager?"

Savich remembered thinking someone had been standing in the master bedroom window at Gatewood, looking out over the water, waiting for Victor to return. He didn't know what to think. Until he could figure this out, better to keep it to himself. He said, "That could be, Sala. It's been bothering me, too."

Ty took a sip of her coffee and looked out at the lake again. She didn't think she'd ever see it in the same light she had before Friday morning. She could picture Octavia Ryan's body floating among the bones and skulls lying on the bottom, many of them covered by years of sand and reeds. She said, "The only real clue we have so far about all those bones is that gold belt buckle. We have to hope we'll get a call identifying it when Dillon shows it on TV."

Sala scooted his chair a bit closer and propped his feet on the deck railing. "I remember a Serial in Boston who murdered twenty-four people—maybe more, no one knows—over about nineteen years. One night a young punk stole his Prius from his driveway, decided to take it for a joy ride. When he brought the car back, he decided to see if there was anything worth stealing in the trunk, and he found a body wrapped in a shower curtain. Thankfully, after puking up his guts, he called the cops."

Ty said, "Who was the Serial?"

"A newspaper editor, well respected, married, lived what you call a normal life. They found his souvenirs in a locked cabinet in his basement."

"What happened to him?"

"He put a gun in his mouth when the cops moved in. I guess what I'm saying is it's not always excellent police work that cracks serial cases. It's happenstance, a snitch, or most of the time, as you know, an errant parking ticket—remember how they caught the Son of Sam? Or, in this case, it was a joy-riding juvenile delinquent."

Sala slept for three hours that night in Ty's guest bedroom before the nightmares pulled him under. Ty found him sweating and heaving, and without a word, the two of them dragged the mattress out on the deck. They settled in and watched the moon hovering over Point Gulliver, watched dark clouds drifting in and out of the moonlight.

27

WILLICOTT, MARYLAND
MONDAY, NOON

Shops closed, and townspeople congregated in Bleaker Park in the center of Willicott, many seated on blankets, since the white-painted wooden benches had been nabbed early. It could have been the Fourth of July or another day of the book festival, except most of the people gathered looked deadly serious. Savich looked out at the hundreds of curious faces, saw some of the adults handing out sandwiches to their kids. He wished parents hadn't brought their families, not with the gruesome details he'd have to lay out. TV vans, camera crews, and anchors, most of them beautiful younger people, were already poking their mics into faces for comments. Everyone already knew about all the bones found in Lake Massey and the murder last Friday, but he supposed the news about the Star of David belt buckle hadn't yet made it through their grapevine. The camera crews were ready, and they were going live. The regional TV stations would carry a special news bulletin, and, of course, a live stream on the Internet.

Savich waited for Willicott's mayor, Robert—Bobby—Bleaker, namesake of his great-grandfather, who'd donated the park to the town after World War I, to finish his introduction, then stepped to the microphone set on a conductor's stand in the middle of the quickly erected stage.

Mr. Maitland had decided Savich would do better without him. No reason to overwhelm. Savich spoke for twenty minutes, walked everyone through the murder of Octavia Ryan, the attempted murder of Agent Sala Porto, and the finding of the bones at the bottom of Lake Massey. He saw some of the parents put their palms over their children's ears when he couldn't avoid graphic descriptions. He told them what the FBI forensic anthropologists were doing, that it would take time. He didn't say the phrase *serial killer*, but he didn't have to. Every adult understood very well. They were afraid, and that was a good thing. They would take greater care now, of one another and their children.

Finally, Savich held up the Star of David belt buckle. The cameras zoomed in. He waited a beat, then said, "This belt buckle very possibly belonged to one of the people who was murdered and thrown into Lake Massey. As you can see, it's large and made of gold and decorated with a Star of David. If you recognize it, please call the hotline appearing at the bottom of your screen." He repeated the number twice and also announced the hotline number for Victor Nesser again. "We need your help. Thank you. Are there any questions?"

There were scores of questions, shouted all together, some of them planted by Savich. He wanted to be sure everyone present knew what he wanted them to know and set aside rumors that might actually hurt the investigation. When they started getting off topic, and one of the press actually asked about the environmental precautions they took while dragging Lake Massey, he closed it down. He repeated the phone numbers for both hotlines once again, thanked everyone for coming, then stepped away from the microphone. He watched the pandemonium of dozens of news people jumping on their cell phones, others madly typing on their laptops and iPads while they talked through headsets.

Ty was convinced the hotline would get a call quickly about the Star of David belt buckle, but it didn't happen. Instead, there was a call about a Victor Nesser sighting in Peterborough, Maryland. Savich and Sherlock drove off to check it out themselves.

28

PETERBOROUGH, MARYLAND

Savich and Sherlock drove to Herm's Crab Shack at the end of Clooney Street in Peterborough, a ramshackle diner in a semi-industrial area. Despite no air-conditioning and unappealing surroundings, the place was jammed. Two overhead fans lazily stirred the humid air in its one long room. The customers sat at family-size wooden tables set cheek by jowl on floors covered with sawdust. The smell of fried food filled the air. A buxom waitress, her broad face shiny with sweat, greeted them, turned, and shouted, "Frankie! Get yourself out here. The FBI wants you. It's about the call your father told you not to make."

Frankie Hooper was tall and skinny, maybe twenty years old, with the long arms of a basketball player. He threaded his way between tables to Savich and Sherlock, grinning hugely. They followed him out through the back of the restaurant into a tree-filled patio, past more people chowing down on fried lobster. They stopped beneath a full-leafed oak tree off to one side, happy for the shade. They didn't need to get him started, Frankie spoke fast and low, like he was afraid he'd forget it if he didn't spew it all out at once. "This young dude came in three hours ago, kinda early for fried lobster—that's our specialty. My granny brought the recipe over from Maine when she married Granddad a thousand years ago. Anyways, I saw his face on TV at least a dozen times, so I knew what he looked like. He looked real seedy, like he needed a bath. Ma thought he looked like one of the students at the community college." He paused, beamed at them, leaned forward. "I know it was him, Agents, that guy, Victor Nesser. I'm sure about that."

"Describe him for us, Mr. Hooper," Sherlock said, "other than his looking seedy."

The description Frankie gave of Victor included only what he could have seen on TV. That was worrisome.

Sherlock gave Frankie her sunny smile. "Did he say where he was going?"

"Nope. He didn't talk to anybody. He chowed down on three fried lobsters. It wouldn't have surprised me if he'd burst himself wide open, he ate so much, and he ate really fast. And you gotta face it, fried lobster isn't in one of the five food groups."

Savich said, "Did he have a girl with him?"

That drew Frankie up short. He pondered, then brightened. "I'd forgot. Yeah, I remember now, she ate a fried lobster, too. She was taller than he was, not very pretty."

Sherlock asked, “Was she younger than him? Older? What color was her hair?”

Frankie looked flummoxed, but only for an instant. “She was wearing a ball cap. I couldn’t see her hair. She was about his age, I guess, maybe twenty-five, younger, I can’t be sure. We were starting to get really busy with the lobster brunch crowd, so I really didn’t pay them much mind. It was only after I saw you on TV and they showed his photo on-screen. He’d left, but I knew it was him so I called right away.”

Savich asked, “How did he pay for his meal?”

“Cash. He pulled out a hundred-dollar bill. You don’t forget seeing a hundred-dollar bill.”

Savich and Sherlock thanked Frankie and headed for the Porsche.

An older man with a bag of takeout in his hand shouted, “Nice wheels, man!”

“Thank you,” Savich said and couldn’t help it. He turned, smiled.

“You like compliments to your baby more than to yourself,” Sherlock said as she automatically studied the street.

“I’m shy, you know that, but my Porsche isn’t.”

Sherlock said, “Okay, so Frankie made lots of it up to please us, but I think he did see Victor.”

Sherlock turned on the AC when Savich fired up the Porsche. “Why do people have this need to make themselves the star of the show?”

He laughed, wove the Porsche back onto the street and toward the highway. “Well, if Victor really was there eating fried lobsters—three of them—he might be sleeping it off in a motel nearby."

"Could be. Not worth a grid search, though."

Sherlock pulled out her cell and called the Victor hotline. "We followed up on your call about Victor Nesser from Peterborough. He's probably not here, but give the local motels a call, make sure they have his photo. Thanks, Dirk." She sat back, fanned herself. "Nearly no traffic. Too hot to be out today."

"Everyone's eating fried lobsters with Frankie and his mom, sweating their eyebrows off."

A bullet slammed in through the Porsche's driver's-side window, missing Savich by inches, and burst out Sherlock's window. She thought she felt the heat of the bullet, it passed so close.

Savich pressed the accelerator, and the Porsche leaped forward. Sherlock twisted around, yelled, "I see him, a dark green Kia. It's Victor. No cars between us. Get him, Dillon!"

Three more shots, all wide.

Savich turned the steering wheel, let the rear wheels slide, and drove straight toward Victor.

Sherlock leaned out the shattered window and fired nonstop at the windshield of the Kia. She saw Victor's face, contorted with rage, then she saw fear, then panic. "What, you putz, you didn't think we'd fight back?" She emptied her magazine, shoved in a new one.

"Hold on!"

She fell back into her seat when Savich took a hard left. She saw a woman's white face as they passed her old baby blue Buick with an inch to spare, heard her horn blasting. A white lab came out from between two oak trees and ran into the road in front of them, an older man behind it, yelling as he tried to pull on its leash. Savich swerved, but it was too late. The Porsche hit a fire hydrant and blew a front tire, bounced back into the street. Thankfully, the hydrant didn't explode. She saw the Kia behind them again, a flash of Victor's face, then it screeched around the corner and he disappeared.

"Sherlock, are you okay?"

She was breathing hard and fast, her adrenaline in orbit. "Yeah, I'm okay. You, Dillon?" She was already dialing 911. She identified herself, gave the description of Victor's Kia, their location. To Savich's surprise, she added, "I got the first three letters on his license plate. RPL, Virginia." She answered questions, then punched off her cell. "They're sending patrol cars our way. We could get lucky yet."

Savich lightly cupped her cheek in his hand. "We're both okay. Good going with the license plate. I'm surprised he hasn't ditched the Kia yet. And really surprised he came at us at all. Why? He couldn't think he'd kill us here, in the middle of Peterborough. Why didn't he keep on driving?"

"All good questions. At least Frankie did see him." Sherlock smacked her fist against the glove compartment. "I shot a whole clip into his car, Dillon, but I missed him. The look on his face, we scared the crap out of him. The gall of that lady driving on our street. A good thing you missed her. The lab's okay, too. Not so much the fire hydrant. We'll see if the city of Peterborough dings the FBI."

Savich laughed, couldn't help it. He reached over, studied her face, felt her arms. "I'm okay. Really. Look, we've got company."

They looked over at three teenage boys running toward them, one of them carrying a soccer ball.

"Hey, dude! You guys all right?"

Sherlock called out, "We're fine. Is everybody okay back there?"

The three teenagers looked at one another, then back at Sherlock. "Yeah, but we heard the pops, the crash. Hey, you got shot at, didn't you? Busted the windows, and I see bullet holes. Oh, dude, your Porsche—the front bumper's all crunched in."

Savich wasn't surprised, but still he felt that news like a punch to the gut. No hope for it. He and Sherlock climbed out of the Porsche, pulled out their creds, and introduced themselves.

The teen holding the soccer ball dropped it and crowded in. "Wow, were you scared? Who was after you?"

"Thanks for coming over, guys, but we've got calls to make." Sherlock looked up to see the older man holding his beautiful white lab beside him, staring at them. She trotted over and identified herself, apologized.

Savich studied his baby, ran his hand over the damage, and kicked the flat front tire. His insurance company was not going to like this, but not less than he did.

29

HAGGERSVILLE, MARYLAND
MONDAY EVENING

Gunny Saks chewed slowly on her mama's chicken parmigiana, savoring the taste of the hot cheese in her mouth. Mama had pulled it fresh out of the oven only five minutes before with the cheese still bubbling. Monday was always parmigiana night, and she'd looked forward to it all day while she sorted the mail for the post office mailboxes and hauled packages in from the loading dock to the staging area where Mr. Klem sorted them into the route hampers for the carriers.

She hummed before she swallowed each bite, a childhood habit. As she chewed, Gunny savored her mama's secret ingredient, a special mozzarella from Trenton, New Jersey, made and sold in small batches by an old Italian grocer Mama had met twenty years ago. Mama had sworn her to secrecy because, she explained, she had a reputation to uphold. Gunny didn't understand this, but she kept her word. She knew about secrets, knew how to keep them. One thing everybody knew was her mama was the best baker in town. Dozens of people lined up every morning except Thursday in front of her mama's bakery, Heaven Sent, for one of her bear claws or croissants or sinful cinnamon rolls, with dribbles of warm icing snaking over the sides. Gunny loved to lick off those dribbles of icing while her mother shook her head at her, said it wasn't fair that Gunny never gained an ounce.

Gunny spooned up some mashed potatoes—good, but not as good as the parmigiana. She swallowed, took a drink of sweet tea, cleared her throat, and said, "Something worries me, Mama."

Lulie Saks looked at her daughter over the top of her glasses. If asked, Lulie would say Gunny normally looked dreamy, placid, but looking more closely at her, Lulie did see worry in her daughter's beautiful light blue eyes. It concerned her because Gunny rarely focused on anything long enough to worry. Lulie did her best to make her daughter's life stress free, simple, and straightforward, to lay out everything for her so she wouldn't suddenly get confused, wouldn't get frustrated. So what if Gunny wasn't the sharpest knife in the drawer? She was a good daughter. And so beautiful, she could have been a model. Tall, slender, with rich, wavy mink-brown hair, white skin. If only—no, she wouldn't go there. It wasn't fair to Gunny, and it was a waste of time. Besides, Gunny was perfect the way she was. She worked hard at the post office and even helped out at the bakery on weekends.

Gunny didn't say anything more, only kept eating slowly, chewing thoroughly as Lulie had taught her.

It was time to help her daughter along again.

"What worries you, sweetie? I know you're not overworked at the post office these days, what with everyone writing emails and not letters, and fewer catalogues than last year going through the postal system. So that means things are slow, right?"

"Work is fine, Mama. But I did hear Mrs. Chamberlain tell Mr. Klem it was a good thing post office workers are all federal employees, so none of them could be fired. Mr. Klem says postal employees are like cowboys, they work until they ride off into the sunset. He laughed and said something like 'Yep, unless one of the carriers screws a pooch in front of the post office. With fifty witnesses.' " She'd mimicked Mr. Klem perfectly.

"Mr. Klem said that?"

Gunny nodded. "Mr. Klem says all sorts of things. He's teaching me his router system, you know, which packages go in this or that route hamper. He said it'd take a while, but I think I'm learning. And all the carriers are really nice. The parmigiana's really good."

Lulie stilled. "Thank you, Gunny. None of the men are bothering you, are they?" Since Gunny had turned fifteen, boys had swarmed around her. She was beautiful and kind and she was guileless. Lulie knew some of the boys and men meant well. But to others, once they realized Gunny was simple, eager to please, it made her an easy target. Gunny might have been an easy target once, but Lulie and Gunny's godfather, Chief of Police Danny Masters, had made a point of teaching her what to do if a boy or a man behaved in a certain way around her. There'd been incidents over the years, sure, but Gunny hadn't forgotten. Now, at thirty, she knew how to take care of herself.

But what about a husband? Kids? Lulie wanted to cry, had cried over the years alone in her bedroom so Gunny wouldn't hear her and be worried. But there was little chance of a family for Gunny, and it broke Lulie's heart.

Gunny said matter-of-factly, "No problems from men, Mama, not since Mr. Gibbs. I told him I was sorry his wife didn't understand him, but if he didn't leave me alone, I would kick him and then I'd call my godfather—Chief Masters." Gunny snapped her fingers and gave Lulie a big grin. "Poof, he backed away like I'd shot him. He's fine now. It always works when I say Uncle Danny is my godfather."

Lulie was shocked and appalled. Mr. Gibbs was the owner of Providence B&B. Married forever, four grown kids. That paunchy idiot had harassed her daughter? "Well, I'm going to speak to him, you can count on that."

"Please don't, Mama. Mr. Gibbs has stayed away from me for a real long time now. Please don't worry."

Her daughter didn't want her to worry? Was that why Gunny hadn't told her? She felt a spurt of pride. Gunny had dealt with him, but even so, Lulie burned. Take the lecher to a dark alley and beat the crap out of him, or tell his wife, a sweet woman with no spine? Both had appeal.

Gunny said, "That press conference today over in Willicott, did you see it?"

Lulie shook her head. "I heard talk about it from Mrs. Tucker this afternoon. All those bones at the bottom of Lake Massey and that federal lawyer they found in the lake. It's very hard to believe. You're not scared, are you?"

"No, it's not that. It's about the belt buckle with the Star of David they found." Gunny carefully cut another bite, eased it into her mouth, hummed while she chewed. Then, "Well, that's what worries me, Mama, the Star of David belt buckle. They found it with all the bones, and I don't see how that could be right."

"Why couldn't it be right, Gunny?"

More silence from Gunny. *Move it along, come on, sweetie.* Lulie drank some tea with its hint of mint and lemon, exactly as her mama had taught her to make it. She thought about the work she still had to do this evening as Gunny gathered her thoughts and ate her dinner. Patience, you had to have a bucketload of patience with Gunny or she'd get frustrated. Finally, Lulie said, "I could understand why all those bones would bother you, Gunny, but why do you care so much about a Star of David on a belt buckle? It sounds very strange."

A light briefly shined in Gunny's blue eyes, her father's eyes, then dimmed.

30

Patience, patience.

"What about the belt buckle, Gunny?" Lulie asked again and watched her daughter delicately pat her mouth with her napkin, like Lulie had taught her, and scrunch her forehead, thinking hard.

Come on, Gunny, out with it.

"The Star of David belt buckle, Mama, the one they found with all those bones. I don't see how it got there."

"What? Oh, I see. Do you know whose belt buckle it was, Gunny?" Of course, if Gunny had seen it, dozens of other people had seen it as well. So what was the problem?

Gunny said, "It belonged to Mr. Henry."

"Henry LaRoque? Goodness, what a memory you have.

He's been gone for what—five years? What a fine man he was, so friendly, so helpful. Do you know his bank gave me my first loan to remodel Heaven Sent? Gunny, wait, don't you think the buckle only looked like Mr. Henry's? I mean, how could it be his?"

Gunny shook her head, raised a hand, and lightly pulled on the long French braid her mother plaited for her every morning, a sure sign she was stewing about something.

"Gunny, if it was indeed Mr. Henry's belt buckle, then dozens of other people must have seen him wear it, not just you."

"That's not true. I might be the only one who ever saw it."

"But how could that be possible?"

"Mama, you know you always told me how important it is to keep a secret? Well, this is a secret. But maybe, since Mrs. Chamberlain and Mr. Henry were special friends, I could ask her about it. Maybe he showed her, too, maybe she can tell me what to do."

Lulie nearly fell off her chair. *Special friends?* Half the town knew Henrietta Chamberlain, Gunny's supervisor and the real power at the post office, had been Mr. Henry's lover for years, until he'd died, and had chuckled at the pairing of the same names—Henry and Henrietta. She was floored Gunny knew about it, too. She could picture Gunny asking Mrs. Chamberlain about the belt buckle, picture Mrs. Chamberlain's embarrassment focusing back on her daughter. But mostly she could picture Mrs. Chamberlain's pain at being reminded of how horribly Mr. Henry had died. How could it even be true? She said in her firmest voice, "Now, don't you go bothering your supervisor, Gunny, unless she brings it up, all right?"

Gunny frowned. She didn't say anything more. Lulie watched

her lovingly place the last bite of parmigiana in her mouth, heard her hum, and wondered, as she often did, what her daughter was thinking.

While she waited for her to figure out the words she needed, Lulie looked around her remodeled kitchen with its shiny appliances and the large granite island, made to her exact specifications, perfect for her daily baking. For the past three years, she hadn't had to go into Heaven Sent at dawn every morning to work. No, she simply rolled out of bed, made herself a pot of coffee, and whipped up cinnamon buns and raisin muffins and the half dozen other pastries she served each day, right here in her own kitchen. It had cost her—well, it had cost Andrew—a buttload of money, but he'd been willing to pay it. After all, it was to his advantage she keep quiet about Gunny's paternity, and of course she would. She didn't hold it against him—in fact, she liked him, admired what he'd accomplished—but she knew he'd never be part of his daughter's life. He couldn't be, not without the very good chance his own life would be ruined. It was also true Andrew didn't want her or Gunny to have any financial worries. He'd insisted on paying for her to remodel the 1960s two-story house set in the middle of a large lot covered with maple and oak trees on East Hilton Street Lulie had inherited from her parents seven years ago. But she was the one who paid Ray Lee, the big-eared teen down the street, to keep the lush grass mowed weekly. She'd filled the hanging flower baskets with petunias and impatiens bursting out now in the middle of the long hot summer.

Lulie sighed and thought again about her nightly bookkeeping ritual, an endless stream of crap to do for a dozen different government agencies, and all the while the government buffoons preached how they loved small businesses. She wondered who looked at all the papers she churned out. She saw a faceless bureaucrat, probably yawning, balling up her work, banking it off the wall into a government wastebasket. No one cared, but it didn't matter. One of them might, and who knew when or if that would ever happen. So she had to do it or risk paying huge fines, maybe lose her bakery, maybe even go to jail.

"All right, Mama."

What was all right? She'd forgotten. Oh yes, Mr. Henry's belt buckle. And a secret. What secret? Like many other citizens of Haggersville, Lulie felt indebted to Mr. Henry LaRoque, who'd founded the First National Bank of Haggersville. "Yes, that's best, Gunny."

Lulie left Gunny to wash the dishes, her nightly chore, while she went to her small study to toil on her computer, the part of owning a small business she hated. Every few minutes she cursed the government, couldn't help it. She tried not to curse out loud because she knew Gunny had sharp ears and she didn't want her to hear talk like that.

Gunny heard her, of course, and she smiled. Words she wasn't allowed to say. She wondered if she'd ever be old enough to say what she wanted. She turned to survey the spotless kitchen, ready for her mama's baking at dawn tomorrow. Perfect, everything was perfect. She turned off the light, went to her mama's study, and kissed her good night. As she walked up the stairs to her room, she thought about the TV show that was waiting for her—*Elementary*. Her mother said the show had been on for too long and the plots were getting silly, but Gunny didn't care. She couldn't get enough of Jonny Lee Miller, even though he was bald now. When you loved someone, she'd heard Mrs. Chamberlain say, you overlooked small flaws.

Before Gunny fell asleep, she thought again about Mr. Henry's Star of David belt buckle. She knew the one she'd seen on TV was his, not one that looked like his. She remembered when, years ago, she'd visited him with a cake for his seventy-fifth birthday. The housekeeper, Mrs. Boilou, had shown her into Mr. Henry's study. He was polishing something. He looked up and smiled at her, considered, then beckoned her to him. That's when he'd seen the cake, and they'd all had a slice. After Mrs. Boilou had left, Mr. Henry had shown her what he'd been looking at, his golden Star of David belt buckle, and asked her if she didn't think it was very fine indeed. Of course she'd said yes. He'd told her there was no other belt buckle like it in the world. And then he'd told her she wasn't to tell anyone else about seeing it. It would be their secret. Could she keep this secret? Of course she could, she knew all about keeping secrets.

Mr. Henry had always been kind to her, often given her a small packet of gummy bears when he saw her in the post office or at her mama's bakery. Once he even came out of his office at his bank to say hello and give her gummy bears.

Mr. Henry was dead five years now, and still she'd kept his secret, until tonight, when she'd told her mama. But she'd seen his belt buckle on television, and how could that be? What should she do? Go to her godfather? He'd listen to her, but what could he do? No, she'd speak to Mrs. Chamberlain, Mr. Henry's very special friend, even though her mama said she shouldn't. Maybe Mr. Henry had shown her his belt buckle, too, and she'd kept it a secret, as Gunny had. Maybe Mrs. Chamberlain would know what to do.

31

PRINCE WILLIAM FOREST PARK
VIRGINIA
MONDAY EVENING

Victor was still shaking from what Lissy had done. He couldn't believe she'd awakened him from a sound sleep in the shade of those thick oak trees down the block from that fried lobster place and claimed Savich and Sherlock were inside. He didn't believe it, not until he saw Savich's red Porsche. They were there, only fifty feet away from him. Someone had recognized him, someone had called Savich.

They'd waited until the agents left, and Lissy had followed, staying back until they were on a street with no cars coming in either direction. Lissy was screaming in his ear to shoot them, but he'd said no, no way. She'd pulled out his Glock—well, actually, the agent's Glock—and let loose. And nearly gotten both of them killed.

So I didn't get them. It was still fun, shot holes in that red Porsche of his, and he smashed in his front fender—bet he cried and wailed and carried on like a little girl. And he got himself a flat tire, too. That'll slow them up some. Bet it'll cost him a bundle to fix his baby.

Victor waited for the hammer to drop. It had been Lissy's fault, the whole debacle, but he knew she'd turn it around on him.

If I hadn't had to drive, I could have shot him and that redheaded bitch. Okay, I'll admit it, I was surprised when he did that turn and came straight at us, Ms. FBI Agent shooting at us like that.

"She nearly got me. I got glass in my face, Lissy. Now they know for sure what car we drive. We've got bullet holes for the world to see. Someone will call us in." He added more twigs and wadded-up papers to the embers in the fire pit.

Savich was fast, Victor, made that turn faster than Mama threw a hammer at the mailman for ogling her. If they'd been in our lame-butt car and we'd had the Porsche, I'd have got both of 'em. They'd be dead meat.

Victor groaned. "Fact is we were lucky, Lissy. If that old man hadn't chased his mutt across the road in front of him, Savich wouldn't have swerved and hit that fire hydrant. They'd have got us, Lissy, you know it. Why not admit it? We barely got out of there." Victor laid his palm over his heart. "I still feel like I want to throw up. That was way too close. I hope we're safe now, but if anyone saw us drive in here, they could tell everyone."

Screw any loser who saw us. Doesn't matter. We're safe. I got us out of there fast, and you know something? It really was fun, got my blood pumping, made me forget those staples in my stomach.

Victor frowned into the small fire pit. The fire wasn't hot enough yet to heat up the beef enchiladas he'd bought ready-made at a market in Lewiston that morning. On the other hand, he wasn't really hungry, not after Sherlock had nearly shot his head off, so close he almost puked up the fried lobsters. His heart began pounding a mad tattoo again, and he rubbed his hand over his chest, hoping to slow it.

Got some heartburn, do you? That's what you get, gorging yourself on all those lobsters. They weren't bad, never had fried lobster before. And they didn't make me queasy, not like you.

"Shut up, Lissy."

Hey, you're still shaking. You are such a wuss, Victor.

He wanted to slap her—not hard, because he knew those staples still hurt, only a little slap, to get her attention, make her realize she owed everything to him. Instead, Victor poked the burning twigs with a stick, stirred the embers, and tucked in some more balled-up newspaper. Sparks flew, the paper caught fire, and then the twigs, and warmth spewed out. He set the enchiladas on a bit of tinfoil on the grate. He leaned back on his elbows and sighed. "I really wish you hadn't taken a chance like that, Lissy. We could be dead or back in Central. I hated all those crazies and those guards, always giving you the stink-eye."

Wuss, wuss.

He ignored her, breathed in the smell of the enchiladas. "You said I didn't think enough, went too fast at that book festival with the chocolate bar, but you did the same thing today. No thought at all. You roared ahead, didn't pay any attention to anything I said. Didn't think they'd turn on us, did you? You thought they'd try to run, but they didn't."

You gotta take your chances when they're offered up, like Mama said, not cower and hide. But only when there's a chance of it paying off, Victor, not like that stunt of yours at the book festival. You take chances when it's smart, and this was smart.

"Would you shut up! I don't care what your mama said. She's dead, Lissy, long gone. There's only you and me now, and yes, we've got to be smart. You don't pick up a gun and start shooting. You know we've got to plan, and I'm good at it. No more hotdogging, okay, by either of us."

Like I said, if we'd had the Porsche and not this pitiful Kia, they'd be dead. And now the Kia has bullet holes all over it.

"I'll buy another car tomorrow morning. It's too dangerous now to drive the Kia around."

You paid five thousand dollars for that old Kia, said you didn't want to steal a car and always have to be looking over your shoulder. Now you're going to buy another one? Where'd you get the money to buy it? It's not from Mama's stash back home, so where'd you get the money?

Victor gently lifted the tinfoil holding the two enchiladas with a fork, careful not to spill the juice, and laid it on a flat rock in front of him. "One for me, one for you, Lissy. Shut up about the money, okay? Why should I tell you where I got it? You never told me where your mama hid the money we took from those banks. Half a million bucks has to be buried at her house somewhere, and you wouldn't tell me. Why not tell me now?"

She was silent, and then he heard laughter in her voice. *You know, I'm thinking those fried lobsters weren't very healthy, Victor. It's a good thing we're young, or we'd keel over of heart attacks. I want to pick where we eat next time.*

"Yeah, sure. But you'll order a bucket of french fries, so crispy they walk right into your mouth. That's healthy?"

She laughed. *Maybe. Victor, we heard on the radio today how Octavia Ryan's going to be buried in that fancy Catholic cathedral in Falls Church tomorrow morning. It's going to be a big to-do, lots of big muckety-mucks boohooing for her. My mama always told me you plan really good, then you go for surprise and shock and WHAM—the bugs freeze, can't think straight, doesn't matter if they're big-assed important bugs, they're terrified, scared out of their buggy wits.*

"Lissy, you know I already have a plan, just looking for the right time and place to make a big splash. You know I'm smart. I know how to do stuff, know where to buy stuff to make it happen. First I was thinking the Savich house, I decided taking the little boy was better, it would really make them pay for what they took from me." He ate a bite of enchilada. It was cold in the middle, but he didn't care. "This cathedral? Now, I think it's perfect. Don't doubt me, Lissy, this time it's going to be huge."

She didn't demand to know what he was planning. She said only *Let's kill us some bugs, then.*

32

FALLS CHURCH, VIRGINIA
TUESDAY MORNING

There was standing room only for Octavia Ryan's funeral mass at Our Lord of the Fields. Family and friends were pressed together in the pews or standing against the nave walls. Sala saw Savich, Sherlock, and Mr. Maitland walk in together and take their seats well behind the family. He saw a lot of FBI agents he knew, some he didn't. And many of the lawyers Octavia had worked with, some he'd worked with, some he'd seen in passing. Octavia's mother and father walked like cardboard cutouts, deep in shock, two of their grown children flanking them, both grim and pale-faced. Because of an insane young man bent on revenge, a family was shattered.

Sala wondered what his own family would have done if he'd

simply disappeared from that rental cottage in Willicott, leaving no clues, no leads. His dad would have eventually moved on. He had his feet firmly on the ground, but Mom—his mom would never have stopped looking. She'd have searched until she died, he knew it to his gut. Sala supposed there'd always be terrorists eager to kill those who didn't agree with them and there would always be Victor Nessers, just as twisted. Octavia had saved Victor from life imprisonment or the lethal injection, and he'd killed her coldly, without remorse, because she'd called him weak, manipulated by his sixteen-year-old Lolita girlfriend. Sala simply couldn't get his brain around the madness. He wanted very much to put his hands around Nesser's neck and wring the life out of him. He felt Ty take his hand, squeeze lightly.

He drew in a deep breath, looked straight ahead at the people in front of him, most wearing black, most sincerely distressed by Octavia's death. No, get it right—her murder. Her coffin was covered with a blanket of pink hydrangeas, her favorite flower, her sister had said. A large color photo of her taken four months ago was propped against an easel. She was smiling wildly, standing on the courthouse steps, pumping her fist in the air. She looked beautiful, insanely happy, ready to burst out of her skin. Sala remembered that day, the day she succeeded in her prosecution of an embezzler and a murderer, one of Sala's cases. He'd met her in the course of that case, worked with her, and when it was over, when she'd won, he'd taken her to celebrate with clam spaghetti at Florintine's in Foggy Bottom.

At that moment a bright shaft of sunlight speared through a beautiful stained-glass window, striking the easel and Octavia's face. Sala stared at the picture of the woman he'd known very well. They'd been good for each other in their short time together. He'd still been grieving for his late wife, Joy, and Octavia grieving an aunt lost to breast cancer and, of course, the death of her marriage.

I'm sorry I failed you, Octavia. Sala accepted that he'd been the only one who could have saved her, but he hadn't. And now she was gone. He felt the pain of it burrow deep. Yet again, Ty squeezed his hand.

He wondered if Octavia would have gone back to her ex-husband after all. He stilled. Wasn't that her ex-husband standing at the edge of the nave? Octavia had shown Sala a photo of him on her phone. It had shown a tall, fair-haired man in his early forties, gym buff and smiling, his arm around her, hugging her tight. Now his shoulders were hunched forward, his face pale and set, as if carved in stone. He never looked away from Octavia's coffin. Bill Culver was his name, Sala remembered. Culver looked utterly alone. Sala pointed as he whispered to Ty, "That man over there is Octavia's ex-husband. Try to save an extra seat."

Ty watched Sala weave his way toward Bill Culver near the back of the church and lightly touch his shoulder. The two men spoke. A few minutes later, Sala brought Culver back with him. He leaned down, introduced her. "And this is Chief Ty Christie." He didn't add Ty had seen Culver's ex-wife murdered on Lake Massey.

Ty took Culver's hand. His skin felt cold and dry. He looked frozen, his grief deep and raw. "Mr. Culver, please sit with us." The three pressed together in a space meant for two, but their neighbors didn't mind, probably didn't even notice.

They sat quietly, listening to the organist play a slow requiem Sala didn't recognize. Culver said, his voice nearly breaking, "That was one of Octavia's favorite organ pieces. I wonder if they know that." Sala looked down at his clasped hands and waited until the organist began another piece before he leaned toward Culver. "I know this is a very hard time for you, Mr. Culver—"

"Bill, please, Agent Porto."

Sala nodded. "Call me Sala. You know about Victor Nesser?"

Culver stiffened, his eyes narrowed, and his mouth became a tight seam. "I saw his face all over TV and on the web. I couldn't believe it. I mean, how could he kill her after what she did for him? Is he insane?"

"That's the working hypothesis. Did Octavia ever talk to you about him?"

Culver looked down at his polished Italian loafers and nodded. "It was toward the end of our marriage, but both of us were still trying to resolve things in counseling. We were still civil.

"I remember Octavia felt sorry for him, said he was the saddest young man she'd ever seen, that he didn't seem to care what happened to him. She said he'd focus on inconsequential things, like the guy in the cell next to him snoring, but mainly he complained about his ankle, said the FBI had shucked him off to a know-nothing intern who didn't know an ankle from an elbow and he'd limp forever. But Octavia told me he barely limped. She hadn't even noticed it until he'd complained about it."

Sala felt his stomach drop. "Do you know the intern's name?"

Culver shook his head. "I think I remember Octavia saying Nesser was treated at Washington Memorial. They took him there right after he was brought back from wherever it was the FBI caught him and that crazy girl he was with. Why?"

Because Nesser might go after him, that's why. "Do you remember if Nesser told her he was angry at the defense she'd used at his competency hearing?"

Culver nodded. "She told me Nesser said to her face she was a lying bitch and how dare she announce to the world he was nothing but a pitiful pawn? She was worse than that worthless lawyer from L.A. he'd fired. I remember Octavia couldn't believe it. She'd saved him from a trial with a jury that would have, justifiably, found him guilty of murder and bank robbery, even though he only drove the car. And he did shoot a police officer, but thankfully she didn't die. He should have gotten life imprisonment or a lethal injection. That's the law. Sorry, you know that. But she got him committed instead." Culver shook his head. "She told me he was smart, so I suppose she was right. He escaped that mental hospital, didn't he? Supposedly high-security? And he killed her because she simply pointed out he was a naïve putz who fell for a teenage Lolita." He struck his fist against his open palm. "He needs to be put down."

"I agree."

Culver looked blindly ahead at the crowd of people, their heads bowed or staring straight ahead, some speaking quietly, and then at the spear of light still shining on Octavia's face. "How many dead bodies did he and his crazy girlfriend leave behind?"

Sala knew, but he only shook his head.

"Octavia truly believed he'd been abused, both emotionally and physically, manipulated by his sixteen-year-old cousin. Lissy Smiley was her name—sorry, you know that, too. Octavia said Victor denied the physical abuse, said his father only hit his mother. When it was over, I remember she cried because she felt so bad he was upset with her. But she hoped he'd come to understand it was the only defense to get him out of jail in this lifetime. I remember I asked her if he would ever recognize it as the truth, if he would ever see what happened with clear sight. She had to admit he probably wouldn't, he was too damaged. She did consider the sentence a victory. I remember clearly she believed true justice had prevailed. And now she's dead." His breathing stuttered. "Because she didn't realize how truly crazy he really was."

Sala understood the man's fury, his pain. He understood how helpless he felt. He didn't hesitate, leaned close. "Octavia told me she was giving serious consideration to coming back to you."

Culver's eyes blazed, then the light died out again, and he shook his head back and forth. "No, she never said anything like that to me. I thought it was over. Did she really tell you that?"

"Yes, she did."

Culver laughed, low and bitter. "When was this, Agent? Surely not when you were sleeping with her? Aren't you any good in bed?"

The fury of Culver's words jolted Sala, but then he calmed. He, too, would be out of his mind with anger at the man who'd been sleeping with the woman he wanted to come back to him, the man who had also failed to save her at crunch time. "No," Sala said, "I guess not."

Culver shook his head. "Sorry, none of this is your fault. The thing is, Octavia never knew what she wanted, but it was always something else, always something she didn't have. I tried to understand, I really did, because I worshiped her. She had a great career, and when her grandmother died, she inherited millions from her offshore accounts." He paused. "But it wasn't enough. I wasn't enough." Culver looked down at his clasped hands and drew a deep breath. "I can't believe she's dead, that I'll never see her again, never make her favorite strawberry margarita for her." He raised dazed eyes to Sala's face. "Did she really say she was coming back to me?"

She hadn't exactly, but Sala nodded.

When the organ music stopped, Father Francis McKay moved to stand at the podium. He paused a moment, looked out at the hundreds of mourners, and then began Octavia's funeral mass. To a Protestant, the mass was like a choreographed dance, everyone knowing what to do when. It was long and slow and infinitely soothing. In the homily, Father McKay spoke of Octavia's passion for justice, her love of her family and of all the people whose lives she'd touched in her too-short life.

Family and friends spoke next, filling the air with pain and raw emotion. Like Father McKay, they spoke of her kindness, her deep and abiding love for her family, and what she felt was her mission to help find justice for those unable to find it for themselves.

As he listened, Savich held Sherlock's hand. He felt such rage at Victor Nesser, he knew if he'd been there, he'd have killed him. Justice long overdue. He knew he'd have to get in line.

After communion, the mass ended, and everyone prepared to follow the hearse to bury Octavia at Forest Lawn, where the first of her family, a great-grandfather, Damian Ryan, had been buried in 1907.

"The Lord be with you."

"And with your spirit."

"May almighty God bless you, the Father, and the Son, and the Holy Spirit. Amen. The mass is ended, go in peace."

Savich saw Sherlock wipe her eyes and hugged her against him. Mr. Maitland stood to embrace family and friends, a rock in a massive tide of pain. Savich wondered how Victor knew where Octavia would be on her last weekend. Everyone believed he'd been following her, but she hadn't noticed. And why should she?

Sherlock had frowned. "But Octavia would have noticed, Dillon, if he'd followed her there," she'd said. "She dealt with very bad people."

Of course, a lot of people knew about Victor Nesser, but none had spoken to him or seen him. None admitted to telling anyone outside of work of Octavia's plans to spend the week in Willicott with Agent Sala Porto.

Octavia's funeral procession assembled. Six men, all colleagues of hers, took their places beside Octavia's coffin, waiting for the priest and the celebrants to lead them down the aisle and outside to the hearse. Father McKay, his two deacons, and a single altar girl stepped out in front of the coffin as the organ began to play "*In Paradisum.*" There was no conversation, only people standing, waiting to leave their pews to fall in behind the coffin as it passed. As the procession started down the aisle, there was a deafening explosion. Stained-glass windows shattered inward, showering people with glass. The music soared. The building heaved, the pulpit shook, and Octavia Ryan's photograph toppled off the easel.

There was pandemonium.

33

Mr. Maitland was already yelling into his cell phone. Savich jumped onto the pew, cupped his mouth, and shouted, "Everyone, stop! Stay calm. Father, pallbearers, move Octavia's coffin as quickly as you can out of the church. Those FBI agents near the exits, lead people out safely. All other FBI agents, take a pew and form a line. People, if anyone in your line is hurt, help them. Everyone, do not panic."

Sherlock grabbed his arm, "I smell smoke, Dillon. The church is on fire!"

He shouted again, "Cover your mouths, do not inhale the smoke. Quickly now! Move! We will all get out of here—"

There were already sirens in the distance.

Savich heard the flames now, smelled the gas from the pipes in the basement. The church would come down fast. He felt the building heave beneath his feet, watched the pulpit crash forward onto the floor and roll down the six deep steps into the nave. The thick old timbers overhead creaked.

He shouted, "Keep walking. Do not run, take care of those around you. We will all get out of here."

Mr. Maitland pressed forward to reach Octavia's mother, who was standing stunned, shocked immobile, staring up at the beams, leaning into her daughter. "Mama, let's go, please."

Mr. Maitland took Mrs. Ryan's hand and gently led her from the pew. He weaved his way toward the nave exit, leading the dozen family members to safety, and ran back into the church. He saw Savich lifting a sobbing old woman into his arms. People moved aside for him as he carried her out of the church, gave her to an agent, and ran back in.

The cathedral was thick now with smoke, billowing up from the basement, the heat of the flames burning the air. Savich pulled a handkerchief away from his face and shouted, "Keep your faces covered! Everyone, you're doing great! Keep moving and help anyone who needs it." Another stained-glass window burst overhead. People coughed and moved. Children were screaming, parents were trying desperately to protect them from the fire that was raging closer and closer.

A wild-eyed man with a camera around his neck was screaming, "We're going to burn to death! I can feel the fire coming right under my feet! We're going to die!" He shoved people aside to get to the exit. Savich grabbed his arm, jerked him around, and cold-cocked him. Savich handed him off to two men in line, who dragged him between them.

The air was choked with thick, acrid smoke, the heat from the closing fire fearsome. Not much more time, Savich knew, before the building collapsed, before the flames engulfed all of them, but the lines of mourners kept moving out the exits. Savich saw Sherlock leading a line of people through the opposite side door. She was safe, too.

Fire trucks, police cars, and ambulances jammed the street a block away from the church. It was too hot to get closer. Police and firefighters ran forward to help agents with the last of the stragglers and help the injured away. The fire was blazing hot and fast, a scene from hell, flames licking into the sky, the smoke black and thick, gushing out of the inferno.

Sala saw Bill Culver walk quickly to the hearse. A huge spear of stained glass had stabbed through the hood, and it wouldn't start. The hearse, once black, was now covered with gray ash. Sala saw Octavia's brother wave Culver off, saw his expression was hard with dislike and distrust, but Bill ignored him. The pallbearers pushed the hearse forward, away from the building.

The fire burned so hot, people kept moving away, staring at the once-beautiful cathedral so quickly reduced to rubble, trying to make sense of what had happened. Ty heard a small boy ask, "Papa, what happened to God's house?"

There were screams and shouts when the roof, blazing brighter than the sun, collapsed, and rancid smoke gushed into the air.

Ty saw a young woman, tears streaming down her face as she rocked a baby. Why was she alone? Where was the rest of the family? Ty hugged the young woman and her child close and eased her into a crowd, whispered to an older couple, "Please, comfort her as best you can and keep the reporters away from her." People were coughing, some hacking up the smoke that had filled their lungs, and she prayed they would be all right. EMTs were circulating, tending to those with burns or smoke inhalation. Ambulances screamed in and out of the scene.

Ty saw a reporter closing fast on Octavia's family, a mic in his fist, his eyes shining with excitement. Nothing like pain and tragedy to bring out a soulless vulture. She started forward to steer the reporter away, but she saw Mr. Maitland move to stand between him and the family, a rock. The reporter was yelling about freedom of the press, but Mr. Maitland didn't move. She thought he snorted.

Ty heard someone shout terrorists had blown up the cathedral. That's when it hit her hard. There was no doubt in her mind Victor Nesser had set the bombs. Was he here, watching and gloating, pumping his frigging fist? She lightly laid her hand on the arm of an older man whose breathing was too fast. "Take shallow breaths, slowly. That's it. Everyone got out. It's over." She prayed that was so. Thankfully, the man's breathing slowed. Still, he held on to her hand like a lifeline. "Where is your family?"

"My son, he's with Octavia's coffin. I'll be all right." Still, Ty found another couple, brought them over to stay with him.

Sala's cell phone rang. He was about to let it go to voice mail but then saw the call was from Dirk, the agent now manning the Star of David belt buckle hotline.

"Dirk, Sala here. What's up?"

"I heard about the explosion, the fire. Are you guys all right?"

"Yes, we think everyone got out, no life-threatening injuries, I don't think, but the cathedral is badly damaged, burning. The area is cordoned off. Firefighters and cops are everywhere, but things seem under control. What's happened on your end?"

"A woman called me, name was Gunny—didn't give her last name—to see what she should do about Mr. Henry's belt buckle, and the *secret*. Then I heard something in the background, movement, and then someone's harsh breathing. I heard Gunny gasp, and the phone went dead. I think something violent could have happened to her. I called her number, but no answer. I'm thinking her phone got smashed."

Sala felt a surge of adrenaline. "Where did she call from?"

"She was near the corner of Fourth and Maple in Haggersville. This was three minutes ago. I called the police in Haggersville, spoke to Chief Masters. I could tell he was really upset when I said her name, and he was out the door fast. I think you and Chief Christie should get there as soon as possible."

"We're on our way. If you hear anything from the chief, give him my cell." Sala caught up with Savich, who was speaking to a teenager dressed in cut-off denim shorts, a baggy T-shirt, and sneakers, and she was over-the-moon excited. Savich saw him, raised a hand. Sala stopped and listened.

"I was skateboarding with some kids down Pulman Avenue, a block from here. I think I saw the guy who bombed Father McKay's church. That fire was so cool—" Her face froze. "I'm sorry, I didn't mean it like that."

"I know," Savich said. "It's all right. What's your name?"

"Ellie, Ellie Corrigan."

"Okay, Ellie, tell me what you saw."

"I saw a guy standing beside an old banged-up green car—I think it was a Kia, like my brother's. He was watching the church burning and listening to people screaming, watching them run. He was hollering and waving his fist, like he was happy, and then I heard a girl laughing, and she yelled out, 'Wham! Kill the bugs!' " Ellie shuddered. "She sounded crazy wild. Do you want me to come with you and give a statement? Like on TV, you know?"

Savich felt a cold chill. Those were nearly the exact words Lissy's mother had said during the bank robbery in Georgetown. *Kill the bugs.* Lissy probably learned it at her mother's knee. No, there had to be an explanation, had to be.

"Yes, I know. Ellie, you said it was really banged up. How?"

"It had all these scratches and what looked like holes—" Her eyes popped. "Bullet holes? Were all those holes from bullets?"

He nodded. "Did you see the Kia's license plate?"

Her face fell. Savich quickly pulled out a small notebook from his coat pocket and handed it to her. "It's okay. Ellie, write down your cell number and your address. I might be calling you later. And yes, tell your parents how much you helped the FBI."

She grinned really big, showing perfect white teeth. Savich watched her hop back on her skateboard and steer toward the teens who'd been watching them.

Sala said, "Nesser?"

Savich nodded. "Did you hear? She said she heard a girl's laugh, heard her yell, 'Wham! Kill the bugs!' "

"I heard."

"Victor's still driving the green Kia. We still don't have a license plate, but how hard can it be to find?"

They both watched Ellie Corrigan get swallowed up in the small knot of kids, doubtless telling them she'd seen it all.

Sala said, "Here's Ty. Hey, are you okay?"

She pushed her hair out of her face. "Yeah, I'm fine." She looked back at the crowds of people. "I saw a lot of bravery back there. Sala, you look ready to jump out of your skin. What's going on?"

34

ON THE ROAD TO HAGGERSVILLE, MARYLAND
TUESDAY

Ty punched on her flashers and pushed her Silverado to its limit when they reached the interstate. Who cared about a little shimmy at one hundred miles per hour? Traffic wasn't heavy at this time of day on a Tuesday, but still, cars melted out of her way. She said, "I can still hear the screams, smell the smoke. Sala, Dillon said as far as he knew, there were no serious injuries, a lot of smoke inhalation, some minor burns." She said, "We were very lucky."

"What was amazing is there wasn't all that much panic. I imagine every federal agency wants in, at least until Mr. Maitland informs everyone it was Victor Nesser, our own homegrown terrorist. The crazy shite. The girl who saw him said he was driving a banged-up green Kia, the same one from his shootout with Savich and Sherlock yesterday. You can bet everyone's looking for him."

Ty's attention was on the road, but she gave him a quick look. "You didn't have to come with me, Sala. I know you'd prefer to go after Victor."

"You're doing near one hundred ten," he said. "Keep your eyes on the road. I'm where I belong. Now, the Google map shows Haggersville is in a valley about thirty miles from Willicott, as the crow flies. I see small lakes, windy roads, heavily forested lands enclosing the town."

"Sala, I've lived here for three years. Haggersville is in my backyard. I know all the shortcuts, you just hang on. And thank you. I appreciate you being with me."

"Okay. Now, did you know Haggersville has four thousand year-round residents, population explodes to over fifteen thousand in the summer, like Willicott?"

"Sounds about right. That shortcut exit is coming up. It shaves off maybe ten miles."

Sala's cell rang. HPD showed up on his screen. A man's deep voice asked, "Is this FBI agent Sala Porto?"

"Yes."

"This is Daniel Masters, chief of police, Haggersville. I found Gunny unconscious behind a dumpster in the alley at Maple and Fourth, exactly where the hotline agent told me he'd last spoken to her. She was unconscious. An ambulance rushed her to our community hospital." Emotion rode thick in his voice. "Someone struck her on the head. If the agent hadn't called me immediately, she might have died." He swallowed. "She's still alive, that's all I know. In case you're wondering, Gunny's my goddaughter."

"Chief Masters, what's her full name?"

"Leigh Ann Saks, but she's been Gunny most of her life. The agent who called me said you were on your way. He also said Gunny had called your hotline about that Star of David belt buckle. Like everyone else, I saw the press conference. But I've never seen that belt buckle before, so I don't understand how Gunny could have known anything about it. I called Ms. Saks—Lulie, her mother—immediately. We'll meet you at the hospital. Oh yes, I found Gunny's cell phone smashed beside her." He paused, then, "I can't help thinking whoever overheard her talking to the hotline agent about that belt buckle had to be scared enough about it to try to kill her. But why? What could Gunny possibly know about anything dangerous to do with that frigging belt buckle? I don't know."

"We need to find that out, Chief. We'll meet you and Ms. Saks at the hospital, but first we'd like to go by the crime scene." He listened a moment, then punched off.

"She's alive and at the hospital. Chief Masters has no idea how Gunny could know anything that would cause someone to try to kill her."

She slowed the Silverado. "Exit coming up."

Ty pulled into Haggersville nineteen minutes later and drove slowly through downtown on Clover Street. Tourists strolled along the sidewalks, licking ice cream cones, going in and out of shops, arms loaded with shopping bags.

Sala consulted his GPS and told her to turn off Clover onto Maple and head east toward Fourth. It was a part of town for the locals, not flocks of tourists deciding where to have a late lunch. They passed a small strip mall with a pharmacy, clothing boutique, and post office. At Fourth and Maple there was a home supply store and a cleaners. Between the two was a deep pass-through alley connecting to the next street.

At the alley entrance, they saw Chief Masters had put up a cross strip of yellow crime scene tape. He'd marked the asphalt with white chalk where he'd found Gunny behind the single dumpster. Ty blocked the alley entrance with her Silverado, and she and Sala walked the area. Since it was open, the alley didn't smell of garbage and was kept fairly clean. Ty said, "He probably walked up behind her from the next street, heard her speaking to Dirk on the hotline, and hit her on the head without anybody seeing him, left her for dead."

"And smashed her cell phone."

They walked out the back of the alley, looked around. Nothing much to see, maybe a half dozen cars parked up and down Fifth Street. There was a 24/7 convenience store directly opposite the alley.

"Bingo," Sala said. While he trotted across Fifth to speak to the store owner, hoping they had a security camera showing the alley, Ty called the Haggersville Community Hospital and identified herself. Gunny was in surgery, as yet no word on her condition. The nurse paused, then added, "Chief Masters and Ms. Saks are in the surgical waiting room. This is an awful thing, Chief Christie, an awful thing. Gunny isn't all there mentally, if you know what I mean, but she's such a sweet girl and so pretty. She's young and strong, that's what I told Lulie."

Ty thanked the nurse, punched off her cell, closed her eyes, and prayed. *Please, Gunny, hang tough.*

Sala jogged back, shaking his head. "Sorry, the camera hasn't worked for six months, and they haven't bothered to get a new one. No one there saw anything."

35

HAGGERSVILLE, MARYLAND
TUESDAY

Luke Putney, twenty-three-year veteran postal carrier for the Haggersville Post Office, liked his nickname: Mr. Gossip. He saw himself as the center of the information wheel. He saw it as his duty to ensure the good people on his postal route were kept fully informed. He prided himself on never being discreet. His last big bomb should have been a doozy. He'd outed Gill Pratt, owner of Penny Barrel Bar, a loud dog, and a silver BMW. He'd discovered, quite by accident, or nearly, that Pratt had a penchant for hard-core porn magazines. It hadn't been Luke's fault the plain brown envelope was ripped, or nearly. Luke had to hand it to Pratt, he'd spun things to his advantage, what with giving out a free beer and a porn magazine to each man who came into his bar until the furor died down.

Luke didn't really see the exposé as a failure, though. He'd gotten several free beers and a free porn magazine himself. He hadn't shown the magazine to his wife, doubted most of the other men had, either.

Now he had a new bomb and he couldn't wait to drop it. He was sure to get some emotion, some outrage, out of Susan Sparrow about Gunny Saks's attempted murder. Gunny and Mrs. Sparrow had a history. Gunny had worked for her at the crematorium for a while. He was primed to see the look on her face when he told her the news, not many people had heard about it yet.

Luckily, Luke had a small package that wouldn't fit in the mailbox, so he had an excuse to go to the front door. He'd checked to make sure it was Mrs. Sparrow's black Lexus in the driveway, not Landry Sparrow's white-as-snow Mercedes. Imagine making enough money for a car like that by putting people in an oven.

Putney rang the bell, anticipation running high. Sure enough, Susan Sparrow answered the door in jeans and a T-shirt covered with a big apron. The smell of chocolate chip cookies wafted out of the house.

"Afternoon, Mrs. Sparrow," Luke said and gave her a small salute.

Susan knew from the gleam in his eyes Putney was bursting to tell her something. She didn't like him, thought him a vicious little man. She smiled politely. "Thank you for bringing up my mail, Mr. Putney. Excuse me, I have to hurry to take my cookies out of the oven. Good day to you." She held out her hand.

Luke was fast. "You haven't heard, Mrs. Sparrow?"

"I really don't have time to talk right now. May I have my mail, Mr. Putney?"

"Imagine, Mrs. Sparrow, our Gunny was nearly killed, hit on the head by an unknown assailant. That's what they're saying at the police station." He said it again, savoring the words: "Unknown assailant. Yep, poor Gunny's in surgery, and the word is she might not make it. Last I heard from Sandy at the police station, Chief Masters got a call from an FBI agent, and he was out the door. He found her and got her to the hospital super fast. He's Gunny's godfather, you know—or maybe more," he added, his voice confidential. "Lulie never talks about who Gunny's dad is." He was surprised she looked indifferent to his news, and peeved. Where was the outrage?

Susan knew, of course, this was why he'd come to the front door. He'd wanted to see her reaction. And she hadn't given him one. She saw the frustration on his face and was pleased. She took her mail and the small box from his still outstretched hand. "I will pray for her." Susan tried to shut the door, but Luke wasn't about to let her off his line.

"The chief's at the hospital with Ms. Saks. Sandy said it all has to do with that weird belt buckle they showed on TV yesterday in Willicott. I was working, so I didn't see the news conference. But my Myra said the belt buckle was this big gold Star of David, though she's got cataracts, and I can't swear she saw it right."

"Thank you, Mr. Putney—"

"Poor Mrs. Chamberlain at the post office—you know, she's Gunny's supervisor. Well, she runs the place, truth be told. She's all upset, of course. Everyone at the post office is upset. Gunny might be simple in the head, but she's a sweet girl. Mr. Klem said we all need to pitch in to buy some flowers and he hoped it wasn't for Gunny's funeral."

Putney watched Susan Sparrow's face closely. She didn't look ready to burst into tears. She looked impatient. With him.

The gall. Here he'd gone out of his way to give her news about someone who'd worked for her, someone she should care about. When she'd married Landry Sparrow, a few of the older biddies had said right away she'd latched onto him for the Sparrow money. Even his Myra had said when the announcement came out, "Imagine, Landry's nearly old enough to be her father. Well, maybe not quite, but there's at least fourteen years between them. It won't work out any different than Prince Charles and that poor Princess Diana. What some girls will do for money." She'd shaken her head, even looked mournful. Although he'd never say it to her, Luke wished at the time he could have a wife fourteen years younger who looked like Mrs. Sparrow. She was on the petite side, with dark hair and brown eyes and the whitest skin. And she was usually nice to everyone—well, you'd have to learn to be nice, wouldn't you, if you needed to convince people to cremate their grandmas?

She gave him a serene smile. "Again, thank you, Mr. Putney, for bringing me the package and my mail."

"Didn't Gunny work for you for a while?"

He was tenacious, she'd give him that. She wasn't about to say anything at all to this gossip-mongering buzz saw. They stood staring at each other. Susan smiled again. "Good day, Mr. Putney. Oh my, you made a mistake. This package isn't for me, it's for

Mrs. Prentiss down the block." Susan handed him back the small package.

Putney took the package and studied the address. "Ah, you're right, Mrs. Sparrow. Sorry about that mistake." She let the door close in his face. Luke hated to leave with an empty tank, but maybe he hadn't. Had Mrs. Sparrow looked alarmed? Frightened? Maybe that's why she didn't want to talk about it? He'd have to think that over, see what her neighbors thought. He walked down the flagstone steps to his white truck. He had a lot more mail to deliver. The day was young, and the afternoon spread out pleasantly before him.

36

Susan Sparrow heard the sound of quiet breathing behind her as she turned back toward the kitchen. It wasn't Landry, he was meeting with the Carters at the crematorium. It was Eric. He'd come in through the kitchen, heard her speaking to Putney, and stayed out of sight. If he hadn't, there'd have been gossip about her and her brother-in-law tearing up the sheets before Mr. Putney finished his route today.

He was grinning. "Now that idiot Putney will tell all the people on the rest of his route you didn't show any concern at all about what happened to Gunny, and why was that?"

Susan shrugged. "I learned very quickly never to show any reaction to anything Mr. Putney tosses at me."

"Doesn't matter, he'll make something up. At least you didn't give him any fodder. Hey, I think the cookies are nearly done. They smell great. Can I have one?"

She laughed as she looked up at her brother-in-law. Eric looked like a bad boy with the beard scruff on his face. Ripped jeans, a black T-shirt showing off his muscles, and scuffed low-heeled black boots finished off the picture. "You're back early. I thought you were fishing with your buddies until tomorrow."

He shrugged, turned away, walked to the kitchen. He wanted a beer with his cookie. Susan followed him and watched him open the fridge, twist the cap off a Bud, and take a long drink. He wiped his hand over his mouth, walked to the oven, and breathed in. "I've always loved chocolate chip cookies. Mom's were great. She used them as bribes, mostly."

"To keep you from breaking heads at a bar?"

"Yeah, maybe that, too. Mainly it was little stuff, like getting me to put the toilet seat down."

"Why'd you come over here, Eric?"

"I wanted to see Landry. Then I realized he was with the Carters, going over their memorial service at the crematorium. He's known them forever. He really likes them."

Susan put on oven mitts and pulled the cookie sheet out of the oven. The cookies were fat and soft, the way both Landry and Eric liked them. She did, too, she supposed. She put the cookies on a rack to cool, saw Eric's eyes fasten on them, shoved one on a napkin, and handed it to him. He said absolutely nothing, inhaled, took a small bite, and groaned. He'd always thought chocolate chip cookies fresh out of the oven had to be what heaven smelled like. "Gotta say, Susan, those are as good as Mom's." He paused a moment, grinned. "Do you know, from the age of seventeen, I always put the toilet seat down?"

"So does Landry. Your mom used behavior modification on both of you. I'll have to remember that."

"Yeah, that Skinner dude started it all." He held out his napkin for another, chewed slowly. "Better than beer, and that's saying something. Do you know, to this day when I eat a chocolate chip cookie, I have this compulsion to go to the bathroom and make sure the toilet seat's down?"

She shook her head at him, couldn't help the grin. "Come on, Eric, why'd you really come home early?"

He wiped his mouth, shrugged. "Really? I came home because I was bored. Carlos snagged himself a mistress—how, I don't know, had to be through divine intervention. Anyway, his wife found out. Now Carlos says his life's no longer worth living. Maroni was busy telling him to tuck his money away where she can't find it, do it fast. Otherwise he'll get skinned like Maroni did in his last divorce."

"I hope she nails his hide to her wall. Did you hear what Mr. Putney was telling me?"

"Yeah, but I already knew. I was pumping gas when I heard about Gunny getting hit on the head in that alley between Kim's Dry Cleaners and Lucky Hammer. It's all anyone's talking about."

"I hadn't heard, so believe me, Mr. Putney was eager to tell me, of course. He doesn't think she's going to survive. Or maybe that's what would make his story better. Do you know how she's doing?"

Eric took another swig of his beer, set the bottle on the counter, lifted another cookie from the sheet. "No, only that she's in the hospital. Did you see the news conference the Feds held in Willicott yesterday?"

"Sure, some of it." She leaned against the counter. "I can't imagine why anyone would hurt Gunny because she knew who owned a belt buckle. I mean, why?"

He walked to the sink and washed his hands. He said over his shoulder, "Who knows? Well, maybe Gunny does."

She looked at her brother-in-law, married and divorced in his twenties, and now forty, four years younger than Landry. Landry said Eric looked tougher than a lumberjack and was probably meaner. He had survived Afghanistan. Her husband looked his polar opposite, tall and slender, an aristocrat with his blade of a nose and high cheekbones. She watched Eric pull out his cell. "I'll tell you what, I'll call the hospital, see if Gunny is still alive. I always liked her. I remember once this putz tried to put the moves on her at the crematorium, some idiot there for his uncle's memorial service, and I stepped in." He paused, added, "I asked her if she was okay, and she said she knew how to protect herself, Chief Masters had taught her. She's a beautiful girl." He shrugged. "It's a pity she's so slow."

Susan listened to him speak to Marjory, once a high school girlfriend, now in hospital administration. He listened, thanked her, and hung up. "All she knows is Gunny's in surgery, no word yet. Gunny's mom and Chief Masters are walking the floor. I tell you, Susan, it makes no sense."

37

HAGGERSVILLE COMMUNITY HOSPITAL
TUESDAY

Only four people were seated in the waiting room of the Haggersville Community Hospital ER, none of them looking particularly sick, very different from the ERs Sala had been to in Washington, D.C. Ty and Sala identified themselves to Nurse Grady at the desk. Her eyes sparked, and she leaned over the counter, told them Gunny's mother was Lulie Saks, who owned the Heaven Sent bakery, and that Gunny was simple. Nurse Grady didn't know how Gunny was doing, she'd only been in surgery with Dr. Ellis less than an hour now. "She didn't look good when they wheeled her into the CT scanner. She was unconscious, and blood was caked over the back of her head. Someone left her to die in that alley. I'm praying she makes it. Everyone is."

Nurse Grady's eyes followed an older gentleman leaving the ER with a cane, watched a woman beside him hold her hand out, ready to steady him if he needed it. She leaned close. "Gunny's always been a good girl—well, she's not a girl any longer, she turned thirty last week. She's always been slow, bless her heart, but nobody ever minded that. You just had to remember to shift into a different gear and go with her flow. I don't know if she was born slow, but I suppose a doctor might have done something wrong, though I don't know for sure. Poor Lulie, she was so scared for her daughter. Did you stop at her bakery?"

Sala said, "No, we're just getting into town."

Grady said, "There are usually at least a dozen people inside. It's a good name, a good place. It's right next to Sunny Day, Sherry Hanson's boutique. I think the boutique does good business because they're next door. Lulie makes the best éclairs in Maryland."

Nurse Grady gave Ty and Sala directions to the surgical waiting room on the third floor. Like all hospitals Sala had visited in the city, there was constant movement, the hum of air-conditioning, the voices of caregivers on the intercom, techs wheeling carts. A nurse carrying a covered bedpan showed them the waiting room.

It was small, with a single window looking out over the parking lot. The floor was covered with an off-white Berber carpet, the walls painted a pale green, a line of Monet prints at eye level, a Nespresso machine that looked older than Ty on a small table in the corner. As good a place as any to wait for life-or-death news. A man and a woman sat next to each other on the single sofa, the man holding the woman's hand, speaking to her quietly.

"Chief Masters?"

He looked up. Ty saw the sheen of unshed tears in his eyes and something else—rage. He squeezed the woman's hand and rose. "Yes, I'm Masters, Chief Daniel Masters."

Ty immediately stuck out her hand. "Chief, we've spoken on the phone a couple of times. I'm Chief Ty Christie from Willicott. This is FBI agent Sala Porto." Sala automatically showed the chief his creds and shook his hand. Masters nodded to Ty. "Nice to finally put a face to the name." He introduced them to Lulie Saks. She started to stand up, but Masters gently pressed his hand on her shoulder. "No, stay seated, Lulie." Lulie Saks looked to be near fifty, about the same age as Chief Masters, her lustrous dark hair not yet showing any gray, but it was sprinkled with confectioners' sugar, making her look vaguely like Christmas. She was wearing skinny jeans and a white camp shirt that came nearly to her knees with daubs of colored frosting and splotches of chocolate on the front, black ballet flats on her narrow feet. She was blessed with high cheekbones and was really quite beautiful. Did her daughter look like her? Her dark eyes were red from crying, her fair complexion pale from fear and anxiety. She looked from Ty to Sala. "Please, have you heard anything?"

"I'm sorry," Sala said, and perjured himself without hesitation, "we've heard nothing yet, which Nurse Grady assured us was good news."

Lulie was trembling so badly she was glad Danny had made her stay seated. She might have fallen over. She continued to look up at Agent Porto, a lovely young man near Gunny's age, tall and well-built, his eyes and hair as dark as hers. She saw concern on his face that warmed her.

Perhaps Sala wouldn't have done it if he hadn't been so close to death only days before, but he came down on his haunches in front of Lulie, took her shaking hands in his, and warmed them. Strong, capable hands, Lulie thought. Hands that could also roll dough and decorate strawberry shortcakes. Lulie shook her head. She was losing it. She felt Danny's big hand, warm and comforting on her shoulder. Danny's hands were too big and rough to deal with delicate pastry dough. She laughed, swallowed.

Sala said, "We're here to help, Ms. Saks. Did Chief Masters tell you about the call from the FBI agent manning the hotline?"

She nodded. "Please, thank the agent at the hotline for calling Danny—Chief Masters—right away."

Sala said, "We will. Our agent was very concerned, contacted Chief Christie and me right after he called Chief Masters. Ms. Saks, this is very important. Please tell us why Gunny told the hotline agent she didn't know what to do about recognizing the Star of David belt buckle. Do you know what she meant?"

Lulie looked into the young man's very kind eyes. It was a solid question. She could do this. "At dinner last night, Gunny told me she was worried, but it took me a while to get out of her what she was worried about. Gunny does things in her own time. Please understand, she's not quite like other people. She's slower, you have to be patient while she gets her thoughts together. She asked me if I'd seen the press conference, but I hadn't. I had been told by a customer about the murder of that federal prosecutor in Willicott and about all those bones found at the bottom of

Lake Massey, but Gunny wasn't worried about the murder or the bones. She was worried about Mr. Henry's belt buckle. She said it was a secret, whatever that meant, and she didn't know who to talk to about it. That was it. I couldn't get anything else out of her. Well, I did tell her not to bother her supervisor, Mrs. Chamberlain, at the post office." Lulie paused. "You know, now I remember Gunny never said she wouldn't speak to Mrs. Chamberlain, so I can't be sure she didn't. Gunny said Mr. Henry might have showed the belt buckle to Mrs. Chamberlain, too, since she was his special friend."

Ty said, "The belt buckle belonged to a Mr. Henry? Special friend? And Mrs. Chamberlain was his special friend? As in they were lovers?"

Lulie nodded up at the young woman. Imagine, so young and she was a police chief. "Yes, forever, well, until he died five years ago."

"Maybe," Ty said slowly, "someone overheard her speaking to Mrs. Chamberlain, someone who works at the post office or was there to conduct business? And that someone followed Gunny when she took her break, to keep whatever Gunny knew from reaching the FBI?"

"And this someone tried to kill her to protect himself? But from what?" Lulie shook her head. "It's a stupid belt buckle. Who cares?"

"Someone obviously did," Sala said. "A lot."

Chief Masters said, "I haven't spoken to Mrs. Chamberlain, and I need to do that."

Ty said, "Would you mind if we spoke to her, Chief?"

"That's fine with me. This is all part of your case over in Willicott. I can use the help."

Lulie's voice shook. "Danny said whoever hit her left her behind a dumpster in the alley between Kim's Dry Cleaners and Lucky Hammer."

Sala moved to sit beside Ms. Saks as she continued, her voice liquid with tears. "I can't believe Mrs. Chamberlain would have anything to do with the attack on Gunny, so maybe Chief Christie is right, maybe someone did overhear. But who? A lot of people go in and out of the post office. It's sort of a social spot, a place where people talk, drink their coffee, and exchange gossip. Any one of them could have noticed Gunny speaking to Mrs. Chamberlain, overheard what she said."

Masters said, "Or one of the postal employees could have overheard, Lulie. We'll get hold of the video that covers the lobby. We'll find out who was there. If Mrs. Chamberlain knows anything herself, I'm sure she'll tell Chief Christie and Agent Porto. Of course, Gunny could have mentioned it to someone else, too, the wrong someone."

"It's all my fault."

Sala heard the horrible guilt bubbling out through the pain, and he understood, too well. He tried to keep his voice calm, matter-of-fact. "How do you figure that, Ms. Saks?"

38

Lulie hit her fist against her knee, sending confectioners' sugar raining down from her hair. "If only I'd kept after her to tell me what worried her about telling a secret! A secret Mr. Henry asked her to keep? Why, for heaven's sake? The man's been dead for five years. He sure doesn't care. She only told me a little of it. Why not everything? I'm her mother. I'm supposed to give her good advice." She gulped, closed her eyes tightly. "I know it's difficult for her, and I'll admit it, even though I try to be patient, to wait her out, to gently push and prod, last night I had so much work to do—bookkeeping for the bakery, tax forms to fill out before I went to bed. If only I'd pushed her, made her talk to me, made her tell me why she was worried about Mr. Henry's belt buckle, but I didn't. I didn't. I shut her down. Now my daughter might die!"

Ty took her hand. "Listen to me, Gunny will not die. Chief Masters got her here in a hurry. Agent Porto and I will make you a promise: we will find out who did this, and Chief Masters will keep Gunny safe until we do, right, Chief?"

Masters stared at her, shook his head at himself. "I hadn't thought that far ahead. Yes, of course I'll keep her safe, Lulie. And the chief's right, there's every reason to hope Gunny will pull through this."

Lulie rose. "I've got to make a call. There's someone who needs to know about this."

They watched her pull her cell phone out of her jeans pocket and walk out of the room, shoulders straight, head up. They heard her speaking low into her cell.

"Chief, do you know who she's calling?"

Masters said to Ty, his voice clipped and hard, "Probably her daughter's father. Gunny's illegitimate, but Lulie has never told anyone who the father is, not even me. Believe me, my wife and I have wondered, everyone has wondered, but Lulie hasn't said. And I can't remember who was around her thirty-one years ago. But what does it matter?" He laughed, shook his head. "I know lots of people in town think I'm Gunny's dad, but I'm not."

Sala said, "But you've looked after her, looked out for her."

Lulie walked back into the waiting room as quickly as she'd left. She looked stronger, more in control. She accepted a cup of Nespresso from Ty. "Would you like cream? Sugar?"

"No, black is fine." Lulie sipped and felt the hit of caffeine. She sat down, set the cup on a side table, and looked straight ahead. Sala said, "Ms. Saks, may I ask who you called?"

"Gunny's father, but don't ask me for a name. It's an arrangement we have. But he deserved to know what happened to his daughter." She blinked up at Ty, then turned to stare at a Monet print on the opposite wall.

Ty rose. "I'll see if we can get an update." She was ready to throw her weight around, but she didn't need to. Everyone at the nursing station was just as worried about Gunny but could only promise to get word as soon as they could.

A nurse walked into the waiting room a few minutes later, eyeballed the four of them, and said, "Lulie, Dr. Ellis said he'll come talk to you when he's finished with her surgery, another half hour or so." She didn't tell them Gunny's heart had stopped twice on the operating table and they'd brought her back. No parent needed to hear that, not from her.

Lulie felt the words gum in her throat, then burst out, "But, Carole, Gunny will be all right, won't she?"

"I promise you, Dr. Ellis is one of the best neurosurgeons in the area, and it's good news he's finishing up. Would you like to call her minister or her priest?"

Lulie's heart jumped. She could hear her voice rising as she said, "You want to call her minister? He thinks she's going to die, doesn't he?"

"No, no, Lulie, believe me, it's more for reassurance, a comfort for you."

Lulie felt her mind nearly crack. No, she wasn't going to let fear numb her brain. She had to hang tough, that's what Andrew had told her. Lulie said, her words clear as a bell, "Gunny is strong. She will survive. Chief Christie told me she would.

There's no need to call Reverend Whorley. We'll wait right here. Carole, please go take care of my daughter."

Nurse Carole Jones looked at Chief Masters. "Dr. Ellis wanted me to tell you if you hadn't found Gunny as fast as you did, Chief, she wouldn't have had a chance. He said to keep the faith." She nodded to Lulie and left.

Lulie turned to Chief Masters. "I didn't thank you, Danny. I'm sorry."

Masters only nodded and suffered Lulie squeezing his hand so hard his fingers turned white.

Good, Ty thought, *Ms. Lulie Saks has pulled herself together. Because of Gunny's mysterious father?* Her dark eyes were focused, intelligence shining clear, the sheen of tears gone. As for Ty, she had prayed, promising endless good deeds if Gunny pulled through. She said, "Ms. Saks, it's obvious Mr. Henry is the key to all this. It also seems for whatever reason he told Gunny to keep the belt buckle a secret. You said he's dead? Could you explain this to us?"

Masters said, "He's long dead, five years now. Mr. Henry LaRoque was his name. He founded the First National Bank of Haggersville back in the early eighties. His wife died of cancer some time ago. He retired after that, some ten years ago, if memory serves. His son and only child, Calhoun LaRoque, took his place as president. I don't know if Mr. Henry kept his hand in, but I doubt it. He believed everyone should be able to do things the way they wanted, and he wouldn't interfere unless Calhoun asked him to.

"People liked Mr. Henry. He continued to be active on the town council, but he didn't want to be mayor, joked he had too many secrets. You'd see him walking nearly every day down Clover Street to the post office, where he had a group of friends who liked to chew the fat, sometimes played some poker. He was what my grandma would have called a gadabout, very gregarious, always liked to know what was going on. He knew everybody, their families, their kids, their pets. Everyone loved him. Gunny said he was always kind to her, gave her gummy bears."

"So what happened to Mr. Henry LaRoque? Was there anything unusual about his death?"

Lulie shuddered. "Unusual? It was horrible. He was murdered five years ago. Horribly. Who would do such a thing to that fine old man?"

39

Ty's mouth dropped open. She stared at Lulie Saks.

Lulie said, "No one was ever caught. You never even had a single lead, did you, Danny?"

Masters shook his head. "Not that mattered. No one could remember Mr. Henry having a single enemy. So I couldn't pin a motive on anyone. There were a few whispers about his son, Calhoun. I remember there'd been some friction between them, but I never really understood what it was about, and no one else did, either. But it can't have been that serious, because when his father was murdered, Calhoun was distraught, seemed out of his mind with grief and anger. And, after all, Mr. Henry had made Calhoun president of the bank, left him alone to run it the last five years of his life. He left the bank to Calhoun in his will, left him everything, in fact, including the mansion, but since Calhoun had already built his own house on the other side of town, Mr. Henry changed his will to leave the mansion to the city of Haggersville. It's used for town council meetings, conferences, things like that. Most of the rooms were cleaned out and modified, but Mr. Henry's study was left the same as the day he died." Masters blew out a breath. "It still keeps me awake, his murder, the way he was killed. His case is, naturally, still open."

Lulie said, "What was done to him was horrible."

Masters said, "Let me tell them about it, Lulie. Mr. Henry lived in a grand old mansion on a huge lot on Black Forest Lane, at the edge of Haggersville. The killer probably came in through the oak forest at the back of his property in the middle of the night. The alarm system wasn't all that great, so the killer easily disarmed it and went into Mr. Henry's house and up to his bedroom. He struck Mr. Henry on the head, stripped off his pajamas, and tied him spread-eagled to the bedposts. What followed was hours of slow torture, no other way to describe it. He was stabbed thirty times with a serrated knife, the M.E. said. Some of the cuts were deep, some shallow, but the goal was obvious—to inflict as much pain as possible and to keep him alive as long as possible.

"He was seventy-five. Still, it took him several hours to die.

"His housekeeper, Mrs. Dolores Boilou, arrived at her usual time and found him dead, covered with blood. I got to his house at eight a.m. on a Tuesday morning."

He stared down at his clasped hands. "It was a brutal, ugly death. And it was personal, no doubt about that. Someone hated the old man's guts so much he wanted to make him suffer an eternity of pain for what he'd done to him or to someone he loved—whoever that was. But I never could find out who or why. No one knew. The whole town was outraged. No one could believe what was done to him. It was a witch hunt there for a while. It still makes me sick to think about it.

"As for Calhoun, his only child, well, I like Calhoun—I mean, he really tries to be as nice as his dad was. He's always donating to local charities, but the fact is Calhoun wasn't born with his daddy's charisma and his kindness. He's eccentric, which means, I suppose, he can't be called crazy because he's rich."

Lulie said, "I think Calhoun likes to shock people, make them shake their heads at what comes out of his mouth. I guess he learned quite young he'd never have his father's natural gift for making people like him, so he's found his own way to make himself memorable."

Masters nodded. "I agree with that, Lulie, but Chief, Agent, I'd swear Calhoun is harmless. I couldn't even begin to see him killing his dad in such a vicious, brutal way—well, in any way, really. He said he was home in bed with his wife, and yes, I know, she alibis him."

Lulie said, "Danny, no one I knew ever seriously considered Calhoun had murdered his father. The consensus around town was a maniac passing through."

Masters laughed. "Yeah, right. 'The maniac did it.' Couldn't be anyone from around here, anyone we know. Had to be an escapee from a Baltimore prison, hyped up on drugs and who knows what all? It made people feel safer to hold tight to that belief. But given the level of cruelty, the killer had to feel over-the-top rage, and that doesn't fit the profile of a drug addict or escaped crazy murderer. Sorry, Lulie, but odds are it was someone local, someone we know, someone who hated Henry LaRoque bone-deep. Also, his murder wasn't spur-of-the-moment. It took time and planning. If only I could have found out the why, I'd have known the who."

Masters clasped his hands between his knees, looked down at his boots. "I called in the FBI, but they couldn't do any better."

Sala said slowly, "And Gunny was struck on the back of the head because she was about to link Mr. Henry to that belt buckle?" He shot a look at Lulie, wishing he'd kept his mouth shut, but if anything, she looked thoughtful. "Agent Porto, you're saying you think the person who killed Mr. Henry struck down Gunny?"

Sala said, "Can you think of another reason?"

"No," Lulie said, "I can't, no."

Ty said, "Let's get back to the belt buckle. Let me tell you, we expected a number of calls to the hotline from people identifying it, but to our surprise we got only one—from Gunny—which has to mean no one else in town knew about it. And that seems to mean he never wore it? If he did keep the belt buckle to himself, for whatever reason, then did Gunny see it by accident? What is it about this belt buckle that made Mr. Henry make her promise not to tell anyone about it?"

"And why attack her?" Sala said. "What would she have told the agent on the hotline that would implicate anyone?"

Dr. Ellis, an older man with a rooster tail of white hair, walked into the waiting room. He was smiling at Lulie. "She's okay, she's going to make it. She hasn't awakened yet, but I believe she will recover in time, Lulie. She's through the worst of it."

Masters pulled Lulie against him when she started to cry and hugged her hard. He couldn't help it. He wept with her.

40

HAGGERSVILLE POST OFFICE
TUESDAY

The post office lobby was crowded, but no one seemed much interested in mailing letters or packages. They were talking about what had happened to Gunny Saks. Postal employees knew the most, it seemed, and they were holding court.

When Ty and Sala walked in and asked for Mrs. Chamberlain, the buzz of conversation stopped dead, all eyes on them.

Sala smiled, gave a little wave. “Chief Christie and I—I'm Agent Sala Porto—we've come from the hospital and we're happy to tell you Gunny's surgery went well. It looks like she'll be all right. She'll recover.”

There were murmurs and sighs of relief, most of them sincere. Ty and Sala were the new center of attention, until it was clear they had no more answers.

A woman's piercing voice rang out, a whipcrack to it. "This is a United States post office, not a coffee shop! Everyone, back to work!" Conversation died on the vine. A formidable woman in her late fifties, Sala would say, tromped toward them in sensible low heels and a plain gray dress that showed, to his surprise, an amazing cleavage. Her glasses hung on a gold chain around her neck, and her hair was permed and sprayed to immobility. She looked no-nonsense, like a Bears linebacker with breasts. Sala imagined everyone knew not to tangle with this woman.

After Sala and Ty showed her their creds and asked to speak to her privately, Mrs. Chamberlain gave one last death look to the postal employees still hanging around in the lobby, then said, "Come this way."

Ty and Sala followed her through a swinging gate past the fourth window. A thin-as-a-straw older window clerk started to say something, saw the look on Mrs. Chamberlain's face, and seamed his lips. Sala didn't blame him. *Smart move, dude.*

"Pay no attention to Hughes. He's been here as long as I have, but he's never going to leave the window, never wanted to. He can sort mail for boxes faster than anyone I've ever seen, but he prefers to sell stamps and weigh customer packages. He and Luke Putney try to outdo each other with gossip."

They followed her into the bowels of the post office, aware of postal employees watching their every step.

Mrs. Chamberlain stopped abruptly and gave the stink-eye to a man in close conversation with a young woman. She said in a death-ray voice, "Mr. Klem, you must get back to work or Mr. Murcheson might find out how you spend your time on the job." Mr. Klem nodded once to the young woman and turned away. Mrs. Chamberlain continued. "Mr. Murcheson is our postmaster, brand new and scared of his own shadow, sent to us from way up north around Boston. He doesn't know how we do things here in rural Maryland yet, so he does what I tell him to, naturally. Right now, I imagine he's in his office, with the door locked. Who knows what he does in there." She stepped around them and walked into a small windowless room with three surprisingly healthy ferns along one wall next to her very nice wooden desk. A small library of postal books were lined up precisely on the wall behind it, some looking old enough to have been published under Eisenhower. A laptop, a landline, and a paperback novel were the only items on her desk. She sat down and motioned them to the two chairs facing her.

Her look was complacent. "Welcome to my office of twenty-one years. I assume you've come because you have questions about Gunny and her job here. You may begin."

Ty nearly giggled. It was close. Sala knew it, too, and so he covered for her, bless him. He sat forward, but before he could speak, Mrs. Chamberlain said, "I hope there's no question about Gunny's hospital bill. All Gunny's medical bills will be covered by the federal government. Dr. Ellis and the hospital never have to worry about being paid."

Sala looked so taken aback, Ty quickly said, "No, we realize there'll be no problem with Gunny's health insurance, Mrs. Chamberlain. We need to know if Gunny spoke to you this morning about the belt buckle we showed on TV yesterday. She told her mother it belonged to a Mr. Henry LaRoque."

"Oh, I see. Well, yes, Gunny sidled up to me about eight thirty this morning, asked if she could speak to me. Naturally I was busy, but I told her to go ahead, tell me what was on her mind.

"It was nothing, really. Gunny said she was worried about Mr. Henry's belt buckle, the one the FBI showed on the television. I told her Mr. Henry didn't have a belt buckle like the one you showed on TV, and I should know—"

Sala saw a slight flush on her cheeks but let it go for the moment. He could accept Mr. Henry hadn't worn the belt buckle. But that his own lover hadn't ever seen it? He said, "Let's say Mr. Henry did have a gold Star of David belt buckle, and Gunny saw it. Did she tell you why that worried her?"

"I honestly don't think Gunny ever saw such a thing. She gets things wrong sometimes, fantasizes. She's a dear girl, but her brain doesn't always—well, work smoothly. She tunes out suddenly, then she comes back, I guess you could say. Fact is, she's slow, Agent Porto, but I suppose you already know that."

Ty asked, "Why was he called Mr. Henry?"

"It was a sign of respect, an endearment. He was a caring, generous man, and you'll not find anyone who disagrees. Mr. Henry handled the mortgages, business loans, financial assistance of all kinds for most of the people in town.

"Now, I told Gunny I was sure Mr. Henry didn't own such a belt, that she was mistaken. She didn't say anything more, only frowned and looked confused. I knew I had to be patient, knew there was more, so I asked her, why all this concern about a belt buckle she saw on TV? She said it had to do with a promise she'd made Mr. Henry, and she didn't know whether she should tell anyone."

Mrs. Chamberlain gave a deep sigh and shook her head. "But before I could ask her anything else, we had an emergency. One of the mail sorters went on the fritz, and I had to make some calls, schedule repairs, reassure Mr. Murcheson, calm down Mr. Judd and set him and his people to sorting the overflow mail by hand. When I finally came up for air, I asked where Gunny was. Mr. Judd told me he'd seen her leave. It wasn't her break time or lunchtime, either, but he said he didn't stop her. He said she was clutching her cell phone in her hand, seemed to be repeating something to herself, which she does sometimes, but he couldn't hear what she was saying. I forgot about it, to be honest, something I very much regret now, after what happened to her. Of course you know Chief Masters found her in an alley, badly hurt. But still, Agent Porto, Chief Christie, why someone would hurt her doesn't make any sense to me. I know Mr. Henry did not own that belt buckle shown on TV, I would have seen it." She sighed. "I know, I know, the fact that someone tried to kill Gunny means there had to be something to what she was saying, but I don't know what it could possibly be."

Ty said, "Mrs. Chamberlain, this is very important. Where were you when Gunny asked to see you about Mr. Henry's belt buckle? Who was around you?"

Both Ty and Sala saw kindling outrage. "Oh, I see. You want to blame one of my employees for striking down that poor girl? That is outrageous, and I won't have you suggesting it!" She curled her heavy white fist on her desktop. "My people are always underfoot, even where they shouldn't be, and I'm telling you, none of them would do something like this. Everyone likes Gunny. She doesn't have an enemy in the world." She shrugged. "So maybe Mr. Henry did have a Star of David belt buckle. I never saw it, and no one else ever saw it, to the best of my knowledge." She met their eyes. "I will be honest here. After Mr. Henry's poor wife died some fifteen years ago—cancer, you know—he and I became close. Not many people knew at the time, and we both preferred it that way. I am a very private person with certain standards to maintain, Mr. Henry as well. As I said, I never saw him with this belt buckle. He always wore red suspenders. Ask anyone.

"And to answer your question, I don't remember seeing anyone in particular. When Gunny came up to me in the lobby, there were customers around—I don't remember who specifically—checking their boxes, chatting, the usual, but to be honest, I didn't pay any attention." She paused, frowned. "I remember Gunny got really close when she spoke to me, like she was worried someone might overhear her. I don't know really, maybe I'm remembering it that way now because of what happened to her. I don't suppose your hotline got a lot of calls about this belt buckle?"

Sala said, "The hotline got only one call about the Star of David belt buckle, and that was Gunny's."

Ty said, "Which leaves us with quite a mystery."

Mrs. Chamberlain fiddled with a pencil, threading it between her heavy fingers. "Chief Masters should have ideas about this. He was the one who investigated Mr. Henry's murder five years ago. He's Gunny's godfather." She lowered her voice. "You probably already know Lulie's never said who Gunny's father is. Of course, some people believe Chief Masters is her father. His poor wife, Molly, has always been clueless, so I suppose it's possible."

Sala wasn't about to touch that. He said, "You spoke of Henry LaRoque's murder five years ago. Is there anything you'd like to tell us about it?"

She lowered her head, the memory of it still strong.

Ty said, "Given the manner of death, it's obvious someone hated him. Do you think somehow Gunny could have connected his belt buckle to his murderer?"

"Mr. Henry's death, what was done to him, it was despicable. But as for Gunny connecting anything to his killer, it simply isn't possible. Listen, Gunny performs simple tasks here at the post office. I hired her because Chief Masters asked me to." She paused. "But I have to say, in the five years she's been here, she's done her various jobs well enough."

Ty said, "Where did Gunny work before she came to the post office?"

"Once she graduated high school, she worked full-time with her mom for a while. Before she came to the post office, Susan Sparrow hired her to work at the Sparrow Crematorium. This was right after Susan married Landry Sparrow. Then she came here to the post office."

"What did she do at the crematorium?" Sala asked.

"Some reception work and she passed out cookies after memorial services, things like that. You'd have to ask Susan Sparrow what her other tasks were. Why do you ask?"

Ty smiled. “Collecting information. Do you know why she left?”

“I never asked her directly, but I got the impression it was too depressing for her.” Mrs. Chamberlain fell silent. She looked to be studying a large citrine cocktail ring on her pinkie finger. “Mr. Henry gave me this ring on my birthday seven years ago.” She met their eyes. “It all comes back to why someone tried to kill Gunny. I don’t see how Gunny could know who murdered Mr. Henry. Because of the stupid belt buckle?” She huffed out a deep sigh. “You know they couldn’t have dredged up Mr. Henry’s bones from the bottom of that lake in Willicott along with that buckle. His family had him cremated.”

41

PRINCE WILLIAM FOREST PARK
VIRGINIA
EARLY TUESDAY AFTERNOON

The air-conditioning in Sherlock's stalwart Volvo was on the fritz. According to the temperature on the dash it was ninety-one degrees. *Inside or out?* Sherlock wondered. And not a single cloud in the sky.

Savich was driving the familiar route to Quantico, with the Prince William Forest Park adjacent to it. He and Sherlock had visited the park a couple of times when Sean was younger, spending the day hiking the trails, showing Sean the eastern box turtle, picnicking on the edge of the North Fork of Quantico Creek. He didn't remember it being this hot. Actually, he couldn't remember any other day being this hot. No one had been more surprised than Savich when they got a call from a park ranger thirty minutes before.

As he turned into the shaded park entrance, with the forest pressing in, Sherlock said, "Finally, a call about the Kia."

They'd put an APB out on the green Kia immediately after Victor had shot at them in Peterborough, but there'd been no calls. Savich pulled up close to the ranger kiosk, got out of the Volvo, and slipped his Glock into his pocket so he could take off his jacket. He and Sherlock waited for a single car filled with a father, mother, and three young kids, all laughing, talking, and arguing, to pass through. They'd hoped Ranger Harmon would be there, but she wasn't. Still, they identified themselves, showed the young man with thick black eyebrows their creds.

Terry Menard studied them, then looked up, head tilted to the side. "Agents, what can I do for you?"

Savich said, "We need to know where to find Ranger Sionna Harmon. She called us."

Terry perked right up. "Oh yes, this is about that terrorist who bombed the cathedral in Falls Church? I've seen his photo—it's all over TV and the Internet. He sure looks like a wuss, doesn't he? As harmless as my terrier Milo. None of us saw him though, only Sionna—well, you can speak to her yourself. I'll give her a heads-up, tell her you're here. She's doing an hour in the visitor's center."

Savich parked Sherlock's Volvo and they walked quickly out of the insane summer heat into glorious air-conditioning and what looked like controlled pandemonium. Families and children, happy to be out of the sun, crowded around the exhibits of the park's history and its geology, the kids shouting questions to a docent. Savich asked for Park Ranger Sionna Harmon.

A tall, leggy black woman with buzz-cut hair strode to them, everything about her screaming efficiency. They introduced themselves. "You called us about the green Kia," Sherlock said.

"That's right. Sorry, but I never saw Victor Nesser. Last night, before I left, I walked through the parking area as I always do, my last duty of the day, looking for anything hinky, I guess you could say. I saw a banged-up green car and wondered about all the nicks and holes, wondered how it could still drive. And I forgot about it. Then this morning a police officer from Dumfries was here drinking my coffee, telling us about the news, and he happened to mention the green Kia. After he left I went back and took a look. It was the Kia. That's when I called you." She paused a moment. "Look, I've asked, but no one saw him come in."

Savich said, "Nesser probably drove the Kia in while you were on break. He did the same thing at a park in Maryland."

"Well, that makes sense. Parks aren't prisons, and we aren't guards. He could have snuck in if he was lurking, watching to see when I or another park ranger left the kiosk for a break. There are lots of places he could have parked out of sight." She paused. "I didn't look closely, but I was wondering. Are all those nicks in the car bullet holes?"

"Yes," Sherlock said.

Harmon's dark eyes studied Sherlock's face. "I'm guessing it was your bullets in the Kia?"

Sherlock only nodded.

Sionna shook her head, ran her tongue over her lips. "This is beyond terrifying, Agents. Our park is full of families. So many kids who'd make hostages."

Savich said, "Let's go look at that Kia."

They followed Sionna past the kiosk, where Terry Menard was busy processing a line of cars to enter the park. The Kia was the very last car in the parking lot. Savich pulled his cell out of his pocket and called a forensic team to Prince William Forest Park to go over it.

Sionna's cell phone rang. She listened, punched off. "That was Ranger Menard. Sure enough, one of our visitors, a Mr. Jules Dunn, reported his car was stolen from the parking area, a blue Honda SUV."

Savich met with Mr. Dunn, an insurance salesman from Leesburg, at the visitor's center, got all his information, phoned it in, and got another APB going for the local area. When Ranger Harmon told Dunn who'd stolen his old blue Honda SUV, the man's eyes bugged wide. In the next instant, he turned to tell his wife and three teenage sons. The oldest boy grabbed his hand and shook it. "Wow, Dad, the terrorist dude stole our car! We're going to be on TV. Way to go!" Mr. Dunn grinned, did a high five, and Mrs. Dunn turned perfectly white, Sherlock saw, a more intelligent response. The three teenage boys were still excited, hooting and hollering, when their dad looked at his wife and stopped grinning. The reality of what had happened was beginning to sink into his brain. Savich said, "Local law enforcement will be on the lookout for your Honda. You'll have to go in and file a report. Ranger Harmon will help you with that."

Mrs. Dunn said, “We won’t see the car again, will we, Agent Savich?”

Savich shook his head. “Doubtful, but what’s important is you’re all safe.”

When the Dunn family was seated in the visitor’s center waiting for a police car, Sherlock said to Ranger Harmon, “We’re going to try to find his campsite, but chances are slim he left anything useful.”

Harmon said, “Would you like me to go with you? I’m a sworn officer, you know, and I have a gun for situations like this. I do know how to use it.”

Savich said, “Thank you. If we need your help, you can count on us calling out fast and loud.”

Harmon showed them the main trail and left them to it, though it was clear she still wanted to come with them. As they walked into the woods on a well-marked path, Savich called Ollie Hamish, his second in command in the CAU, who gave him the latest news on the church bombing aftermath. When Savich punched off, he said, “Looks like everyone is going to make it. No critical injuries reported. Needless to say, the politicians are lining up to get their outraged sound bites on the bombing of the church on the six o’clock news. Same old, same old.”

Sherlock pointed. “Look at those red maples and the Virginia pines. We need to bring Sean back here.” She fanned herself. “Let’s wait for some cooler weather, though.”

They started walking quietly, alert for any sound that wasn’t right, and soon heard footsteps and several voices. Like Savich, Sherlock carried her jacket over her arm, her Glock in her pocket.

She eased it out. A family—husband, wife, two young kids—appeared around a curve in the trail ahead of them, hauling tents and camping equipment. They looked happy—well, the kids looked happy. The dad looked stoic, the mom tired and sweaty. Sherlock pressed her Glock against her leg. No sense scaring the bejesus out of them. Everyone said hi and walked on. They passed into a large designated RV camping area where people sat around in portable chairs, drinking sodas and beers, some grilling hamburgers for a late lunch. Sherlock breathed in deeply, heard her stomach growl.

They walked to the far end of the camping sites, then followed a trail that led through poplars and white oaks so thick they formed a canopy overhead to block the sun. A blessing.

They found what was probably Victor's campsite some twenty yards beyond where camping was allowed and a Snickers wrapper, nothing else. The ashes in the freshly dug fire pit were cold. Victor had been gone a long time and he'd swept the area down.

As they trudged back, Sherlock said, "How long do you think it'll take Victor to dump Mr. Dunn's Honda, and steal another car?"

42

Victor didn't steal another car. He dumped the Honda SUV that smelled like sweaty teenager socks in Alexandria and called a taxi to take him to Koons in Tysons Corner, where he paid seven thousand dollars cash for a dull brown 2009 Chrysler 300 LX. He gave a little wave to the salesman as he pulled out of the lot. It didn't matter his face was all over TV and plastered in every cop shop in the area. No one would recognize him. He was no longer a clean-shaven young man with short brown hair. He couldn't help his pale complexion or his size—skinny, his chinos hanging off his butt—but he'd changed as much as he could. Now he wore a longish dark brown wig and thick glasses with clear lenses, plus a bit of a goatee that was, unfortunately, coming off bit by bit, but he didn't care. The goatee had been Lissy's idea, and it itched. No more baggy chinos, either. He was wearing tight blue jeans and a black T-shirt under an open plaid shirt. The jeans itched, too, but Lissy assured him he looked sexy now, not at all like a nerd.

I really like the new you, Victor. I always wanted you to walk on the wild side. Yum, love those tight jeans. I hadn't realized you have a butt. Now you're my dark, dangerous avenger and you'll help me send that bastard, Buzz Riley, straight to hell. While we were suffering in that stinky psych ward, all those rules and having to sit through all those sessions with those idiot shrinks, he was having a big time, all free and happy after he killed Mama. Well, we're going to end that. Right between the eyes, Victor, or maybe in his mouth. I really like that. Lights out!

"We already checked his house once, saw his old car was locked up tight in the garage. I'll bet you Savich told him to get out of town."

He heard her huff out a breath, then, *You're probably right, but that doesn't mean we can't come after him again, later, when he thinks he's all safe from us. You did good with the church, Victor. Blew the sucker sky high, exploded it off its foundation. To see all those bugs flying out of there, trying not to get burned to a crisp, it was fun.*

"It was fun, Lissy, but you heard the radio. No one bit the big one, only minor injuries. I thought what with the fire bursting up through the church floor, they'd all go up in flames, but it didn't happen." Would she blame him? Call him incompetent? He waited, tense, already feeling his blood burn.

She whispered softly against his face, *The way you put that bomb together, such tricky work, Victor. I was amazed. And how you knew where to fix it to the gas pipe in the church basement, that was so hot. And you made sure no one saw you. Don't feel bad. You know the FBI agents are paid to not panic. They're supposed to be cool and save lives. So they did their job, nothing great about that. You still sent them a powerful message: screw with us and see where you end up.*

You did good with this car, too, dull brown so nobody will notice it. But why won't you tell me where you're getting all this cash? You peeled off all those hundreds from a big wad in your pocket. Why won't you tell me where you got it?

Victor sped up to pass an old Mazda, then immediately slowed again to the speed limit. "I'll make you a deal, Lissy. You tell me where your mama buried all the bank robbery money in Fort Pessel and I promise to go back in a week or so and let you kill Buzz Riley. That's a good deal, isn't it?"

She huffed and went silent.

43

FIRST NATIONAL BANK OF HAGGERSVILLE
TUESDAY AFTERNOON

Ty pulled her Silverado into the parking lot at the end of West Clover Street between the Midas Hair Salon and the First National Bank of Haggersville. The bank was a stately, older two-story redbrick building, well maintained and important-looking, a place where you could be more confident than not your money would be safe.

Sala waved at the salon. "Midas hair? Does that mean they dye your hair gold?"

Ty said, "I tried pink once as a teenager, but never gold. Think it's too late for me to give it another shot?"

Sala laughed, gave her hair a tug. As they crossed the parking lot, Ty phoned Lulie Saks at the hospital. Gunny was out of post-anesthesia care, but she still wasn't coherent. It might take some time, Dr. Ellis had told Lulie, before Gunny could be questioned and make sense. Both Lulie and Chief Masters were with her, and Officer Romero Diaz was seated outside her cubicle in the ICU. Gunny was safe and secure.

Ty slipped her cell back into her pocket. "The killer will know soon enough Gunny's alive, if he doesn't already know, which he probably does. He couldn't afford to let her talk to the FBI, so he either goes into the wind or tries to kill her again in the hospital." She sighed. "Of course, if the killer knows she didn't see him, he might think he has more time."

Sala said, "If he's afraid she knows something that could bring him down right away, it wouldn't matter if she saw him or not. I honestly don't see how she could know who hit her on the back of her head. I'm hoping she heard something distinctive, smelled something, maybe a cologne she recognized, something like that."

"I've always believed there's a lot of faith involved in law enforcement, otherwise you get ground under." After a moment, she said, "You know what? In the short time I've known you, I realize you're always situationally aware, know who and what's around you. I've got to learn that."

"Well, maybe. My older brother was also in Afghanistan, still is. He taught me before I went in. Saved both our lives. All you have to do is clear out your mind, look and really see, listen and really hear. But none of that mattered with Victor Nesser."

Ty reached out, touched his arm. "You can't see in the dark, Sala, plus you were sound asleep. Teach me, okay?"

He studied her hand a moment, her long fingers and short buffed nails, a strong hand, a capable hand. He looked back into her serious face and smiled. "Yes, all right, I will do my poor best."

"Speaking of poor best, Victor didn't manage to kill anyone in the church this morning. Only minor injuries reported so far. I wonder what he thinks about that? That he failed?"

"Or maybe he's happy he showed the world what a badass he is."

Sala held one of the big glass double doors open for a man in Bermuda shorts and flip-flops, and he and Ty followed him into blessed air-conditioning.

"Wowza," Ty said. "Would you look at the gold-veined brown marble floor?" She swept her hand around her. "It's like a 1930s art deco Hollywood set. What a shine. Everything meant to impress."

A dozen or so desks and chairs were arranged artfully along the walls. There were old-fashioned windows, tellers on high stools manning each station. All of the bank employees seated at the desks were dressed sharply. People waited in a snaking line, peeling off whenever there was an open window. It seemed quiet and orderly, old-fashioned and really quite civilized.

Sala said, "I hope Al Capone doesn't burst in with a tommy gun."

She smiled. "I'll bet the bank was built in the thirties, and everything is authentic. They've buffed it up, made repairs, and kept all the original stuff. It's like stepping back in time. Would you listen to me, I've already lowered my voice to a whisper."

"Do you know, I can't remember the last time I was actually

in my bank. I do all my banking online now. But maybe I'd change my mind if I had a bank that looked like this."

Ty flashed to Harry Potter's Gringotts Wizarding Bank. This layout was pretty close, minus the goblins manning teller windows and the huge chandeliers hanging overhead. They heard people talking to one another, all whispers, like they were in a cathedral, and more than once they heard the name Gunny Saks.

They stopped at the security station, a beautifully carved art deco podium. A tall redheaded man with blue eyes and a big smile stood beside it. He was dressed in a well-pressed dark blue guard's uniform. Sala thought he looked about as forbidding as a poodle, even with the SIG in his holster.

They introduced themselves, showed Mr. Nathaniel Hoolihan their creds, and were directed toward the ornate staircase at the far end of the lobby. "Mr. Calhoun's office is right behind the big bank of windows overlooking the floor."

Ty looked up. "Why would he have all those windows? Seems to me it would be distracting."

Mr. Hoolihan cleared his throat, leaned close. "When Mr. Calhoun became president, he broke out the wall and had those big windows put in. It lets him look down onto the floor, see the customers that come in every day—that and he likes to see we're all doing what we're supposed to. It wasn't that way when Mr. Henry was running things."

Sala bent close to Ty's ear as they mounted the beautifully shined staircase. "So Mr. Calhoun LaRoque has already seen us. Does he know who we are, I wonder?"

"I'll bet he does by the time we get to his office," Ty said. "Are you ready to meet Mr. Eccentric?"

"As in 'too rich to be called crazy'? You bet."

At the top of the stairs they were met by a very pretty young woman wearing three-inch stilettos, a pencil-slim black skirt that wouldn't allow for an extra pound, and a white silk blouse under a matching black jacket. She had spectacular dark hair in wild curls around her head down to her shoulders. She gave them a huge smile showing straight white teeth. "I'm Courtney Wells, Mr. Calhoun's senior private assistant. Mr. Hoolihan called up, said you were FBI, that it was important you speak immediately to Mr. Calhoun. Is this about Gunny Saks? Did she die yet?"

Ty smiled. "No, she didn't die. And yes, we'd like to see Mr. LaRoque immediately. Thank you, Ms. Wells."

Courtney was too young to hide her disappointment. She huffed, turned on a skinny heel, and walked to a magnificent mahogany door, opened it, and stuck her head in. "Mr. Calhoun, the two FBI agents I told you about are here to see you." She stepped back, waved them in.

They walked into a big square office directly out of a fashion magazine in the 1930s. The magnificently carved desk, the chairs, the sofa, and the museum-quality credenza behind the desk were all classic art deco. On top of the credenza sat a series of framed photos—the frames art deco, of course—all of the man himself and his wife, from their twenties to the present, a photo chronicle of their lives together. Behind the big desk sat Mr. Henry's one and only child. He slowly rose and gave them a smile. Calhoun LaRoque looked to be about Ty's father's age, but unlike her dad,

Calhoun was at least six foot three and skinny as a toothpick. He was dressed in a bespoke dark blue suit with narrow white pinstripes, a white shirt, and a bright red power tie, like a uniform in its way, like her father's blue Washington State Patrol captain's uniform with its black bow tie.

Calhoun LaRoque had a head of thick pewter-gray hair with a few strands of black still woven in. His eyebrows were dark and thick over deep brown eyes. He waved at Courtney and very nicely asked her to close the door behind her.

Courtney left the door open a crack. LaRoque cleared his throat, loudly. She closed the door with a snap.

Calhoun said, "Courtney used to listen at the door, so I saw to it they put in a thicker one. It steams her not to know everything before anyone else."

"Why didn't you fire her?" Sala asked.

A dark eyebrow went straight up. "Didn't you *see* her, Agent Porto? She's drop-dead gorgeous, the most beautiful girl in Haggersville. Looking at her every day, believe me, it offsets her small, er, lapses, makes her mistakes seem nearly insignificant. She's worked for me since she was nineteen. She's twenty-three now. Did you see all that hair? She knows I like it in curls flying everywhere, so she's careful to keep it that way. Now, I know you're federal cops. Is this about poor Gunny Saks?"

44

Calhoun LaRoque hadn't taken a breath. Into the brain and out of the mouth. Sala loved being surprised by people, their various incarnations never failed to amaze him.

Calhoun rose as Sala stepped forward and handed him his creds, shook his hand, introduced Ty. "Chief Christie is from Willicott, and I'm FBI. We're not here to speak to you about Gunny Saks, sir. We're here to ask you about your father, Mr. Henry LaRoque."

A dark eyebrow shot up. "Mr. Henry? Why, for goodness sakes? The old man's been gone longer than Courtney's been able to vote. He's old news. Wait, has Chief Masters discovered something after all this time?"

"No, sir," Ty said.

Calhoun sighed, sat down again, and waved at two plush green leather chairs facing his desk. "I was all geared up to talk about Gunny Saks. That's the story of the day, what everyone wants to know. Oh well, up to you, up to you. Sit down."

He sat forward, folded his hands, and tried to look the dignified, serious, concerned banker, but he couldn't pull it off. He looked too excited, like a kid on Christmas morning, and they heard his toes tapping beneath the desk. "At least can you tell me if she died?"

Did the man have no filter at all? Ty said, "You'll be pleased to hear, sir, Gunny will be all right. The surgery was successful."

"Huh. Well, good. I suppose these things happen, even in Haggersville." Calhoun's voice dropped to low and confiding. "I had surgery once myself. They took out my gallbladder. I'll tell you it hurt pretty bad there for a while." He smiled. "But I got better really fast because my wife hauled me out of bed and walked me all over the hospital, kept telling me I'm a great healer and besides, only weaklings need a gallbladder. She was perfectly right. What would you like to know about Mr. Henry?"

Ty settled into the very comfortable chair. "You can tell us why you were at odds with your father, Mr. LaRoque?"

"Me? At odds with Mr. Henry? Who told you that? He was a popular old man—well, he wasn't old when I was a boy, I don't guess. Growing up, he was too busy to spend much time with me. I don't remember his ever throwing me a baseball or football. He never came to my basketball games, probably worried the bank would go under if he didn't give it all his attention. He was that caught up in it. He was either holed up in his study or out and about, particularly in the evenings. Very popular, my father, but I guess you already know that.

"Come to think of it, looking back, I don't think he particularly liked me. I don't know why, but there it is. But then again, he didn't particularly like my mom, either. He started sleeping with that scary Mrs. Chamberlain at the post office even before my mom died, at least that's what I heard later. That went on for years, until the old man finally died, although to be fair, that wasn't his decision."

"Died?" Sala repeated slowly, an eyebrow raised. "No, it wasn't his decision. We understand your father was murdered, brutally."

"Yes, you're right, of course. I never understood why the murderer had to kill him in so horrible a way." Calhoun looked down at his Breitling watch, realized that wasn't smart, looked up again. "I mean, a bullet would give you the same result, right? My father is still greatly missed, ask anyone in town. I remember there was standing room only at his memorial at the crematorium." Calhoun paused, frowned down at his Montblanc pen. "Now that I think about it, and to be completely honest here, the old man was a real son of a bitch to me. But we pretended we got along well enough for the most part, no dramatic fallings-out."

Ty said again, "A son of a bitch? How so, Mr. LaRoque—"

"Calhoun, please."

Ty leaned forward. "Calhoun. How was he a son of a bitch?"

"You heard me. He was Santa Claus to everyone in town, but nothing for his wife or his son, not even his time. He never visited me at Dartmouth, gave me only enough money to keep food in my mouth. Wouldn't you say that qualifies?"

Yeah, Ty guessed, *it does*, but she said, "I can see his behavior hurt you."

"Yeah, but here I am whining and he's been gone for five years. I didn't even see him much until my wife and I moved from Baltimore back to Haggersville when he surprised me by putting me in charge of the bank, said he was retiring.

"I think he had to put me in charge, no choice, since he was big on tradition, and I was his only kid. He decided to will me this bank and his money. He knew I was smart and wouldn't run his bank into the ground. You see, I managed a bank in Baltimore for twenty years, showed him I could do it very well." Calhoun paused a moment. "I wish he'd sent me some of that money when I was in school or starting out.

"So in the end, I guess that has to mean he wasn't really disappointed in me, doesn't it? He would have even left me that monstrous house of his, except I told him I didn't want it."

He began weaving the Montblanc through long, thin fingers. "He left his house to Haggersville. They've kept his study like a shrine to him, haven't touched a thing. I think my old bedroom is a storage room now. Last time I looked, there were boxes of copy paper stacked up in there. All my posters of Wilt were gone."

Sala said, "Did your father know what you thought of him?"

"Oh sure, when I was an adult making my own living, I told him. It didn't seem to bother him much. I remember he laughed at me, told me to get over it. That's about it." Calhoun rose, an obvious dismissal that Ty and Sala ignored. He sat back down and sighed.

Ty said, "Mr. LaRoque—Calhoun—who do you think murdered your father?"

"I haven't a clue, Chief. Chief Masters never had a clue, either. No one had a clue. My dad had no enemies, like I've said, everyone loved him. Ask anyone around town."

"Did you love him, Calhoun?"

"I suppose I did, early on, since he was my dad. My wife always laughed at the stories I told her about how he treated my mom and me. She said he had crazy wiring and to forget it."

Sala said, "Did you ever see your father wear a large Star of David belt buckle?"

Calhoun drew back. "I've heard talk about a weird belt buckle they found in the lake, and that's why Gunny Saks was struck down. Do you really think it belonged to Mr. Henry?"

"Yes," Sala said, "I assume you saw him wear it?"

Calhoun shook his head. "Gunny made a mistake, understandable since she's—" He waggled his fingers to his head and rolled his eyes. "It couldn't have been Mr. Henry's. He always wore suspenders, even though he didn't need them to hold up his pants. He was skinny, like me. I bought him an alligator belt once for Christmas, but he never wore it. Only red suspenders. He always said real men wore suspenders, like his father did before him. I'll bet he was even cremated in those red suspenders." Calhoun stopped cold. "Now isn't that odd? He never suggested I wear suspenders, never gave me any, so I never have."

"I haven't, either," Sala said.

Ty asked, "Why do you call your own father 'Mr. Henry'?"

"Hey, that's what everyone's always called him, my mom, too."

Sala said, “You said Mr. Henry was cremated. What did you do with his ashes?”

“His ashes? Oh, I scattered them in Baltimore, off Fells Point into the Patapsco River. It was storming that day, and I didn’t want to motor all the way out to the ocean.”

“Do you still have the urn?”

Calhoun thought about that a minute, frowned. “I think I donated it to the thrift store. I mean, poor people die, too, so why not have a really nice urn for their loved ones’ ashes? Mr. Henry’s was the best money could buy, ceramic, as I recall.”

When Sala and Ty left, Courtney Wells tossed her beautiful curly hair at them and nodded toward the stairs. Ty gave her a big smile, whispered, “He can’t wait to tell you everything.”

Ty said to Sala, “The man’s certifiable.”

“Or he likes to play-act at being certifiable.”

“And he gets away with it, which would mean he’s not at all stupid.”

“No, Calhoun is anything but stupid. Both he and Mrs. Chamberlain agree Mr. Henry never wore belts, only red suspenders. So how did his belt buckle—according to Gunny Saks—end up in Lake Massey with all those bones? It’s got to mean Mr. Henry wasn’t cremated after all, that his bones were there at the bottom of Lake Massey.”

“And he was wearing the Star of David belt buckle when he was thrown in. Or,” Ty added, “Gunny Saks is wrong about all of it, and we’re chasing giraffes. But someone did try to murder her.”

Her cell rang. It was Lulie Saks. Gunny was fully awake, and there was something very different about her.

45

HAGGERSVILLE COMMUNITY HOSPITAL
LATE TUESDAY AFTERNOON

Sala and Ty paused to speak to Officer Romero Diaz, sitting outside Gunny Saks's cubicle in the ICU. He was late twenties, buff, too handsome for his own good, a heartbreaker, Ty bet. He assured them they shouldn't worry, nobody was going to hurt Gunny. His voice changed when he said her name.

"You care about her," Ty said.

Diaz said, "Sure, we grew up together. I always thought she was a sweet kid, and so beautiful. Nobody's going to get near her." He touched his fingers to his holstered Beretta.

Ty and Sala squeezed into the small cubicle space to stand next to Ms. Saks and Chief Masters.

Lulie looked up even as she kept stroking her daughter's face.

"Gunny fell asleep again after they gave her a pain medicine in her IV. She had a bad headache." She paused a moment, getting herself together. "They say she had a blood clot—a subdural hematoma, pushing on her brain. Both her surgeon and the nurses say her vitals are good now." She paused, swallowed. "She'll be all right."

"You said she was different?" Ty said. "What did you mean, Ms. Saks?"

Chief Masters said, "Actually, I told Lulie she was different. Lulie'd stepped out for a minute when Gunny opened her eyes. She looked confused for a second, then she smiled at me and called me by a nickname that nobody's called me for years—BBD, stands for Big Bad Dan. I didn't even know Gunny knew that name."

"Did you call him by that nickname, Ms. Saks?" Ty asked.

"Yes, like everyone else did when he was younger, before he became Chief Masters, but it stopped when Gunny was a little girl." She touched her fist to his arm.

Chief Masters plowed his fingers through his thick hair. "Yeah, yeah, when I finally decided to grow up—no more bar fights and speeding my Mustang through town, generally scaring the crap out of people."

Lulie said, "I really liked that Mustang."

"Yeah, I did, too, but my dad was hooting and cheering when I finally sold it." He paused a moment, then picked up Gunny's still, pale hand, a lovely hand, with long, narrow fingers, clear-polished short nails. "Like I told Lulie, Gunny's smile, the way she looked at me, spoke to me, she seemed different somehow.

She was taking me in, focused on me. I've never seen Gunny look at me like that. There was real awareness in her eyes. Then she sort of whimpered deep in her throat, whispered her head hurt, and I called the nurse. Like Lulie said, the nurse injected something for pain in her IV, and she fell asleep again."

"Gunny was hovering on the edge of sleep when I came back in, and she didn't speak any more," Lulie said to them. She drew in a deep breath. "I don't quite understand what you mean, Dan. It is strange, though. She called you BBD after all these years? The first thing she said when she woke up and saw you?"

He nodded. "I've been thinking about it since you called Ty, Lulie. Let me say when Gunny smiles, it's always sweet, loving, and you know there are only kind thoughts behind that smile, no sarcasm, no irony. There aren't any layers to Gunny's smiles. Everything is right there, for all to see."

"What he's trying to say in a nice way is Gunny is simple. Everything's on the surface. She's guileless, open, childlike, I guess you could say."

He nodded. "Okay, but not this time, Lulie. When she smiled at me, she was here, with me, and her eyes were alive with emotion as she tried to remember what had happened, put together where she was. I'll tell you, her eyes seemed to penetrate right into me—I don't know—sorry, I'm not explaining it well."

Lulie lightly laid her hand on his arm. "We'll see soon enough when she wakes up again."

Sala said, "Before she does, can we talk a minute about Henry LaRoque? Both Mrs. Chamberlain and Calhoun LaRoque told us his father was cremated."

Lulie blinked at them. “Mr. Henry? Yes, that’s right, he was cremated at the Sparrow Crematorium. They also have memorial facilities and most everyone in town was there. There wasn’t a viewing because of the way he was killed.”

Chief Masters said, “He looked like he’d been through the Spanish Inquisition. They had to keep him covered.”

Lulie said, “Oh, I see, you’re wondering how his belt buckle ended up in Lake Massey with all those bones. How that’s possible? He really was cremated, though. Could Gunny have been mistaken?”

Sala said, “Then why would anyone have tried to kill her, Ms. Saks? Her being attacked was all about that belt buckle. She said she did see it, and for whatever reason, Mr. Henry told her to keep it a secret, made her promise not to tell anyone, including you. Neither Mrs. Chamberlain nor Calhoun ever saw that belt buckle. They said he only wore suspenders.”

“That’s right,” Chief Masters said, “red suspenders. But why would he show this particular belt buckle to Gunny? Why would it be a secret Gunny had to keep? It was his, after all.”

Lulie said, “Why wouldn’t she tell me about it after he was murdered five years ago? I mean, what would a secret matter after he was dead?”

Chief Masters squeezed her hand. “I bet she forgot, Lulie, and it simply slipped out of her head. Seems to me Gunny’s always lived in the here and now, that is, when she could focus. She’s always accepted whatever comes her way, doesn’t question it. You tell her to do something, she does it, and then she forgets about it.”

"Yes, that's true," Lulie said. "But why would Mr. Henry swear her to secrecy? Why would Mr. Henry care? It's a stupid belt buckle, nothing more. That's why her story seemed so strange to me."

Ty picked it up. "Mrs. Chamberlain told us Gunny worked at the Sparrow Crematorium before the post office."

"Yes, she did," Lulie said. "Mrs. Sparrow—Elaine Sparrow, Landry and Eric's mother—hired Gunny to assist Mrs. Chugger at the reception desk. She greeted people, handed out cookies at the memorials, occasionally answered the phone. You know, odds and ends, nothing too taxing." She paused. "After the Sparrow parents died and Landry married Susan, she became Gunny's boss. Gunny really liked Susan, but it bothered her seeing dead people, especially seeing them shoved into an oven and burned up. I asked her how that was possible, I mean, her job didn't require she be near the actual cremations. Turns out she'd been in the wrong place at the wrong time and it freaked her out. Susan told me she was sorry about losing Gunny. She told me Gunny was very good with grieving family members, very empathetic and gentle. Then Danny, you got her hired at the post office."

Chief Masters nodded. "Lulie, Gunny squeezed my hand. She's coming around again."

Gunny felt light against her eyelids, not too bright or hurtful, but soothing and warm, comforting. She felt no particular pain in her head now, only a sort of heaviness, like a weight bearing down on her, and wasn't that odd? She slowly opened her eyes, looked up into her mother's beautiful face, then at her godfather and the two strangers behind them, a man and a woman, both about her age, both focused entirely on her, their expressions serious. Were they from the church? Was she dying?

"Gunny? Baby?"

Her mother's voice, like sweet clear bells, like when she was reassuring her after a nightmare or when she'd told her how wonderful she was when Gunny managed the grades she needed to graduate high school. When was high school? It had to be a long time ago, hadn't it?

She heard her mother's voice again, next to her cheek. "Can you speak to me, Gunny?"

Gunny. She suddenly remembered the bag race when she was six years old and all the kids had to hop toward a finish line with garbage bags belted under their armpits. She'd stumbled all over herself, and Bertie Wyman had called her a gunnysack. And it had stuck. It was better than the other names the kids called her, like dummy and doofus. She'd never complained to her mother because she didn't mind those names as much as the names she'd heard adults call her, like simple but always very sweet. After the garbage bag race, Gunny was what everyone called her, her mom included. Her mom said it was charming and fun, even though she realized now her mom had hated it, and was only trying to make the best of it. But she'd accepted being called Gunny, really hadn't given it much thought.

Now, though, she realized it wasn't right. Gunny wouldn't do. She wanted her mother to know it, wanted her godfather to know it, too. She whispered, "Mom, please call me Leigh. That's my name. Leigh Ann Saks. Gunny sounds like some sort of marine. Gunny was okay when I was a little girl, but not anymore."

There was utter silence. Leigh heard her mother suck in her breath. She felt the weight of their stares, the many unspoken questions hanging in the air, heavy as the weight on her head.

"It's been a long time since I was a child, Mom," she whispered. "I'm an adult. I'm also thirsty."

It was her godfather who spoke first, his voice soothing as the soft light. "Not a problem, Leigh. It might take me a little while to get used to it, so be patient with me." He put a straw in her mouth. "Slow, Gunny—Leigh—real slow, okay, sweetheart?"

It felt like heaven, and she wanted to drink the entire glass of water fast, all in one long gulp, but she felt pain building up somewhere in her chest and stopped. "Thank you," she whispered. Her mother lightly touched a Kleenex to her mouth.

"Do you have any pain?"

"Not really, I was drinking too fast." She smiled up at her godfather, then beyond him to the good-looking man and woman. "Who are you?"

46

Lulie kissed her daughter's cheek and straightened. "Honey, let me introduce you to FBI agent Sala Porto from Washington and Chief Ty Christie from Willicott."

They moved forward and held out their identification so she could see. She really liked what Chief Christie was wearing—black jeans, a tucked-in white shirt, a sharp black jacket. She had such cool hair, dark brown with curls down to her shoulders and the prettiest green eyes, a mossy green, maybe. She was taller than Leigh, fit as a marine, her godfather liked to say, which was a big compliment. Agent Porto was tall, hair and eyes as dark as an archangel's, his cheekbones knife sharp, his face expressive. He was very good-looking indeed. She smiled, nodded. "It's nice to meet you both. Are you here because of my accident?"

Lulie moved out of the way so Ty could stand close to Leigh. Ty took her hand and saw uncertainty in her eyes, but also awareness and complete focus on what Ty was about to say. Chief Masters had said when she'd awakened, she was different. Was this what he'd meant? She said, "Someone struck you on the head, Leigh. We're here to find out who did. Can you remember hearing or seeing anything to help us find out who struck you?"

"Someone hit me on the head?" A sharp jab of pain made her close down for a moment. She raised her hand and felt the thick bandage. Slowly, never looking away from Ty, she shook her head.

Leigh didn't look slow, she looked baffled, completely understandable after being knocked unconscious.

Leigh looked toward her mother. "Mom, I don't understand. Someone hit me? Why? I'm Miss Goody-Two-Shoes, even you've called me that. Why would anyone hate me enough to smack me on the head?"

Sala took Chief Masters's place. "Ms. Saks, I'm afraid someone did strike you, knocked you unconscious. You've had surgery, but you are not to worry. It all went well, and Chief Masters has assigned Officer Diaz to guard you. He's right outside the cubicle."

A small smile bloomed. "Romero? Guarding me? I remember he belted Keith Morton when he tried to kiss me. I really wanted Romero to kiss me when I was sixteen." She paused, and a shadow of regret, of sadness, flitted over her face. "Then he grew up, and I didn't."

Ty squeezed her hand, couldn't help it. She said, "Do you remember leaving the post office this morning?"

Leigh slowly shook her head, winced, closed her eyes, and leaned back against the hard pillow. "Where did you find me?"

Sala said, "Chief Masters found you behind the dumpster in the alley between the dry cleaners and a hardware store."

"Lucky Hammer," Chief Masters said as he lightly smoothed Leigh's hair back from her forehead to cover some of the white bandage. "An FBI agent manning the Star of David belt buckle hotline called me, and I got to you really fast and brought you here to the hospital. You were in surgery for three hours. Dr. Ellis swears you're going to be fine, no worries."

Ty said, "Do you remember walking to the alley to make a phone call, Ms. Saks?"

Leigh slowly shook her head. "I'm sorry, but it's all a blank."

"What is the last thing you do remember?" Sala asked her.

Her brow furrowed. "I remember speaking to Mrs. Chamberlain, but I don't remember—wait, I had some question, I think, about Mr. Henry. But why would I? I mean, Mr. Henry's been dead for a long time now, so why would I be asking Mrs. Chamberlain a question about him?" She gave a tiny shrug. "Whatever it was, I suppose I thought she'd know since she and Mr. Henry were sleeping together a long time before he was killed."

Lulie couldn't believe what she was hearing. Gunny—Leigh—speaking about Mrs. Chamberlain and Mr. Henry's affair? Not their being special friends, no, sleeping together, saying it like an adult would. She felt like the one who'd been smacked in the head. What was happening with her daughter?

Ty thought about showing Leigh a photo of the belt buckle on her cell phone to spark her memory, but instead, she said, "You were thinking about Mr. Henry because there was a press conference yesterday in Willicott. An FBI agent held up a belt buckle, a special one with a gold Star of David. It was found with a lot of human bones at the bottom of Lake Massey. Anyone who recognized it was asked to call the hotline, and you did, Leigh. In fact, you were the only one to call the hotline with any real information. You were knocked down before you could say much to the agent speaking with you. He thought something had happened to you on the telephone and called Chief Masters immediately, who found you in that alley. Then the agent called to alert us, and we got here as quickly as we could."

Chief Masters closed his eyes against the enormity of what could have happened if not for that FBI agent who had cared and acted.

It was as if Leigh had read his mind. "If you hadn't found me, I could have died, right? Thank you, Dan, for saving me."

It was unnerving for him now to listen to this young woman he loved but had always believed to be special—yes, simple, unable to function in this big bad world without the kindness and protection of others. Where was that girl?

"You're welcome," he said. "The bottom line, sweetheart, is now you'll be around to wipe drool off my chin in the misty future."

Lulie laughed. "My chin as well. Are you in pain?"

"A little bit. My head, it feels like a block of concrete is perched right on top pressing down. Mom, in the misty future, you might have buttercream frosting on your chin, but never drool."

A man's voice came from the entrance to the cubicle. "What's this about drool? Whosever it is, never mind."

After introducing Ty and Sala and Leigh to her surgeon, Lulie said, "Dr. Ellis, I'm glad you're here. I suppose the nurses called you because Gunny—Leigh—is awake? But she doesn't remember anything about what happened."

"That's not uncommon, Ms. Saks. It's almost expected after the kind of trauma she suffered. Post-traumatic amnesia often clears in a day or two."

Lulie lowered her voice. "Dr. Ellis, I don't know how to put this, but Leigh seems even more awake, more with us than usual. It's as if she's more aware than ever of everything around her."

He nodded. "That's good to hear, actually. Patients can seem hypervigilant sometimes soon after brain trauma, a sort of self-protective response, you might say. I would say it's nothing to be concerned about. She'll be herself again soon."

Lulie didn't give up. "What I mean to say, Dr. Ellis, is that for those of us who know Leigh very well—you've never met her, of course—she seems, well, very focused, different, in a good way, I guess, but none of us quite understand what it might mean. To be blunt, before she was knocked in the head, she was simple, but now she's not."

Dr. Ellis stared at her, then over at Chief Masters, who nodded. "That is perplexing, Ms. Saks. Tell you what. Why don't you let Leigh and me talk about that together while I do my neurological exam? If you would all leave me alone with her now. We'll have plenty of time to talk later."

Dr. Ellis ushered them out and snapped the curtain closed over the cubicle entrance, and they found themselves standing beside Officer Diaz.

He stood. "Is Gunny going to be all right, Ms. Saks?"

Lulie smiled at the handsome young man her counter girl Glory wanted desperately to notice her. And Leigh had wanted him to kiss her when she'd been sixteen? "Her name is no longer Gunny, Romero, it's Leigh. That's her real name and that's what she wants to be called now." Diaz cocked his head to one side, and Lulie patted his arm. "You'll get used to calling her Leigh. She doesn't remember anything about what happened yet, but she might soon. Please keep a close eye on her, all right?"

"I told you, no one will get past me, Ms. Saks," Diaz said, and tried his best to look ten years older and Rambo-tough.

There was a commotion at the large central nurses' station, and they turned to see a tall man dressed in a bespoke light gray pinstripe suit striding toward them. Sala recognized him from a law enforcement meeting on the Hill. It was the chairman, Congressman Andrew Mellon. What was this about?

"Who is that?" Chief Masters said aloud.

Lulie said simply, "He's Congressman Andrew Mellon. I called him, Danny. He had a right to know what happened. I admit it, I'm surprised he came, rather than sending an aide." He was walking toward her, his eyes never leaving her face. Lulie realized it gave her a spurt of pleasure, and wasn't that odd after so many years? It was the first time Andrew had ever come to see her in public. She walked quickly to him, and he took her hands. Everyone watched him bend his head down to speak to her.

He had a right to know what happened. What did she mean? Ty watched the tall, distinguished man with his dark gray-flecked hair take Lulie Saks in his arms and hold her close, whisper against her hair, comfort her. Then he handed her a handkerchief to wipe her eyes. She gave him an unsteady smile, took his hand, and brought him over to them.

"Andrew, I would like you to meet Leigh's own trio of cops." She introduced everyone. "They're here to find out who hurt her. I guess I should introduce you as Congressman Mellon."

Congressman Mellon raised a patrician black brow. "Andrew is fine, Lulie. Now, what are the FBI, the police chief from Willicott, and the police chief of Haggersville doing together here in the matter of a young woman struck down in an alley?"

Lulie said, "Like I was telling you, Andrew, it's pretty complicated."

Mellon nodded. "I was notified by our liaison of the press conference being held in Willicott, which is in my district and therefore of interest to me. I saw it. Agent Porto?"

As Sala was bringing the congressman up to date, Dr. Ellis came out of the cubicle, saw a well-dressed stranger had joined the group, and automatically nodded to him. He said to Lulie, "Ms. Saks, there is nothing significantly wrong with her neurological exam. She needs rest, which is the best thing for her right now." He nodded to the group and walked toward the central nurses' station.

"Sir," Ty said to Congressman Mellon, "I recognized you, of course, since you're our representative, but I am surprised you would actually come here in person to find out about a constituent's medical condition."

He gave her a charming smile, warm and inviting, showing a slightly crooked eyetooth. "Of course I'd come, Chief Christie. I've known Lulie and her daughter for some time. Lulie and I need to talk."

47

ON THE ROAD TO FORT PESSEL, VIRGINIA
TUESDAY EVENING

Victor, why are we on I-95? You know I hate all this traffic, all these cars piled nearly on top of one another, all these losers trying to get home to their boring little houses to their boring little kiddies. It's fricking rush hour, turn around and let's go back to Washington. I want to drill that murdering Riley right between his stupid eyes.

"I told you, Lissy, I won't let you kill him unless you tell me where your mama hid the bank money. I told you, too, it seems Riley's gone to ground, probably Savich warned him to stay away for a while. So we'll go to Fort Pessel first, to your mama's house. You show me the money, and in a couple of weeks, I'll even let you drive back to where Riley lives."

If I tell you, you swear you'll let me pump a couple of bullets in his brain?

"Yes."

Victor felt the touch of her wet mouth against his cheek, the lick of her tongue. He felt a surge of lust, then a sort of familiar settling down all the way to his soul. He remembered her mama's journal, a thin white book she'd kept hidden in a small hidey-hole behind the baseboard under her bed. He'd been watching her unawares. When she'd hidden it, he'd snuck it out and saw she'd listed all the banks the gang had robbed, the guards they'd murdered, the people they'd killed who'd interfered, the amount of money stolen from each bank, and how much she had left after paying out everyone's shares. All of it entered in Jennifer Smiley's spidery black handwriting. He hadn't had time to read all of it, didn't know if there was any clue about where she'd hidden the money. If he could get to that notebook, maybe he wouldn't need Lissy to tell him. Then again, it was risky going back there, and maybe the FBI had already found the notebook. Still, it was a smart hiding place, so maybe not.

"Lissy, do you remember your mother's little notebook?"

No, I didn't even know Mama had a notebook. Why are you talking about that? You're putting me off, aren't you, Victor? Listen, I'm hungry, we had only a couple of tacos for lunch. When my stomach growls, it makes those awful staples pull, makes them hurt.

"I know you love Southern fried chicken and mashed potatoes, so we'll stop and get you some."

Forget the mashed potatoes. I want grits, Victor. I haven't had grits in way too long. Hey, I really like the whiskers and the glasses, makes you look all badass and dangerous and smart. Turns me on. After dinner, let's stop a little while.

Again he felt her warm breath, felt her lick his cheek.

He shook his head at her. "Come on, stop it, Lissy, you almost made me rear-end that car. Look, we're nearly out of rush hour now, all the worker bees are starting to peel off. Don't lick me again, not yet, okay? I'll find us a place to eat dinner."

And no one will recognize my guy. You really look hot, Victor, and maybe a little bit mean. Just right.

He was whistling when he walked into the Golden Goose Diner in the small town of Winslow, Virginia, and slipped into a cracked leather booth. A pretty blond girl with a pencil tucked over her right ear, wearing shorts and a skimpy top, came to his table, looked him up and down and grinned. "Hey, you ready for some barbecue?"

"No, not tonight," Victor said. "Fried chicken, a double order, ah, and some grits." He saw Lissy was smiling really big. He added to the waitress, "Lots of butter in the grits, please."

Both the portions were huge, and when the last chicken wing was only bones, Victor pressed his hand over his belly. He was stuffed and felt faintly nauseated. Too much fat. He thought of all that fried lobster, and all the fried chicken he'd eaten in his short life. Lissy should have been happy, but she wasn't.

That little bitch is flirting with you, Victor. She keeps coming back here, pressing closer and closer, talking to you in that slutty voice. You let her see that wad of cash on purpose, didn't you, to get her interested? You want to have sex with her since I have staples in my belly and it hurts too bad? You sleep with her, Victor, and I'll shoot her ass.

He'd never before seen Lissy jealous and realized it made him feel hot, like a chick magnet. He pulled back his shoulders, gave the waitress a big smile when she came over, and handed her a hundred-dollar bill. "I'm Victor, and your name tag says Cindy. That's a real pretty name. Hey, keep the change. Maybe after work you'd like to have a glass of iced tea with me, cool down? Or we could go somewhere."

Cindy Wilcox made a snap decision. Victor looked nice, sort of sexy with that long hair and goatee. Fact was, she was bored. She looked at her iWatch, a gift from her married brother last Christmas. "Thirty-five more minutes, and I'll be done here. Hey, I'll ask Chuck real nice if I can leave early, how's that?"

"Sounds good. Why not bring me a glass of iced tea, and I'll wait for you."

Victor watched Cindy sashay back behind the counter and fill his glass with more tea, squeeze in some fresh lemon, plunk in the ice cubes. He breathed in deep when she leaned over to set his tea on the table, felt her breast brush his arm. The feel of her was amazing. She smelled like roses. He knew Cindy had seen the cash and knew, too, she wanted some of it. He didn't blame her, didn't think less of her, stuck in this hick town in a hick diner with crap air-conditioning and grease floating in the air. He could take her to a nice cool motel and see. Or maybe it would be best to go to her place. He felt Lissy's anger, thick and hot, pouring over him, into him, heard her hissing in his ear, and that felt even better than good.

He smiled, glanced at his own watch. "I've got some time before I have to be on the road again."

Ten minutes later, Victor followed Cindy's ancient faded green Mini Cooper as it twisted through a half dozen quiet, unlit streets. It was late enough that there wasn't much traffic and no screaming kids. They were all inside, watching TV, then off to their beds for the night. She pulled into the driveway of a middle-class duplex in a not-bad neighborhood, turned off her Mini Cooper, got out, and walked to his car, hips swaying. He stepped out of the Chrysler.

Cindy said, "Hey, not a bad car, except for the color. Why'd you get a vomit-brown car? It's like a rental nobody would ever steal."

Victor said smooth as silk, "That's why exactly. I had a car stolen once, a beautiful white Mustang, so all I buy now are ugly-butts. Never got one stolen again."

"Did you live in a bad neighborhood?"

Victor thought of Jennifer Smiley's house at the cul-de-sac in Fort Pessel, only three or four hours' drive southeast of Winslow. It wasn't a bad house, a bit run-down, and the neighborhood had been mainly white, hick, and nosy. "Yeah, maybe," Victor said, and stared at her breasts.

48

Cindy laughed, fully aware he was looking his fill at what her mother called her "assets." She knew she looked good. There was no way he would get back on the road tonight. She'd made up her mind while she'd helped clean up Chuck's greasy kitchen so he'd let her go early. She'd see if the skinny cute dude with all his cash might be her meal ticket out of this lame town. He was better-looking than the paunchy middle-aged man she'd met two years ago on the casino floor in the Mandalay Bay in Las Vegas. He'd scored ten grand at blackjack and laid his eyes on her nubile self, and she'd kissed him, congratulated him, told him how lucky he was. He'd taken her shopping, and she'd come home with two designer outfits, a diamond bracelet, and three pairs of Louboutin shoes. She'd left the dude smiling. It would be the same with

Victor—she'd butter him up, make the right promises to get him to offer to take her with him, didn't matter where. She imagined there was more than ten thousand in that roll of cash he'd flashed at dinner, and she intended to have a blast with him until it was gone. She'd leave him smiling, too. "I'm going to turn on the air conditioner the minute we get upstairs. It'll cool down pretty fast. Come on, Victor, let's forget the iced tea and have a little bourbon. That's my favorite."

Victor stood behind her while she unlocked her front door, surprised to hear Lissy whispering in his ear. *You want to have some fun, Victor? All right, let's go play with the little slut.*

Why wasn't Lissy still jealous? It made him mad. Time to turn up the heat. He whispered under his breath, "Nah, you don't want to play with her, Lissy, but I do. She's really pretty. Time to enjoy myself. You need to leave us alone."

You think you're going to screw her? Fat chance. Once we're upstairs, well, you'll see. It's time for me to have some good old-fashioned fun, too, not just you.

"You already had your fun today. We blew up a church, Lissy, this morning. Wasn't that enough for you?"

Yeah, we did, but hey, did you manage to kill anybody? Haven't heard you did. That precious FBI agent you locked in the closet at Gatewood, there he was, all hale and hearty, and even old Octavia's coffin made it out okay. So nope, I'm not about to miss more fun. I do like you looking dark and dangerous. I guess the little slut agrees with me. But you need some more glue or your beard's going to molt off.

"Did you say something, Victor? Ah, at last, this heat makes the door sticky. Come in, come in. You open windows for air, and I'll put on the air conditioner."

Victor walked into a small entrance hall that held a side table with a mirror over it, covered with a stack of mail that looked mostly like bills to him. Poor Cindy, tips must not be very good at the diner.

He followed her into a narrow living room with a small dining area and a one-person kitchen beyond. Cindy had movie posters all over the walls, mainly Justin Timberlake, the putz. It was hot and stuffy, so he quickly opened a couple of windows and let the fresh air flow over him. He waited. Lissy was quiet. Maybe she was jealous again?

He felt a hit of lust when Cindy came out of the kitchen carrying a tray with two shot glasses filled with what looked like bourbon. No iced tea chaser, fine by him. Victor liked the way her blond hair fell over her left eye and she had to constantly push it back. She handed him his shot glass, then lifted her own and tapped it to his. "Here you go, Victor. Bottoms up."

They drank the bourbon straight down. Victor thought his throat would explode, it was so hot. Not good bourbon, some rotgut. He managed not to spit it out.

"Would you like to listen to some music? I'll get us some more bourbon in a minute."

He felt Lissy coming near, and nearer still, getting ready to talk, her breath hot, rancid, and he knew there was nothing he could do to stop her. She didn't want to play, didn't want him to have fun. She'd fooled him, and now she was going to take Cindy down.

The empty bourbon glass went flying when the first kick hit

Cindy's left leg. She stumbled back, yelled, "Why'd you do that? What's wrong with you?"

Cindy was strong, she was fit, but she knew she couldn't win if he really came after her, not in the long run. She'd invited the monster into her apartment herself. Fear paralyzed her for a moment, then fury. She kicked out, aiming for his crotch, like her brother Simon had taught her. But he was bent to the side as he ran at her, and her foot struck him full strength in the belly. He lurched back, grabbed his stomach, and keened, as if she'd shot him and he was dying. He screamed, but it was high, more like a wail. *"You bitch! You kicked me right in my staples!"* A knife appeared in his hand. She hadn't even seen him pull it out of his pants pocket, and she backed up into the kitchen. He continued to scream at her, cursing her, his voice still high, hysterical, not making sense. Then he ran at her, trapping her in the kitchen. The knife was raised high over his head, and she saw tears running down his face. She grabbed a skillet off the stove and hit out at the knife, knocking it aside for a moment, but he backhanded her, knocked the skillet out of her hand. The knife was coming down at her again. She kicked out, but again she missed, got his thigh. *"You puking little bitch!"*

She kicked out once more, and this time she got him firmly in the crotch. He stood frozen, the knife in his fist, and he stared at her, then crumpled to the floor, moaning and holding himself, rolling over, cursing and crying. Cindy ran, tried to pull open the front door, but it was stuck again, and her hands were slippery with sweat. She yanked and pulled. She heard him stumbling to his feet. She heard the click of a bullet being chambered.

49

SAVICH HOUSE
GEORGETOWN
WEDNESDAY MORNING

Sherlock poured Cheerios into a *Transformers* cereal bowl before realizing Sean wasn't there to eat it. He was still at his grandmother's house. She stood in the center of the kitchen, staring down at the bowl, and cried.

She felt Dillon pull her against him. She burrowed her face into his shoulder and cried some more.

She hiccupped, got a grip on herself, and finally pulled away. "I'm sorry, I don't know what came over me." She knuckled her eyes. "Crying like an idiot, it never helps. What's wrong with me?" She looked up at him and felt another tear slide down her face. "Dillon, I miss Sean so much, and it's all because of that psycho Victor Nesser. We've got to find him, Dillon. This is personal. I'd like to shoot him, maybe dump him in Lake Massey, let his bones lie there forever."

Not a bad idea. Savich said, "Last night I dreamed Sean and I were throwing a football in our backyard. I threw the football over the fence, and Sean took a running leap and cleared that fence by a good foot, howling with laughter." He stopped cold. He wasn't about to tell Sherlock that right before he awoke, he'd realized Sean hadn't come back. Savich had vaulted the fence to find him, but he saw only fog and shadows. Like in his vision at Gatewood. Savich closed his eyes against the fear he felt. She was right. They had to find Victor and end this. At least Buzz Riley was safe, visiting one of his kids in Chicago rather than flying to Saint Thomas. As far as Savich knew, he and Sherlock and Sean were the only people left in Washington on Victor's hit list.

He pulled her close again, kissed her hair, felt her shudder. She said against his neck, "I would have liked to see Sean jump that back fence. Where was Astro?"

"He was barking his head off, cheering Sean on. But he wasn't Astro, he was a thirty-pound bulldog, and he couldn't move very fast." His cell phone sang out "Shape of You" by Ed Sheeran.

He looked down at the ID. "It's Sala."

"He's calling this early, it's got to be important."

"Sala, what's going on in Willicott?"

He listened as he watched Sherlock carefully stack Sean's favorite *Transformers* cereal bowl back in the cupboard then splay her hands on the counter, as if for support. Then she straightened, shoulders back, head up, and he saw the steel in her. "You said the chief of police, who's also Leigh Saks's godfather, said she's different? Her mother agreed? Different how, exactly?"

Finally, he said, "Okay, Sherlock and I will drive up to Haggersville. Give us a couple of hours. We'll see you at the hospital. If anything comes up in the meantime, call me."

He punched off his cell. "This sounds interesting." He told Sherlock what Sala had said about Leigh Saks. "Let me call Ollie, make sure everything's on track at work. Maybe we'll get a lucky break and someone will spot Victor again."

But there hadn't been a lucky break by 10:30 a.m., when Savich and Sherlock walked into the Haggersville Community Hospital ICU. They saw a young officer on guard outside one of the cubicles. He immediately rose and held up his hand. Savich and Sherlock pulled out their creds and introduced themselves. A tall man came out of the cubicle, his bespoke suit wrinkled, his eyes tired. Savich immediately recognized Congressman Andrew Mellon.

"I heard your name, Agent Savich. I know who you are and have greatly admired your career." Mellon shook Savich's hand. He turned then. "You must be Agent Sherlock." He beamed at her, pumped her hand. "Saving all those lives at JFK. It was amazing. I'm one of your biggest fans."

"Thank you."

Mellon said, "Agent Porto told us you were coming here to see my daughter."

Savich's eyebrow went up. "Your daughter? Leigh Saks is your daughter?"

"Yes, she is."

Sherlock gave the congressman a long look. “So it took her nearly being murdered for you to come and acknowledge her?”

He took the blow and nodded. “Yes, I know. It was past time. Thirty years past time.” He straightened. “But I’m here now. I’ll do what I can to help.”

Savich said, “We’re glad you’re here, Congressman. Agent Porto told us Leigh’s godfather and her mother said she’s changed.”

Mellon nodded. “I’d always understood she was slow, perhaps simple, but since I’ve never been part of her life, all I see is the young woman I met this morning for the first time. There seems to be nothing simple about her. As you know, she was struck on the head, had surgery. Both Lulie and Chief Masters say she’s no longer the same person since she woke up. She told her mother her name wasn’t Gunny, it was Leigh, which is indeed her name of record.”

He pulled open the curtain of one of the cubicles, beckoned for someone to come out. Mellon said, “This is Leigh’s mother, Lulie.”

They introduced themselves to Lulie Saks, showed her their creds. She leaned in, her voice almost a whisper. “Agent Porto told me he’d asked you to see her. He said you might understand what has happened to her.” She searched Savich’s face. “It is true, she is different, completely different. I hope you have some idea of why she’d changed. Agent Porto said you were very talented in, well, seeing past the obvious. At understanding people. The doctor didn’t seem to really grasp the situation yesterday. Come in and meet my daughter. She’s been in and out.” Lulie drew a deep breath. "Andrew and I told her he is her father. She'd never met him because neither he nor I wanted his wife and children to suffer from the situation, but now everything's changed. He came because she'd been hurt."

Congressman Mellon said, "Lulie is protecting me, and some of it will remain private, though I'm not sure for long. I was selfish, concerned about my father's threat to stop supporting my political career and afraid to let it be known I had a daughter out of wedlock, afraid of the effect on my wife and my family, too concerned my other children would be scarred from this relationship. But they're adults now, out on their own. They'll adjust. When Lulie called to tell me Gunny—Leigh—had been nearly killed on the street, all my excuses were no longer important." He paused, gave them a big smile. "My daughter's what's important now."

Lulie said, "Needless to say, finding out Andrew is her father came as quite a shock to her. But she took it all in, wanted to know everything."

He shook his head. "I only hope she'll come to forgive me, perhaps even someday to accept me." He laughed. "She didn't even know I was her congressman. Isn't that a kick in the ego?"

Lulie gave him a light tap on the arm. "She'll come to know you, Andrew, and she'll come to accept what happened. She has a good heart, trust me. It's time for you to meet her, Agent Savich, Agent Sherlock." Lulie pulled back the cubicle curtain.

Leigh was awake. Her head hurt, but not too badly anymore, the pain reliever they'd given her still swimming happily in her bloodstream. She was still sort of floating up near the ceiling from the medication, feeling utterly calm, a lovely feeling she knew wouldn't last. She opened her eyes to see her mom and her—father. Yes, that distinguished man was her father. She was thirty years old and she'd finally met the man who'd had an affair with her mother all those years ago. He'd come when she'd gotten hurt. That said something good about the man who always sent money but never brought himself into her life. He was tall—important for a politician—and handsome, but she hadn't seen any of herself in him. She didn't know what to think of him. Yet. She had so many questions, endless questions she wanted to ask both of them. They stood aside, and she watched a big man walk to her. He was several years older than she was, his complexion dark, maybe Mediterranean, his hair and eyes dark as well. He was tough-looking, a man, she knew intuitively, no one would mess with. He smiled down at her, a very nice white-toothed smile, and she felt a jolt. He wasn't only built, but he was also hot, and she assumed he knew it. Most good-looking guys she'd met in her adult years had known very well their effect on women and exploited it. She gave him a tentative smile in return, then looked beyond him to a tall, slender, very pretty woman about her own age. She looked like a princess, fine-boned, with beautiful curly red hair and fairy-tale blue eyes, wearing no-nonsense black slacks, a white blouse, a black jacket, and low-heeled boots on her feet. This woman wouldn't suffer fools gladly, any more than the man would. She, too, was smiling at Leigh.

She looked between them, then said matter-of-factly, "You're married, aren't you? Who are you?" Was that her voice, all insubstantial and paper thin?

50

Savich cocked his head at the young woman with her head swathed in a white bandage. Despite the pain meds he knew she was on, he still felt the pull of her. "My name's Agent Savich, she's Agent Sherlock. Yes, we're married. We have a little boy. He'll be five in September. It's the first thing out of his mouth whenever he meets someone new. And you're Ms. Leigh Saks. Agent Porto asked that we come here to speak with you." Savich took Leigh's hand between his. He again felt the pull of her. She was looking at him, searching his face, probing. This young woman was considered simple yesterday?

When the FBI agent took one of her hands in his, Leigh felt the warmth and, oddly, utterly safe. She looked up into his dark eyes and felt a different kind of jolt, a kind of recognition, a feeling of connection. "I saw you on TV Monday."

"You saw me talking about the belt buckle?"

She nodded. "I'm told that's why I was hit on the head."

"Could you tell me what happened?"

Leigh felt a flash of pain, but then it fell away. She saw a door trying to open in her mind, knew what was behind that door, but she wasn't ready to remember it, not yet. She gave her head a slight shake. "Did you meet my father? I just met him myself. I never knew him. Mom never talked about him. But now he's here, and he promised me we'd see each other from now on." She closed her eyes a moment, whispered, "Everything seems so very strange. I nearly died, and now I have a father."

Savich lightly squeezed her hand and felt something he rarely felt—a bond, vague and undefined, but still there. He said only, "Don't push, Leigh. I know you're not ready. There's no rush, all right?"

How could he know she wasn't ready? Leigh said, "Does your son look like you or like Agent Sherlock?"

Sherlock had taken a position on the other side of Leigh's bed. She said, her voice calm and easy, "He's a carbon copy of his father, which I've never thought was fair. I mean, I did all the work. You're very pretty, Ms. Saks. Our son would tell you that you look like a princess within a minute of meeting you."

"Me, pretty? A princess?" Leigh touched her fingers to the white bandage around her head. "Shall I consider this my crown, then?" She wasn't aware her mother was staring at her, mouth agape. As for the tall, aristocratic man looking at her, the man who was her father, he was smiling at her, and in that smile, she suddenly saw a flash of herself. But how could she smile back? She didn't know him any more than she knew these FBI agents.

So many questions were swimming around in her head, floating in and out, and an occasional jab of pain where the surgeon had cut into her head, and wasn't that a gruesome thought? "Mom said my dad came because he heard I was hurt. I wished all my life he'd come, but he never did until now. I thought he was ashamed of me. If so, I can't blame him. I mean, I was no Einstein, more on a level with Einstein's dog."

"No," Mellon said, "that wasn't it at all."

"Good, I'm very glad to hear it. Since you're a politician, I imagine you can explain why you never recognized me, but I'm hoping you won't feel the need. I don't want any more mysteries, any more uncertainties, any more half-truths. There are so many now I feel like I'm drowning. Isn't my mom beautiful, though? She's the best baker in Haggersville. Oh goodness, sorry for going on like that, even though it's true. The nurse said the medicine would make my brain squirrelly or maybe like a hamster who's fallen off his wheel."

"Your brain is functioning beautifully," Sherlock said. "It's tough recovering from surgery. I know. Now, you have some pain and you're tired, so please tell us to leave when you want to go to sleep, all right?"

Leigh gave a little nod. "So far, so good. Of course, you have questions for me, questions are everywhere, aren't they, bubbling around in my brain. But maybe I can answer yours."

Savich said, "Leigh, you said you saw me on TV Monday. Do you remember I asked anyone who could identify the Star of David belt buckle to call our hotline?"

"Yes, I remember, and I did call eventually. But that didn't end well, did it? I believe I managed to tell the man on the hotline it was Mr. Henry's belt buckle and it was a secret, but I don't know if it was of any real help. And help with what exactly, I'd like to know?"

"Let's stop there a moment," Sherlock said. "Please think back, Leigh. You were speaking on the hotline. Did you hear anything? A voice? Breathing? Did you smell anything, an aftershave, a cologne?"

Leigh shook her head. The door in her mind remained firmly closed. "I'm sorry, Agents, but all I can tell you for sure is that I was speaking and then I felt a horrible pain on my head, and I was gone. I woke up here to see Danny standing over me."

Savich said, "Not a problem. The agent on the hotline said you identified the belt buckle as belonging to Mr. Henry."

She nodded. "That's right. It's strange I'd be the one to see it and no one else. Why didn't he show it to other people, too?"

Lulie said, "We don't know why, Leigh, but you seem to be the only one who ever saw the Star of David belt buckle. Chief Christie said you were the only one who called in about it."

Leigh thought about this a moment. "How odd Mr. Henry never showed Mrs. Chamberlain his precious belt buckle, and here they were lovers for years. I guess because I was only a twenty-watt bulb, he thought it was safe to show me. But why would it be such a big mystery?"

Sherlock leaned close. "You're going to help us find out. Leigh, when did you first see the belt buckle?"

"I saw it only one time, not long before Mr. Henry died—well, he was brutally murdered, wasn't he?" She stopped when she heard her mother's indrawn breath. "Mom, of course I knew about it, no one talked about anything else for weeks. I wasn't a total moron. I listened and heard everything." She shook her head. "Poor Mr. Henry, it's hard to believe some monster would do that to him. My godfather—that's Chief Masters—he took a lot of grief when he couldn't find the murderer. He still feels guilty, bless him. Everyone seemed to like Mr. Henry so much, but obviously that wasn't the case. Someone wanted to make him suffer. What had he done? It must have been really bad." She paused, lightly touched her fingertips to the bandage again, and seemed to pump herself up, forcing herself to continue. "You wonder where I saw the belt buckle. That, I remember. I'd gone to his big house to take him a chocolate cake Mom had made for his birthday. His name was in cursive in thick red frosting all across the top. He'd given her another loan for new equipment for the bakery, and she wanted to thank him.

"Mrs. Boilou, his housekeeper, told me he was in his study, and she took me there. She said he'd be really pleased to get that cake, since he had a real sweet tooth. She said she'd bring plates and forks and he could enjoy it right away.

"Mr. Henry was seated at his big mahogany desk and he was polishing something. He looked up, and I saw he was startled at the sight of me. Then he smiled when I held out the cake for him to see. He smiled and laughed, told me he couldn't wait. Mrs. Boilou came in, and Mr. Henry cut us all pieces of cake. She left, and he and I ate ours together.

"When he finished, he tapped his stomach and sighed. Then he told me to come over to him. He showed me an odd-looking belt buckle. It shined gold, like it was from heaven. He told me I was the only one he'd shown it to, the only one who'd ever seen it before. He said it was unique. 'Just imagine, it's a Star of David.' He laughed, said he wasn't even Jewish, but it didn't matter, it was his pride and joy.

"He held it out to me, and I took it. It was heavy, and I asked him if it was pure gold. He said yes it was, and he polished it every single week, made it shine bright as the sun. He said it brought back wonderful memories, precious memories he'd cherish forever. He told me sometimes he would hold the belt buckle and remember how incredible he'd felt when he took it. It was his now, and it would always be his. Then he brought his face close to mine—I remember his breath smelled like sugar and Mama's cake—and he whispered the belt buckle was to be a secret between him and me and that meant I wasn't to tell anyone about it. Before I left, he made me promise again not to tell anybody about seeing it, even my mama. It was our secret, only ours. I never told a soul, until—"

"—until Chief Christie found the belt buckle at the bottom of Lake Massey along with dozens of bones," Sherlock said. "Your memory of all of that is incredible, Leigh."

Lulie said, "It was five years ago, Leigh. How could you remember everything in such detail?"

Leigh looked briefly baffled, then she smiled. "It surprised me, too, Mom. All I did was think about that afternoon, and it was crystal clear, the words he spoke, everything that happened, the expression on his face."

She looked up to see Agent Porto and Chief Christie come into the cubicle. It was a tight fit.

Sala said, "You're looking good, Leigh. Chief Christie and I were standing outside the cubicle. I hope you don't mind we were listening. Mr. Henry said he *took* the belt buckle. Do you know what he meant? Did he say who he took it from?"

Leigh said, "No, sorry, but I'm sure that's what he said. Do you think he might have stolen it?"

"We don't know yet," Ty said. "How do you feel?"

"Better than I did yesterday." She smiled at them both, then said to Ty, "You were looking for that poor woman's body, and you found this, too."

Ty nodded. "Indeed we did."

"You've met my father?"

Sala nodded. "We met Congressman Mellon last night."

"My mom says I might as well vote for him now. As far as she knows, he's one of the honest politicians on Capitol Hill."

Andrew laughed, amused by his daughter's insult. "Your mom's right, kiddo. I'm sure you can see my brain's working a mile a minute to come up with ways to seduce you into voting for me."

"Keep my mom happy and keep your promises. But then again, maybe what you said was spin, and that would make you a very good politician."

Lulie stared at the poised young woman, still trying to come to grips with the fact that she was Gunny.

"Thank you, Leigh. A deal like that is a good start."

Sala said, "Do you remember speaking to Mrs. Chamberlain?"

Leigh shook her head. "Poor Mrs. Chamberlain, she always

tried to be kind and patient, even when I see now she wanted me to go home and never darken her door again. When I told her about the belt buckle, she didn't believe me about seeing it, very understandable, of course, given who and what I was. Then I left."

Savich said, "Can you tell us what you did then, Leigh?"

"I remember walking, trying to decide who to tell or if I should tell anyone at all. I mean, Mr. Henry was long dead. Then I remembered the hotline and knew I had to call. I remember I turned into the alley next to Kim's Dry Cleaners. I had my cell phone in my hand, I called the hotline, then nothing. The door's still closed."

"How did you know the number?" Sherlock asked.

She shrugged. "I guess I must have memorized it. Sorry, I can't remember anything else, even now that I don't seem to be Gunny anymore."

Savich said, "What do you mean, you no longer seem to be Gunny?"

The air seemed to go out of the room. No one made a sound, all eyes were on Leigh.

51

Leigh looked surprised, then thoughtful. She said slowly, "Before, the world always surprised me. It seemed to keep changing. I thought I was beginning to understand something, and then I suddenly forgot what it was, forgot even what everyone was talking about. I tried, but somehow I couldn't seem to finish a lot of things, couldn't say what I really felt before things suddenly slipped away. It was like I was waking up again and again, and no one else had gone to sleep. I thought it was normal for me, normal for Gunny.

"I could never get things to fit together. What I was thinking would be gone before I could focus on it, make it mean anything. I had this sudden 'all gone' feeling and suddenly I was confused again." She shrugged again and smiled. "Now, I guess I'm like everyone else. I can think and talk and make sense like you do. I'm a different me now, but what's great is I'm here all the time now. Mom, don't be scared. I'm not crazy. Think of it this way—it's like I've rebooted my computer and now I've got lots more gigabytes."

Savich lightly laid his hand on her forearm, above the IV line. He felt warmth and strength, and awareness. Because she'd been struck on the head? Or because of something the surgeon did during surgery? He liked what she'd said: *I've rebooted*. She was staring at him, and he felt in that moment that she was looking into him, aware of his thoughts, his feelings. To his shock, she whispered, "You're very worried about something, aren't you, Agent Savich? It's like a black slick of grease over every thought you have." She squeezed his fingers.

Savich opened himself to her, but all he felt in return was a comforting warmth. He closed his hand over hers and slowly, he nodded. "Yes, you're right. I am very worried."

She said matter-of-factly, "You'll find the killer, Agent Savich. You'll find him for us."

"Thank you." Savich slowly rose. "If that door opens, Leigh, call me." He handed her a card, smiled down at her. "I like the reboot, but you know what? I would have liked you as Gunny, too."

"But not in the same way, Agent Savich, not at all in the same way. There's so much for me to learn now, to understand, to *see*." She looked over at her mother, then her father, and finally, she smiled at Ty and Sala. "All of you, thank you. I will try to remember something that can help identify who hit me so you can find Mr. Henry's murderer." She paused a moment. "You're all very kind." She closed her eyes, and they watched her breathing slow, watched her relax. Odd, but Savich knew the moment her mind eased into sleep. The power dimmed, grew quiescent.

Savich said quietly to the group, "Let's talk outside."

When they'd stepped beyond Officer Diaz's hearing, Lulie said, "She's herself, but she isn't. I don't know what to do." She shook her head, and a tear slipped out of her eye. Andrew pulled her against him. "Shall I bring in psychiatrists to examine her?"

Savich said, "No, no need to do that. Leigh seems fine. She's dealing with all the changes she described, all by herself. She doesn't need help. What she needs is time to integrate all the new facets of herself, to fully understand what it's like to be normal. All the important parts of her, her kindness, her love for you, her empathy, they all seem to be there. I have no idea how this happened, but the result is remarkable, a miracle, if you wish.

"You should ask the neurosurgeon if he's even seen anything like this or understands how or why this happened. But the fact is, it did happen. She'll find her way, come to terms with her new self and her new abilities. She'll be bringing a lot more awareness to bear on how she looks at people and the world. As I said, I know she will reintegrate herself in time into that new world."

Sherlock said, "Ms. Saks, you can believe Dillon. Leigh will do fine, I promise you."

"But how can you possibly know that? Neither of you is even a doctor."

A bit of hostility, a bit of snark. Savich gave Lulie a blazing smile and said without pause, "No, we're not, and you should certainly speak to them. But I think you'll find we're right about this."

Lulie spurted out a laugh and shook her head. "Agent Savich, I saw something happen between you and my daughter. You somehow connected with her. I'm not sure how, but you did."

Savich said, "Yes, I believe I did. Leigh's in a good place. Congressman Mellon, it's good to see you again. I'm very glad you came to your daughter."

Mellon said, "After Lulie called me, I told my wife about Leigh, told her I was coming to see her. Glynn already knew about Lulie and Leigh. She'd known for a long time but had never said anything to me or anyone else. She patted my hand, told me I was doing the right thing. Then she flat-out floored me. She said she and the boys would welcome Leigh if I brought her to meet them." He shook his head. "Now as for the politics of it, there's no good way to announce it, spin it, as my daughter said. Still, it's better I do it soon, rather than wait for the tabloids to do it."

Savich said, "I've always found it's best to be candid with the media, less chance for those with a political bias to twist your words."

Mellon gave a crooked grin. "There is always political bias, Agent Savich, now more than ever. I've never met anyone in Washington who doesn't have an agenda, but maybe, in this case, you might be right. It's probably the best alternative."

"You've already seen one miracle today, Congressman, namely Leigh. Maybe you'll find yourself another."

"Maybe so." He shook Savich's hand and turned to Lulie.

Lulie said, "I'm thinking your wife may not mind having me around after she tries one of my éclairs, Andrew."

He regarded the woman he'd loved so madly thirty-one years

before, remembered how he'd always enjoyed her wit. "Now, that's a good possibility. I'll take her a box."

Savich said, "The door is still closed on Leigh's memories of what happened immediately before she was hit on the head. I'd like to bring in Dr. Emanuel Hicks tomorrow morning. He's an FBI psychiatrist and a renowned hypnotist. If she did see or hear anything, it's possible she'll remember it under hypnosis."

Lulie looked at Andrew, then slowly nodded. "I'll speak to her about it when she wakes up. I can't imagine she wouldn't want to try, Agent Savich."

Ty looked down at her Timex. "Sala and I need to go speak to Leigh's former employer, Susan Sparrow, at the Sparrow Crematorium, see what she has to say."

"We'll go with—" Savich was interrupted by Neil Diamond belting out "Sweet Caroline."

"Savich."

Sherlock watched his face light up like a Christmas tree. "Thank you for calling me so quickly, Chief. We'll be there as soon as we can." He punched off and slipped his cell back into his jacket pocket. He wanted to pump his fist, but instead, he said, "Ty, Sala, Sherlock and I have to go."

"Tell me it's about Victor Nesser," Sala said.

"It is indeed."

52

WINSLOW, VIRGINIA
WEDNESDAY

Savich pulled the Volvo smoothly against the curb in front of the Winslow police station, set between a fire department and a big parking lot. He checked his Mickey Mouse watch. "Under two hours from Haggersville, excellent time."

She patted his arm. "You did well. Buck up, you'll have the Porsche back in a couple of days."

"Can't be too soon."

"Suck it up."

Together, they looked up and down the main street. Winslow was small, a dot on a map, High Milsom Street and three or four streets of set-back middle-class homes, most of the yards a lush Irish green from all the rain. It was hot, the humidity a killer, like a heavy wet cloud sitting on their heads.

They walked into a long, narrow room, cold as a refrigerator, and shuddered with pleasure. An older man in a dark green uniform looked up from his desk behind a high counter directly opposite the front door. "Can I help you? Oh, you must be the FBI agents Chief Pearly called. I'm senior deputy Hubie Pearly, the chief's cousin. One of my boys, Dom, works here, too. He's smart. He'll move right up, and I reckon someday we'll have another Chief Pearly. Right this way, Agents. The current Chief Pearly's in the back with our young victim. Poor kid, on top of everything else, she's got crappy parents. That sounds harsh, I know, but it is what it is."

They followed Hubie Pearly past four empty desks, a unisex bathroom, a water cooler, and a small kitchen to a glass-walled office. Inside they saw a portly man in a brown uniform sitting opposite a young woman whose pretty face was leached of color, her eyes red from crying. She was wearing what was probably the chief's leather jacket over a top and shorts, flip-flops on her narrow feet, her toenails painted a bright orange. The chief was holding her hands, speaking low to her.

Hubie tapped on the window and opened the door. "Anson, the FBI agents are here. Fancy that, one of them's a girl." Hubie stopped cold, looked back at Sherlock, and stared. "Oh geez, sorry, ma'am—Agent—I shouldn't have said that."

"Probably not," Savich said. "My wife, actually. Chief Pearly?" He identified himself and Sherlock, handed the chief their creds. Chief Pearly studied them. To their surprise, he handed their creds to Hubie, who studied them a full thirty seconds before he handed them back to Savich. "Yep, now I remember—your name, Sherlock. Imagine, here you are, in the flesh. You sure are pretty to be so tough. You're famous among law enforcement around here, you know."

No, Sherlock didn't now, but she nodded.

"Well now, 'scuse me. I'll leave you to it, Anson." And Hubie was out the door.

Anson Pearly slowly rose to his feet, assessing them with clear, intelligent gray eyes. "Forgive my cousin, he sometimes runs off the rails a bit." They all shook hands. He turned. "This is Ms. Cindy Wilcox. She might not be the heroine of JFK, but she is the heroine of Winslow today, saved herself from that maniac who blew up the cathedral in Falls Church. When she described the man who attacked her, told me he called himself Victor, I remembered the BOLOs, showed her his picture. She said it was definitely Victor Nesser, knew it even if he was wearing a disguise."

Sherlock looked at the teenager huddled in a chair, her blond hair tangled around a pretty face. She was staring at them. "Ms. Wilcox?"

Cindy stared up at Sherlock. "Yes, I'm Cindy."

Sherlock gave her a big smile and patted her arm. "You must be very resourceful and smart to escape Victor Nesser. I agree with the chief, you're a hero." Sherlock drew her up out of the chair and hugged her. "You're alive, and I've got to say that makes me very happy. I know you're still shaky with the shock of what you went through. Victor Nesser is a very scary man, but you survived, Cindy. You beat him. You're here and you're safe and you can talk to us. Can you tell us about him, tell us what happened?"

Cindy shuddered and hung on to Sherlock. "My mom and dad were here. She yelled at me, said it was my fault for inviting a stranger to my apartment. We argued, and they stalked out. My older brother, Hank, he's an army sergeant in Afghanistan. I know he would have come and hugged me like you're doing. Even if he'd agreed with my folks, he would have stayed with me." She hugged Sherlock tighter and started crying. She wheezed out, "It was my fault, really. I did flirt with him. He—Victor—was nice and polite, and I thought maybe he'd give me some of that huge bankroll he had. But then the second he got to my apartment, he turned into a monster." Cindy put her face against Sherlock's hair, tightened her arms around her, and wouldn't let go.

Sherlock rocked her, whispered against her tangled hair. "You're all right, Cindy. You survived and learned not to trust someone you don't know well." She eased her back to look at her face. "No matter what anyone says, you saved yourself from a very bad man. You did it, no one else. Now it's time for you to get ahold of yourself and tell us exactly what happened so we can catch him, make sure he never tries this again."

A lone tear streaked down Cindy's pale cheek. Slowly, she nodded. "Yes, yes, I can do that."

Sherlock said, "You said the photo the chief showed you was Victor, but he looked different. How?"

"His hair was dark brown, on the long side, and he had glasses, with black frames that made him look smart, you know? And he had this pathetic beard. He was so nice to me, so cute—he left a hundred-dollar bill, and his dinner was only twenty dollars. I saw him pull it out of a big rubber-banded roll of hundred-dollar bills. But it wasn't all about the money—well, some of it wasn't. I liked him, I really did. He was sweet and very respectful. And then he changed, so fast. He wanted to kill me."

53

"I'm going to record this, Cindy, is that all right?"

Cindy had already described everything to Chief Pearly, answered his questions over and over. Now she realized why Chief Pearly had made her repeat things. He'd done it on purpose, to help her remember all the details. She could tell it all easily now, in logical order, thanks to him. She described how Victor had followed her to her apartment in a mud-brown Chrysler, described exactly where she'd been standing in her apartment when he'd come at her.

Sherlock said, "That first time you kicked him, you said you meant to kick him in the crotch, but you got him in the belly. He screamed at you that you'd kicked his staples?"

"Yes. But what staples? Had he just had surgery? He didn't

act like he'd been in pain at all, not until I kicked him. He bowed in on himself, and I could tell I'd really hurt him. He screamed at me, but it was strange. His voice was high-pitched, and he sounded crazy mad."

Sherlock felt the saliva dry in her mouth. She looked over at Dillon. He didn't look surprised.

Chief Pearly said, "Cindy, are you sure you heard him say 'staples'?"

Cindy nodded. "We talked about this, Chief. It had to be surgical staples. I mean, what other kind could there be? Then he came at me again, and again, and I finally managed to kick him in the crotch. That sent him to his knees, howling. I ran to the front door, but it was really humid and the door stuck. He was screaming at me in that mad, crazy voice again. I looked back, saw he had a gun. I knew I couldn't get the gun away from him." Her voice hitched. "I kept pulling on the door, and it opened just as he fired. I swear I felt the heat of the bullet as it went past my head, and see? On my neck? The Band-Aid? When the bullet slammed into the door, splinters came flying out. I ran and ran all the way to Chief Pearly's house on Gleason Road. He went back to my apartment, but Victor was gone."

Chief Pearly said, "Cindy, you said he was driving a mud-brown Chrysler."

She nodded. "Like I told you, Chief, it didn't occur to me to look at the license plate number. I'm sorry."

"Yes, but you remember the plate was white, which means the car's registered in Virginia. Agent Savich, you said you think it could be headed to Fort Pessel, Virginia?" Chief Pearly pinned Savich with a look. "How do you know he's headed to Fort Pessel?"

"It was a home of sorts to him for a while, but basically, it's my gut talking."

Savich knew Victor might already have been to the Smiley house and dug up the bank robbery money as soon as he'd escaped. He had shown off a thick roll of hundred-dollar bills to Cindy last night. Then why would he go back? If he already had all that money, not just a roll but a suitcase full, why was he still here? There had to be a reason, besides revenge. Savich already had agents camped out at the Smiley house in Fort Pessel, watching for any sign of Victor.

He studied Cindy's pale, very pretty face. "Cindy, I'd like you to tell me as best you can exactly what Victor was like when he attacked you and you kicked him in the stomach."

"It was sort of like that old movie about that weird guy who was two people—*Dr. Jekyll and Mr. Hyde.*" She shrugged. "That sounds crazy, but really, all of a sudden, he looked like he wanted to rip off my face. I remember his eyes, they were darker, slitted, and mean, really mean. The change in him, it was scary, terrifying." She swallowed. "Do you believe me?"

Savich said, "Yes, I believe you."

Sherlock said, "So you were hoping this cute guy with his wad of bills could be your ticket out of Winslow?"

Cindy's eyes fell to her flip-flops. "Well, yes, I guess."

Sherlock looked at the girl who'd survived Victor Nesser. "How old are you, Cindy?"

Her eyes went to Sherlock's face. "Twenty. On August twenty-ninth. I'm a Virgo."

"Virgos with guts are really good at applying themselves, Cindy. Sounds like you could make a top-notch Virgo."

"How?"

"First thing, figure out what interests you. If you don't know, go online and look at some of the curriculums of the state schools in this area. You could take some required classes this fall. It would help you figure out what you want to do."

Cindy looked at her in amazement. "You want me to go to college? Some dumb state school? My folks would laugh at me, tell me I'm wasting my time. My friends would laugh at me for trying to be a geek, and worse. As for my sister, she'd tell me to marry Jimmy Folks and have babies." Cindy actually shuddered.

"Would your brother Hank laugh?"

Cindy didn't even pause. "No, I guess Hank would tell me to get off my butt and go for it."

Sherlock hugged her. "There you go. Maybe it's time for you to be more open to things, to make a change. Skype Hank, see what he has to say. The important thing is not to waste this wonderful life you've been given, not to sell yourself short. Look at what you already did—you saved yourself from a very scary man."

Cindy stared at Sherlock, then she laughed. "I'm not about to sell myself short, not anymore. And I'm not about to waste my time sitting on my hands in some dorky classroom with other kids who don't give a crap about the history of the world. No thank you. I have better things to do."

“What sorts of things, Cindy?”

“Well, before last night, before that crazy man Victor, I couldn’t make up my mind. I realize now I was too scared to take a chance, but it’s like you said, Agent Sherlock, I’m a hero. I saved myself. No more doubts, no more being scared. I’m not going to put up with all these local hicks shouting at me all the time. ‘Cindy? Get me catsup.’ ‘Sweet cheeks, get me another beer.’ ‘Hey, cutie, wanna go out with me?’ ” She shuddered. “No more. I can do better than that. From today on, I’m going to be Tennessee. Yeah, Tennessee Wilcox—that name has guts, not a name to mess with, not like Cindy. The creeps can get their own catsup. And I’m going to save my money and go back to Las Vegas.” She beamed at Sherlock, hugged her again, and gave the chief back his jacket.

Back in the Volvo, Savich turned on the air-conditioning, leaned over to pat Sherlock’s arm, kissed her, and cupped her face in his palm. “Good try, sweetheart. Tennessee has a real ring to it. Perfect for Las Vegas, don’t you think?”

54

SPARROW CREMATORIUM
HAGGERSVILLE, MARYLAND
WEDNESDAY

The Sparrow Crematorium was a modern two-story white stucco building with beautifully kept grounds, standing in the middle of a small park of pine and maple. Cars were tucked discreetly to the side with a dozen or so sitting under the blazing sun, most with sunscreens across the windshields. There was no hint of smoke or cinder in the air, maybe because they cremated at night. Like most people, Ty knew they burned bodies in an oven, then scooped up the ashes and put them in an urn of the family's choosing. And like most people, she didn't want any more particulars.

Sala and Ty walked a long flagstone path toward the main

entrance set beneath two white Doric columns. No one seemed to be about.

"I've never been to a crematorium before," Ty whispered. "All that white, it looks so clean, so—sanitary."

"I guess that would relieve my mind if I planned to cremate one of my family, and that's the point. Ty, pull up, I want to talk a minute. Let's catch some shade under that oak tree." The shade felt good, relieved the nearly skin-searing heat a bit. Sala said, "Here's the thing about Mr. Henry LaRoque being cremated here: I can't help but remember that crematorium in Noble, Georgia, the Tri-State Crematory. They weren't burning bodies like they were supposed to, they were throwing them out like refuse on their property. I remember people even reported seeing bodies next to the building, but the local sheriff kept claiming everything was fine.

"It's a textbook case, right? Lots of papers written about it, FBI profilers chewed it over, and yet I still don't understand why they did it. Why didn't the owners simply cremate the bodies like they were paid to do? Running the ovens costs that much? If so, why didn't they simply pass the cost along? If it was only about greed, then why not at least bury the bodies deep? No one would have ever known what they did. It was rank stupidity—imagine dumping dead bodies like so much trash close to their facility. Didn't the owners think people would notice? Didn't they consider they'd be reported?"

He paused, looked out over the peaceful lawn. "And now we find a whole lot of bones in Lake Massey. And the belt buckle in among all those bones. And we are at another crematorium."

Ty said, "I remember the owner, Ray Brent, served twelve years in prison. And of course many families sued in civil courts. But it's not enough for what he did—for years. I remember thinking he should have gotten life imprisonment."

Sala said, "There's flat-out crazy, like Victor Nesser, and then there's evil, people who are so perverted there don't seem to be any limits, like Brent."

Ty said, "Sala, I get it. We'll find out if the Sparrows dumped those bodies in Lake Massey. Doesn't exactly look like that kind of place, though, does it?"

"Neither did the Tri-State Crematory in Georgia." He studied her face, summer tanned, her intelligent green eyes with absurdly long lashes, her curly dark brown hair blowing around her face, her stubborn chin and the line of freckles marching across her nose. Sala realized he admired her. More than that, he was grateful to her. "It's all about helping the victims for you, isn't it? Most recently me." He squeezed her arm. "Thank you, Ty."

Ty lightly touched her fingertips to his hand. "And thank you for being here with me. Now, let's go have a talk with the Sparrows. I saw you on your iPad on the way over here. Did you find anything interesting?"

They looked up when an older couple walked past them, their heads close together, in quiet conversation. He waited until they were out of hearing. "I looked up the Sparrow Crematorium, established by the current owners' grandparents in the mid-sixties. The parents, Elaine and Jonah Sparrow, were both killed in an auto accident five years ago, clearing the way for the current owners, their children, Landry and Eric. Landry, the older son, is forty-four years old, and he's married to Susan. She's thirty, married Landry nearly six years ago. A pretty big age difference between them."

"So Susan married Landry Sparrow before the parents died in the auto accident."

"Yes. Their car ran off a bridge into the Kersey River about thirty miles east of here during a bad snowstorm. It was ruled an accident. What a suspicious mind you have, Chief Christie."

"No, not really. So now the younger generation is running things." Ty waved her hand around her. "This place looks up-to-date, modern, well maintained. It's in a beautiful setting. It looks prosperous, like they're doing well financially."

"And not all that far away from Lake Massey."

"Sala, to be honest here, a Serial makes the most sense to me, not another rogue crematorium dumping bodies they were supposed to burn in the oven."

"Easy enough to determine," Sala said. "We can have some of the urn ashes they returned examined, verify they're human."

Ty frowned at him. "I never thought of that."

He grinned at her, chucked her chin. "Well, I'm FBI, and you're only a lowly police chief."

They were both smiling when they opened the wide white double doors and walked into the foyer of the Sparrow Crematorium to be hit in the face with cold air. It was wonderful.

"Nice place," Sala said. The white walls were wainscoted with dark wood, making a beautiful contrast. There were flowers on a single table, a mirror behind it. It was like a lovely home, except that at the end of the foyer was an obvious reception area. An older woman with beautiful gold hair streaked with thick hanks of white sat behind a mahogany desk, watching them approach. The area was softly lit, soothing, Ty supposed, for the mourning families, reassuring them they were in the right place, doing the right thing.

It was very quiet, the older couple who'd passed them outside nowhere to be seen. Where were the owners of all those cars in the parking lot? Perhaps at a viewing? Simply standing here in this building made Ty uncomfortable. Was it because of a human's natural fear of death and being forced to face it? Was being burned in an oven better than being buried under six feet of black earth? The dead person wasn't there to care. It was so quiet, she noticed her own boots clacking across the rich dark oak floor.

The woman gave them a full, warm, very sympathetic smile. "How may I help you?"

Sala pulled out his creds and handed them to her. She studied them a moment, then looked at Ty's ID. "I've been expecting you. Mrs. Chamberlain at the post office called to tell me you'd be coming to speak to Susan because of Gunny. Oh yes, forgive me, I'm Ms. Betty Chugger. Ever since Mr. Chugger ate himself into a heart attack and keeled over while he was fishing in his boat, eating a hot dog, I decided I wanted to be called Ms., not Mrs. I guess that makes me all modern now. I hope you're not here to tell me Gunny's dead?

Ty said, "No, she'll be fine, but she isn't called Gunny anymore. It's Leigh, Leigh Saks."

"Leigh? Why Leigh? Why did Lulie change her name?"

Sala said, "Leigh herself changed back to her birth name, told her mother she was no longer Gunny, she was Leigh. That's her real name, Leigh Ann Saks."

"Fancy that," Ms. Chugger said, shaking her head. A beam of sunlight from the skylight overhead speared down on her hair, making it look like spun gold. "After a blow to the head, it's a wonder she even remembered her real name. Well, strange things happen all the time, don't they?"

"Indeed they do," Ty said. "Did you personally work with Leigh, Ms. Chugger?"

"I hate to say anything about a person who could die—"

"We told you, ma'am, Leigh is going to be fine," Sala said. "Were you working here when Leigh was?"

"Oh yes. Gunny—Leigh—worked here about a year before she left to go to work at the post office. You ask me, that was a favor to Lulie, hiring poor little Gunny—Leigh. Sorry, she wasn't Leigh then, she was Gunny, but all right, I can call her Taylor Swift if she wants. I remember you had to explain everything to her slowly, usually twice, but when she learned, she did simple tasks well. She's a lovely girl, beautiful like her mother, Lulie—silly name, but Lulie's such a superb baker, no one cares." Ms. Chugger shook her head. "It's a pity, but Leigh was born simple, or the idiot doctor who pulled her out of Lulie must have ruined her brain, whatever. Poor child.

"I remember Lulie called Susan to tell her Gunny admitted she couldn't stand working here any longer, too many nightmares about seeing people on that conveyor belt headed into the oven." She looked put out. "There's nothing depressing or scary about it, I assure you. Everything is done with great respect. Landry oversees that part of our services. He always says a prayer for the deceased. Besides, if Gunny—Leigh—ever saw anything, she wasn't where she was supposed to be."

"Thank you, Ms. Chugger," Ty said. "We'd like to see Susan Sparrow now."

Ms. Chugger nodded over her left shoulder. "She's in the second office to your right. Both the boys are with her."

"Boys?"

"I mean both Landry and Eric Sparrow are with her. I'm old enough to be their mother, so yes, they're still boys to me."

Ty said under her breath as they walked down the wide hallway, past former Sparrows' portraits on the walls, all the way back to the mid-sixties, "Didn't you say Landry was forty-four?"

"I guess if you live in a small town, you stay young until all the older folks die off. Then you graduate to being an adult."

Ty paused a moment to look at the painting of a handsome middle-aged man and woman identified by a gold plaque as Elaine and Jonah Sparrow, who'd died in the car accident and were the parents of the current Sparrows.

"They were fine people," a woman said from an open doorway down the hall. "I'm Susan Sparrow, do come on back."

55

Susan Sparrow was a looker, no doubt about that. Her hair was black as a raven's wing, her eyes brown, her skin a lovely white, and a figure to stop a Mack truck. "Betty buzzed me," she said. "Do come in, Agent Porto, Chief Christie. My husband and brother-in-law are here, as I'm sure Ms. Chugger told you."

Ms. Chugger's boys, Ty supposed when two men slowly rose to face them. Susan Sparrow said, "Let me introduce you to my husband, Landry Sparrow, and Eric Sparrow, my brother-in-law. And as I already told you, I'm Susan."

They shook hands, passed their creds to the three Sparrows. Susan said, "Do sit down and tell us what we can do for you. First, though, how is Gunny?" Susan Sparrow waved them to a lovely gray sofa with a coffee table and three chairs facing it. On the coffee table Ty saw a pile of magazines—the top one *Funeral Business Advisor,* which sure sounded better, she thought, than, say, *Crematorium Weekly*.

Ty sat down and sank into the soft gray leather. "She's going to be fine. I must tell you, she announced she's changed her name back to Leigh now, her birth name."

Landry Sparrow sat forward in his chair, and said in a clear tenor voice, "Why would she do that? That doesn't sound like the Gunny we all know." Ty looked closely at the good-looking man dressed in a gray pinstriped suit and black tie. He was fit, his hair a dark brown with touches of gray at his temples. On the Wowza scale, she put him at an eight.

Susan said, "It sounds more adult, I guess."

Landry shrugged. "Whatever she wants to call herself now, we're all pleased to hear she's awake. It was a terrible thing, someone hitting her on the head. Do you know who it was?"

"Not yet," Sala said. "Ms. Chugger tells us you oversee your deceased clients in the crematorium oven, Mr. Sparrow? Could you describe the procedure?"

Susan said quickly, "We have a variety of procedures, rituals, actually, and they vary depending on the client. More than one person is required to see the operations are carried out professionally and with respect. We all take part."

"A pity our clients don't know how well we're taking care of their corporeal selves." Eric Sparrow grinned and poured himself a cup of coffee from the antique silver pot on the table. He held up the pot, but there were no takers.

Landry said, "Our clients are actually the families of the deceased. Only they can truly appreciate how well we take care of their loved one's corporeal remains."

Eric toasted his coffee cup at his brother, still grinning. Unlike Landry, Eric looked like the proverbial bad boy, tough and good-looking—well, tough and a little dangerous-looking, and Ty wondered how efficient he'd be in a bar fight. He wore a slouchy black Hugo Boss jacket over a tight black T-shirt that showed off his muscular chest. Ty knew Hugo Boss, her older brother was an acolyte. Eric had beard scruff on his face and wore his dark hair on the long side. He had a blade of a nose, obviously never broken. His eyes were as dark as his brother's, his hair nearly the same dark brown. He was too young to have distinguishing gray at his temples. He lounged back in his chair, the coffee cup in his hand, and gave Ty the once-over. He was very thorough. Then he saluted her with his cup. "You're really a police chief?"

Ty was tempted to crack her knuckles, but didn't. She cocked her head at him. "Why do you ask, Mr. Sparrow?"

"Well, you're very pretty, for one thing, not at all like Chief Masters, with big feet and hair on his knuckles. Now that's a man I don't like to mess with. He beat the crap out of me years ago, and I haven't forgotten. I deserved it, of course, and he didn't pull any of his punches. But you, Chief Christie? I'd like to mix it up with you."

"Whatever it is you mean by that, Mr. Sparrow, it's a good bet I'd break your jaw," Ty said, and gave him a smile, with teeth.

Eric Sparrow's dark eyes shined. Before she could belt him or maybe laugh, Landry said, "Now, you were asking about how we care for the remains of the deceased during their cremation? It's very straightforward. A final, more economical coffin rolls on the conveyor belt into the oven. It is very clean, very efficient. I understand that was the reason Leigh Saks quit, she accidentally saw a cremation, something she was not meant to see." He paused a moment, frowned. "I guess it hits too close to home for some people, if you know what I mean, particularly for someone like Gunny—Leigh. It is not one of my favorite activities here at the crematorium."

Sala said, "As in you can imagine yourself inside the coffin heading into the oven?"

"That's right. Some people can't help it."

Eric said, "I usually try to think the deceased deserves it, but you can't count on that always working."

"Eric, stop it." Susan tried to wipe the smile off her face, but couldn't. She cleared her throat. "Agent Porto, Chief Christie, we are very pleased Leigh is recovering. Since you're not asking us about her time here, I imagine your being here has to do with your finding that Star of David belt buckle with the bones at the bottom of Lake Massey." She paused and looked down at her hands, so tightly clasped in her lap her knuckles were white. "It's all over town now that the buckle belonged to Mr. Henry LaRoque, and that brings up concerns."

Before she could say anything else, Landry said in a clipped, hard voice, "My parents put up with enough sneers and snide comments when the story about that unspeakable crematory in Georgia broke some years ago, but it's outrageous if you seriously think something like that could happen again. Here. We're the ones who cremated Mr. Henry, and then you find those bones and Mr. Henry's belt buckle. So that must mean we don't really cremate our clients' deceased loved ones, but instead, we haul them off to Lake Massey and dump them?" He paused a beat, then his voice sharpened, became impassioned. "We respect our calling, as did our parents and our grandparents. We respect what it means to put your faith in someone who will take appropriate care of a person you loved who has died. We always fulfill our contractual and sacred duties, always. We are not insane, Agent, Chief, nor are we stupid, which I've always believed is exactly what those people in Georgia were."

"Well said, bro," Eric said, still lounging in the chair like a lizard sunning himself. "Throw in evil, and I'd agree one hundred percent. Even if it was an enemy who died, I wouldn't chuck his carcass into a lake, though I might sit back and enjoy burning his worthless ass. It should be obvious to you we run a reputable business here. What else do you want to know?"

Ty said, "Mr. LaRoque's wake was held here, is that right? The night before his memorial service and his cremation?"

"Yes, that's right," Susan said. "Everything was beautifully done. Lulie provided all the edibles for the large group who came to pay their respects and share stories of how he'd touched their lives."

Ty asked, "Did you see his body?"

Eric shook his head. "His coffin was kept closed after he was delivered here by Chief Masters, at his son's request. Calhoun even arranged for the medical examiner to wrap him tightly in a shroud, a service we normally provide ourselves. There was no reason for anyone, including us, to unwrap him, so for his memorial we simply moved him into a better coffin, a very fancy one that Calhoun insisted on renting—not buying—and closed the lid for the memorial service. Afterward we cremated him immediately because, as you know, there was no preservation."

Susan said, "All we can be sure about is that Mr. Henry was not cremated wearing that belt buckle, only the shroud. It wasn't present in the ashes. We have no more idea than you how the belt buckle got into Lake Massey. I would have thought Leigh was mistaken about seeing it, but then someone attacked her, leaving no doubt at all." She leaned forward, her eyes never leaving their faces. "There is no reason to believe we were involved in any of this."

Landry said, "How did Leigh see the belt buckle?"

Ty couldn't think of a single reason not to tell them all of it, and she did.

Susan was blinking rapidly when she finished. "Gun—Leigh remembered this so clearly? She actually said she saw him polishing the belt buckle? The Star of David belt buckle? But how is that possible? I mean, Gunny—Leigh—was always sweet and kind, and she tried so hard. But it took her time to even get her thoughts in order. For her to recount what happened five years ago? In such detail?"

56

Ty said, "Unlike you, we didn't know Leigh before she woke up from surgery. We know she was thought of as simple before she was struck down, but when she came out of anesthesia, she was able to tell her story quite clearly. You'll be more than a little surprised at how well she's recovering."

Landry raised a patrician eyebrow but said nothing.

Susan Sparrow fiddled with the pearls around her neck, a single beautifully matched strand. "I've known Leigh for as long as I've lived in Haggersville, and she was always the same, sweet and very pretty, but you had to be patient."

Eric said, "What I want to know is exactly what she might have said about the belt buckle to freak out the person who killed Mr. Henry enough to try to stop her?"

Ty said, "As I said, all she recounted was that Mr. Henry told her the belt buckle was unique, that when he polished it, it gave him wonderful memories of an earlier event in his life, one he cherished and loved to revisit. There's probably a lot more to that story. He swore her to secrecy before she left. She wasn't to tell anyone, even her mother."

Landry said, "But why would Mr. Henry want the belt buckle to be kept secret? Did he steal it from some museum?"

"We don't know," Sala said. "Not yet."

There was a moment of silence, then Eric said, "Do you know what I remember most about Mr. Henry? Everyone loved him. I've got to say I don't like many folk here in Haggersville, but I liked him, too. I still miss the old dude, actually. And the brutal way he died, that flipped everyone out, including me. Someone had a real hard-on for him. It seemed impossible to me anyone hated him that much."

"But someone did," Landry said.

Ty said, "We're hoping she'll remember more under hypnosis." She found herself watching each of them carefully as she spoke, but saw nothing more than simple interest.

Sala said, "Mrs. Sparrow, unlike your husband and brother-in-law, you're not from Haggersville. When did you move here?"

Susan said, "It's been what? About six years, Landry?"

He nodded, smiling at her. "I met you the first time right after you arrived. Remember, at Mario's Pizza?"

Eric said, "Bro, I heard you were at Mario's with Corey Jameson that night."

"Shut up, Eric, that's old news." Landry turned to Ty and Sala.

"It took me fifty-seven days to convince her to marry me. She was a hard sell, especially since every other single man in Haggersville was after her."

Eric laughed. "You were lucky I was out of the country or I would have convinced her you were all wrong for her."

"Boys, be quiet, both of you." Susan's voice was amused.

Ty said, "Let's get back on track here. You've already considered the possibility people will wonder where all the bones at the bottom of Lake Massey came from."

Landry said, "We're expecting the usual gossip, but no one would seriously think those bones came from here. What makes the most sense to me is a serial killer has been operating in our area over many years, dumping his murdered victims into Lake Massey."

Sala said, "The only glitch in the serial killer theory is finding Mr. Henry's Star of David belt with the bones. Our FBI forensic anthropologist has started DNA testing them. Unfortunately it's impossible to determine which bones were found closest to the belt buckle, and not far from the dock of Gatewood. We'll ask Calhoun LaRoque for a sample of his DNA, since he and his father would share the same Y chromosome. Perhaps we'll get lucky."

Eric said, "Let me say it's impossible his bones will be found. Calhoun LaRoque scattered his father's ashes at sea."

Landry was frowning. "I suppose it's possible the medical examiner sent us the wrong body. Again, none of us unwrapped him to verify."

Sala said, "We'll question the medical examiner, find out what their procedures were five years ago. It's a long shot, though."

Susan looked at them helplessly, splayed her hands. "What else can we tell you? I assure you we did nothing wrong." She stood, and suddenly Susan Sparrow looked like a general. "Now, I want to speak to Leigh Saks. I have known her for a very long time—well, I've known Gunny for a very long time. She has no reason to distrust me. Perhaps she'll tell me something she was hesitant to tell you or something she didn't consider important or simply forgot. It was five years ago. Perhaps I can help us clean up this mess as quickly as possible."

All of them rose. Sala said, "Leigh is under guard now. If you wish to see her, Mrs. Sparrow, we'll follow you. Will either of you gentlemen be coming?"

Landry shared a look with his brother. "I have some business I must see to." He walked to his wife, smoothed her eyebrows with his thumbs. "We're in no way to blame, sweetheart, don't ever forget that."

"I know. But I want this unpleasantness over and done with, Landry. I will not let this family be hurt."

"There's my girl." Landry said to Ty and Sala, "In case you haven't noticed, Susan's a tiger."

Eric said, "Since I already dealt with the Baddeckers about their deceased granddad, the service is set, and there's nothing more to do, I'll drive Susan to the hospital. Besides, I'd like to see Leigh myself. I'm thinking she sounds like a new, improved version, like someone I might ask out on a date. She's your age, isn't she, Susan? Maybe she'd appreciate a younger guy like me rather than a forty-plus old man like my bro here."

Landry smiled at his brother and gave him the finger.

57

HAGGERSVILLE COUNTY HOSPITAL
WEDNESDAY AFTERNOON

Lulie Saks sat with Andrew Mellon and Dr. Ellis in the family conference room. "Thank you for hearing us out, Dr. Ellis," she said. "We know Leigh is doing very well and we're grateful for it, but yesterday you didn't seem to fully understand how much she's changed for the better. It frankly seems miraculous. Now that I've told you more about her and you've spent more time with her, can you tell us whether this will continue? And how it's possible?" She swallowed. "Will she go back to being like she was?"

Dr. Ellis said, "No, don't worry. Leigh will remain the way she is now. I'm sorry if I seemed to dismiss your question yesterday. Leigh was new to me, and so were you. I have to say, she seems quite bright, quite alert, not nearly as you describe her before her head trauma. I've discussed this apparent change with our neurologists and can think of only one plausible explanation. She might have been suffering from some form of partial seizure disorder until now. There are subclinical forms that can be hard to recognize, that even her local medical doctors justifiably could have missed."

Lulie looked like she'd been shot. She clutched Andrew's hand, squeezed so tightly her knuckles turned white. "You mean Gunny—Leigh—was having seizures of some kind all these years, and I, her mother, didn't realize it? Didn't see it? I accepted she was simple—poor sweet child—and I did nothing when I clearly should have? And her doctors missed it?" Lulie's voice climbed an octave. "I could have helped her? A simple medicine could have helped her?"

Dr. Ellis lightly laid his hand over Lulie's. "You are in no way to blame, Ms. Saks. There was no way you could even tell she was having a seizure. Neither could her doctor. You gave her a fine home, you loved her, helped her."

"But I don't understand. How could this happen?"

Dr. Ellis said, "We believe some combination of her recent brain trauma, then the surgery and the anti-seizure medication phenytoin, surgeons routinely give after neurosurgery might have stopped them for now. The focus causing the seizures might no longer be active, or at least be isolated. I can't be more definitive, there's simply no way I can be certain, but again, this is our best explanation. Our neurologists have recommended the very best medication.

"I know it seems like a miracle to you, Ms. Saks, and maybe it is. The brain is an extraordinary organ, and we aren't close to knowing and understanding everything about it, it can behave in mysterious ways. It's sort of like a supercomputer, very complex, its workings very intricate. As to Leigh's leap from slow to extremely bright, part of that is most probably your simple shock at seeing the change in her—the focus, the understanding, the ability to speak fluently with no hesitation."

Andrew said thoughtfully, "It seems like a veil has been lifted, and we're now seeing the true person."

"Exactly. Also, we believe it's possible all these years she absorbed information, knowledge, if you will, from other people, from books, television, movies, who knows, but she couldn't express it with the seizures holding her back. Eidetic memory? Probably not, but an excellent memory nonetheless, excellent retention. Again, there isn't a scientific precedent for this kind of change, and these are our best explanations. Now you have a daughter who will excel in whatever she chooses to do with her life. She's a very lucky young woman who has a great deal to look forward to, with your help." He rose, nodded to Mellon. "Congressman, a pleasure to meet you." He paused at the door, said to Lulie, "What's important is what a fine new world is now open to your daughter. There's no changing the past, but the future?" He smiled. "It's going to be fabulous for her."

Romero Diaz was sitting forward in his chair, assessing every tech, every doctor, every nurse who got within spitting distance of Leigh Saks's room.

He smiled real big when he saw Ty, nodded to Sala, saw Mrs.

Sparrow and Eric coming behind them. *He's a heartbreaker,* Ty thought again. "Anything we should know about, Officer Romero?"

"Dr. Ellis left about thirty minutes ago. Ms. Saks and Congressman Mellon are with Leigh right now. Each left only once for a bathroom break and some coffee. One nurse and two techs went in, then left."

Sala said, "And here is Mrs. Sparrow and Eric Sparrow. They'll be coming in with us."

Romero got to his feet. "Of course I know Mrs. Sparrow and Eric." He nodded to Susan and smiled, shook Eric's hand. "Eric bought me my very first legal beer down at Beer Heaven out on Route Forty-Four."

"Your first three legal beers, as I recall," Eric said, and tapped Romero's arm. "I remember you puked in the parking lot."

"But not on your precious truck," Romero said. "I jumped out, didn't want you to break my jaw."

"At the very least," Eric said. "It was my new F-150."

Susan rolled her eyes. "Every year it's a new F-150. Who knows if it's new or not?"

Eric gave her an appalled look. "How could everyone not know?"

Ty held up her hand. "I forgot to ask you how well you knew Leigh, Mr. Sparrow."

Eric said, "Fact is, I never knew her very well because she interacted primarily with Susan when she worked at the crematorium. Of course, I was in Afghanistan much of that time. Hey, you knew her better, Romero."

Romero felt the weight of everyone's attention on him. "It's weird to think she's different now, smarter somehow. I heard the nurse saying she bet Leigh now had a really high IQ, she seemed that smart. Well, she wasn't smart growing up. I always liked her, thought she was really pretty and it was too bad. Some of the kids made fun of her. I'm about two years younger than her, so I wasn't one of the guys who wanted to take her out." He shrugged, colored a bit. "And I guess guys being guys, they were eager to score, well, to take advantage, until they met Ms. Saks. She had them believing she'd shoot any guy who tried to get fresh with Gunny—with Leigh. I don't remember her ever really dating anybody. They couldn't pass the Ms. Saks test."

Sala wondered if Leigh had ever had a relationship that included sex. Probably not. Had she ever been kissed?

When the four of them entered the cubicle, Lulie turned to them, a finger to her lips. "She's asleep. Dr. Ellis said it's the best thing for her. Chief, Agent, I'm pleased to see you. Susan, Eric, what are you doing here?"

Susan whispered back, "It was my idea, Lulie. I wanted to see Leigh, talk to her. Lulie, you know Mr. Henry's belt buckle was found with all those human bones in Lake Massey. No matter how light a hand Chief Christie and Agent Porto have, no matter what active measures we take, you know some people will wonder if we dumped some of our deceased clients into the lake, didn't in fact cremate them. I'm hoping Leigh can remember more of what was said that day with Mr. Henry about that belt buckle, maybe help figure out why it was in the lake." She paused, looked over at Leigh. "She looks so peaceful. It's hard to think of her as being different now, as being, well, whole."

Lulie felt tears spring to her eyes and swallowed. She didn't tell Susan the medical determination Dr. Ellis had made, it didn't matter. "I hadn't realized the implications, Susan, but now I do. Let me assure you, Leigh hasn't forgotten anything about that day. When she wakes up, she'll be pleased to go over it with you. Now, let me introduce you to Congressman Mellon. He's Leigh's father. He came immediately when I told him she'd been hurt." Lulie said nothing more, just stood back and smiled and watched Andrew take over.

Andrew shook Susan's hand, then Eric's. Eric said, "I voted for you, Congressman, always believed you were a stand-up guy." He looked over at Leigh and smiled. "Glad you came, sir."

Andrew said, "I am, too. Leigh worked for you, Mrs. Sparrow?"

Susan nodded again, but she never looked away from Leigh. She looked the same except for the big white bandage around her head. Her face was beautiful, her skin translucent. Susan said, "Eric's right. It's good you're here. I didn't vote for you, sorry."

He smiled. "I find it hard to understand why some folks don't vote for me. It's always a blow. But I always hope they'll come into the light at the next election." He paused. "I would have thought everyone in this town would know by now that Leigh's my daughter."

Eric said, "The news hadn't yet reached the house of the dead, Congressman."

"Eric, please." Susan looked at Lulie. What did she think about her daughter's father showing up? If she were Lulie, she might have shot him. She said with a warm smile, one she reserved for the bereaved, "I'm so happy for you, Lulie. When Leigh wakes up, may I speak with her?"

"Of course. Look, Susan, I don't want to see the crematorium bankrupted when I'm sure you had nothing to do with either the bones or the belt buckle in Lake Massey. Ty and Sala are smart. They'll figure out what happened, you'll see."

Eric said, "Thank you for believing in us, Lulie."

"Eric, your parents were fine people. They raised two honest boys." Lulie looked over at her daughter, who was awake and yawning, blinking her eyes. "Let me tell her you're here."

Lulie walked to Leigh's bedside, stroked her cheek with her fingertips. "Hello, sweetheart. How do you feel?"

Leigh smiled up at her mother. "I'm okay. Don't worry, Mom."

"Would you like to speak to Susan Sparrow? She and Eric are here to see you. And Chief Christie and Agent Sala."

Yes, of course they were here, Leigh had heard them talking, clear as day. It was strange, but she hadn't been aware she was awake. How odd that was. She called out, "Chief Christie, Agent Porto. Hello, Susan, Eric. I'm glad you came. I'd like to thank you for coming, especially Susan. You were a good boss, very patient with Gunny—with me." She waited until Susan stood beside her. "Forgive me, but I'm still floating on the ceiling. But the pain medicine should clear out soon, and I'm hopeful of a soft landing." She studied their faces. "I understand you must be worried about what people will think of the crematorium. And of course you realize many people don't think all that deeply, they prefer always to latch onto the most titillating answer. But everyone knows the Sparrow family. You have no need to worry."

58

Susan could only stare at the young woman she'd known for as long as she'd lived in Haggersville. Her eyes were a bit blurred from the drugs, but her voice—no longer was her sweet voice diffident, uncertain, always pausing to see if someone else wanted to speak. Now her voice was strong, confident, and what she'd said about people? "Yes, that's it, exactly," Susan said. "Chief Christie and Agent Porto told my family you'd changed your name from Gunny back to your given name, Leigh. I'm glad you did. It's a lovely name."

"Yes, it is, isn't it?" Leigh looked beyond her, smiled. "Hi, Eric, it's nice of you to come." She patted the other side of her bed.

Eric walked to her, lightly touched his fingers to her hand. He couldn't help it, he stared at her as his sister-in-law was doing.

Leigh asked, "Susan, do you have any idea how Mr. Henry's belt buckle could have gotten in the lake?"

Susan knew she had to stop gawking at this young woman. "No, I don't. Nor do Landry or Eric."

Eric said, "We told the chief and agent that none of us saw his body. It was delivered in a shroud from the morgue. We moved him in his shroud into a closed coffin for the memorial service. Then he was cremated. We never saw a belt buckle, and it definitely wasn't among his ashes."

Susan shrugged, looking helpless. "We're at a loss."

"I see," Leigh said. She remembered vividly what she'd heard had been done to Mr. Henry.

Susan leaned close. "Leigh, I'm sorry to ask you, but could you please tell us about that afternoon you first saw the belt buckle? We're hoping, praying, you'll remember something else that happened in that meeting, something that might help Chief Christie and Agent Porto."

Sala said, "Give it a try, Leigh. Think back to that afternoon with Mr. Henry. Picture it again. You're there. You're eating birthday cake. Is Mrs. Boilou in the study with you and Mr. Henry?"

"No, I told you, she took her slice of cake and left." Leigh continued, her voice calm, and once again she gave a perfect recital of her visit from the moment she'd walked through his study door carrying his birthday cake to when he'd sworn her to secrecy about the belt buckle. "And so I left, went home, and told my mom how happy Mr. Henry was with his birthday cake. There was no problem about keeping the belt buckle secret. I forgot all about it until Agent Savich showed it Monday on TV."

Eric said, "This was Mr. Henry's seventy-fifth birthday, right?"

Leigh smiled. "Mom put a big blue sugar seventy-five on top of the cake." She paused, then, "Do you know, Susan, I didn't wonder then, but now it seems strange he had a Star of David belt buckle when he wasn't Jewish."

Sala said, "I checked his background, no mention of Jewish relatives or ancestors. Both Ty and I found it odd as well."

Leigh said, "I see him so clearly, so very proud of that belt buckle, and he kept polishing it over and over again. And caressing it, which was creepy, now that I look back on it. It was like a valued prize he'd won. He told me how the belt buckle brought back wonderful memories of the first time in his life he knew what was important to him. And he kissed the belt buckle. Now, that really was creepy.

"Thinking about it now, I wonder how a Jewish belt could represent what was most important in his life? Where did he get it? Who gave it to him or sold it to him? Or did he steal it?"

Ty said, "All excellent questions. But a stolen belt buckle? How can that have been so important to him?"

Eric said, "It's amazing you can remember so clearly everything Mr. Henry said after five years."

Leigh said, "Do you know, it doesn't feel amazing, not any longer. It feels, well, natural." She felt pounding in the back of her head, a constant, but the pain meds were still hanging in, keeping the worst of it at bay. Thankfully, the meds weren't strong enough to fuzz up her brain.

Andrew said, "Leigh, if Mr. Henry said words you didn't understand back then, how can you know what he said now?"

She couldn't say Dad, not yet, maybe not ever. Chief Masters was more her dad than this man who'd fathered her. "Sir, all I know is when I pictured Mr. Henry saying those words, how his mouth moved, well, suddenly each word was clear."

Lulie smiled. "I know that might make all of you uncomfortable, but Dr. Ellis said Leigh might have had a kind of partial seizure disorder and with the surgery and medication, it's under control now. If I can accept it, then you must as well."

Eric grinned down at Leigh, and the bad boy came through loud and clear. "Maybe someone went after you because they were jealous of you?"

Leigh patted the white bandage wrapped around her head. "Not yet, Eric. Let me get the handkerchief off my head, my hair washed, and a touch of lipstick on, hey, then maybe somebody'll be jealous."

Leigh had made a joke, an actual joke, and everyone laughed except her mom and Susan. Lulie couldn't help it, she kept gawking at her daughter. As for Andrew, he looked proud.

Eric said, "You think the person who struck Leigh down might still believe she knows something to incriminate him or her that Leigh hasn't thought of yet? That's why you have Romero guarding the door?"

"That's right, Mr. Sparrow," Sala said. "We're not going to take any chances."

Leigh said, "I appreciate that, Chief Christie. Susan, Eric, I'm being hypnotized tomorrow. We'll see if any more comes out. If so, Chief Christie will let you know." She smiled at Susan, who was still staring at her. She said, rich humor in her voice, "Susan, it's okay. I know I'm a surprise to you, but it's still me." She turned to Ty. "What does Mrs. Boilou have to say? Does she remember that day five years ago? Maybe remembered something I didn't?"

"We can't get in touch with her," Sala said. "Vacation at her sister's, we were told."

All the uncertainties were reaching critical mass in Ty's brain. She felt exhausted. She wanted to crawl in beside Leigh. Then her phone buzzed with a text from Dillon.

You and Sala come to dinner at my house.

Important. An hour and a half?

She texted back. *What's on the menu?*

Time to take a risk.

Count us in.

Ty looked up to see Lulie was crying, her face against Andrew's shoulder. She raised blurred eyes to Ty. "Even now Leigh's still in danger."

Thankfully Leigh hadn't heard this. She'd fallen asleep again. Eric and Susan Sparrow were standing silent, looking on. What were they thinking? Ty put her hand on Lulie's shoulder. "Ms. Saks, this will all be over soon. Chief Masters will keep Leigh safe." Ty smiled. "Maybe when Leigh wakes up again, she'll have the solution."

Eric said, "After seeing her now, I wonder what she'll decide to do with her life."

Lulie hiccupped, gave a ghost of a smile. "Maybe a rocket scientist?"

"Or a politician," Eric said, shooting a look toward Leigh's father.

59

SAVICH HOUSE
GEORGETOWN
WEDNESDAY NIGHT

Ty set down her fork, sat back in her chair, and patted her stomach. "I'd drive to Maine for that lasagna, Dillon. It's so much better than mine, I want to steal your recipe then shoot you so I'm the only one left who knows how to make it."

Sala said, "You don't have to worry about me shooting you, Savich. I'll sign over my paychecks to you if you'll cook for me."

Savich laughed and looked at his wife, who was drumming her fingers on the table, lips seamed. He gave her a moment, knew she wouldn't be able to help herself, and, sure enough, in the next second, out came "And what about the garlic toast? You didn't think it was the best garlic toast you've ever eaten?

And the Caesar salad? Wasn't the dressing spectacular enough for you guys? Weren't the croutons cheesy enough, crispy enough?"

Savich said, "Ty, so Sherlock's hair doesn't burst into flames, start with how you'd drive from Montana to eat her garlic toast and the salad. Go."

Ty, no slouch, said, "Forget Montana. I'd sail over from Hawaii, Sherlock. I gotta say, your amazing Caesar salad left your husband's pathetic attempt at lasagna in the dust."

Sala said, "Your garlic bread, Sherlock, it was so good I didn't want to eat anything else, especially Savich's excuse for lasagna. What I said, ah, I was only being polite."

Sherlock looked from one to the other, nodded. "Well done, both of you. Dillon, don't you dare laugh," and she threw one lone remaining crouton at her husband. "Yeah, yeah, you're the king. And now I'll have to listen to these two go nuts over your coffee." She rose, hands on hips. "But you wait. In a little while, if I think you're worthy, I'm going to let you try my apple pie. Picture it, hot and bubbling straight from my magic oven, topped with French vanilla ice cream."

After the table was cleared and kitchen cleaned up, they adjourned to the living room with cups of Savich's amazing coffee and Savich with his tea, which neither Ty nor Sala complimented since they weren't stupid and they wanted Sherlock's apple pie.

Sherlock said, "Let's begin with Victor Nesser. We need some new eyes and perspectives on this problem. To catch you up, some more specifics about what happened in Winslow. Cindy Wilcox, the teenager who saved herself, said Victor was like

Dr. Jekyll and Mr. Hyde, one minute respectful and nice, but as soon as he stepped into her apartment, he turned into a monster, screaming at her, cursing her, intent on killing her." She drew a deep breath. "Dillon believes he understands what it all means and how it's related to everything else that's happened."

Savich said, "Sala, remember the girl's mad laughter you heard at Gatewood?"

"Not something I'll easily forget."

Savich leaned forward. "It couldn't have been Lissy, she's dead. I'm the one who killed her, so I didn't understand what was going on. Dr. Hicks believes Victor was broken after Lissy died. His losing Lissy so devastated him that his mind fragmented. Now, given what happened with Cindy, I can think of only one answer. The only way Victor could deal with her loss was to integrate Lissy into himself."

"A split personality?" Ty asked. "A Dr. Jekyll and Mr. Hyde?"

Savich nodded. "I think the only way he could survive was to keep Lissy alive. I think Victor becomes Lissy and then himself again. That's what Cindy told us, if you think about it. And that means they were already together in the psychiatric hospital. There's nothing in any of the doctors' records, which means Victor was able to hide it from them. And now, on the outside, Victor and Lissy each have his and her own scores to settle."

Sala was shaking his head. "But the laughter, Savich, it sounded like a girl, a real girl, not a guy trying to imitate a girl."

Savich took a sip of his Earl Grey tea. "That must mean she literally takes him over, that Victor becomes Lissy—not only her voice and the way she speaks, but also her way of looking at things, everything. I can't explain it and neither can Dr. Hicks, but what other solution could there be?"

Ty said, "So Victor is somehow channeling Lissy Smiley? He becomes her?"

Savich said, "It's tough to come to grips with it, but consider what happened. Victor stops for dinner at the diner in Winslow, Virginia. The pretty young waitress, Cindy, sees his big wad of hundred-dollar bills when he pays the check, and yes, obviously Victor wants her to see the money. She flirts with him, invites him back to her apartment. She wants to persuade him to take her with him and share all his money for a while."

Sherlock picked it up. "It would have pissed off Lissy, and that's why she appeared, tried to kill Cindy. Dillon hasn't said it, but Lissy was a natural-born killer, a psychopath without a shred of conscience or remorse for her victims.

"Cindy described Victor's voice becoming higher, crazy mad, out of control. She said he even looked different, his face changed, his eyes darkened. When Cindy kicked him, he screamed she'd kicked him in the staples, and he grabbed his belly and went down in pain."

Ty's eyebrow went up. "What staples?"

Sherlock said, "Lissy had major surgery to repair a ruptured duodenum. Her incision wasn't healed yet when she died, and the staples were still in."

Sala said slowly, "So Victor's Lissy stayed frozen in time, so now when she takes over, she is exactly as she was before you shot her?"

"Evidently."

"Now my brain is ready for a vacation. Or apple pie." He looked hopefully at Sherlock.

"All right, maybe all of you are worthy enough. Dillon, come help me. Let these two geniuses think about this."

Savich was carrying a tray with ice cream and plates on it and Sherlock the apple pie like a trophy for the winner when they came back. Sala breathed in the smell of hot cinnamon and wanted to weep.

Ty said, "Forget these unworthy men, Sherlock, marry me instead. I'll give you my all, which admittedly isn't much, but I promise I'll always be there for you."

"Hmm. All right, I'll consider it." Sherlock began cutting pie slices. "If Astro were here, he'd be bouncing around like a tennis ball, barking his head off."

Savich spooned the ice cream atop each slice and handed out the plates.

After a bite, Ty closed her eyes in bliss. "I hated Dillon's lasagna. It was swill. Now, this pie is ambrosia."

"I wouldn't give Savich's lasagna to my cat," Sala said, "and that's saying something. If given the chance, Lucky would eat my socks out of the hamper."

Sherlock laughed and patted his shoulder. "Music to my ears. Now, listen while you eat, okay? Sala, you dealt with Victor, plus you heard Lissy's laughter. You already know something about her. Let me emphasize: Lissy had no self-control. If she thought of something, she did it, no mental brakes, no thought to consequences. It was always about the pleasure of the moment, and it often involved killing someone."

Savich said, "Now, Nesser. He was sent to live with his aunt Jennifer Smiley when her sister, Victor's mother, and his father, a Jordanian, decided to return to Amman. Jennifer's very young daughter, Lissy, seduced Victor. From that night on, he loved her to his soul, would do anything for her. Let me emphasize here, Lissy drove the bus.

"Did Lissy love Victor as much as he loved her? Yes, I'm sure she did. Victor was damaged before Lissy, and he was destroyed after she died."

60

Sherlock said, "Sala, let me ask you this. Which of them do you think murdered Octavia? Victor or Lissy?"

Sala said without pause, "It was Victor. It felt like a man's anger."

"And which one decided to lock you in a closet to die?"

"It had to be Victor, of course, who dragged me unconscious up to the third floor at Gatewood. As to which one decided to leave me to die in that closet, I don't know, but I did hear a girl's crazy laughter in there. So maybe it was Lissy." He closed his eyes a moment, and Ty saw he was stiff as a board, back in that closet reliving the hopelessness, the knowledge he was going to die, and of course the guilt that he hadn't saved Octavia. She lightly touched her hand to his arm.

Ty decided it was time to turn off the guilt spigot. Turn off the horrible images of him left in that closet to die. She leaned over and jerked his pie plate away.

"Wait! Oh, no you don't!" And he was back. He waved his fist at her, ate the last bite of pie off his plate.

Savich was remembering how he'd seen Victor walking up the path toward Gatewood, how he'd looked up at Savich standing in the second-floor master bedroom window and pumped his fist. Had Lissy not been with him when he'd rowed Octavia out in the boat and killed her? Evidently not. And that was interesting. They could be apart as well as together. Had Victor imagined he was seeing Lissy in that window?

Savich said, "Let me take the bomb at the church yesterday. Before Sherlock and I brought down Victor, he tried to bomb us, so I'm sure he did the work. He had the expertise. But I bet Lissy loved the idea of blowing up the church at Octavia's funeral. Lissy loved drama, loved making a statement. What could be more dramatic than destroying a church full of people? Killing as many as she could? She had to be dancing, waving her fist."

Sherlock picked it up. "Remember Norm, from Norm's Fish and Bait in Bowman, near Greenbrier State Park, where Victor went in to buy junk food Sunday morning? Victor saw his face on TV. He didn't kill Norm, he panicked and ran. Lissy would never run. She'd yell, 'Lights out!' and kill everyone in sight. So it was Victor at the Fish and Bait in Bowman."

Ty said, "Okay, then it had to be Lissy who tried to shoot you guys in Peterborough after she saw you talking to people at that fried lobster place where Victor had lunch. It was spur-of-the-moment, over-the-top. I mean, it's broad daylight, and there you are, the enemies. She went hard at you to get you, kill you dead."

"Yes," Sherlock said, "that's classic Lissy. Thank heavens it wasn't Lissy who came into the children's tent at the book festival. It was Victor, and I'll admit what he did had to be spur-of-the-moment and really out of character for him. I mean, his weapon was a big chocolate bar."

Savich said, "Winslow happens to lie in a direct route to Fort Pessel, where Lissy and her mother lived and where Victor lived with them. It's where we believe Jennifer Smiley hid her half-million-dollar share from the bank robberies. We know Victor has a big wad of cash, so it makes sense he knew where the money was hidden, and he retrieved it." He ate the last bite of pie, regretfully set his empty plate on the coffee table. "If this is true, can you guys think of any reason why Victor would go back to Fort Pessel again?"

"Not unless he didn't take all of it," Sala said, and scraped up the last tiny bit of apple pie from his plate and looked like he wanted to cry.

Sherlock took his hand. "Come with me, Grasshopper. I think I have one slice of pie left, and it's got your name on it."

"Suck-up," Ty called after him. He waggled his fingers without looking back.

Savich sighed. "And here I was thinking about having that last slice for myself in bed tonight."

When Sherlock and Sala returned, Sala hugging a plate to his chest with one small slice of apple pie on it, Savich had to laugh. It looked like he was holding a life jacket. "We told you how Victor gave Cindy a hundred-dollar bill to pay for his dinner at the diner. Let's say we can trace the hundred-dollar bill to one of the bank robberies. That would leave us with the same question—why go back to the Smiley house if you already retrieved the money? No one's lived there for over two years. The bank foreclosed and has been trying to sell it. It's probably not habitable by now."

Ty said, "Sentiment? No place else to go? Someplace you—and Lissy—know and feel safe? Or maybe he didn't take all the money, and he's going back to make another withdrawal, like Sala suggested. His own personal bank." She waved her hand, frowned. "On the other hand, the bank could sell the place at any time, and then it wouldn't be safe to go back. And Victor would know that." She looked beyond Savich's shoulder.

"What, Ty?"

"Oh, well, this is probably stupid—"

"Spit it out, Christie," Sala said, "or I won't give you my last bite." There was a sliver of pie on his fork, and he waved it in her face.

"All right, but don't call me crazy. What if Victor never knew where Jennifer Smiley hid the money, maybe Lissy never told him, or she herself didn't know where her mother hid the stash. So maybe he got his wad of cash someplace else or from somebody else."

Savich said, "No, that's not crazy at all. Actually, we checked all convenience store robberies around the time Victor escaped, but none in the area fit the bill."

Sherlock said slowly, "Let's say he didn't rob anyone. It would be a huge risk for him. He escaped, he's on everyone's radar. What you said, Ty—what if someone gave him the money?"

"But why on earth would anyone give Victor money?" She smacked the side of her head.

"No, wait," Savich said. "Victor didn't have any friends, any benefactors, rich or otherwise. Maybe someone paid him money to do something for him."

Everyone stared at him.

"You mean like commit a crime for him?"

They all considered that possibility.

Savich said, "It's possible. Victor's crimes garnered lots of publicity, and maybe someone paid attention. Regardless, I already have agents at the Smiley house in Fort Pessel in case Victor shows up."

"Here's for your twisted brain." Sala handed Ty his fork with the final sliver of apple pie balanced on it.

Savich soon realized they were tapped out on Victor, and no wonder. Everyone was exhausted. He looked at his Mickey Mouse watch. "We've got some good ideas going, but you guys have an hour drive ahead of you. Let's call it quits for tonight. I'm looking forward to bringing Dr. Hicks to the hospital tomorrow to hypnotize Leigh. If anyone can help her remember if she saw anything in the alley before she was struck down, it's Dr. Hicks."

"You'll like Dr. Hicks," Sherlock said. "He's an Elvis impersonator. He stuffs a pillow in his pants because he's skinny. He goes to all the events dressed like the King. He sounds like him, too."

Savich said, "Let's add that he's the very best hypnotist we've ever worked with. If he really likes you, it's possible you might get him to sing 'Blue Suede Shoes.' "

"I wish I'd thought of hypnosis," Sala said. "I guess that's why they pay you the big bucks, Savich."

"Right now, I'd rather have more apple pie."

61

WILLICOTT, MARYLAND
WEDNESDAY NIGHT

It hit her so hard, Ty took a turn too fast and skidded on the rain-slicked road. She couldn't see clearly enough through the rain-fogged windows or the windshield to find a familiar landmark, so she prayed as she slowly, carefully managed to straighten her truck out of the skid. She stopped the truck in the middle of the empty road, briefly rested her forehead against her clenched hands on the steering wheel.

"Ty, are you all right? What happened?"

"My heart's pounding out of my chest. Sorry about that. Sala, a thought just hit me, made me jerk the steering wheel. Listen, Haggersville is a lot like Willicott, and a lot of people heard us talking about Leigh Saks and her hypnosis tomorrow. Everyone who heard us tells someone else, and on and on it goes. The person who struck her down, maybe they'll try again before she can be hypnotized. And there's only one deputy guarding her."

Sala punched a number on his cell. "Chief Masters? Ty and I are concerned there's only one guard on Leigh." Ty listened to him explain their concern, then, "Thank you, Chief. Good night. We'll see you tomorrow at the hospital."

"Neither of you questioned my judgment at all," Ty said.

A dark brow went up, but Ty didn't see it, she was watching a small Fiat pass. When they were driving again, he said, "That's because you've got great instincts, Ty. I don't know whether the hypnosis will help, but neither does the killer. And with Leigh more cognizant now, able to understand better, maybe she'll be able to put something more together about what happened, with or without hypnosis. So you nailed it. Protecting her is our priority." He turned to face her. "But next time you get inspired like that, try not to be driving in a downpour. You can stop worrying about it now. Chief Masters is on it." He paused a moment, looking out into the rain. "You know, Ty, this still feels like a Serial to me, but maybe something more, too, something we're not seeing, something we don't yet understand. I still wonder if it comes back to the Sparrows."

She whipped the steering wheel left to take the exit to Willicott, skidded, and straightened. She gave him a manic grin. "Sorry again. I nearly missed it. You're right. But the Sparrows aren't throwing their clients in Lake Massey, not those three people we met. Their parents? Nah, it doesn't feel right, either. Well, I could be wrong, it's happened on rare occasion, but not this time."

He held on as she turned onto the twisty lake road that

wound through and around hills and crossed bridges over deep gullies, always hugging the lake. There was scarcely ever any traffic at night on this road and none tonight, what with the heavy rain that had started right after they left Washington. Who would choose to drive in this weather with no guardrails and the occasional fifty-foot drop?

Sala said, “The lake looks like a black hole through the rain and the shadows of those hills.”

Ty drove around a curve and there, right in front of her, was something huge and black. She slammed on the brakes, sawing the steering wheel to avoid a skid this time. The brakes stopped them hard a few yards short of a large construction truck, sitting like a dark monolith in the middle of the road. A few more yards, she thought, her heart galloping, and they could have been badly hurt, her truck bashed in on them.

“You okay?”

“Yes,” she said, her hand over her kettledrumming heart. “I’d like to know why someone parked a fricking construction truck in the middle of the road on a dark, rainy night, no hazard lights, no nothing. This really burns me. I’m going to go bust some chops.” She jerked open the door, but before she could jump out, Sala grabbed her arm and pulled her back in, slammed the door closed. “No, don’t move. I saw this too many times in Afghanistan. It’s an ambush. Kill your lights.”

She did. “What? An ambush? Us? Who would want to ambush us?” Her breathing hitched. “You’re thinking the killer’s worried we know too much? But Sala, there would be lots more cops to take our place. Why try to kill us?”

He shoved her down. “We’ll talk about it later. Call 911, Ty.

Get your people here as fast as possible." He listened to her speak to her dispatcher, Marla Able, then punch off.

"Do you have a bullhorn?"

She stretched over the seat and pulled it out from the back.

Sala opened his window and shoved the bullhorn out and shouted, "Whoever you are, drop your weapon, put your hands on your head, and come out. We've called for backup."

There was silence, no answer. He pulled her down to the floor of the truck beside him. She said, "I've never made all my five foot ten inches fit into such a small space before."

He patted her back. Good, she'd made a joke.

"Sala, maybe I can slowly back us out of here."

"Nah, no reason to take a chance. Let's wait for your deputies. Charlie, right?"

"Yes, and Paula and Doug." Ty started to whine about cramping up, but she thought of the three or four inches Sala had on her and the fifty pounds and said, "So you think he was expecting us to get out of the truck, come and investigate."

"That was what he'd be counting on, yes."

"Thank you for stopping me, then. I was about to jump out of the truck and run to that huge behemoth, all full of righteous indignation and anger. I could be stone-cold dead."

"Ty, listen."

There it was, the faint blast of a siren.

Ty's cell rang. Charlie shouted, his voice hyped with adrenaline, "Ty, are you all right? What's happening? I'm nearly there."

"Charlie, it could be your siren scared him off. If you see a car or a truck hightailing it away from our position, go after it. We're fine. Are Paula and Doug close?"

"They're some minutes behind me, both had to come from home. I see a big honker construction truck in the distance sitting in the middle of the road and part of your truck behind it. I'm going to approach from my side. Meet you there?"

Ty called her other two deputies, sent them to Willowby Road to cut off that exit. She punched off, said to Sala, "Time to find out if you're right, Sala."

She pulled a flashlight out of the glove compartment. They stepped out of the truck, using the doors for cover, and into the deluge.

They heard Charlie's siren nearly to them.

"If the attacker is still around, he's an idiot," Ty said. They saw the bright lights of Charlie's truck illuminate the big black construction truck in the middle of the road.

Charlie left the lights on but turned off the engine. Ty shouted, "Charlie, you see anything? Anyone?"

"No! Not a thing. No one's here."

Slowly Ty and Sala, guns at the ready, walked to the construction truck. Charlie's flashlight lit up the inside. He opened the truck door and leaned in. When he straightened, he raised a piece of paper in his hand. "Look at this, Ty."

Ty and Sala read the big block letters:

BROKE DOWN. IN TOWN.

The three of them looked at one another. Charlie said, "Well, guys, better be safe than sorry, my mom always says. Hey, Chief, you okay? Looks like a false alarm. I'll go find the truck driver, get him taken care of, okay?" He pulled out his cell. "I'll give Paula and Doug a call, tell them false alarm and to go back home."

Ty could only nod. She saw that Sala was holding himself stiffly, and he was quiet, too quiet. She took his arm. "Let's go home, Sala, have a nice cup of tea. This little adventure might have put a white hair in my head."

He nodded, but didn't smile.

62

Ty found herself nearly mesmerized by the slap and glide of the windshield wipers, metronome steady. She'd laughed about Charlie's call reporting he'd found the truck driver in the all-night diner on Route 37, drinking a Bud and full of apologies. She'd fallen silent, watching those windshield wipers.

Sala was staring straight ahead, sitting very still, like if he moved, he'd shatter. She opened her mouth but shut it. *I saw this too many times in Afghanistan.*

When he saw the construction truck sitting in the middle of the road, had he been thrown back into his horrific experiences there with ambushes? He'd reacted immediately. On top of what he'd gone through in Afghanistan, then being tied up and left to die in the closet at Gatewood, no wonder his mind went to the worst-case scenario. Was it automatic? Was it a form of PTSD?

The rain came down heavier, and Ty slowed her Silverado to a crawl. They drove through Willicott, deserted, very few lights on. She said, "Sorry, I didn't even ask you if you would prefer to stay at your place in Washington."

He didn't look at her, simply kept staring out the windshield. "I wouldn't."

"Good. You want to know why I'm glad you're with me? I like having you at my cottage to share my morning coffee, to eat my grilled cheese sandwiches with me at midnight. And when we're lying in the dark waiting for sleep, I like talking with you about the important stuff and unimportant stuff, it doesn't matter.

"You could have easily saved our lives tonight, Sala. The thick rain, the dark night, the huge truck in the middle of the road, it could have been an ambush. So it was a simple breakdown tonight, who cares? You took action, no dithering about, no questioning yourself. You acted. It was your vigilance in Afghanistan that saved your life. It could have saved our lives tonight."

"I should have questioned myself. The whole thing was nuts—an ambush on a road in Willicott, Maryland? Not likely."

"Do you forget we're closing in on a murderer?"

He shrugged. At least he was talking. She wanted to tell him again she admired his brain, the way he could analyze another person quickly, come to a conclusion that was usually spot-on.

She flip-flopped her hand. "Believe me, what happened tonight was better than an ambush, but, Sala, if it had been the murderer out to kill us, you saved our bacon. You're a hero."

He shrugged.

She turned into her driveway, turned off the engine, and twisted in the front seat to look at him. "Sala, I'm no doctor, but it seems pretty obvious to me after what you went through in Afghanistan and then being left to die at Gatewood, what happened tonight is perfectly logical."

"No, you're not a doctor."

She drummed her fingers on the steering wheel. The rain poured down, a gray curtain enclosing them. "I guess what I'm saying is I'm very glad you were with me tonight." She grabbed her umbrella. "You're going to have to run, it's the only one I have," and she dashed out of the truck to her front porch, unlocked the door, and ran inside, Sala on her heels.

She could help him simply by being with him, sharing with him, distracting him, keeping him completely involved, which he was. She turned to him at the front door of her cottage and said simply, "I want you to stay with me for as long as you want."

He started, then smiled down at her. "Thank you. Do you know, until you mentioned it, I hadn't even thought about my place in Washington. I think my coffee might be as good as Savich's, which means it's lots better than yours. If you let me, I'll prove it to you tomorrow morning."

She laughed. "Okay, my Turkish sludge isn't for everyone. You wait until you taste my hot chocolate this winter."

This winter. That made her blink, but she realized she meant it.

She gave a momentary thought to his sleeping in the guest bedroom. She wasn't about to tell him she wanted to keep an eye on him, that she worried about nightmares. Without discussion, they pulled the guest bedroom mattress into the middle of the living room and sheeted it. Because the rain had cooled the temperature, Ty got a couple of blankets. She changed into pajama boxers and a T-shirt with ONLY THE PITIFUL LIE TO A COP emblazoned on the front. Sala stripped down to a black T-shirt and his black boxer shorts. Before adjourning to the mattress, they went into the kitchen and stood staring out the window at the fog-shrouded lake and the flat black sky, like two old married people at the end of the day, with their jammies on, winding down in the dark night. And like two old married people, they set their cells into a charger, climbed under the covers on the mattress, and settled in. The sound of the rain was steady, soothing.

Sala said, "Tell me about your deputies."

"Paula and Doug are both older, been on the force for over ten years, both mainly still on the job to make ends meet. They're good with the locals since everyone knows them, and they get along with most. Knowing the two of them, they're having a blast, even though the ending with the truck driver drinking a beer is anticlimactic. I know it's hard to believe, but until now, Willicott hasn't been what you'd call a big crime center."

He laughed. "And Charlie Corsica?"

"He's young and he's not a dummy. Actually, he's bright but needs a lot of work. He plans on being police chief one day. I forgot—hold still." She came up on her knees, turned on a lamp, and examined the small bandage on his head. It had survived the pounding rain. "I'll change the bandage to a Band-Aid tomorrow, put more antibiotic on the stitches." She leaned back on her heels, gave him the once-over. "Now what we both need is a good night's sleep."

She gave a big yawn and settled in.

"Ty?"

"Yes?"

"About tonight. What happened—I saw that construction truck and felt a surge of fear. It was overwhelming, sent me immediately into combat mode, made me jump to conclusions."

"Yeah, it did. Thank you."

He snorted out a laugh and fell silent. "You're not going to let me point out what I did was crazy, an overreaction, are you?"

"Nope. You did the right thing. If you want to keep beating yourself up, do it on your own time. I think you should call the forensic anthropologist at Quantico tomorrow, see if he's harvested DNA off any of the bones yet. It's probably too early, but worth the call. What do you think?"

"I'll make the call. We'll see."

It was a start. She'd keep distracting him. Ty turned on her side to face him. "I haven't told you, Charlie did a standard background check on each of the Sparrows, found nothing to raise any red flags."

She was pleased when he said, "We should go deeper. I'll call Dillon, ask him to put MAX on it."

She said, "The brothers are so different from each other. Landry is suave, the crown prince in a three-piece bespoke suit, and Eric a good-looking brawler if I ever saw one. Both have degrees in business from good schools, both raised by loving parents." She paused. "Now, Susan is different. I read her bio. She was born Susan Ann Humphries, Nashville, Tennessee, orphaned when she was a kid and raised by her aunt and uncle, both dead now. She took their name—Hadden. Went to school there, eventually moved to Haggersville. Nothing yet about her parents. Oh, shoot me, I'm trying to dissect every shadow I see. Sala, do you think Eric regards Susan as more than a sister-in-law, that he'd like to see his brother go away?"

"Not that I could tell," Sala said, and she was pleased to hear he sounded sleepy, "but family dynamics aren't ever straightforward. They're always a drama unfolding. Those brothers, though, I think they're close, they care about each other a great deal. And Susan? She's maybe the dark horse, isn't that what you're thinking?"

"Or maybe I'm only making myself crazier." Ty fell silent, listening to Sala's breathing as it slowed into sleep. Maybe he'd be able to sleep through the night for once without Octavia's death creeping in to stir up another nightmare and bring it all back. Add the unexpected incident tonight—no, he'd dealt with it fine. It was unfortunate you couldn't control what you dished up to yourself to terrify you out of your wits at night. Without thought, she leaned over and whispered, "You're a good man, Sala. I hope you have good dreams. Good night."

63

HAGGERSVILLE COMMUNITY HOSPITAL
THURSDAY MORNING

Ty and Sala introduced themselves to Officer Romero's replacement, an older grizzled man named Gene Fuller, sitting in the hallway outside Leigh's door on the surgical floor, where she'd been transferred, a hunting magazine on his lap. He showed them in so they wouldn't startle his partner, a female deputy dressed in a brown uniform sitting in a chair, her back to the single window. They weren't surprised to see Lulie Saks standing beside Leigh's bed. She'd probably slept here the previous night.

Lulie smiled at them as they walked in. "Good morning, Agent, Chief. Andrew had meetings back in Washington he couldn't miss. As for my beautiful daughter here, Leigh's feeling better, and she's excited about getting hypnotized." She turned back to her daughter, patted her hand.

Leigh gave them a little wave. She no longer had a white turban wrapped around her head. She patted the smaller bandage. "Now this looks more discreet, don't you think. They shaved off hair from the back of my head for surgery, but who cares? I've got enough hair left to cover it so people won't gawk."

Sala saw Lulie blink, still not used to this bright, articulate woman who was her daughter.

Leigh nodded toward the female deputy. "This is Officer Adele McGowan. She won a shooting championship in Kingsburg, Maryland, two years ago. I've known her forever. Hey, Adele, believe me, I'm glad you're here."

Adele McGowan stared a moment at Leigh, still a bit disbelieving, Ty supposed. She gave them a small salute, exchanged introductions, and continued watchful.

Sala said to Leigh, "Glad to hear you have no problem letting Dr. Hicks rummage through your memories with you."

Leigh laughed, then frowned a bit at a lick of pain. She waited, and the pain eased. "What a way to put it, Agent Porto. No, like Mom said, I welcome it. Will he be here soon?"

"Anytime now," Sala said.

Ty said, "I saw you wince, Leigh. How do you really feel this morning?"

"Honest, I'm fine. Have you learned anything?"

Sala said, "Yes, we've been busy. We have a lot to nail down before we make any announcements."

She understood immediately and nodded. "Fair enough.

There are ears everywhere, everyone would know everything."

They heard voices, turned as the door opened again. "Ah, here's Dr. Hicks," Sala said, "and Agents Savich and Sherlock."

Leigh looked up at a tall man with beautiful dark eyes, kind eyes, eyes that saw a great deal. She said to him, "When Agent Savich called me a little while ago, he told me you impersonate Elvis and you're really good."

"That I do, Ms. Saks." He studied her face as he shook her hand, careful of the IV in her wrist. "For someone who had surgery such a short time ago, you look fit as my guitar."

"As fit as a 1956 Gibson J-200?"

Dr. Hicks grinned like a schoolboy. "Actually, a Martin D-18 is my preference. Did you know Elvis purchased that same fine instrument in Memphis in '55?"

"I didn't know that. Will you send me tickets to your next performance?"

"You can be sure I will. Are you ready to proceed, Ms. Saks? It's painless, I promise you."

"Please, Dr. Hicks, call me Leigh, particularly if you're going to go dumpster-diving in my brain."

He was charmed. "I've never heard what I do described in quite that way before. But you don't seem at all worried, and let me reiterate you don't need to be. I know you still have some pain, Leigh—"

She waved that off. "Only a bit, Dr. Hicks. The meds help dial it down if I need them."

"Very well. I can help you with that later myself. I understand,

Leigh, you've been through a great deal. Agent Savich has filled me in. You understand your surgeon, Dr. Ellis, thinks you had a seizure disorder for a very long time, and it's under control now? Does that worry you?"

"Yes, both Dr. Ellis and Mom told me. All I really know is I'm different now, Dr. Hicks, but I'm very happy about it. Ecstatic, really, and no, I'm not worried at all. I know I'll keep my new self."

Dr. Hicks looked into her very pretty eyes and saw intelligence shine out at him. And humor. The truth was, he didn't know if Dr. Ellis was right about the seizures. He rather would like to believe her transformation was a miracle. He believed in miracles. He smiled at her. "I can't wait to see what's inside your head."

"I think a lot of folk would also like to know that. Onward, Dr. Hicks."

"Very well. What I want you to do, Leigh, is simply relax that busy mind of yours, and then Agent Savich will ask you some questions." Dr. Hicks pulled out the shiny gold watch that had belonged to his grandfather. "Look at the watch, nothing more, and relax. All you have to do is listen to my voice and look at the watch. Let your mind empty and float away, into my voice, all right?"

"I'll try, but it might take a while. My brain is so full, so many ideas, so many questions."

He only nodded. Leigh began to follow the movement of the swinging gold watch, wanting to laugh at the silly thing that was supposed to empty her brain into the ether. Then, without warning, she began to feel warmer. The world became smaller until it was only the gold watch swinging in front of her and there was only her and Dr. Hicks. She yielded herself to it.

Dr. Hicks nodded to Lulie and said to Savich, "She's under and very quickly, too. I find creative people are a treat to hypnotize." He looked back at Leigh's mother. "Does she sing or paint? Something like that?"

Lulie slowly shook her head. "No, but she always loved books, all kinds of books in the house, even though I knew she never understood much. Still, she'd go cover to cover. Maybe it was the words themselves that fascinated her. Not the pictures, most of the books didn't have pictures. I read to her every night." She shook her head. "And she knew about Elvis's guitars? I remember I went through an Elvis phase, had all sorts of books about him around the house. She was very small, but I'd see her turning each page slowly, studying them. There were pictures, so that's what I thought she was looking at."

Leigh must have taken in a lot of those words, and now, perhaps, she had a deep reservoir of knowledge to draw on. Hicks said, "Tell me, Leigh, do you remember when you first read about Elvis and his guitars?"

"Elvis," she repeated slowly. "I was a little girl. Mama was humming one of his songs, 'Heartbreak Hotel,' I think, and we were dancing. She had lots of books about Elvis. I remember I read all of them—well, looked at all of them."

"You obviously did more than look. Now, our first order of business—you will have no more pain in your head."

She looked perplexed, then in the next moment, she looked

quite pleased. "No, there's no more pain. Thank you. It's very nice. It's tough being brave, but I hated seeing Mama so scared for me."

"You don't have to be brave anymore, Leigh. Your mother's not scared now." Dr. Hicks nodded to Savich.

Savich leaned close. "I'm glad you feel good now, Leigh."

"I feel better than good, Agent Savich."

"I would like you to go back five years and revisit Henry LaRoque, the day you took a birthday cake to him."

"All right."

"When you walk into his study, you're going to see more, hear more, observe more. You're very alert now. You're seeing yourself. Are you in his study now?"

64

"Yes," Leigh said. She paused, shook her head. "How odd. I always thought Mr. Henry's study was so grand, so big and imposing, but it's not. It's a nice room, sure, with dark woodwork and lots of bookshelves built in, but it's not Versailles. All right, there's Mr. Henry, and he's welcoming me, admiring Mama's beautiful cake. She knew he was a chocoholic, knew her cake would please him.

"Oh my, it's all so clear now. I realize Mr. Henry feels sorry for me, and that's why he's so very kind and gentle with me, like an uncle with a small child." She added without irony, "I see how he considers it a reward for the poor, simple girl to see his prized possession, the Star of David belt buckle, all gold and shiny."

"Does he say anything you haven't already told everyone?"

She frowned. "No, I've already told you all exactly what he said to me. But it's how he acts, the way he holds the belt buckle, keeps running his fingers and hands over it. I see it makes him remember wonderful things. It's his treasure, his valued prize. He's not sure if showing me the belt buckle is smart, but he wants to show it off, to brag, even if it's only to me. He watches me closely until he's convinced I'll keep his secret. He's not worrying much now."

"He never gave any indication of where he got the belt buckle?"

"No, but the belt buckle, it's everything to him."

Savich nodded to Ty and she stepped forward. "Leigh, Chief Christie here. Do you think the belt buckle was a trophy for some competition he'd won?"

Leigh said, "Perhaps. It's certainly a prize to him, a special treasure."

Savich said, "Is there anything else you see or feel?"

She thought about this, shook her head.

"Now let's come forward five years, to Tuesday. Are you with me, Leigh?"

"Yes, of course."

Savich saw she looked completely relaxed, her expression untroubled, not a hint of pain, thanks to Dr. Hicks. "Leigh, before we go back to the alley, tell us why you decided to call the hotline."

"Gunny was so afraid of breaking a promise because she should never do that, but she—well, I—knew something was badly wrong, knew Mr. Henry's belt buckle shouldn't have been at the bottom of Lake Massey with all those bones. He was cremated, so what was the explanation? I told Mama, but she was stressed with work. And the last thing she needed was for me to keep piling on and worry her even more. I did think about asking Mrs. Sparrow, too. I had worked for her at the crematorium and I really liked her. If anyone could explain why the belt buckle ended up in the lake and not cremated with his body, she would know, wouldn't she? I mean, had he been wearing the belt when they scooted him into the oven? But what if he hadn't, then where did the belt buckle come from? My brain went round and round until I thought of calling the hotline myself. I thought they would tell me what to do."

"Okay, Leigh, you leave the post office, and you walk into the alley. I want you to see everything on a different level, look at yourself, keep your senses wide open."

"Yes."

"Why the alley?"

"I didn't want anyone to overhear." She added matter-of-factly, "They'd think I was crazy as well as stupid."

Sala asked, "What do you see in the alley?"

"She has her cell phone in her hand. No, it's me, of course, it's Leigh and I have my cell phone. My palms are sweaty. I'm so afraid I might say something wrong or stupid to the hotline person and they'll be mad at me and hang up on me. I'd put the hotline number into my phone so I wouldn't forget it. A man answered, and I told him I knew about Mr. Henry's Star of David belt buckle, told him I was breaking a promise and he had to tell me what to do. I could hear the excitement in the agent's voice, like he thought he might have hit the jackpot with me.

"He asked me for my full name, but I couldn't tell him, simply couldn't get it out. That was the old me, of course. That was Gunny. Thinking about the secret, how mother had always said keeping a secret was sacred, and she—I—froze. Then a monstrous pain in the back of my head, and I woke up after surgery in the ICU." Leigh was quiet a moment, then said in a voice filled with wonder, "Gummy bears—I told the agent about Mr. Henry giving me gummy bears."

Lulie took her hand, lightly stroked her long, slender fingers. Leigh wore only one ring, the gold Celtic knot on her pinkie finger.

"Go back to the alley now, Leigh, before you were struck," Savich said. "You're outside yourself. You're now an observer, reporting on what you see, what you hear. Look around you. You see yourself, but what else? A shadow? Someone at the other end of the alley? Do you hear something? A shuffling sound, footsteps?"

Leigh closed her eyes. "She doesn't hear anything, but she feels something's close, something worries her. Yes, she hears light footsteps, coming from behind her, coming toward her."

"Do they sound like a man's or a woman's footsteps?" Sala asked.

Leigh's smooth, serene face changed into an impatient frown and her voice became annoyed, clipped. "They sounded a little like high heels, Agent Porto, but if I knew that for sure, I would have told you."

Lulie grinned, couldn't help it. She whispered to Ty, "That's my girl."

Ty smiled. "No, that's her mother."

When it was obvious the well was dry, Savich nodded to Dr. Hicks, who took Leigh's hand.

"Leigh, it's me, Dr. Hicks. I want you to tell me something.

When you were thinking back in time, you spoke many times of yourself as Gunny, as if she were a different person. Can you explain that to me?"

Leigh looked thoughtful, as if considering an interesting experience. "I know full well Gunny is me and I'm Gunny, but I'm not really, am I? My eyes see differently now, more like yours do, Dr. Hicks."

Dr. Hicks said, "A lovely way to say it. When you wake up, Leigh, you will continue to feel no pain. You will remember everything. Three, two, one. Wake up, Leigh."

Leigh's eyes opened. She looked thoughtfully at each person in the room, then turned back to Dr. Hicks. "How is it possible? I don't have any pain at all. And I remember your telling me I wouldn't."

"Think of me as your own personal magician," Dr. Hicks said.

"Will you marry me, Dr. Hicks?"

"If my wife ever leaves me, I'm yours. Now, do you remember which guitar Elvis traded in for his new Martin D-18?"

"Of course, in Memphis in 1955, he traded in his Martin 000-18. To be able to impersonate the King. That's amazing. I want to come and see you perform."

He leaned down and lightly kissed her cheek. "I'll be sure to let you know about my next Elvis gig. You're an amazing young woman. I'm very glad I met you and I look forward to seeing what you make of your life from here on out."

65

FORT PESSEL, VIRGINIA
THURSDAY AFTERNOON

I didn't want to come back to this pissant town, Victor. Nothing good ever happened here, well, except you came.

"I had to beg my parents to leave me here. You remember I couldn't stand to be around them, with my old man knocking my mother around and the stupid woman never doing a thing about it. And then my dad wanted to move back to Jordan to be with his fricking foreign relatives? Can you imagine what that would have been like? For me, an American? Even your mama hitting me on the head with a hammer wasn't as bad as staying with those two pathetic losers."

You hit me sometimes, Victor.

"Only when you riled me, Lissy. You know I never hit you

hard. Now, you said you hurt really bad after Cindy kicked you in the belly, right in the staples. We need to get you some pain pills, and this is as good a place as any, plus I know where old Mrs. Kougar keeps them."

You can't waltz into Kougar's Pharmacy like you did last time, Victor. Don't you remember how she showed up and nearly shot you?

"Yeah, yeah, she surprised me. I still got you pain meds, enough to last you, didn't I? We'll hunker down at your mom's house and wait until it's dark. Maybe we can stay until they stop looking for us. I looked up the house on the Internet. No one's bought it, so the bank still owns it. It's all empty, waiting for us."

Listen, Victor, I want to go with you to the pharmacy when the old witch is still there. You can tie her up, and we'll take the pills and listen to her whine and threaten and then WHAM! I'll shoot her old head off, watch her few brains run all over.

"It's broad daylight, Lissy. There'll be people in and out until she closes."

Didn't matter last time, did it? She came back after closing and nearly killed you. She deserves to have her brains splatted. I deserve to be the one to do it. Hey, you hear that siren, Victor?

"Don't speed up, Lissy! We're only a couple of young people driving around. The cops aren't after us here. Listen, they're peeling off. Go slow, now. Head for your mom's house."

Yeah, all right. We can lie low for a while. I'll take the meds and feel better. But you know that little bitch Cindy described our car to the cops, maybe she even got the license plate. So you know Savich is looking for us.

"Sure, let him look. Why would he come down here? They'll go haring around some other state parks. Look, Lissy, I know we need another car, but I'm running a little short on cash. Everything I had to do in Washington to get Savich's house plans, all that research on how to disable that alarm of his, the bomb and the gun, all the Willicott arrangements, the two cars I bought—it cost a whole lot."

That's easy, Victor. Let's steal us a car, no more shelling out our money to buy another butt-ugly one. Maybe this time we can spot a nice little Fiat. I like racing stripes, you know that.

"It's way too dangerous. I've still got enough money to buy another car, but I'd like to have a cushion left. Don't forget we'll need enough of a stake for a new life, Lissy. It would be easier if you told me where your mama hid the bank robbery money."

She was silent, then, *You swear if I tell you, we can go kill Riley?*

"You're not thinking, Lissy. You know it's too dangerous for us in Washington right now. We've got to wait. I'll go to the Boggert Used Cars here in Fort Pessel, buy another car there."

You never told me where you got all the cash. A whole buttload. Where'd you get it, Victor?

"I'll tell you after you tell me where the robbery money is hidden."

Silence, then, *Okay, maybe. We'll get some pain meds for me tonight.*

"Yes, but no more killing, Lissy, so that means I'll go alone. You can't control yourself, so you'll wait in the car or at your mom's house."

Can we sleep in the house, not outside like last night?

"I don't see why not. You can keep your clothes on, you know I don't like seeing those ugly staples."

66

GEORGETOWN
THURSDAY AFTERNOON

Savich sat quietly in the Volvo, waiting for Sherlock to get some aspirin at the CVS across the street. He was thinking about the agent Victor had shot in Fort Pessel two and a half years ago. Cawley James had been lucky.

It was now down to a manhunt. Savich knew to his gut where Victor was going next. If he was wrong, so be it. It wouldn't matter in the long run.

He pulled out his cell and called Agent Reed, one of the three FBI agents stationed at the Smiley house in Fort Pessel, for an update.

"Todd, Savich here. Talk to me."

"The three of us are in place at the Smiley house, with me

inside, two outside surveilling the grounds. You know the house is on a cul-de-sac bordering on a mostly maple and oak forest, lots of places to hide. The house is pretty ramshackle, looks every bit like no one's lived here since Jennifer Smiley went down in that last bank robbery. The bank repossessed the house and owns it now.

"We're on it, Savich. All of us remember what happened last time, when Cawley James got shot. What I don't get is why you think Victor's coming back here."

Savich said, "I think he was headed to Fort Pessel all along. He still needs the money he thinks is buried there, or he'd have been long gone by now. He'll have to dump the Chrysler, buy another car, or steal it. I called the local dealerships, and I've got the local police chief on alert for any stolen vehicle reports. Can't be sure which way Victor will go." *Which way Lissy will make him go.* Savich wondered if he should tell the hard-nosed agent, a fifteen-year veteran known as Black 'n' White in his field office because he never saw any grays in life, that he was looking not only for Victor but for Lissy sharing his body with him, probably appearing whenever she wished, or whenever Victor needed her to. Since Todd knew Lissy was dead, Savich could see him staring at his cell, wondering if Savich was losing it. Savich settled on, "Reed? Be careful. Victor isn't known for crazy violence, but he can change in a flash. As if he flips a switch, he morphs in an instant."

Agent Todd Reed was silent, thinking about what Savich had said. Victor could morph, get violent? Well, of course he could. He said, "Well, I've found most criminals can become crazy violent or not, depending on the circumstances."

"Yes, but Victor is different. Believe me on this, Reed. You might not know until it's too late, so be ready. Don't hesitate like Cawley did. I've seen Victor turn on a dime, trust me. No one wants history to repeat itself. He was in Winslow and it's only a three-hour drive to Fort Pessel. If that's his destination, he could already be there, so be on the lookout."

"We'll be ready. I went over myself earlier to the two local used car dealerships here in Fort Pessel, not a surprise there's only two since more folks are shopping online nowadays. They'll call me if they have a dull brown Chrysler 300 LX come in. And I'll check in with Chief Wen."

"He remembers what happened the last time we tried to get Victor there in Fort Pessel. Yes, call him as a courtesy. Remind him to keep this quiet. Call me if you spot Victor, Todd, and don't forget the access road behind the Smiley house."

"We've got everything covered. Don't worry, Savich."

When Sherlock came back to the Volvo, a small bag in her hand from the pharmacy, he said, "You okay?"

"Sure, I already popped a couple of aspirin." She paused. "I was thinking it was a lovely day to see another part of the country, like Fort Pessel. What do you think?"

Sometimes it was scary how well she knew him. "I figure we can be there by dark."

"Onward, then." Sherlock leaned her head back against the seat rest and said, "Did you tell Todd we're coming?"

"No, but we spoke and I gave him lots of warnings. Sherlock, remember when Cindy kicked Victor and he screamed about her kicking the staples?"

“Yes, but I guess Lissy was the one who screamed it. I see where you’re going with this.” She said thoughtfully, “Last time Lissy was in pain, Victor robbed a local Fort Pessel pharmacy for meds. Are you having Todd cover the local pharmacy?”

Savich shifted the Volvo into gear and eased onto the highway. “It’s more important to keep the Smiley house well covered.” He gave her a crooked grin. “And we could be totally off base. It’s only a guess, really. You and I will check out the pharmacy.”

She leaned over, kissed him, and gave a big yawn. “Wake me when we get there.”

67

FORT PESSEL
THURSDAY AFTERNOON

You're being butt-stupid, Victor. Worry, worry, worry, that's all you do. There's no reason for the Feds to be at Mama's house, not this time around.

"We didn't think they'd be here last time, either, but they were. We nearly got caught. We were lucky. This time I'm not going to take any chances. Now shut up, Lissy. I'm going to be very careful. The FBI isn't stupid, Savich isn't stupid. I have this feeling he knows Fort Pessel is where we're headed."

Yeah, okay, you're right. This time. I should have shot that teasing bitch Cindy the minute we stepped in her dippy apartment, put a bullet between her slut eyes. Then she wouldn't have seen our car and we wouldn't need a new one again.

"But you didn't do that, did you?"

She got me good, I'll admit it. You realize she came onto you only because she wanted your money, Victor. Why do you think she took you to her apartment? Guys are so easy.

"Yeah, I guess we are." He laughed. "And proud of it."

Well, my fault, I shouldn't have missed when I shot at her. The bitch. You know, I didn't hit her because I hurt so bad. Victor, I really need those pain pills.

"I know, Lissy, I know. As soon as it's dark, as soon as Old Lady Kougar closes the pharmacy, I'll get them for you. Try to relax, okay?"

Victor drove slowly. He'd heard her moan quietly in her sleep. He knew she hurt and he hated it. He hadn't known she'd go after Cindy, but he should have. Violence was like meth to her. She was an addict, she craved it, and this time she'd paid for it. Who would have guessed Cindy could kick like that? And she'd gotten him good, too, right in the groin, knocked him silly.

He turned onto the single-lane access road that ran along the forest line and eventually behind the Smiley property. He'd rarely seen anybody else drive this road. Still, he was careful. He saw the potholes were bigger since the last time he was here, the forest encroaching nearly to the asphalt. It was where he'd parked when he and Lissy had first come back for the bank robbery money, before they'd faced down Savich and Sherlock and he'd believed his life was over. Victor shook his head. He didn't want to remember, didn't want to think about what had happened that day, how his life had simply exploded. Only it hadn't, not really. His life had become his again, with Lissy. Things would be different this time, and everything would turn out fine. He'd planned through each step since he'd escaped from that psych hospital. Well, there'd been some mistakes along the way, sure, but he was done with that.

Victor realized he no longer wanted vengeance against Savich. There were many more important things for him and Lissy now. It simply wasn't worth taking the risk. But he also knew Lissy wouldn't let him leave until she killed Buzz Riley. That was all right, he could live with that. It was so important to her to avenge her mama. But then that would be the end of it. They'd be on their way to Montana, a nice long road trip. Maybe they'd go to Big Sky, buy a small piece of land, and have enough money left over for a good start. He didn't know what they'd do, but it didn't matter, the dream of the future warmed him, centered him. But first he had to find the money, even if Lissy wouldn't tell him where her mama had hidden it. He had to find that ledger, he knew to his gut it would give the hiding place.

He saw no one on the access road, not FBI, not any locals. He parked the Chrysler off the narrow road, maybe a mile from the Smiley house, and said quietly to Lissy, "I want you to stay here and keep quiet. I'm going to take a good look around, make sure everything's safe for us."

Take a gun, Victor. If you see anyone hanging around, you gotta shoot 'em before they get you. You've got to come back to me.

She didn't realize he'd taken the gun from her when she was asleep. He wouldn't tell her, either. He would be careful, but there'd be no shooting, not if he could help it. Lissy was the one who loved guns and killing. He didn't mind, everyone loved something.

Before he got out of the car, he said, "Of course I'll come

back." At least in Montana, she could shoot bears or whatever there was out there in the Wild West, and no one would care. He quietly closed the car door and stood perfectly still for a moment, letting the July heat seep into him, the endless summer humidity flood him like a shower. He heard birds, some scurrying forest animals, probably squirrels, maybe foxes.

He remembered Agent Porto at Lake Massey and shook his head at how lucky that man was to be alive. Of course Victor would have shot him if he'd had to. Sure, he would. Hadn't he killed the bitch lawyer? Whacked her over the head, dumped her overboard? He didn't feel much of anything about that now, except maybe relief it was over and he'd done it all himself, without Lissy hissing in his ear, trying to take over. He wouldn't have gone out of his way to kill her if it hadn't been worth it. All that money waved in his face. Of course he'd agreed. He'd told her the truth once they were in the boat and she was rowing him out onto the lake. He remembered the strange look she got on her face. Well, she was dead and gone now, no use thinking about it.

But he couldn't forget Agent Porto. He hadn't wanted to kill him. Let him wake up and find Octavia Ryan gone. What could he do? He didn't know who Victor was, hadn't seen his face. Victor had wanted to leave him in that cottage, but Lissy reminded him he couldn't. Porto could wake up, and he knew too much. She kept at him, telling him over and over Savich would figure out it was him. It was her idea to leave him in that closet. *Let the big guy suffer. Let him realize he's going to die and there's nothing he can do about it.* She'd taken the agent's gun from Victor once already, used it to try to kill Savich and Sherlock in Peterborough. When was that? Tuesday? Yesterday? Victor shook his head. He felt a moment of disorientation and panic. He stopped cold, squeezed his head between his hands. Where was he going? What was he doing? He felt a sharp slice of bitter pain, then everything righted. Had Lissy voodooed him? Now, there was a thought. If she could, he wouldn't put it past her, to punish him for leaving her in the car, keeping her from having her fun.

Victor waited a few more minutes. Everything seemed quiet. He hadn't heard or seen anyone. Lissy was snuggled back in the car, waiting for him, maybe asleep. He left the road and walked slowly and carefully across the spongy forest floor, grateful for the thick tree branches overhead. He stopped when he reached the back of the Smiley house. He'd thought he'd be pleased to see the place where he'd spent the happiest months of his life, but what he saw was dilapidated wood that needed painting, a trash-strewn yard, and a moldy tire hanging from the lower branch of an ancient oak tree. He remembered pushing Lissy in that tire, remembered her screaming at the top of her lungs, and her mother yelling at them, "Stop that hootin' and hollerin'!" He remembered he and Lissy had stopped, and they'd wandered into the forest, only holding hands until they were sure her mom couldn't see them, then made love in the cool shade of an oak tree, its branches canopied overhead, the air warm on their young bodies, a perfect afternoon. He sighed and kept his eyes open for any sign something wasn't right. He looked into the kitchen window, saw no one there. The house was empty.

Then Victor saw something, a movement, a shadow.

He held perfectly still, barely breathing, something he'd

learned in that hospital so the crazies, the bullies, the predators wouldn't notice him. After a while they hadn't, for the most part. He'd become an expert at stillness. He'd also learned not to speak to Lissy when any of them came around, only fade slowly into a wall.

He saw movement again in the kitchen window, then a man, a big man dressed in a white shirt with his sleeves rolled up, doing something at the sink.

Victor knew the man was an FBI agent. He also had no doubt Savich had sent this agent, probably two or three of them, to wait here for him to show up. How had Savich known Victor would drive on to the Smiley house, after the debacle in Winslow? Did he also guess he would come back for the money? He cursed himself for the big mistake he'd made with that waitress, that cute little Cindy, who turned out not to be a wimp but a ballbuster, literally. She'd given them away. Winslow was too close to her, too close to Fort Pessel. Yeah, he'd screwed up, wanting to make Lissy jealous so she'd appreciate him more, not rag on him so much, and look what had happened. If Lissy had killed her, that would have been okay. No one would have known it was them, but Cindy escaped. They'd taken off like bats out of hell, his heart yammering in his chest for a good fifty miles. As for Lissy, she'd bowed over with that kick to her belly. She'd cried at the pain and raged at her failure, blaming him, of course, because she was the one who'd had to shoot at Cindy and she'd hurt too badly to aim properly, and the girl had gotten away. He'd do things differently if he could, and wasn't that always the problem with the past? You looked at it over your shoulder and knew you couldn't change it.

How many agents were here? He kept his eyes on the man in

the kitchen. He saw him turn and speak to someone else. So there were at least two agents? Did the local police chief have deputies doing drive-bys?

What to do?

Victor waited until it was dark, past nine o'clock, when the crickets were loud and steady. It was cooler, finally. No lights went on in the house, but Victor saw flickers, knew the agents were awake, watching, waiting.

It was time to get Lissy's pain pills, then he'd decide what they'd do next. If she continued to refuse to tell him where the money was hidden, screw it, he'd drive away. He wouldn't take her to kill Buzz Riley.

She said first thing when he opened the car door, *You've been gone forever, Victor. Hours and hours. You've been watching the house, haven't you? They're here, aren't they? The Feds are here, waiting for us?*

"Yes, they're here. Don't worry about it, not yet. Now it's finally dark and the pharmacy is closed. Remember, Lissy, you stay in the car when we get there. I'll get the pills."

But if Old Lady Kougar comes in like she did last time, you'll need me.

"No, I won't, not this time. Stay in the car." Okay, he'd give it one last try. "It's time to fish or cut bait. If you tell me where the money's hidden, not only will I let you kill Buzz Riley, I'll buy you your little red Fiat."

All right, I'll think about it. Maybe I do know, but don't screw up this time, Victor. I really want that red Fiat.

68

CHIEF TY CHRISTIE'S OFFICE
WILLICOTT, MARYLAND
THURSDAY

Sala was leaning back, his head pillowed in his arms, his feet propped up on Ty's desk. "All right, let's pull out the puzzle pieces we found today and see if we can fit them together. We're getting there, Ty. I can feel it."

Ty took a sip of her coffee, set the cup down precisely in the middle of her desk, eyed Sala's big feet, and smiled. She ticked off on her fingers. "We checked out the people who moved to Hagersville within a year of Mr. Henry's murder. There were seven families we spoke to but found nothing to tie them to LaRoque. Three of the families had accounts at Mr. Henry's bank, but by then he'd already put Calhoun in charge. None of them had even met him before he was killed. They'd heard about his murder, of course, but there was no reaction at all among any of them that rang false."

Sala said, "Those are the negatives, Ty. Let's put it out there: we already know about one person who moved to Haggersville not much longer than a year before his murder—Susan Sparrow. I know you think she's in the mix for it, because"—he counted off on his fingers now—"we saw her on the videotape with a whole lot of other people at the post office the morning Leigh was hit on the head. She didn't lie about being there, because we didn't ask her, but why didn't she mention it? Leigh thinks she heard high heels before she was struck down, so it was probably a woman. And Susan Sparrow was one of the people who dealt with his supposed cremation."

"But we have no motive," Ty said.

"Patience, Chief. You know I asked Dillon to set magic MAX into running a deep background search on Susan after we spoke with her. He left Ollie Hamish, his second in command, on the task before he and Sherlock left for Fort Pessel. Savich thinks Victor went back there." At the mention of Victor's name, Ty saw him stiffen up. She stood and walked over to him, lightly rubbed his shoulders. Odd, but he relaxed almost immediately.

"So we wait to hear from Ollie?"

He nodded.

She sat back down behind her desk. "Okay, let's say it was Susan who followed Leigh and hit her on the head. Where does that get us? We have Susan and the belt buckle in the lake. What's the connection?" She began tapping her fingertips on her desktop. "Why hasn't Ollie called?"

He started to tell her to be patient again, when his cell rang. "Speak of the devil, it's Ollie."

He put his cell on speaker. "Glad to hear from you, Ollie. We've been going round and round here. Tell me you've found something."

"Yeah, I've got two things for you, actually, one of which will blow you away. We texted pictures of the belt buckle to our liaison at the Israeli embassy. He forwarded them to a friend who's worked for years at the Holocaust Museum. The friend remembered it, knew the artisan's brother quite well. He recalls the brother crafted it for an Israeli colonel, and he was surprised it ended up in the States. He's contacting the family for us, trying to find out how it could have gotten here. I might have more for you on that tomorrow.

"Now for the blockbuster: MAX's background check on Susan Sparrow. On the surface, everything seemed normal, a woman born Susan Ann Hadden in Nashville, Tennessee, thirty years ago. An only child, middle-class parents, nothing until her parents were killed in a small-airplane accident when she was fifteen years old and she was adopted by the mother's sister and her husband. Both her aunt and uncle died when she was seventeen, left her enough money to attend college at Purdue, where she majored in business, made good grades. She had a solid employment history, worked in Saks management in Chicago, then moved to Haggersville, met and married Landry Sparrow. She's been active around town, raising money for the hospital, and is apparently well liked." He paused and said, "MAX went deeper and found that Susan Hadden Sparrow never existed. She's a legend, a fiction created some twelve years ago. There's no record of her parents, no record of an aunt or an uncle, no record of an adoption. We don't know who and what she was before she became Susan Hadden. She was savvy enough to hire someone to fill in the details of her life well enough to make it all seem real."

Ty pumped her fist in the air. "You didn't hit gold, Ollie, you hit platinum. Oh yes, I'm Ty Christie, police chief in Willicott. So, who is she? Who is Susan Sparrow?"

"We have no idea."

Ty said, "That snazzy FBI facial recognition program, could you run Susan through it? We might get lucky."

"Already did. Sorry, guys, nothing there. If she did do something criminal when she was a teenager and was arrested, her photo should have been in the database, unless it was sealed by the court. I couldn't find her. But you do have enough to take her in for questioning. I'll follow up with you tomorrow about the belt buckle."

When he'd clicked off, Sala said, "The only reason for her to re-create herself is if she had something to hide, something that could ruin her life, maybe someone else's life. Maybe something criminal. Or was she running from someone who scared her so badly she had to disappear her old life completely? Or what? Get sent to jail?"

Ty sighed. "Why did she move to Haggersville? And what did it have to do with Mr. Henry? And she attacked Leigh Saks because she was afraid of what Leigh would tell the hotline about the belt buckle? It belonged to an Israeli colonel. How did the colonel's belt buckle get to Mr. Henry? It's all about the dratted belt buckle, Sala. It's at the core of all of this. If we find out why, we've got our motive."

Sala said, "But that's the point. We still have no motive and no proof. If we confront her with what we know, she could run."

"As of this afternoon, she was keeping all her appointments, working at the crematorium, business as usual. It wouldn't be easy, packing your suitcase while your husband is standing at your elbow, wondering what's going on."

"We need something more to hold her on," Sala said.

Ty thought there was something more she did know, something important, but she couldn't quite grasp it. She had to settle, maybe get some sleep.

69

Ty was sitting on the top stair of the massive staircase at Gatewood mansion. She heard voices from downstairs, from the living room, a shout of laughter. She wanted to walk downstairs and join them, wanted to get closer because they were enjoying themselves so much. But she couldn't move. She tried again, heaving with the effort, but it was like some great force was holding her in place. She felt something that made her afraid, saw something dark casting shadows on the high ceilings downstairs in the entrance hall, darkening its corners. She didn't know what it was, but she knew it was evil. And it was coming closer, to her and to the happy voices talking and laughing. She wanted to warn the voices, but she still couldn't move. She tried to shout to them to run, but nothing came out of her mouth. She covered her eyes with her fists, wishing she could will herself away from there because now she was so afraid, she was scared to even breathe. She felt movement beside her and would have screamed if she could. She opened her eyes and saw a pretty young girl standing over her on the staircase. She wasn't looking at Ty but down the stairs, and she seemed focused on the laughing voices, just as Ty had been. Ty said, "I wanted to go down and laugh with them, but now I know there's something evil down there. It won't let me move. Will it let you move? Can you warn them?"

"I can move, but it doesn't matter, not now. You're right, he's here. They'll all be dead soon." She paused, cocked her head. Ty felt the evil coming toward them.

"No!"

"Ty, wake up!"

Now the pretty young girl was huddled down above her, her back pressed against the staircase wall. Then she ran, up the stairs to the third floor.

"Ty, come on, wake up!" He shook her shoulders, and she moaned, convulsing with fear, trying to pull away.

"He's coming, he's coming! But I can't see his face! Why can't I see him?"

Sala shook her once again, harder this time. Ty snapped awake, her vision blurred, her brain churning. Slowly, the pretty girl faded away, the terrifying blackness faded away. The laughter and voices were last, but then they too disappeared, leaving only Gatewood, standing gray and tall and empty on Point Gulliver, in a soundless world. Ty sucked in air. She stared up at Sala, his face dim in the night. She recognized his scent, his voice, and quieted. She whispered, "He killed them, Sala, and there was nothing I could do, nothing she could do."

She was icy to the touch, and Sala imagined her pupils were dilated from the shock of it, the fear. He grabbed up the single blanket and wrapped it around her, then pulled her against him, rubbed his hands up and down her back. "You're all right, you're okay. You had a doozy of a nightmare, sounded as dramatic and scary as any of mine. That's right, Ty, take slow, deep breaths. I've got you."

She whispered against his neck, "Sala?"

"I'm here."

Slowly Ty pulled back. She was still breathing hard, almost panting, remembering the awful fear, the helplessness.

"Who killed them, Ty? Who were they?"

Finally, she began to calm. She said, "I was at Gatewood, Sala, sitting on the landing stairs, and they were downstairs laughing and talking. I wanted to go down and be with them, but I couldn't move, and I knew something was holding me there. I couldn't escape it. Then a blackness came, and it spread all over the house. And she was there, and she knew as well as I did it was coming. Then she ran away to hide."

As she spoke, the girl's words were beginning to blur and fade away. Ty leaned against him, finally felt her breathing even. Sala said nothing more.

She said against his shoulder, "Sala, before I went to sleep, I was thinking about Gatewood, and I could see the outline of the belt buckle in the water off the end of the dock. And the bones, stretching out, almost to infinity. Then I dreamed I was there, Sala, and the girl at Gatewood was there, too—I know who she was." And Ty told him the story every citizen of Willicott knew, a terrifying story still told to keep the kids away from Gatewood. "She was only fifteen when a madman murdered her father, her mother, her brother, stabbed them and threw their bodies off the Gatewood dock into Lake Massey. They couldn't find her body, though, and some people came to believe she'd murdered them and run away after stealing the money her father kept in his safe."

Sala said, "But she survived."

She settled against him again, nodded against his neck. "Tomorrow morning, before we go back to Haggersville, I want to make a stop at Charlie Corsica's house. I think we've found her."

70

KOUGAR'S PHARMACY
FORT PESSEL, VIRGINIA
THURSDAY NIGHT

Victor drove with his lights off into the narrow alley beside Kougar's Pharmacy, pulled up close to a dumpster he knew was always there, and turned off the engine. It was dark as a pit. One thing you could count on in Fort Pessel—when the sun went, most everything closed down. Even the single movie theater only opened its doors on Friday nights. Of course, the bars outside Fort Pessel were always alive with lights and music. Here in town, near midnight, there were only the streetlights on low wattage, hardly even a car.

He sat quietly for a few minutes, feeling the pervasive heat build inside the car with the AC off. He thought about what he would do now, with the FBI agents at the Smiley house. He had a feeling the bank robbery money could be somewhere near the old, long-unused well, about thirty feet south of the house. But he couldn't be sure, and he couldn't think of anyplace else to look. If only Lissy would simply tell him. It pissed him off she didn't trust him enough, and look what he was doing for her. Stealing more drugs so she would feel better, and yes, finally stop complaining about the staples digging into her belly.

He'd been extra careful this time, even driven by Mrs. Kougar's house on Nob Tree Hill to make sure she was home. Her lights were on, and her lame-butt ancient light blue Impala was in the driveway. Still, he'd waited until he'd seen her shadow moving around upstairs.

He was all set. Break in, fill a Ziploc bag with pills, drive out of the alley, a clean getaway. No worries about an alarm. Before he got out of the car, he said again, "Stay here and out of sight, Lissy. There's no need for you to come in." He prayed she'd listen. He didn't want to have to deal with her craziness tonight, her endless criticism, her trying to give him orders.

She said nothing, which was very unlike her. He said immediately, "I know those staples are really hurting you, Lissy. I'll be as fast as I can. Then you'll feel real good again."

She could have wished him luck, but she didn't. She stayed quiet.

He turned off the interior light, got out of the Chrysler with a tire iron in his hand, and quietly closed the driver's door behind him. He walked to the mouth of the alley and stared up and down the street. The frigging town was dead.

His sneakers made no noise as he walked to the back door.

He eased his tire iron between the door and the frame and pushed down. Old Lady Kougar still didn't have an alarm, but the door held. He bet she'd installed a dead bolt inside. He pulled out the tire iron, repositioned it for more leverage, and pushed down with all his weight. The wood splintered and the door flew open, then stopped again. She'd put a chain on the door. No problem, he was ready for that. He pulled out a metal cutter and snapped the chain. He picked up the tire iron and pulled out his flashlight. He stepped into the back storeroom, filled with unopened boxes of cough medicine, toilet paper, condoms, shampoo, hemorrhoid cream . . . everything the citizens of Fort Pessel could want or need.

He knew the prescription drugs were in locked glass cabinets behind the pharmacy counter, about twenty feet away from the back storage room. He clutched the tire iron in his right hand, his flashlight in his left, and made his way into the store. It wasn't as dark out here as in the closed-in storeroom, what with the large windows across the entire front of the store and the streetlight on the corner. He turned off his flashlight and walked to the counter, paused a moment, listened. Nothing. If Old Lady Kougar hadn't moved them around, he knew exactly where the pain meds were. He unlatched the small gate separating the customers from the pharmacy. His hand was on the gate when he heard a voice from his nightmares.

"It's over, Victor. Lay the tire iron on the floor and put your hands on your head. Do it now."

Savich. Victor couldn't believe it, wouldn't believe it. It was Lissy, mimicking Savich to make him nuts.

"Now, Victor. I don't want to shoot you, but I will."

It wasn't Lissy. Victor jerked around and threw the tire iron where he thought Savich was standing. He heard it strike a shelf, sending merchandise flying to hit the linoleum floor and scatter.

"Victor, you took your shot, and now it's over. Hands on top of your head. I won't tell you again."

Slowly, Victor lifted his arms and tried as best he could to lace his fingers on top of his head and keep hold of the flashlight. He whispered, his voice a croak, as if he hadn't spoken in a long time. "How? How could you possibly know I was here?"

"After Lissy's crazy attack on Cindy Wilcox in Winslow, how can you be surprised?" It was her voice, a voice he knew as well as Savich's. It was Agent Sherlock. She'd shot him in the ankle, tried to cripple him. He thought of Cindy in Winslow and the mistakes he'd made, that Lissy had made—no, it was his fault. He'd been a fool. He'd let Lissy down by flirting with the little waitress, even following her home. Had he expected Lissy would let him have sex with her? He didn't know now, hadn't known then.

Sherlock walked from behind an aisle of hair care products, Savich from the cold medicine aisle. They were here together, the two people he hated and feared most in the world.

Victor, how can they be here? Sure, there was that fiasco in Winslow, but how did they know we'd be here tonight, in the pharmacy?

Lissy hadn't stayed in the car. She was here, hiding behind him, whispering in his ear. Victor was terrified she'd be hurt. He willed her to keep quiet. He whispered out the side of his mouth, "I don't know. You know they're smart."

Sherlock said, "What did you say, Victor? I told you, we went to Winslow and spoke to Cindy. She told us you yelled she'd kicked you in the staples. We knew it wasn't you with the staples. She kicked Lissy. We knew you'd want pain meds for her. You needed them for yourself, too, didn't you?"

A high, manic girl's voice screamed out of Victor's mouth, *"Victor, you puking loser, you brought them here. You should have killed that little bitch, and we'd be safe."*

Savich said, "Victor didn't want to kill her, Lissy, only you did. And you failed. Victor's not the puking loser, you are. The little waitress won, Lissy."

Victor looked ready to explode with rage. Or was it Lissy? Savich needed to get Victor back. "Victor, we know you came for the meds, but you also came back for the money, didn't you? We know you have some money, but you don't have all of it. Where did you get your stake?"

Victor answered him. "None of your business. Lissy still hasn't told me where her mom hid the money, so I had to come find it. But I had enough to take care of your kid before I killed Ryan." Victor stared at Sherlock. "And you, of course. How did you know I was in his room? I didn't make a sound. How?"

Sherlock said, "We had a plan in place if the alarm system went down. My part was to go to Sean's room, and there you were, standing over Sean with a gun and a knife. I wanted to shoot you in the head, Victor, but unfortunately I didn't. If I had, Octavia Ryan would be alive. A huge error in judgment on my part."

Savich said, "Someone paid you to murder Octavia Ryan, didn't they? And here she was one of the few people in the world who cared about you and helped you. Was it Lissy who told you to take the money to kill her? Was it Lissy who told you what to do and you did it? Tell us yourself, Lissy, tell us why he did that."

Lissy screamed, *"That bitch called him weak, a psycho! That bitch called me a Lolita! Victor always wants to please me—well, usually—but I don't control him. No, never. Yes, that cow saved us from prison, Victor knows that. He only did what he had to do to get us out in the world again."*

Sherlock said, "Lissy, we already know Victor didn't hate Octavia Ryan. He killed her because he was paid a lot of cash to do it. Tell us who paid you."

They heard Victor's voice, lower, deeper, with threads of bubbling madness. He laughed. "You're wrong about all of it. That bitch deserved it."

Sherlock said, "She saved you from life in state prison, and you murdered her and dumped her into Lake Massey. That's pretty cold, Victor. How did she deserve that?"

Victor shrugged. "I only did what I had to do, and besides, I had to prove to Lissy I could do it. She even bet me I couldn't, but she was wrong. I rowed Ryan out and told her I wasn't the loser, she was. She was the one being manipulated, not me. She didn't want to believe me, but then she did. She started crying, and I whacked her to shut her up."

Then Lissy's voice. *"I wanted to shoot the cow, but Victor wouldn't let me. See, Victor does what he wants."*

Victor's voice again. "I really don't like guns, Lissy, you know that." He blinked, focused on Sherlock. "I don't want to go back to that psycho jail. Lissy hates it, really hates it, and her staples hurt all the time. I had a hard time getting her pain meds there."

Lissy yelled, *"I won't go back there, Victor! I won't, I won't. I'll die there. The staples, they hurt so bad! Give me the pills, now!"*

It was hard for Sherlock and Savich to get their brains around Lissy and Victor talking back and forth, ignoring them both.

Then Lissy screamed at Savich, *"You should know, you bastard, you kicked me in my stomach, screwed me all up! It's your fault, all your fault! You threw Riley your gun, and he killed my mama!"*

Victor threw the flashlight at Savich and ran for the storeroom, pushed the door open as Savich's bullet struck the wood six inches from his head. "Stop, Victor!"

He kicked the door shut behind him and ran out the back door to the Chrysler, jerked on the door handle.

"Victor, stop right there," Sherlock shouted. She was standing in the mouth of the alley, her Glock aimed at him.

Victor whirled around, but it was Lissy's high, wild voice screaming, *"You bitch! You're fast, aren't you? Well, I'm going to shoot you right between your eyes, soak that red hair in your blood!"*

Victor pulled Sala's Glock from his pants and shot once toward her as he ducked behind the Chrysler. Sherlock hit the ground and rolled.

"Lissy, stay behind me!"

"No!"

Savich couldn't believe it, Victor was running straight at him, firing in a frenzy, screaming in Lissy's high, mad voice, *"You killed my mama! I'm going to send you to hell where you belong! Die, you bastard!"*

Savich took aim as bullets began spraying wildly around him.

There was a single shot, and Victor froze. He turned back to see Sherlock walking slowly toward him, her gun trained on center mass. His brain was cloudy. Lissy was crying. She screamed at him, *"We can't die, Victor! We can't, we can't!"*

Victor fell against the car and began a slow slide.

"Victor, no!" But the words came out of Victor's mouth in a gasp, then dwindled into a low whisper of sound.

The Glock fell to the ground. He grabbed the car door, but his fingers were wet with his own blood and slipped. He fell to his knees, then onto his back.

Savich came down beside him, applied pressure to his chest, but he knew it was no good. Victor looked up at him. He was wheezing, gasping for breath, his throat filling with blood. But it wasn't Victor, it was Lissy who whispered, *"I wanted to kill you first, shoot you right between your eyes. Victor should have done it, but I let him try to steal your little kid. Stupid, but sometimes I had to let him have his way."*

"Lissy, where is Victor?"

Victor felt his blood spreading over his chest, into his chest. Blood filled his throat, bubbled up to pour out of his mouth. Where did all the blood come from? He didn't really hurt. He felt immensely tired, and he knew, he knew. "Lissy?"

I'm here, Victor, I'm here. I'll never leave you. Her voice was soft in his ear.

"I know," Victor said, turned his face against Savich's blood-soaked palm, and died.

Savich slowly rose. He held Sherlock against his side. "Victor and Lissy, they died together."

Sherlock slipped her Glock back onto her belt clip. How

could Victor make his voice sound like Lissy's? A high young girl's? They'd heard her, and she was Lissy, she knew they'd both swear to it. She handed Savich a handkerchief. "Wipe your hands while I call our agents at the Smiley house."

As Savich wiped Victor's blood off his hands, he heard Sherlock say, "It's over. Victor's dead."

They waited together in the alley beside Kougar's Pharmacy beside Victor's body.

And Lissy's.

71

WILLICOTT, MARYLAND
FRIDAY MORNING

Ty pulled her Silverado into the Corsica driveway at 7:30 a.m., too early for Lynn Corsica to have left for the library. Charlie answered the door wearing jeans and a T-shirt, sporting a bad case of bedhead. "Chief! Agent Porto, what's going on? Is something the matter? Let me get my gun!"

Ty grabbed his arm. "No, it's all right, Charlie. Sorry we're here so early without calling, but I need to speak to your mom."

"My mom? But—"

"Didn't you tell me your mom is the smartest person you know?"

"Well, yes, but—" Charlie heard the urgency in her voice, stopped. "My mom's in the kitchen, making me and my dad blueberry pancakes." He added over his shoulder as he trotted away from them, both Ty and Sala on his heels, "Dad's still in bed. He had a late night, some sort of infestation on his prize bougainvillea." Ty knew Mr. Corsica owned the largest nursery and landscaping company in these parts, so there was no need to explain.

This was Ty's first visit to the Corsica home in a very long time. It was a ranch-style 1980s-vintage split-level set in the middle of a large lot surrounded by oaks and maples, and, of course, superbly maintained flowers and trellised roses in boxes, no doubt thanks to Mr. Corsica's business.

"Chief Christie—Ty!" Lynn Corsica, a spatula in her right hand, was walking out of the kitchen toward them, her feet bare, her blue bathrobe flapping around her legs. She stopped and gathered herself.

"Mom, Ty wants to speak to you."

"Yes, of course. All right. How can I help you, Ty?"

Ty quickly introduced Sala then drew out a photo she'd printed from a website and handed it to Mrs. Corsica. "Do you recognize this woman?"

Lynn Corsica looked down at the publicity photo, a head shot of a beautiful dark-haired young woman who looked both serious and kind. "I don't think so." She cocked her head at Ty. "Why did you think I would recognize her?"

"Mrs. Corsica, I'd like you to subtract fifteen years from the woman's face, change the hair color, maybe blond or light brown, and imagine she has blue eyes. Take away the makeup. Focus on her eyes, the shape of her mouth."

Mrs. Corsica studied the photo. "She looks about thirty in

this photo, so I have to picture her at fifteen?" She studied the photo some more, frowned, then slowly, she raised her head. There was wonder in her voice. "It's Albie Pierson, isn't it?"

"Yes, I believe it is," Ty said. "Her family wasn't here long enough for her to be in a yearbook, but I hoped you'd remember her. Can you describe her?"

"She was a pretty little thing, slight, fine-boned, with lovely blond hair like you said, and light blue eyes. She always wore her hair in a French braid, long, past her shoulders.

"I remember clearly she was in the library the very first week her family moved into Gatewood. I gave her a library card myself. Such a sweet smile she had, and she was always very polite, listened when anyone spoke to her. I liked her." She paused. "Then of course her whole family was murdered, and she disappeared. They couldn't find her body, so people being people, some said she murdered her family, maybe she snapped because of sexual abuse, something like that. One of her teachers came forward to say she thought she'd seen bruises on Albie's arms, but I knew none of that was true. I'd gotten to know Albie. I was also a rape counselor over in Bowie before we moved here. I would swear Albie had never been abused. That's what I thought, anyway, but it didn't matter much, since they never found her."

Mrs. Corsica looked down at the spatula in her right hand, dripping batter on the oak floor. "Look at me, keeping you standing here in the hallway. Come into the kitchen and have some pancakes and coffee." She didn't wait for an answer, turned on her bare heel and walked into a bright kitchen, its walls a pale yellow and windows looking out over a beautiful, manicured backyard, with more wildly blooming flowers planted along a white fence.

She waved them to chairs, poured them coffee. "Charlie, you sit, too. We won't wait for your dad. He was still asleep as of a few minutes ago."

She turned back to the stove to ladle more batter into a hot skillet. Ty wanted to get to Haggersville now, face down Susan Sparrow, tell her they knew she was Albie Pierson. But her stomach growled as Mrs. Corsica sprinkled blueberries on top of the batter. Sala grinned at her. They'd only had a quick cup of coffee before leaving the cottage.

Soon they were all buttering pancakes, pouring maple syrup over them, and forking crispy bacon off a plate. As they ate, Mrs. Corsica said, "I haven't thought of Albie Pierson in years. I used to wonder what happened to her, wondered if the monster who'd stabbed her family to death had taken her with him, killed her, and buried her somewhere. Then life happened, as it always does, and we all forgot. Where is she now, Chief?"

"In Haggersville. Her name now is Susan Sparrow."

"You mean the Sparrows who own the Sparrow Crematorium?"

"Yes, those Sparrows," Sala said. "She married Landry Sparrow six years ago and has been there since." He held out his plate for two more pancakes.

Mrs. Corsica served him while her pancakes still lay uneaten on her plate. She said quietly, "Imagine, she's been close by. I'm so glad she survived. Tell me, are you going to arrest her for the murder of her family when she was fifteen?"

"No," Ty said. "She didn't kill her family, no disagreement with you on that. I think it was a stranger, and Albie hid, knowing what he was doing, what he'd done. When she was sure he left, she took the cash out of her father's safe and ran. I don't think she was afraid of the police. I think she ran because she was afraid of the monster who'd murdered her family. We would like to speak to her about that day, and then about something else entirely."

Mrs. Corsica searched her face, then said slowly, "It's all about those bones found in Lake Massey, isn't it?"

"Yes," Ty said. "And who those people were."

"But what does it mean?"

"As soon as we resolve this, Charlie can tell you all about it."

Sala sat back in his chair and sighed deeply. "Thank you, Mrs. Corsica, for the outstanding breakfast. We would appreciate your not mentioning anything we spoke of here to anyone, all right? You too, Charlie."

"No, of course not," Mrs. Corsica said. "You either, right, Charlie?"

Charlie nodded. "Chief Christie's my boss, Mom. If I did, she'd fire my butt."

"Deservedly so," his mother said, and sighed. "But I still wonder what it all means. The belt buckle, Susan Sparrow really being Albie Pierson, and all those bones."

"Give us another day. Thank you very much for confirming Susan Sparrow's identity, and the breakfast was delicious."

They left three minutes later, waved to Mrs. Corsica standing in the open doorway, the spatula still in her hand, an older man now standing behind her, his hand on her shoulder. They walked to Ty's Silverado, Charlie, still barefoot, beside them. "You know everything, don't you, Chief?"

"No, but we have a good start. Give us today, Charlie, to nail everything down."

72

HAGGERSVILLE, MARYLAND
FRIDAY MORNING

Ty turned onto the interstate, flashed a look at Sala. "It's hard to believe all this started only a week ago." A week ago today. And Octavia was dead, and so was her killer, Victor Nesser, shot in an alley beside a pharmacy in Fort Pessel last night.

Sala said, "It's tough to get my head around what Savich told us—Victor and Lissy dying together. He said he spoke to both of them, they were both there. And Lissy spoke to them. It makes my hair stand on end."

"It does sound unbelievable," Ty said.

When they wended their way through morning traffic, finally arrived at the Sparrow Crematorium, Sala's cell phone buzzed. "Porto here. Dr. Thomas, good timing. What do I mean? Nothing, really. What have you got for me?"

Ty stopped, shut off the engine, turned to listen.

Sala said, “A moment, please, Dr. Thomas, let me put you on speaker so Chief Christie can hear.”

“Chief, Agent Porto, the majority of bones we’ve cleaned and examined so far show considerable trauma inflicted near time of death, repeated stab wounds, to be precise. I’m not a medical examiner, but I’d say a similar knife was used—a common six-inch fixed-blade hunting knife, like a Buck. So, Agent Porto, this is not a reprise of the crematory in Noble, Georgia. This is something else entirely.”

Sala said, “So you believe these people were murdered, all of them stabbed to death, and the killer used Lake Massey as a dumping ground.”

“Yes. As I said, we’ve only examined about a third of the bones, but I can’t see the pattern changing.”

“Have you found the remains of a Caucasian man, about five foot ten, seventy-five years old?”

“Yes, there was an older man, probably in his seventies, maybe early eighties. Multiple stab wounds, like the rest.”

“If we provide you with a Mr. Henry LaRoque’s autopsy report, do you think you could make a positive identification?”

“It would be possible, yes.”

Sala said, “And Dr. Thomas, please let us know if you have any luck with the DNA harvesting. We agree the victims are very probably from the area, missing persons or people who were thought to have up and left for whatever reason. It might be our only way to identify them all.”

Sala punched off. “So I bet Mr. Henry wasn’t cremated, he

was thrown into the lake wearing his treasured belt buckle. By Susan Sparrow."

When they walked into the flower-filled entry of the Sparrow Crematorium it was to see Ms. Betty Chugger watching them approach her reception desk. They heard music, a soft harp, from behind a closed door to their left.

Ms. Chugger said, her voice barely above a whisper, her finger over her lips, "We're holding a small memorial service for a lovely woman who lived her entire life in Haggersville. So we must keep our voices down. It was Mr. Landry's mama who insisted years ago we provide this service to the family and friends who wish it. It lessens their fear of something they haven't experienced before, that is, of their loved one being cremated. A kind of closure, Mrs. Sparrow called it. It's a very nice idea, don't you think?" She added without pause, "What can I do for you this beautiful morning?"

Ty said, "We need to see Susan Sparrow."

"Not possible, I'm afraid. Landry said she wasn't feeling well this morning and he'd wanted her to stay in bed. He fears it's some sort of flu. Only he and Eric are here today. Would you like to see them?"

Ty looked at Sala, then shook her head at Ms. Chugger. "Not now, but thank you. We'll be back later."

Sala looked up the Sparrows' home address on his tablet.

73

SPARROW HOUSE
HAGGERSVILLE, MARYLAND
FRIDAY MORNING

Ty pulled her Silverado into the empty driveway of a lovely two-story colonial on Ridgeway Lane, an upper-class neighborhood with spacious front yards lined with maples and oaks. It was quiet, no traffic, no kids, and even though it wasn't noon yet, the air was hot and still. They walked to the front door, listened, heard nothing except the low hum of the central air-conditioning. Sala pressed the doorbell, heard the ring echo through the house. He rang again, waited, and then tried the doorknob. To his surprise, the front door wasn't locked. He pushed the door inward into a dim entry hall. Through an arched doorway to the right was a living room with traditional antebellum antiques, to the left, a businesslike study.

Ty called out, but no one answered. They walked through the dining room to the kitchen, and beyond that through a mudroom to another smaller pale yellow study at the back of the house, probably Susan's.

They walked up the beautiful mahogany stairs, their steps soundless on the Oriental runner, past stylized paintings of nineteenth-century New York and Chicago, evocative and expensive-looking.

They paused, listened, heard nothing.

At the top of the stairs, they split up. Ty walked into an empty master bedroom with more antebellum antiques—a chest, a mirror, a rocking chair—and thick white wall-to-wall carpeting. She looked into a large, perfectly organized walk-in closet, then into the bathroom, another display of opulence, with a Jacuzzi and a double sink in beautiful green-veined marble.

She saw a large white envelope lying on top of three perfectly folded yellow towels in the center of the bathroom counter. It was addressed to Chief Christie and Agent Porto.

She met Sala back at the top of the stairs. He nodded down the hall. "A playroom of sorts, I guess you'd call it—a pool table, some video games, poker table, comfortable leather furniture. Beyond are guest rooms, both with baths. No one up here. What's that?"

Ty held up the envelope. "It was sitting on top of some towels in the master bathroom. It's addressed to you and me, by name."

They sat side by side on the top step. Ty opened the sealed envelope and pulled out three sheets of very fine stationery covered with beautiful cursive. She read aloud:

Agent, Chief, knowing you two, I'll bet it's Friday morning and you've figured out who I really am, not that it matters because I'll be gone, and you won't find me.

I have very little time, so I must hurry. I know I owe you an explanation and answers to all your questions, just as I knew you would find this letter. No, it's more than an explanation, it's my confession.

I confess to being solely responsible for the two crimes I'm about to describe to you. I'm very glad I failed in one of them, namely in harming Leigh Saks. My only excuse is that I panicked and didn't see I had another choice.

As you know, I'm sure, my real name is Albie Pierson. I was fifteen years old when a monster broke into our home and murdered my father, my mother, and my brother. I saw him take off my father's favorite belt. I watched him carry each of their bodies out to the Gatewood dock, watched, helpless, as he dumped them, one by one, into the lake. I knew he would look for me and kill me, too, so I hid in my special spot beneath the stairs until I was certain he was gone. Finally, I walked out onto the dock, following the trail of my family's blood, and stared down into the water. I couldn't see their bodies. I knew to my soul he would come back because he wanted to kill me, too, and I wanted to survive. I took five thousand dollars from my father's safe and ran.

I won't go into details about my life. I look back at that fifteen-year-old girl and I admire her. She grew up in the space of a single hour, and she survived. In the beginning what kept her going was the promise she made that horrible day, that she would find and kill the monster who murdered her family. Then this young girl heard the chief of police in Willicott was looking for her as a person of interest, and she realized some people believed she had killed her own family.

The only way to stay safe until she found the killer was to stay hidden. She moved to Chicago and reinvented herself, became Susan Hadden. She studied and learned and read countless news reports online, but she never read anything that could lead her to the monster who'd murdered her family at Gatewood.

I left Chicago and moved to Haggersville six years ago, on a whim, I told myself, but of course it was because I was desperate to be near where I'd lived so happily with my family, close enough to Willicott so perhaps I'd hear something about those long-ago murders, something that would help me find the monster. But not in Willicott itself, where I might be recognized. And so I settled in Haggersville. I realized I never thought of him as a man or a murderer, but always a monster, the monster.

I was in for a big surprise. I met and married Landry Sparrow. For the first time since my family died, I actually started to enjoy life. My Sparrow in-laws welcomed me. I hadn't known them long when they died needlessly in the auto accident, but Landry, Eric, and I had one another, so our life continued. And the crematorium became as much mine as theirs. I will admit I never in my wildest imaginings dreamed I'd be cremating people for a living. But life can't be predicted, can it? I already knew for certain everything could change in the blink of an eye. As it did again when you found the belt buckle in Lake Massey.

Five and a half years ago, one month after Landry and I married, I found a white envelope in the mailbox with only my name printed on it and a single sheet enclosed. It was written in black ink, block printing, no address, no signature. The writer said he recognized me, he knew who I was because he had my photo. He was sorry he hadn't found me on that magical day fifteen years ago today, even though he'd searched for me. But here I had turned up, right under his nose. He loved Fate, he wrote. And irony. Didn't I find it amusing the police still wanted me for questioning, that some still believed I'd killed my family?

I guess you could say my heart stopped. I thanked heaven I was alone at the time so Landry wouldn't see me with the letter. The monster had found me, not the other way around. And he'd recognized me? My hair wasn't blond now. It was nearly black, and I wore brown contact lenses. He said he was thinking about calling the police himself to see if they'd haul me in and put me on trial for murdering my family in Willicott so long ago, but didn't I know? There was no expiration date on murder?

I could see him laughing when he suggested I take his letter to Chief Masters. He couldn't wait to see how the chief and the fine people of Haggersville greeted my terrible accusation. And against whom? Some imaginary ghost? He suggested the chief would think I'd written the letter myself. And what would I do then? Of course, he was right. I couldn't take his note to the police because it would bring who I really am, Albie Pierson, into the open, ruin my name and my marriage, possibly even end with my being tried for murdering my own family.

He wrote that he'd waited too long to kill me but now he wouldn't have to wait much longer. I'd never know when he would come for me. I knew he was laughing when he wrote that, so pleased with himself that he could terrify me again.

And he had. How could I protect myself? I had no idea who he was. I felt the terror of that long-ago day again when he was searching the house for me, when he was only a thin wall away. And then I realized his recognizing me, his taunting me, was the best thing that could have happened. I was no longer that innocent teenager, hadn't been Albie Pierson hiding beneath those stairs for years. I realized I had no intention of showing the note to Chief Masters or telling anyone, but not for the reasons he believed. I wasn't going to let him kill me. I was going to find him and kill him exactly as he'd killed them. I was going to avenge my family.

How did I find him? I knew after his letter he had to live in town, in Haggersville, the very town I'd moved to. Otherwise how could he have seen me, recognized me? I realize, now, it was he who murdered all of those people whose bones you found in Lake Massey. He was completely insane. I made a list of all the older men in town who'd lived here a long time. I bought a handgun, but I still had no good plan.

I wondered, since he was taking such pleasure in taunting me, torturing me, would he become careless? So I ignored his letter. I knew he'd see me, see if I was upset or find out I was planning to leave. I showed no response. I went about my business as if nothing had happened. He'd left the first letter in my mailbox on a day he knew I'd be the first one home so Landry wouldn't see it. I set up a video camera looking out over the mailbox in case he left another. A week later he wrote another letter, this one shorter, describing most everything I'd done the day before, most all of my movements. The second letter he left at the crematorium after hours, just inside the front door, again with only my name on the envelope. What he didn't know, of course, was that I'd set up a camera there, too. And there he was, clear as day, leaving that envelope, walking away with a jaunty step. It was Mr. Henry LaRoque.

He was on my list of possible suspects, but needless to say, I was still shocked.

I confess to killing Mr. Henry LaRoque five years ago. I broke into his house late at night, surprised him, and tied his hands and feet. Then I stood over him and stabbed him wherever I wished, for well over an hour. At first he couldn't believe I'd actually found out who he was, that I'd actually had the guts to come for him. Soon he was begging to tell me everything I wanted to know if I'd end it. I told him I would if he told me why he'd done it.

Between his screams on that very fine night, the last night of his miserable life, he gasped out that my family were his first victims, said they showed him what joy there was in killing, helped him lay out his plans for all the pleasant golden years ahead of him, and he loved them for it. It was magical for him, killing the new family at Gatewood exactly where another family had been butchered.

Then that evil old man told me things I never expected to hear, things that hardly seemed possible, yet I wasn't surprised. He told me he kept a journal, detailing exactly what he'd done and to whom and when, and he told me about his box of treasures, each tagged so he'd always remember the day, the victim. He kept it all in his study, hidden behind some old theological tomes no one ever looked at. He admitted he'd taken off my father's belt before he'd thrown him into Lake Massey. He didn't know I'd seen him do it. That Star of David belt buckle given to my father by an Israeli colonel years ago, his thanks for saving his daughter from a suicide bomber in a café in Jerusalem. LaRoque said it was his favorite, his reminder of that day, the first day of his journey when he'd stripped that belt off my father's body, wrapped it around his hand, and put it in his jacket pocket to keep it from getting more blood on it. By this time he was delirious with pain, nearly insane with it, begging me to end it. I knew he was dying now, but I didn't give him a final stab in the heart and end it. No, I left him there to think about how I'd killed him, the teenager he hadn't managed to find.

Your much-beloved Mr. Henry LaRoque was a serial killer, and he was proud of it. He basked in it to the end. That old man, that monster, claimed he'd butchered people for years and thrown their bodies into Lake Massey. Fifty-one people, he said. He was proud of how easily he'd fooled everyone in town.

He was Mr. Henry to them all, so popular he never had to pay for his own coffee.

I have never had a single regret about killing him. I think he couldn't help writing me that note when he realized who I was. After all, I was the girl who got away, the only person who'd seen what he'd done, the only person who could appreciate who and what he was, what he'd accomplished. Would he have tried to kill me? Or would he have taken more pleasure from my knowing he might?

When his ruined corpse was delivered to the crematorium, I unwrapped him, gloried in what he looked like now, in death. I took my father's belt and put it around his pants, replaced his body with another's due to be cremated. I drove Mr. Henry and his precious treasure to the lake and dumped him where he'd dumped my family, off the end of the dock at Gatewood. I'd finally avenged them. Perhaps now they could rest in peace. Against all odds, I'd kept my promise and I'd killed him.

I was the one who struck down Gunny—Leigh Saks—with a brick, a spur-of-the-moment reaction to being terrified of what she would tell the FBI hotline about that belt buckle. What could she possibly have said? I didn't know what he'd told her that long-ago day. But I'd heard she'd seen Mr. Henry with that belt buckle, and I knew it might lead them directly to me. I didn't have time to question Leigh myself. I acted. Now, of course, I realize she didn't know anything that would have implicated me. All she did was watch that profane old man polishing and fondling my father's belt buckle.

I am grateful Leigh survived. I am grateful that whatever

it was in her brain that had made her simple miraculously corrected itself. I have no understanding of how that happened. But I wish her the best in her new life. Perhaps one day she will consider I did her a favor.

I hope you are alone in my house, that neither Landry nor Eric is there with you. I've written to them separately. The pain it will bring Landry makes me want a magic wand, to wish away that any of this ever happened, that I ever came to Haggersville. But I did. He will have to face it, deal with it, as I will.

Again, my husband and my brother-in-law have no idea what I have done or who I really am. They are innocent of any wrongdoing whatsoever.

Yet again I have to leave my home.

I predict the two of you will prosper.

She'd printed out her name, then signed it

Albie Pierson, aka Susan Pierson Hadden Sparrow

74

VITA-MAX CORPORATION
CRANSTON BUILDING, SUITE 202
TYSONS CORNER, VIRGINIA
SATURDAY AFTERNOON

When Ty and Sala stepped off the elevator on the second floor of the older Cranston Building, they didn't see anyone, understandable since it was the weekend. They heard whistling, followed it down the hall to a door that was cracked open. They walked in to see Bill Culver packing boxes. Ty had thought he'd looked good in the suit he'd worn at Octavia's funeral, but he was even more good-looking today, dressed in jeans, boots, and a black T-shirt tight enough to show off pecs that rivaled Eric Sparrow's.

He looked up, puzzled a moment, then he smiled and stepped forward. "Agent Porto and Chief Christie, whatever are you two doing here?" The smile fell off his face as if on cue when they didn't answer him. He splayed his hands in apology and said in a low voice filled with emotion, "There was no time on Tuesday to thank you for caring enough to invite me to sit with you." He squeezed his eyes closed a moment. "And then that explosion, all the chaos, a terrible thing. A miracle no one was killed."

"You never left Octavia's coffin," Sala said.

"Of course not. How could I? She was the woman I loved, the woman who would have come back to me if that crazy young man hadn't killed her. I saw on TV he was dead, killed where he'd lived once, in Fort Pessel, Virginia. Thursday night."

"Yes, that's right," Ty said. "Why are you packing boxes, Mr. Culver?"

A smile bloomed, then disappeared quickly. He shrugged. "The timing is regrettable, but my lease is up. I've bought a small building not far from here, offices for the additional staff I've been planning to hire and a bigger distribution center for the three new Vita-Max stores I'm going to be opening over the next six months."

Sala whistled. "That's an expensive plan. It would keep me up nights wondering how I was going to pay all the bills."

Culver laughed, but sobered immediately. "You're right, of course, the financing would have been tight, but Octavia's lawyer called me last Wednesday to tell me Octavia never changed her will. Still, I was stunned. When we married we agreed I would be her sole beneficiary and she would be mine. But then when we couldn't resolve our differences and she left, I naturally assumed she would change her will."

Sala said, "Octavia told me about the bequest from a relative, a complete surprise. What is the amount, something near five million dollars?"

Culver nodded. He shrugged again. "Of course, I'd much rather have my wife back."

"Would you really?" Ty had spoken very quietly, but Culver immediately turned on her.

He stared at her, his face tightening with anger. "What do you mean by that, Chief Christie?"

It was Sala who answered. "I told you at Octavia's funeral she had decided to go back to you. It must have come as quite a shock, since you'd paid Victor Nesser twenty thousand dollars to murder her. Of course, if she had come back to you, you would simply have waited until it was safe to pay someone else to murder her later, say, after your second honeymoon. No reason to share all that money, was there?"

Culver's hands gripped the edge of his desk so hard his knuckles were white. He was shaking, and not from rage. "That's outrageous! How dare you come in here making accusations like that! I loved Octavia, do you hear me? Loved her! I will grieve for her the rest of my life. The two of you—you disgust me. I want you both out of here right now."

Ty smiled at him. "It turns out, Mr. Culver, the twenty thousand dollars you withdrew on three different dates from your bank, Third Republic of Virginia, right here in Tysons Corner, was from the bank vault. It also turns out Victor Nesser paid for his dinner in a town called Winslow with a one-hundred-dollar bill that matches a sequential serial number from one of those bills you withdrew from your bank. He had a few dozen more hundreds in his pants pocket when he died."

He looked blank for only a moment, then he said, smooth as honey, "I admit that's strange, if it's true and not some kind of mix-up at the bank. But that money I withdrew? I pay people with cash all the time, some of my suppliers prefer it. He could have gotten the bills from anywhere. He didn't get them from me."

Sala continued, his voice expressionless, "We examined the prison logs at Central State Hospital while Victor was there. They videotape visits to patients who are violent offenders, did you know that? Guess what? There you are, Mr. Culver, right there, a few days before Victor escaped. It was foolish of you to go there yourself, rather than hire someone else to contact him. But you're not all that smart, are you?"

Culver opened his mouth, but Ty raised her hand. "Mr. Culver, spare us. It also wasn't bright of you to tell us you hadn't known you were still Octavia's beneficiary. One phone call to her lawyer, and that lie stood up and saluted. You knew it very well, made sure to confirm it before you arranged to help Victor escape and kill her. Your cell phone puts you there near the grounds the night he escaped. Were you ever afraid he might go crazy and murder you, Mr. Culver? After all, he was incarcerated in a high-security mental facility. Or Octavia had told you all about him, and you were certain he was harmless, at least to you? You picked him up, gave him the twenty thousand, all in one-hundred-dollar bills, and took him to the Klondike Motel and left him there."

Culver's hands were fisted, his jaw working. He looked like he wanted to smash Ty's face. "You listen to me, I didn't mean what I said exactly. I was still grief-stricken when her lawyer called me. I don't really remember what he said or what I said. You're twisting everything."

Sala was breathing hard, so enraged he wanted to leap on this man. "If I had known what you are, you bastard, and Octavia had told me she was going back to you, I would have tied her down to protect her."

"She was coming back to me—you told me so at her funeral!"

Sala shrugged. "I lied. I felt sorry for you, so I lied."

Culver grabbed up a box cutter, saw Sala beckon to him with a wave of his fingers, and slowly put it down.

"Good move, Mr. Culver," Ty said.

"Listen to me, both of you, I didn't kill her. It was that Nesser. You know he did it. I only visited him at the hospital because Octavia was concerned about him, asked me to check on him, see that he was doing okay, nothing more than that. It was a simple favor."

Ty shook her head back and forth. "Mr. Culver, more lies won't help you. I'm sure Octavia told you all about him, told you how unstable he was, how easily manipulated. When she got her inheritance, you realized what a mistake you'd made. You tried your best, but you didn't think she believed you'd really change when you swore to her there'd be no more gambling, no more women on the side. Then you remembered Victor, remembered how he'd hated what she'd said about him in order to get him committed to a psychiatric hospital and not sentenced to life in prison. You offered Victor twenty thousand dollars in cash, offered to help him escape if he would murder Octavia for you and disappear."

"Go away, both of you. I have nothing to say. I want to speak to my lawyer."

"Oh, you will, Mr. Culver, you will. But first, Agent Porto will read you your rights."

Sala wanted to beat this man with his bare hands, but instead he drew a deep breath and read Culver his rights. "A couple of agents will be arriving in a minute to take you to the Hoover Building. You will need a very good lawyer, but I don't know how you're going to pay him. All the money Octavia willed to you? You're never going to see it."

"No! You have no proof of anything! You're jealous because you couldn't get Octavia and her money for yourself!"

Ty saw Sala was about to leap on Culver. She laid her hand on his arm, felt his muscles tensed, felt the rage in him. She was more than grateful to see Agents Fulton and Droban walk through the office door.

Sala was shaking when they left Culver's office to the sound of Culver cursing. Ty stopped him by the elevator. "Sala, I'm so sorry, so very sorry, but it's over now." She hugged him hard, whispered against his face, "You held it together. You didn't beat him to death."

He said against her hair, his voice catching, "He's going down, Ty. The man who killed Octavia is going down."

She said nothing, only held him close as he wept.

EPILOGUE

TY CHRISTIE'S COTTAGE
WILLICOTT, MARYLAND
SATURDAY NIGHT

Sala took a drink of Ty's Turkish espresso, settled himself against the sofa cushions, and patted Lucky, his fifteen-pound black-as-midnight cat with beautiful green eyes and one tattered ear, who was licking her tail even as she arched her back into his hand. She seemed perfectly content to be in a new place, sitting like a queen in the middle of a sofa with a new human ready to worship her.

Ty said, "Time to change those butterfly strips on your head again, Sala, make sure you're healing okay."

"You changed them Wednesday." Sala touched his fingertips to where Dr. Staunton had placed three stitches. Had it only been since last Saturday? He flashed on being bound in the closet and said immediately to distract himself, "Ty, thanks for the worry, but I'm fine. If you have a Band-Aid, I'll put some disinfectant on the stitches and cover them."

She looked at him thoughtfully. "It is sort of cozy having you with me, Sala, but I'm in charge here. Get your fingers away, I'll do it."

When she'd smoothed down the Band-Aid, she stared at the faded bruises and welts still visible on his wrists, felt a punch of anger. "Do your wrists still hurt?"

He shrugged. "No, good to go."

Ty laid her palm on his cheek. "Do you know what I think is the most amazing thing about this whole incredible week?"

He was still stroking Lucky's back, but all his attention was on her. He cocked his head in question.

She looked him in the eye. "That you survived, Sala. You survived and you're going to be fine. That makes me very happy."

He smiled, and perhaps he stroked Lucky's back a bit faster. Lucky gave him a look, stretched out to lick his hand, then broke out in a symphony of purring. *The vagaries of fate.* "I've always known intellectually that none of us can have a clue when our world is going to be turned upside down. When my wife died, I didn't think I could handle it, but time passed, and the pain and grief slowly receded. And now this. Octavia murdered, my nearly dying. Ty, the truth is, I'm still a mess. There's been so much. The nightmares won't go away all that soon."

"Then isn't it great I'm a light sleeper?" She yawned. "Not

quite time for sleep yet, though." No, she thought, it was time to simply enjoy breathing in the soft clean air. The heavy rain of the previous night had dropped the temperature, and presented an incredible clear sky, a sickle moon, and a dazzling array of stars. The crickets gave their nightly performance.

EPILOGUE 2

SAVICH HOUSE
GEORGETOWN
SUNDAY NIGHT

Three Dizzy Dan's pizza boxes were open on the coffee table in the Savich living room, smells of piping-hot cheese and Sherlock's favorite, pepperoni, wafting through the air.

Sean was finally in his bed, hopefully asleep, after thirty minutes as the star of the show without a word about the week the adults had managed to survive.

Savich took a final bite of his vegetarian delight pizza and settled back. He'd taken Ty and Sala through all their questions about what had happened in Fort Pessel. He said now, "No one has a clue about where Jennifer Smiley hid the bank robbery money. With the fresh publicity about it, the bank will be dealing with treasure hunters swarming over the property again and digging holes everywhere, not to mention what they'll do to the interior of the house. Publicly the bank is declining to get involved, but I'll wager bank employees are out there digging with the rest of the treasure hunters." He paused, took a drink of his Dos Equis.

He looked over at Sala, dressed in chinos, a black T-shirt, and sneakers, and thankfully, saw that he finally looked calm and settled. He wasn't surprised Sala had more or less moved to Willicott with his cat and was living in Ty's cottage. And who knew where that would lead?

Sherlock said, "So how's Lucky doing?"

Sala said, "This morning Ty gave her slivers of baked chicken breast. After that offering, she settled under her hand for a good petting. That's progress."

Ty said, "Give me three days, and she'll spend more time with me than with *señor* here. By the way, we saw Leigh Saks, her mother, father, and her father's wife today at Lulie's bakery, her first day out of the hospital. Congressman Mellon's wife was very pleasant. She was eating Lulie's éclairs at a fine clip, along with the rest of us."

"And Leigh?" Sherlock asked. "How is she doing?"

"She was smiling a lot," Sala said. "Needless to say, everyone was eager to see her, to talk with her. Lulie told me Leigh's thinking about politics and working for her dad in Washington. It was his idea. It would be a whole new life for her. She seemed excited about it."

Ty said, "Leigh was amazing. I think she was amused everyone suddenly wanted to speak to her, well understood their interest, but she didn't really show it. She was gracious and kind."

"That's great to hear." Sherlock added, her hand hovering. "Okay, guys, there's one last slice of pepperoni pizza." But she didn't wait, she snagged it up and took a big bite.

Savich leaned forward. "So you were in Haggersville today. How are Albie Pierson's husband and brother-in-law dealing?"

Ty said, "Landry and Eric were in denial at first, but after reading the letters she wrote to them, they've had to accept it. They're devastated. What's amazing to me is she managed to lead a normal life for five years after she killed LaRoque."

Sala shrugged. "And why not? It was the life she had before LaRoque became a threat to her again. And it was over. She avenged her family. It ended for her when she strapped her father's belt to LaRoque's body and threw him off the dock at Gatewood."

Ty nodded. "Just as he did her family. Still, for five years she had to live with the world praising Mr. Henry when she knew the truth."

Sala said, "She had to pay that price to stay safe, to keep who she was secret. Chief Masters hasn't released the facts of the case yet, said he wasn't going to until he'd gone over all the evidence with the district attorney."

"Have they contacted all the families of the victims from LaRoque's journal?" Savich asked.

"They've been going over his journal and his box of souvenirs, and yes, they've started to contact the family members before they release the names. The chief said drama was running high in town, with rumors about why Mrs. Sparrow was missing without warning, but that will be nothing compared to the uproar when he announces the truth about Mr. Henry being a serial killer. And he's already told Leigh Saks, in confidence, that it was Susan Sparrow who struck her down."

Sherlock asked, "What did Leigh say?"

Ty said, "When she got the whole story out of Chief Masters, Leigh said no way would she press charges. She said she couldn't imagine what Susan had lived through. She wished her the best since Susan hadn't killed her—and look what she'd given her, a rebooted brain. She said she hoped Landry, once he got over his shock, would be proud of her, and maybe in the future, who knew, Susan would contact him and maybe they'd get together again."

Sala looked directly at Savich and Sherlock. "Chief Masters told Ty and me he isn't going to commit any resources to finding her. Are you both on board with that?"

Savich and Sherlock didn't hesitate. They nodded and raised their glasses in a toast. "To justice. Long overdue."